D0499737

2.00
+

This Bird Flew Away

Lynda M. Martin

Thanks!
Lynda Mar...

Black Rose Writing
www.blackrosewriting.com

© 2010 by Lynda M. Martin

All rights reserved. No part of this book may be reproduced, stored in a retrieval system or transmitted in any form or by any means without the prior written permission of the publishers, except by a reviewer who may quote brief passages in a review to be printed in a newspaper, magazine or journal.

The final approval for this literary material is granted by the author.

First printing

All characters appearing in this work are fictitious. Any resemblance to real persons, living or dead, is purely coincidental.

ISBN: 978-1-935605-92-8

PUBLISHED BY BLACK ROSE WRITING

www.blackrosewriting.com

Printed in the United States of America

This Bird Flew Away is printed in Times New Roman

Edited by Kathryn Lynn Davis

www.thisbirdflewaway.com

Acknowledgments

The writing of this story is the culmination of several years of thought followed by many months of concentrated work, and it would not have been possible without the help of others – as is true of all human endeavors. First and above all, I must thank my partner in life, Jim, for his constant support in all the ways one can support another. Thank you, your love and belief in me is humbling.

Second, a special thank you to my granddaughter, Paige, who provided much of the authenticity of the teen-age Bria's voice and who so kindly read my many rough drafts, providing me with her special insight into the fictitious girl's possible emotions. Most of all, dear Paige, thank you for reminding me of the poignancy of that special time when one is no longer a girl but not yet a woman.

I owe a tremendous debt to my editor, Kathryn Lynn Davies who so kindly and patiently taught me so much about the craft of writing and cheered me on throughout the process. Dear Kathryn, your generosity in sharing your knowledge, your tact and your positive approach taught me to believe in myself and my work. Thank you. Words fail me.

My early advance readers also deserve my heartfelt thanks. In particular, Jack Hunsucker, Peg Cole, Cisca Jensen, Tami Schindler-Klassen, Paige Klassen, Ita Kinsella, Amanda Severn, Brenda Cole, Rebecca Emrheit, James McCrae, Tammy Lochman, Ronnie Sowell, Harriet Goodchild, Sue Mackender, and the readers over at Fair Critters. Your opinions and insights were invaluable. Speaking of advance readers, to my dear friend Rafini Loewchen, a particularly heartfelt thanks for arguing against my stand so vociferously, I knew I was on the right track.

Lastly, thank you Reagan Rothe and the others at Black Rose Writing for inviting me to become a new member of their publishing family.

.

Forward

Bria is a fictional character, as are all the others found in these pages, but she was conceived from the copious case notes I still keep decades after the writing. Thirty years dedicated to child protection left me grieving for all the children who did not receive the help they deserved, who went through life scarred, humiliated and ashamed – and you are legion. To you, all of you, I offer this story, as true a depiction of a vulnerable childhood, the crimes committed against you and the process of healing as my inadequate skills allow me to write.

How many are you? Official statistics, while disturbing at twenty to twenty-five percent of girls and eight to ten percent of boys, reflect only reported cases. I had the great honor of being invited to an international conference of child protection workers some years ago, where world-wide estimates suggest seven of every ten girls, and four of every ten boys are sexually exploited by the age of sixteen, and horrifying as those figures are, most professionals consider them to be conservative.

In true life, I make a practice of discussing this subject with every woman I've come to know, and to date I've met only two who tell me they made adulthood without some form of sexual abuse. You are in the majority. May we learn to bring our secret out into the light of day.

The case discussed here involves child trafficking for the sex trade, often discussed as a problem of modern times. Nothing could be further from the truth. This horrific industry is as old as humanity, and an evil I first encountered twenty-five years ago. Many imagine it only affects foreign children – another misconception. Today the FBI estimates 100,000 American children are trafficked each year, primarily girls with an average age of eleven.

Bria's story is one of optimism, the healing power of love, the strength of the human spirit, the connection of family and the triumph over evil.

May her story lead you on a similar voyage.

With gratitude to the girls it was my great privilege to meet, the journeys we shared and the love we found.

May God bless us all,
Lynda M. Martin

One:
"I know you're not supposed to say hate at a funeral."

1967
Bria

According to Auntie Peg, if you couldn't hear my voice then I must have my nose in a book. That's exactly how Jack found me, curled up in a chair with *Nancy's Mysterious Letter* in the basement of his father's house. I was trying to be invisible. After such a difficult day, I felt far too prickly to be nice to him, even though I'd eagerly awaited his arrival since morning.

"Hey, Carrot Top, remember me?" He flung himself into the chair beside me. A cloud of stale dust flew up and floated down to make grey patches on his dark suit. He looked the same, maybe a little heavier, more of a man than he had last time I saw him. Still his angular face was familiar and my heart jumped in recognition of my one-time good friend.

"Of course, and my name is Bria, Bria Jean—not Carrot Top." Did he think me such a featherbrain as to forget him in only three years?

"Sorry." No he wasn't, not one bit. His eyes crinkled up as if he was secretly laughing at me inside.

Was he? The thought filled me with a flash of rage. "How would you like it if I called you Big Nose?"

"You can if you wish, sticks and stones and all." He shrugged as though my spiteful words couldn't pierce his skin.

"I don't want to. It wouldn't be polite." I was secretly relieved my insult hadn't hurt his feelings, since he was the only one likely to pay attention to me out of the whole horde of folks upstairs. But he *did* have a big nose. Yes, and it had grown a new bend close to the end as if refusing to go anywhere near his mouth. He had a real grownup face now.

"You're right. So let's be polite and start over. Hello, Bria Jean, how are you doing?" He stuck out his hand and gave mine a gentle squeeze.

"Okay."

"Your mother said you were sick earlier and unable come to the service with the others. I looked for you."

"I just didn't want to go. It made me throw up."

"Understandable." He nodded and his shaggy black curls fell over his face, almost to his eyes. "So why are you down here in the basement all by yourself?"

"Too many people up there." I pointed to the bare joists and beams above our heads. *Was he looking at me funny?* I drew my long, skinny legs under my new navy blue dress and retreated farther into the depths of the old wing-backed chair.

"No joke." His eyes roamed the cave-like room, the stacks of boxes, old toys and discarded furniture. "Kind of lonely down here, isn't it?"

"No."

"So, you're simply *sitting* in this gloomy basement?"

I held Nancy Drew across my face as a shield. "What does it look like I'm doing? I'm reading."

"Won't you talk to me instead?"

"You want me to?" Astonished, I glanced up and stared directly into his black eyes. "All day long I was told 'shut up,' same as always. Auntie Peg says I blather."

"I like blathering."

Again, he had the air of someone privately amused, and I wondered what I'd said he found so funny. A warm flush heated my face and my pale freckled skin burned red the way it always did when I was embarrassed. *Could he see it?* I squirmed with insecurity, which made me madder yet. "Well, you must be the only one."

"What're you reading?" He spoke gently, and his smile changed, became softer and directed at me, not for himself. I felt better.

"Nancy Drew." I showed him the cover, happy to have a safe subject to discuss. "Number eight." I was an addict.

"Really?"

"Yes. There's no pictures, you know. This isn't some baby book. You have to read it."

"Amazing." He leaned forward, peering at me intently. "How old are you now?"

"I'm almost ten."

"That would make you nine."

"I'll be ten in two months." Jeeze, he'd already become a grown-up, always correcting. I liked him less, and a pang of disappointment seared through my heart and almost made me cry.

"October birthday, same as me." He waited for me to say something, and when I didn't he went on in a hearty way. "I'll be twenty-three. What day is yours?"

I glared at him from under my lowered eyelids and snapped, "Tenth."

"Wow, mine's the twelfth. We'll have to send each other cards."

"Like Christmas?" This pricked my conscience, and I remembered a promise to Auntie Peg I'd forgotten. "Oh yeah, I'm supposed to say thanks for the Christmas cards. Although, I hope you don't mind me saying, but I thought the last one kind of babyish."

"You're welcome." He was smiling again, and for the first time I noticed he had the funniest smile, all off to one side. The other half stayed frozen where it was, without moving a bit. It was puzzling. I didn't remember that. "Did you get mine?"

"Yes. I particularly enjoyed the last one. Did you make it all by yourself?"

"I used crayons. Doesn't take a genius. I ran out of money."

"Oh, well thanks anyway." He stared at me, as though measuring my frame for a bike or something. "You know, you're quite a surprise."

"I am? Why?"

"First I was looking for a cute as a puppy little girl, but I remembered the last time I saw you, you were a string bean with gaps in your smile. And then…"

"And then what?"

"I come down here and who do I find? A big girl, almost ten, reads mystery novels."

"Girls grow up," I informed him.

He laughed a real laugh, not one of those polite ones grown-ups give a kid when you're trying to be cute. "Yes they do but I don't think you're quite finished yet."

"I hope not." I glanced down at my stringy self, all the way to my overly big feet. "I don't want to be like this forever."

He smiled his strange half smile again, kind of nervous, as though he couldn't figure out what to say next. Then he got an idea. "Hey, how about you read to me?"

"What? Are you kidding?"

"No." He clasped his hands in front of him, pulled up his eyebrows and in a wheedling tone added, "Please?"

"I suppose, seeing as you asked so nicely. Should I start from the beginning or do you want me to fill you in on the story so far?"

"Not necessary."

"But you won't know what's going on."

"Oh, I'm sure I can catch up with it." He sat quietly, waiting for me to begin.

"I should tell you I never read aloud before; my auntie says books are sent by God to keep me quiet. So I might not be any good. Are you sure?"

"I'll make allowances. Please honor me with a reading."

I opened the book to page eighty-two with considerable ceremony and began, my voice a little quavery at first.

Jack listened, nodded in all the right places and raised his black eyebrows in suspense at the appropriate times.

I concentrated so hard, I didn't hear my mum calling me, and by the time I did, her voice sounded sharp. That spelled trouble with a capital T, and I'd already had enough for one day. "Oh-oh."

"Call to the trough." He got up, turned, bowed and offered me his hand. "Shall we go to the table, young lady?"

"Only if we must." I meant it. I'd sooner shovel my dog's poop from the yard than go into that herd of people. Then I tried out a phrase I'd found when I tried to read Auntie's Jane Austen books. "Though I have exceedingly little appetite."

He choked on a strangled chuckle. "You really are a precocious thing, aren't you?"

"Maybe." I suspected it meant an annoying, big-mouthed, pest of a kid someone told him to look after. Hadn't babysitting me been his job all the other times Mum left me with Mary? "I don't know that word."

"It means you are older than your years."

"Well that's certainly possible. Auntie Peg says I'm getting too big for my britches."

He threw back his head, opened his mouth and a big laugh shook his whole body. I climbed the stairs filled with satisfaction and proud I'd amused him so well, he being a grown-up and all.

***

There was no place for me upstairs. The house was packed. Someone sat in every seat in the living room, and little groups of people stood around holding plates in hand, attempting to eat standing up. The dining room, too, teemed with bodies, just as crowded. The chairs had been pulled back to sit against the walls and all were occupied.

The table itself had disappeared from view, laden with platters of meat—corned beef, red and thickly marbled, swimming in a lake of dappled juices; a huge bowl of mashed potatoes; another of carrots; steamed cabbage; pickled beets and two different salads. The volume of food was enough to take your appetite clear away—as if the squeeze of all those over-dressed, funereally grave people didn't do the job alone. I thought of escape but Mum spied me.

"Finally." She sagged against the doorframe, one hand on the small of her back, the other on the pregnant belly swelling under her black dress. "You come when you're called, understand?"

"Yes, Mum." I prayed no one noticed how mad I'd made her yet again. I glanced around but everyone studiously ignored us. "I'm sorry. I didn't hear you."

"You need to eat."

"I'm not hungry, honest." I begged but I should have just shut my big mouth and saved my breath for better things. She wouldn't listen.

"Eat."

"But—"

Her finger flew to her lips in an all too familiar hush gesture. "You need to eat. Bria, don't argue. I'm pretty much up to the limit with you today."

"Yes, Mum. Only a little though, please?"

"All right, a little."

Success, hurray, I gloated. I could get off without meat.

But she pointed at me. "Make sure you take some of everything, not only the things you like."

"Where should I eat?" I spread my hands and waved them around the crammed room.

"Get some food and go find a corner in the kitchen."

"Can I go outside?" Jack's younger brothers and the other boys ate out in the yard, free from supervision, and I envied them.

"Not in your good dress."

"How 'bout downstairs?"

"Bria Jean." Bria Jean meant business, time to zip it closed, not one more word; I knew that. I crossed my useless arms over my chest.

"Now!"

Jack's mum, Auntie Rose, came bustling over, all helpful and smiley. "C'mon Bria, darling, let's get you set up. Here we are." She picked up a plate, ladled out a huge dollop of mashed potatoes, some cabbage and to my horror, a thick slab of corned beef, glistening with fat. I'd never get that down my throat without gagging.

"No, Aunt Rose, I don't like—"

"Thank you, Rose." My mum snagged my upper arm, swung me around, and marched me across the dining room into the kitchen. She swatted my bum the whole way. She plunked me in a chair at the chrome legged table, took the plate from Rose and slapped it down in front of me. "Now, listen. You thank the Lord and Aunt Rose you're not going hungry today and you eat this. Do you understand?"

"Yes, Mum."

"Good." She disappeared into the dining room.

Not one of the women hustling back and forth from the kitchen spoke to me as I sat simmering, staring at the slab of corned beef, hating it, hating her, hating a world that forced a girl to eat things she didn't like or want. I'd whipped myself up into quite a state, complete with tears and quivering lips when another chair landed beside me and Jack sat down.

The traffic slowed as all the guests filled up, leaving us alone. He nudged my upper arm. "Will you look at what she gave me? Carrots! I hate vegetables." Indeed his plate held no meat. "Would you consider trading me half of your corned beef and potatoes for some of these?"

"I'll eat them all if you'll eat this." I slid my dinner toward him.

"It's a deal. Thank you very much."

And just like that, I fell in love with Jack.

When we finished, he took both plates and placed them on the pile of used dishes by the sink. "What do you say we try and earn a few Brownie points with our moms and start washing up? I sure could use some. I've been in a whole lot of trouble lately. I'll wash. You dry."

"What did you do?" I caught the dishtowel he tossed to me, always so eager to hear about someone else's wrongdoings.

"Oh, you're much too young to tell."

"I thought you said I was precious."

He chuckled softly. "Precocious: you are, and precious too. However, leave me my secrets."

I nodded. I had plenty of secrets myself. Sometimes I wondered why I didn't puff up and blow away like a dandelion, all the secrets I carried. "Yeah, all the stuff other people aren't supposed to know."

"But generally do anyway."

"Uh-huh." I didn't want to talk about secrets anymore.

Silence lingered a while. I couldn't think of a thing to say, an unusual situation for me. I searched through the clutter in my mind for something safe to tell him. "My mum said you're going be a policeman like your dad and uncles. She says all you Connellys are policemen."

"Only some of us. Let's see, my brothers are all too young. Uncle Pat, Mary's husband, well yes, he's a policeman. Uncle Dan, have you met him? He's a mechanic. And me—I'm still in school and will be for a few more years. I'm going to be a lawyer." He leaned over and whispered close to my ear. "That's why I live at home, in case you wondered."

"Oh, no, I didn't. My big cousins sleep at my auntie's house. Dougie only shows up on weekends, and Rich has his own place, but he's married and they have a baby. The other two come in most nights, but Rob; he's out a lot and you can never guess what he'll do. One time the Mounties came and took him away, but he turned up for breakfast the next morning." I was ready to add, don't ask me why because I don't know since no one would tell me, when I remembered my manners. "Oh, sorry I interrupted."

He shrugged and winked at me. "I talk about my family, you tell me about yours. Quid pro quo, it's called."

"You finish first."

"We Connellys do produce a lot of policemen, but your dad joined the Air Force." His voice changed. "I'm sorry you lost your dad, Bria Jean."

"He wasn't my dad, you know." The words flew out of my mouth before I could stop them—a dangerous lapse and I hastily concocted a cover-up. "I mean I have another dad, my real dad but I never met him. He lives way off in England."

"Does he write to you?"

"No, he's way too busy. He would if he had the time though." I wished it were true. I couldn't meet Jack's eyes while telling such a whopper, and fixed mine on the window.

"I suppose that's the reason Gerry adopted you, your other Dad being so busy."

I was ready to squirm out of my skin; I wasn't a good liar. "Yeah, well, I can't think why."

"My guess: he married your mother and adopted you to be a family, isn't that right?"

"He didn't want me." I blurted out the unbearable truth and my face flamed red-hot in mortification.

"If you ask me, that's his loss. He missed out on a terrific daughter."

"I don't care," I said in affected nonchalance, still staring at the window.

Jack put a soapy wet finger under my chin, turned my head and studied me intently with black eyes I could see myself in. "I knew Gerry long before you or your mum did."

"Oh? How long is that?"

"All my life. He was my uncle, my dad's youngest brother. He wasn't much older than me, only ten years."

"Did you like him?"

"Not a lot. I wouldn't normally say such a thing under the circumstances, but I think I can trust you with the truth. You won't tell anyone will you?"

"No. I won't. I promise." I felt all shivery and looked around.

"I hated him."

I stood still, staring in shock. "Jack, I might be just a kid but I know you're not supposed to say you hate someone at his funeral."

"I wonder why. It seems to me the last goodbye is when we should be most truthful."

Truthful? What did I know about truth? All the way from Calgary to Chicago, Mom drilled me in what I should say, or more importantly, what I should not. Now here was Jack, looking at me with his eyebrows pulled up and a smile on his face, waiting for me to say something on that forbidden subject.

I took my first tentative step out onto the thin ice, hoping it wouldn't crack beneath me. "My mum says now's not the time to talk about the troubles. We have to let Gerry go up to heaven and sit beside Jesus and God with his family's good wishes. I'm supposed to say thank you and shake hands when someone says they're sorry and not one word more."

"What are the troubles?"

"I told you, I'm not allowed to say." My voice came out high and thin, full of lurking tears. "Don't you listen? It's a secret."

No sooner had "secret" popped out of my big mouth than my mother appeared and I jumped in guilty surprise.

"Bria, here you are. I'm going to take you over to Mary. I'm exhausted and I want to lie down."

She hadn't heard. I almost fainted in relief so overwhelming I forgot to protest it was too early to send me to bed, and I wanted to stay with Jack and the best conversation I'd had all day.

Jack must have thought the same thing because he said, "Sandra, why don't you leave her with me? She's helping me clean the dishes. You go on and get some rest. I'll make sure Bria gets over to Mary's."

I finally inhaled when she said, "Thank you, Jack. Would you? Bria, you behave. Do as you're told. Good night."

"Good night, Mum." She didn't give me a kiss, nothing, so she might have overheard after all, and if she had, I'd been in for double-trouble tomorrow. I got scared all over again.

Jack looked alarmed and put his wet hands on my arms. "Bria, what's wrong? You're white as a sheet and you're shaking."

"I don't want to talk about Gerry anymore. Someone might come in." My teeth chattered in my head and my limbs trembled like aspen leaves in the breeze.

He took the towel out of my hands and dried his. "Come with me. We've done our share of dishes. Let's go for a walk. I want to show you something."

Two:
"Quid pro quo."

We went out the back door, through the yard, around the house and into the street. The fresh air was a blessing: clean, cool and sharp in the late summer evening.

I swiveled my head left and right, trying to take everything in. The houses shouldered in on each other, almost identical, two stories, high and narrow looming above the street to form a canyon stretching on forever. The lights blinked on in a series that started behind us, flickered over us, and then ahead until the individual lights were no longer discernable—just a yellowy haze way off in the distance. It was magic. Chicago was the biggest place I'd ever seen.

We walked in silence for ten minutes until Jack turned, and we entered a little park. "This has always been one of my favorite places. Even as a young boy I liked to come here. I'd sit and think on things. Do you ever feel that?"

"Pretty much all the time."

"Do you like this place?"

Laid out in front of me and tickling my sandaled feet, a circle of lush grass formed a lawn bordered by a concrete walking path and completely ringed by ancient trees. The scene would have been dark and scary if not for the old-fashioned lampposts every twenty feet or so.

"It looks like a magic meeting place for hobbits." My soul thrilled at the thought we'd stepped into another world. I gazed up at Jack, wondering did he feel the same. "Do you know about hobbits?"

"Yes, I read that book. Good book." He smiled down at me and pointed to the other side of the circular lawn. "Let's go sit on one of those benches."

We walked around, following the path. He asked, "Can we chat some more? I like talking to you. You're funny and smart."

"Thanks. Me, too. You listen to me. Most people don't. What do you want to talk about, Jack?" We chose a bench and I wiggled in close to him.

"I'd like to discuss Gerry. No one can hear us. I have a lot of stuff to get off my chest."

I considered. "Yeah, but don't ask me to tell the secrets. In case no one told you, I've been in enough trouble today."

"Sure, but I thought, seeing as everybody else is back home toasting to him, 'oh what a great man,' 'gave his life for his country,' 'distinguished himself'—you heard them – we should tell the truth. We know, don't we, he was no saint."

"I guess."

"Don't you think we owe God the other side of the story?"

My heart started pounding and my throat hurt. "I can't say anything to God right now."

"So talk to me."

"I'm not supposed to." My voice quivered.

His arm came across my back, so I obligingly snuggled up. My shoulder nestled in his armpit and he squeezed me against his side. We sat quietly for a few minutes, and I slowly unwound my tensed muscles and my breathing returned to normal. Jack's voice spoke into the evening air. "First, no one is here but you and me. Second, no one said you were in trouble. They said you were sick."

"It's true I threw up, and I don't feel so good, not sick, something else. Mum says I'm acting up. I don't mean to."

"I think I know what's wrong."

"You do?"

He leaned his head close to me and out of one side of his mouth confided, "It's the secrets. They make our insides rotten. And most of the time, secrets are just lies, and living lies makes us feel bad."

"So what do we do?"

"We find someone we trust and share our burden."

"Is that what you want: to tell me your secrets?" I straightened myself up, prepared to receive his revelations.

"Yes." He lit a cigarette, sucked in the smoke and puffed out slowly. "And then you tell me yours. Quid pro quo, remember?"

Surprisingly relaxed now he'd actually asked, I still couldn't comply. I had a paradox. While I was quite happy to besmirch the newly deceased, there remained an obstacle. "What if we made a promise never to tell?"

"Oh, you have a big problem. Let me think a minute."

"Okay." I sat quiet and enjoyed the magic park. A wind blew a hole in the trees, swirled around us, and I shivered, so Jack pulled one arm out of his jacket, covered me and folded me in. The heat of him, seeping through his shirt, warmed me up and the last three years fell away. I was six again and Jack had wrapped me in a towel after swimming, rubbing my arms to warm me up after the frigid waters of Lake Michigan. He was still my special friend. Given a choice, I'd stay wrapped up with him all night.

"I have the solution."

"What?"

"I'm studying to be a lawyer. One of a lawyer's jobs is to keep his clients' secrets. We call this confidentiality. Even if a policeman, a judge, or your mother asks him, he can never tell. That's called privilege."

"Really? What a strange job. I thought lawyers made big speeches in court and found out who did the murder."

"You watch too much television. No, most of the time a lawyer's job is dull, except for keeping secrets. That's important." With his free hand he fished around in his pocket. "So here's what we're going to do: I'll give you a dollar."

"Wow, thanks." I held the bill in my fingers.

"Now you give it back to me." His hand lay out flat, waiting.

"Why?"

"You're paying me a retainer. Now I'm your lawyer. You can tell me, and it will still be a secret. Problem solved. You can keep the promise."

Unsure, I puzzled out all he'd said. "I guess this makes things okay, but you start."

"Gerry was older and bigger than me, and one time he ordered me to steal a candy bar from De Lucca's store. I didn't want to but he twisted my arm so hard, I had to; he hurt me. Mrs. De Lucca caught me in the act and I faced a lot of trouble. I hated him for bullying me into doing something I would never do on my own."

I flipped through my long list of reasons for hating Gerry and settled on something innocuous, something safe. "Gerry called me bad names. He called me a little bastard. He used to yell at my mum 'keep your little bastard out of my stuff' or 'why don't you take your little bastard and go.'"

"Did you hate him?"

"Did I ever." I was caught up in remembered fury and my mouth ran on all by itself. "I hated him most when he hit my mum and made her cry."

Jack upped the ante. "I hated him when he hit me and I cried." He lowered his head until his eyes locked on mine. I couldn't get away. "Did he ever hit you, Bria?"

"Sometimes…mostly, my mum."

"Was he always a hitter?"

"I don't know. I only lived with them for a little while, not long"

"Is that so? Where did you go?"

"To Auntie Peg in Buffalo Coulee, Alberta. My home."

"Did your mum send you away because of Gerry? He must have been very mean for her to give you up to your aunt. What a hard decision for your mother. When did you start living there? Were you happy?"

He asked so many questions I lost track. He wanted to hear all about me. No one else did. I loved my special friend, and I yearned to tell him everything. I was so cozy and warm in our jacket; the craving to stay cuddled up snug against him was irresistible, so I opened my mouth and let the words tumble out.

I had lived in Buffalo Coulee since I was a baby, one of the many things I shouldn't say, according to my mum. She said it embarrassed her to have others think she wasn't a good mum, and they would. People are mean-minded, and loved to wag their tongues.

They'd say she was selfish, travelling to faraway places just to please herself, when the truth was Canadian trained nurses were paid way more money for foreign work, and seeing as she had to send money home to us, this was the most responsible thing for her to do. But others might think she'd do better to get a job at the hospital in Strathmore and live at home.

Didn't she come home whenever she could, she'd ask me with a strange tone in her voice. Did people think her life was all fun and games? She'd done her best to look after me, hadn't she?

I didn't know what to say to make her feel better. I was happy with Auntie Peg, but when Mum came home, everyone else became drab and gray. She always looked like she stepped right out of the TV, so pretty in clothes you'd find in one of my Cousin Lizzie's magazines, and she smelled heavenly. She'd take me with her wherever she went, shopping in Calgary for new clothes in fancy stores where they'd bring her things to try on and she'd twirl in front of me. "Do you like it? Do I look pretty?" We'd go into Strathmore and drink hot chocolate in Baba's Café.

Every head in the place would turn to stare at my glamorous mother. She was fun.

I laughed into the still night, remembering my favorite good time. "One time, in the summer, we picked armloads of buffalo beans—those pretty yellow flowers you find in the ditch, in case you don't know what they are—and I took the flowers into the kitchen and put them in jars of water but they were full of bugs and Auntie Peg made me throw the whole lot out. Still, we sure had fun picking them. They're almost the same color as Mum's hair but mine is more like the black eyed Susans that come in the fall, and I wished my hair could be yellow like hers and she called me her little fire baby, and we laughed and…"

I sucked in a huge gulp of air after my rush of words, reached up with my hand to push some itchy strands of hair from my face, and pulled it away, surprised. It was wet. I touched my face. It was wet too. I felt like I'd just woken up from a strange dream and still my mouth ran on. "She liked to laugh and she played with me then. She doesn't play anymore. She's always mad at me now. She changed." I wiped my cheeks with the back of my hands.

Jack peered down at me, his dark eyes two black holes in his face. He didn't speak for what seemed a long time. "Bria, sweetheart, she's just lost her husband and has a new baby on the way. Don't you think this must be hard for her, more than enough to cause her to change?"

"She changed before, way before."

"When?"

"I don't know. She wasn't home so much once she got married."

"His squadron was stationed in France then," Jack said. "I thought they took you with them."

"I was too little to go, Mum said, so I stayed with Auntie Peg, same as usual, which was fine with me."

I'd heard Aunt Peg fighting with her before she went away. Auntie's voice sounded harsh in a way I'd never heard before. She'd said, *France? You're off to France with some man you've only known a few months. What's wrong with you, girl? You have a child.* My mum sounded whiney, like Lizzy, who was only thirteen, and mumbled something about … *my chance at happiness.* Auntie had walked about the house with a grim face for days.

Mum was gone a long time, almost all of kindergarten. One day she showed up, had another fight with Auntie Peg and moved me to Mary's house in Chicago. "Don't you remember? You took me to the zoo, right?" I flashed him my best adoring smile.

He laughed. "Our big day out together, I'd never seen anyone so excited about being on a bus."

"I was only six, Jack. Give me a break." I elbowed him softly in the ribs. "Anyway, I stayed at Mary's. Do you remember when the whole family went on a picnic and you taught me swimming?" I waited for him to nod. "And then Mum took me back to Auntie Peg, right in the middle of grade one."

"Did she?" Jack sounded annoyed. "All this time I thought you were living with your mother and Gerry. That's what she—" He bit off his words.

"I know." My mum sometimes told lies, an awkward fact of life.

Just after I turned eight, Mum came home and promised me a fabulous life, painting a picture from 'Father Knows Best.' I'd have a Mum and a Dad, and soon a new sister or brother; we'd all live together in a nice house on the base in New Mexico, and we'd be so very happy.

I loved my Auntie Peg and my Uncle Dugald, my cousin Lizzy and even the boys, but how could I resist? She was my mum.

So a little scared, a bit sad but mostly excited, Mum and I boarded a plane and flew into our glittering, sterling silver future. It tarnished quickly. My first disappointment involved school. "Do you believe I was starting grade four at Buffalo Coulee School, but in New Mexico, they made me do grade three all over again, like a dummy? It wasn't my fault I was too young for their stupid school. Talk about boring."

"I can imagine, especially for a clever girl like you. Is that when your mother changed? Did something happen in New Mexico, Bria?"

All the warmth and good feeling flew away, and I went all stiff and cold. "I don't want to talk about that."

Jack sat silent for a bit. His arm under our jacket flexed, and he rubbed my arm. "What happened in New Mexico?"

Oh, how I ached to tell him but when I opened my mouth to do so, a bubble started deep in the pit of my stomach, rose to the back of my throat and with a moan, I leaned over and vomited on the grass.

Jack took out a hanky. "Here, let me." Gently, he cleaned off my mouth.

I wanted to die of embarrassment. Vomit had splashed on his shoes and even up on his pants and, worse, I started bawling like a little baby.

When I finally stopped crying, he picked me up, carried me over to another bench, away from my mess, and set me down beside him as we had been before. He pulled me close and kissed me on the forehead. "Is it so bad? I think you should tell me."

I resisted as long as I could, then shouted. "He was so mean!"

"Tell me," he whispered, holding me close.

Loving the feel of his arm around me, his warmth and his man-smell, I did.

My "Dad," who had adopted me without ever meeting me, was no TV father, and never once called me kitten, mostly 'hey you.' Within a week, I'd had my first of many spankings, though I didn't know why. I soon learned to connect the smell of liquor with a need to hide.

On the other hand, I enjoyed more time with my mum than I ever had before, and we had fun – sometimes. Most afternoons, by four-thirty, she'd start to get nervous, and run through some mental checklist: is the laundry done, supper planned, the house clean, fresh towels in the bathroom, is she prettied up enough? The list was endless. The last item was always, *Bria, try to be good.*

I tried, but was never good enough, or so it seemed. After a few weeks, I'd go to my room as soon as the car pulled into the driveway, not waiting to find out if he smelled of booze, leaving my mum the only target for his discontented wrath. No matter our plots and schemes, things got worse.

I thought of her swollen, bruised eye when she *"hit the upper cupboard door, silly me,"* and the blackish blue blotches on her back. *I fell in the tub*, and her pleading, *don't tell anyone*. Even on our way to Chicago for his funeral, she made me promise, don't tell.

Jack held me close. I couldn't remember the last time anyone did that. "Go on."

"He had tons of rules, but if we were careful, we'd be okay. That was the worst part. For a while, he'd be sweet as pie, and just when I thought things would be better and got happy; boom! He'd come home mad, smelling like whiskey and I'd think oh-oh, here comes trouble. Sure enough, by the end of supper, I'd be in my room with a sore bum, listening to my mum cry."

"Let me guess what happened next. It wasn't enough to follow his rules anymore and no matter how hard you tried he'd be mad all the time. Am I right?" Jack's voice grew hard and edgy and so did I.

"Yes. How did you know?"

In a gentler tone, he said, "I lived with a drunk as a boy and remember all of it: the unpredictable rage, the violence, Mom locking herself in the basement, us kids trying to be invisible. I was frightened all the time. See, you can tell me and I'll understand."

I relaxed again, barely aware of his hand stroking my back, not caring I hadn't understood much of what he'd said. The words wouldn't stay inside me. "I was always so scared. He'd come home, drink his booze, and yell at us. One time he called his supper shit and threw the plates at Mum. If everything wasn't just as he liked it, he'd hit her. Mum would shout at me to go to my room, and I couldn't see but I listened. I was too scared to come out. I wanted to help her, but..." A sob caught in my throat as the memories swept through my mind, more vivid and real than the scene before me.

Jack's face was close, and I felt his warm breath blow on my scalp when he exhaled. "The miserable son-of-a-bitch. I suspected as much." I felt a kiss on the part in my hair.

He spoke softly, almost talking to himself. "I saw him drunk one time, a few weeks before he left for Vietnam. He beat a man and both my Dad and I together had trouble pulling him away. He sent the man to the hospital. He was out of his mind, Bria, crazy mad. Did you ever see him like that?"

Another spasm of retching ripped through me, but nothing came up.

Jack gave me a piece of gum to chew, pulled me as close as could be and murmured, "Tell me, sweetheart. You can't keep these things inside."

Don't tell, said my mother's voice when I closed my eyes.

"Trust me," said Jack, holding me in his warm jacket.

I couldn't stop myself. The blubbering started up again, and I gulped air between sobs and words. As though I was somewhere else, up in the trees perhaps, I listened to the gabble below. The tale pouring out of my mouth shocked even me. "It happened at Easter time. His friends, the other flyers came to our house. They drank lots and yelled, *Vietnam* and *DaNang* and *Kill the gooks*. Mum cooked some food and begged the men to eat. She told me to go to my room, but Gerry said No! I had to sing for them. So, I did. Mom said I needed sleep. Please let me go. Gerry yelled, *Fuck, you're such a drag*. I went to bed and listened.

I fell asleep, I guess, but woke up to screaming. I ran out. Mum was on the floor and Gerry was sitting on her hitting her and hitting her. I grabbed his hair and pulled. *Stop it!* His belt hit me and hit me. Mum got up and smashed the lamp on his head. *Run, Bria, run!* I did. I ran to the neighbors and banged on the door. The man went to our house. Gerry came out. They fought. More people came. I ran in. Mum on the floor—

blood all over her legs. They pulled her up. Blood gushed out—Mummy!
—they took her away and—and left me all alone with people I didn't
know."

When I came back to reality, Jack's arm crushed me against his
chest. His shirt was soaked. His head hung down and his jaw clenched on
and off. "Are you mad at me, Jack?"

"At you? No."

"Was it my fault?"

"No. Never."

"He didn't want me. He hated me and he got mad at Mum. She
wanted me. She *did*."

"Of course she did."

"I should have been better. I'm sorry."

He stroked my hair and used the sleeve of his shirt to wipe my face.
"No, sweet girl, this has nothing at all to do with you and would
probably happen whether you were there or not."

"Why?"

"Because he was a son of a bitch, that's why. A mean minded son of
a bitch—like his brother."

"What brother?" I asked.

"Never mind. Another time, perhaps. Are you all right, now? Can
you tell me what happened next?"

It was getting darker. I looked up at the sky, but instead of the stars I
expected, all I could see was an orangey glow of haze. I made my
decision. I'd share the rest, but never the worst thing: not why I was
going to hell.

"I stayed with Dan and Dee, the people next door, for about a week.
She gave me a bath. She said any man who would beat a pregnant
woman and kill her baby, he'd rot in hell."

"She sounds like a good person."

I had liked her. For a while, we pretended she was my big sister. She
let me stay home from school, and I watched TV and played with their
little baby. He was so cute, and I thought about the brother or sister my
mum had lost. One day Dee took me to the hospital to visit my mum. She
looked bad; her face was all puffy and black and blue and she was so sad
and tired. She wanted me to go back to Aunt Peg's house. I said she
should come, too, but she just shook her head and said *I can't*.

I looked up. "I don't know why she couldn't. Do you?"

"No. Your question is something I've never been able to figure out:

22

why a woman will stay with a man who hurts her."

"Dan took me to see Mum again, and she told me she loved me and I should be good. She made me promise not to tell what happened. And I never did."

"Until now, but I'm glad you did. This is too much for you to carry around." He leaned down and kissed my forehead. "No wonder you've been sick."

"Dan said my mum would get better, but she never did. Do you think she will?"

"I'm sorry but I can't say, not knowing her or what she's lived through. She does seem sad and tired. How long after this did she stay with Gerry?"

"Beats me. No one even told me Gerry went to the war. She doesn't talk to me much anymore. That's why I hate Gerry so much. He took my mum away from me."

"She's here with you now."

"Not like before. She's not the same. I want my old mum back. I wish she had never married Gerry."

He sat quiet for a minute, as though deep in thought about something important. "Do you feel better, now?"

"I guess. Mostly I'm tired."

"Let's go back. I'll walk you over to Mary, so she can put you to bed."

"Can't you put me to bed?"

"No, Bria Jean. A young lady like you? It wouldn't be right."

"Why?"

"I can't honestly tell you, sweet girl. I just know it's so."

I had one more thing to say. "I love you Jack."

He didn't answer. He scooped me up in his arms and gave me a hug. For a moment, I thought he was crying, but maybe he just had to cough.

Three:
"I'm going to hell."

Mary

The minute they walked in the back door, I knew Jack had been successful. My plan had worked. If anyone could breach those thick walls around Bria, it would be him; she doted on him so. If I understood what was wrong, I'd be able help her and hopefully put an end to the night terrors, the screaming and tears, and even more important, her absolute refusal to confide in me—so unlike our Bria.

She gazed up at me with wretched eyes in a red blotchy face. Jack appeared completely spent, but he put on a hearty voice. "Here she is, Mary, tired and wanting her bed."

"Stick around. I want to talk to you." I took her from him and led her up the narrow staircase to her bedroom. "Come on, Bria darling. You can bathe in the morning. Let's get you into your pajamas so you can get a good sleep. Tomorrow's a new day."

She didn't put up any fuss at all, let me wash her face and change her and she slipped into bed with a mumbled "night-night."

"Prayers, Bria. You can say them in your bed tonight."

She clasped her hands as I'd taught her and muttered the childhood classic. "This night I lay me down to sleep, I pray the Lord my soul to keep. If I should die before I wake, I pray the Lord my soul to take. God bless Mum, Aunt Peg, Uncle Dugald, Lizzie and the boys and also Aunt Mary and mostly Jack. Thank you Lord. In Jesus' name we ask this. Amen."

I answered with "Amen," and watched as she brushed some loose hair from her face, heaved a ragged sigh and closed her eyes. I added a silent request of my own. *Please let my sunny girl come back to me soon. I miss her, even her chatter. Amen.*

I straightened the covers, kissed her cheek and went into the kitchen to find Jack. "Well?"

My question reverberated around the small room.

Jack stood beside the table, leaning on one of the well-worn chairs. "Well, what?"

"Don't be a smartass, Jack. You know darn well what I'm asking. Tell me all she told you. How could they wreak such a change in her? It's grievous. And the mother. Have you had a good look at her? What did that bastard do to them?"

"Mary, I'm sorry, but I can't tell you anything." He tried to pawn me off with a tired smile.

I wasn't about to let him get away with that. Something had passed between them, and I wanted to hear. "She didn't talk?"

"Oh, yes." His face was inscrutable.

I lost my patience. "What then? Tell me?" I went over to the cracked and chipped countertop, reached for the kettle, filled it and placed it on the range for tea, making sure to slam it down hard. "She's been in a terrible state since she got here and practically hysterical about the funeral."

He shook his head emphatically and held both hands up. "I can't. I'm under strict obligation not to repeat what she told me. And I won't."

"Are you serious? Come on, Jack, I need to know. How can I deal with problems I don't understand?" In three steps, I stood before him, face-to-face, and glowered as fiercely as I dared.

He fended me off with a light caress on my cheek. "All I can say is this: all your suspicions are correct, perhaps even more than you can imagine. Isn't that enough?"

"I suppose if you insist—"

"I do."

"Damn you, Jack Connelly. May I at least ask if she's all right?"

"No, I don't think so, but she will be." He walked over to the sink, wet a cloth and dabbed at what appeared to be vomit on his pants. "Listen, Mary, I believe there's more, something she isn't ready to disclose."

"Well, perhaps she'll talk to me."

"Now that she's started, maybe so. Be careful what you say. She's wound far too tight."

"All right, Jack." I thought he was pale. "You look tired."

"It was no picnic."

"As bad as that?"

"Yes." His shoulders sagged and his expression hardened. "I'll drop by tomorrow to check on her."

I thought of her mother, how she had ridden the poor girl all day. "I intend to talk to Sandra."

He kissed my cheek and said, "Mary, Mary, where would we all be without you? Good night."

The door clicked shut, and I sent my belated gratitude after him. "Thank you, Jack."

Still tense and dissatisfied, I comforted myself with a small shot of brandy, a little something to steady the nerves and bring me sleep. The boys would be at John's house drinking for hours yet, with my Pat assuredly the last to leave.

***

The bedside clock said two a.m. when I awoke abruptly. I was alone. Pat was still not back. What had awakened me? My befuddled senses strained to comprehend. Then I heard it: sobbing, desperate sobbing from down the hall. I got out of bed, put on my robe and went to her.

"Bria, darling, what's wrong?" I took her heaving body into my arms.

She was unable to talk.

"Do you want your mother? She's just next-door. Shall I get her?"

"No." The single syllable shot out of her mouth as a scream.

"What then, darling? Tell me."

"I can't." The abject misery on her face wrenched at my guts.

"You can. You must."

"No, it's bad."

"Nothing can be so bad. You won't shock me. Aren't I your good friend? You can tell me anything, and I'll still love you." I rocked her slowly and stroked my hands over her frizzy head, down to the end of her thick braid. "Tell me; tell your Mary what's troubling you so."

Her shrill voice filled the room. "You shouldn't love me. I'm bad. I'm rotten. I'm going to Hell."

"No, darling, you're one of God's angels, you are. There's no place in Hell for you."

This only brought on greater sobs. I did all I could, held her in my arms and murmured "hush, hush" in her ear until she calmed. "Bria, tell me why."

26

"It's all my fault. I asked God to take Gerry away, and he did. I did it. Me." She began keening, a thin high wail that went on and on.

Understanding came in an instant. "Do you think Gerry died because you wished it so?"

The answer, when it finally arrived, was swollen with self-reproach. "I didn't wish; I prayed and prayed. I begged God to take him away every single night for two whole years."

My mind reeled. *Oh, sweet Jesus, the poor little innocent.* "And you think God took Gerry to shut you up?"

An absurd image leaped into my imagination of a harangued God, pestered and exhausted beyond tolerance by the continual pleadings of a young girl. In desperate need of peace and quiet, He lifted a mighty finger and selected Gerry's aircraft for annihilation. This, and the quick flight from frightened concern to amusement overwhelmed me, and I began to giggle. "Isn't that a little self important?"

Startled, Bria sat up straight in bed, eyes round as apples, took several deep, shuddering gulps of air and laughed with me, an unnatural laugh increasing in intensity until it became as hysterical as the sobs had been. The sound grated on my nerves. I shook her. "Stop, Bria."

She went deadly quiet, staring straight ahead. Then tears again, but this time good healthy weeping, the kind that washes away sorrow. I busied myself running her a bath and left her to her private grief.

I went downstairs, put two tablespoons of brandy and a spoonful of honey in a glass of warm milk, and gave it to her while we waited for the tub. "Listen darling, I'm going to tell you something. Our Gerry was a rotten little boy—yes he was—the kind of boy quick to hit a smaller kid, quick to kick a dog."

Her red and swollen eyes opened wide. She thought for a minute and suggested, "Maybe he was mad at something."

"We're all mad at something, but most of us learn not to take it out on others. Gerry was one of those people who didn't. I think that was his nature: cruel." I tipped the end of her glass. "Come on, drink up."

She gulped the doctored milk and turned her white mustachioed face back to me. "Yes, he was."

"You can forgive such selfishness in a child, not an adult." I slipped off her pajamas. Her skinny girl's body looked so fragile; the thought of a grown man hurting her filled me with outrage. "Tell me, did Gerry drink?"

She nodded, foiling my attempt to pin up her braid. "Sometimes not for a while. Then all of a sudden—look out. And we had to tiptoe around him, not that anything we did helped much."

"You've learned an important lesson in life. Stay away from a drunken man, particularly when he's mad about something." I finally succeeded in pinning her thick shank of red hair to her head.

She turned to face me and asked, "What if you can't get away? What if you have to live with him, like Mum did?"

"Your mum is a grown-up and made her choices. You can learn from her mistakes. And when you're older and look at men as a woman does, pay attention to how they drink."

I popped her in the tub and kept on talking. "My Pat now, he'll come in the door tonight, drunk and laughing, and I'll help him up the stairs, take off his shoes, put him to bed and that will be that. He'll wake up tomorrow feeling like hell. He won't get drunk again for a long time."

She twirled around in the water. "And he never gets mad?"

"Not once in seventeen years did the drink make him angry. Teary sometimes. Be still now. You're getting me all wet." I scrubbed her slight, bony back. "But John now, Jack's dad, he was always an angry drinker."

"Jack's dad? Was he mean? Did he hit?" She seemed disturbingly interested to hear all the details. *A hopeful sign?*

"Yes. I'm going to tell you a story about our family."

"A secret?" She sounded thrilled with the idea.

"No, everyone knows; it's no secret. Hush now and listen." I washed behind her ears and the back of her neck. "Jack's dad was an angry drunk. Maybe it was his job. Policemen see a lot of hard things, you know."

"Maybe it was his nature, like you said."

"Perhaps, but I blame the drink. It deadens the part of a man that knows right from wrong."

"Was he mean to Jack?" she asked in concern.

"One night, two years ago, while you were away, his dad hit his mother and Jack hit his dad. His dad punched him so hard he broke his jaw and his nose."

"No!" Her face was a study in empathy and she sniffled, on the verge of tears once more.

"Jack stayed in the hospital for two weeks. John joined AA, and he hasn't had a drop since."

"And he never hit Jack again?"

"No, he didn't. He's over there now pouring drinks for everyone except himself. It's bound to be killing him. I admire him. I've read the craving for drink can be very strong."

My assurances brought her no comfort. "But poor Jack."

"Poor Jack, yes." I paused for a bit, waiting for her full attention. "Did something like that happen to you?"

"Yeah. A few times, but I got over it." She gave me a bright smile, genuinely cheerful, and I found this perplexing.

She chattered on while squeezing out the washcloth to make rivulets of water run down her chest. "It wasn't so bad. He didn't break anything in me." Her face turned grave. "Is that why Jack's nose goes off to one side like it does? And did you notice he only talks with half his mouth?"

"Yes. Time for bed now. Out you come." I toweled her down, helped her put on the pajamas and returned her to bed. "Off to sleep, now."

Her last words followed me into the hallway. "Oh, poor Jack."

The resilience of youth, I supposed. At least now, with everything out in the open, I could formulate a plan.

Tomorrow I'd find an excuse to talk to the mother, that silly woman who hadn't bothered to spend even one night in the same house as her distraught little girl.

"Sandra," I would say, "I think you should leave Bria here where she's happy and always has been, where she's spent almost as much time as she has anywhere else, and certainly more than with you. She needs a rest. I'll care for her while you have your baby, and then we can talk about what to do."

Yes, keeping her with me, permanently if I can, is best for her and for me. I'll get Jack to work on it right away.

Four:
"God, I hate it here!"

1969
Bria

September 16, 1969

 God! I hate it here. You wouldn't believe the tension. Jess the Mess! What a piece of work. She's a slapper, a raging tyrant, a petulant brat, self-important, self-righteous, lying, unhappy sour bitch! She's nuts, wacko and mean and her kids are even worse. Anne, older and lots bigger than me, is sneaky as a snake. If I don't do exactly what she wants, she slaps my face, so I can't be blamed for my joy when her mother slaps hers, and that happens all the time. She's fifteen years old and wets the bed, for crying out loud. And Linda, the one in grade two, she's scared of everything. Her eyes never stay still. Jess the Mess calls it her guilty look, but I think she's terrified and looking for a way out. They're all crazy! No one says what is and is not allowed in this place until I've done something. How was I supposed to know I'm forbidden to go for a walk without express permission from her majesty, the Queen of Crescent Heights? And now, here I am, face well slapped and grounded to my room. Again! I have to get Tara away before she gets big.

 I put down my pencil, closed the scribbler I used for a journal, the way Sister Marta, my teacher back at Ave Maria School in Chicago, told me to. "Keeping a journal of your thoughts is like talking to God, and if you're honest in your writing, with time you get a picture of who you are." I had my doubts, considering I was using a scribbler cleverly stolen from the class supply locker.

 I missed Sister Marta. She used to talk to me about books and ideas and always had time to sit and help me in mathematics, which I don't get. At Ave Maria, they didn't worry what grade you belonged in. You worked in every subject at your own speed and when you finished the work, you moved ahead, even if you were way behind in mathematics and science. Sister Marta used my name and remembered stuff about me, not like Miss Coalbins, who calls me Connelly and doesn't know anything.

When I left Ave Maria, I was sorry to quit a school I liked a lot, but at first, I didn't feel so bad because Buffalo Coulee School worked the same way. All the students sat in one room, grades one to nine, so if you grew bored with your own work, you listened to the other kids, and best of all, our teacher, Mrs. McKay, was a neighbor and a friend of our families.

Webster Niblock Elementary is my third school for grade six: Ave Maria last fall; then after Christmas back to Buffalo Coulee; and now, the next year, here I am in Medicine Hat, stuck in the sixth again. Déjà vu?

More kids go to this new school than all the kids in my previous schools put together, including New Mexico. Nobody cares I'm smart in some things. I had to go back a year just for stupid old math. I'm so bored. And Miss Coalbins is not to be trusted, as I found out.

One day at school, learning imagery and metaphors, I wrote Jess was a dragon, because that's how I saw her. Lying quiet in her lair while you tiptoe around, she suddenly springs to life just as you're about to make a getaway and scorches you one for no reason other than you're there.

Miss Coalbins called her and told her. Boy, did I get into trouble. First, a couple of hard slaps and then she sat in a chair with this ridiculous pained expression. I mean honest, her bottom lip quivered. She said, "I demand an apology." Of course I had to give one. I like my face up here on my head.

I miss Mary and being special to someone. My room back on Laflin Street might have been small but totally mine and no one ever came and searched through my stuff looking for trouble. Mary respected my privacy and liked having me around. Even after Tara's birth, I remained Mary's favorite, entirely the opposite of here where I sleep down in the basement and everybody else, Tara included, gets a room on the second floor.

I miss Jack, who always wanted to talk to me and brought me books he thought I'd like. Once he took me to see the White Sox play, and another time to the aquarium. His explanations on things were perfect, easy to understand but not addressed to some dumb little kid. He knew I had a brain and even told me he liked me for my intelligence. Not like here—nobody here knows I'm smart, or cares.

Auntie Peg's is way better than this place. She thinks because they are poor and can't buy us things she has nothing to offer, but at least at her house I could get food to eat if I was hungry. Here, the Mess controls what we eat and when and where. If I felt hunger pangs, I had to ask, "Please, may I have something to eat?" All posh and fancy, like life in some old-fashioned book.

She sat back, deep in deliberation, "I don't know. Supper's ready in two hours, and you didn't finish lunch. If you don't clean your plate at mealtime, you don't deserve anything special."

"I'm sorry," I said, like I do two dozen times a day. "I wasn't hungry then but I am now."

"Oh all right. Get yourself a slice of bread and only one, mind you. You can take some of the strawberry jam."

I ran off to fix my snack, but she called me back. "Bria, have you forgotten something?"

I couldn't think of what at first, but understanding hit me like one of her slaps. "Oh, sorry. Thank you."

"Such dreadful manners." Her eyes grew narrow. "Until you learn common politeness, no, you cannot have extras to eat. You don't deserve treats." Her mouth pursed up and she dismissed me by sticking her face back into the romance novel of the moment.

I stood in front of her a minute, uncomprehending. "So I can't have something to eat?"

"What did I just tell you? No."

So on the way back to my basement room, I grabbed a banana off the countertop in the kitchen and stuffed the purloined booty under my shirt. Halfway down the stairs, I heard the pounding of footsteps above me and quickly threw it through the open-backed steps, into the storage area below.

I was almost at the bottom step when she caught me by the arm. "What have you got?"

I plastered my most innocent look onto my face. "Nothing."

"That bowl held five bananas, and now I count only four." She started frisking me, like a cop on TV.

I stretched out both my arms. "I don't have anything."

She eyed me suspiciously, clearly thwarted in her desire for a thief to punish but climbed back up the stairs, probably to puzzle on the case of the missing banana, and I slipped into my room. Two hours passed before I found the nerve to go and search for the fruit, but by then I didn't want it anymore.

I missed Auntie Peg and Dugald. They were fair and left me alone to do whatever I thought good for me, didn't watch me like the keepers of some miserable jail. I missed Lizzie and the bed I shared with her, where we talked about all kinds of things at night, though I wasn't allowed to approach her at school seeing as she was three years older, and I embarrassed her in front of her friends. I missed the boys, even Rob.

I had a dog back there, Rosco. I hoped he was all right. We had a dog here, too, an old beagle named Kilroy, but he got into almost as much trouble as me. He can't help peeing at night and the Mess tells Frank to beat him for his accidents, which makes me sick. He's just an old dog and the last time I begged Uncle Frank not to hurt him. He stopped and I took Kilroy to my room in the basement and hugged him. I hoped he felt better, poor harmless old dog.

Yesterday, Auntie Peg called to say, "Hello, how are you?"

But Jess the Mess stood beside me the whole time, so I couldn't say much.

Auntie asked, "Are you taking good care of Tara?" which was a perfectly natural thing to ask 'cause at her house, I did a lot of those chores, changed her diapers, held her bottles and put her to bed.

Seeing as she hung around staring at me, I said, "Oh Auntie Jess does that, she takes good care of her." I was not allowed to do those things. "She's growing so fast and getting teeth."

I wanted to say, "Can we come home? I'm so unhappy and I don't think Jess is good for Tara. Please take us back."

But of course I couldn't, not when Jess breathed down my neck. She wanted me to play outside or in the basement all the time and leave her alone with my baby sister, but I tried to watch her enough to know she didn't hurt her. She seemed okay about babies, just not kids that could walk and talk.

Auntie asked, "How is school? Do you like the new one?"

I could only say, "Yes, school is fine." It's not.

"How's the weather been?"

"Good." How would I know, spending all my time in the basement as I did? My teeth ground back all the things I wanted to say.

I got to the one question I burned to ask. "Did I get a letter from Jack or Mary?"

"Yes. I'll send it on to you." She'd said that before, and I hadn't gotten them.

"No, keep it for me until summer." I glanced up at the Mess, at her narrowed eyes and looked quickly away. Somehow, during my settling into Jess's house, my address books and letters disappeared, and I didn't know where the new ones went. I wanted all my addresses back so I'd be able to write to Jack, but I would have to wait.

Finally, I got to the last question, the one I always finished with. "Did you hear from my mum?"

I knew the answer even before she said, "No."

So that left only, "Bye, hope to see you all real soon," in a cheery voice and, "Love you."

Then I had to hang up and say, "Thank you" to Jess, like all was well with the world.

No one had any news of my mum for a long time now. I felt so embarrassed to have to tell people I had no idea where she was. At times, I would be angry at her. At others, I missed her a lot. Sometimes I thought something must be wrong with me, 'cause even my own mother didn't want me.

I wondered about her all the time; what was she doing and where was she? I feared for her, knowing she wasn't well, not at all. When Tara was born, I thought she might get better; she'd be happy to have a new baby and get busy looking after her, but things didn't work out that way. She came home from the hospital and took to her bed. Mary cared for Tara and carried her to Mum to get her feedings. Mary bathed her, changed her diapers and rocked her to sleep.

After a while, Mum seemed to get better. At least I found her up and dressed when I came home from school. She started talking more, normal little pleasantries like, "Oh, hello Bria, did you have a good day today?" Certainly a big improvement, but she still never took care of the baby.

That's why I was so surprised when she told me it was time to go back to Canada. I didn't think so. I thought we should all stay put, especially me and Tara, and I said so to Jack, who agreed with me.

"So why are we leaving?" I asked him, not upset, just curious. I didn't mind going to Aunt Peg's for a while. I missed them.

"Yes, Jack, why?" Mary shouted. She was mad.

"She's the mother, Mary. She has the right to take her children to the country of her birth. There's nothing you or I can do to stop her. Don't you think I would if I could?"

"Does she look like a fit parent to you?"

"Mary." Jack rolled his eyes toward me.

I understood. The old adult conspiracy: don't talk in front of the child, as if they were thinking anything I hadn't already thought. I knew Mary worried about us, and why. My mum was a mess. I tried to comfort her. "Don't worry Mary. Auntie Peg and I will take good care of Tara."

Mary sighed and choked, ready to cry again. "And who, Bria darling, will look after you?"

"I'm almost eleven. I can look after us both."

"Bria, you only turned ten four months ago. You're a lot closer to nine than eleven." Jack always corrected me on the details—stupid man. Didn't he understand that it was more important to make Mary feel better than to be accurate?

At first, things went pretty much as I predicted. Auntie Peg and I took care of Tara, who grew cuter and cuter, gurgling and laughing as soon as you looked at her: so simple and innocent, unaware of the work she made, more than I thought possible of any little creature.

I tried to do as much as I was able because Aunt Peg was so busy. It's not easy running a house for nine people, not in an old place with no plumbing and a biffy outside under the poplar trees.

No one would believe the amount of work involved in looking after one little baby who pees a hundred times a day. You have to pump the water from the well, heat the huge pot on the wood range, boil the diapers, scrub them, rinse them and put them on the line every single day. Even less fun when it's way below zero outside, and the wet flannels hang all night in the kitchen and you get slapped in the face with a soggy diaper whenever you turn around.

Aunt Peg slowly grew mad at Mum, who spent the day laying on the couch in the living room, staring up at the ceiling, seeing God only knows what. Some days she would get up and dressed and try to do stuff. One day she went into Strathmore and came back saying she'd gotten a job at the hospital, but when the big day arrived, she couldn't make herself get out of bed and go, so that was that, as Mary would say.

I missed Mary, but mostly I missed having my own room. Lizzie didn't want Tara in with us, so I slept on a camp cot in the kitchen, beside the baby's box so I would wake up during the night and take her to Mum.

One day, Mum got up and dressed, went into town and didn't come back. We kept expecting to hear from her, but received only silence. Uncle Dugald drove to Strathmore and talked to the RCMP, but they never had anything to tell us.

No matter how much work I did, I still sensed trouble coming. One night Aunt Peg and Uncle Dugald sat me down at the table 'cause we needed to talk. Uncle started out with, "Bria, you're getting to be a big girl now. I want you to be as grown-up as you can to hear what we need to tell you."

This was bad. I waited. My heart waited.

With much clearing of his throat, he went on. "I know you understand about money. Here's the problem: I don't make a lot running the elevator for the Wheat Pool and nine people live in this house."

I had an answer for that. I'd been riding since I was a little kid, and last summer I'd ridden in the rodeos and made some money, which I gave to Uncle Dugald. I loved racing and the more I won the more money he got. The races were where I'd met my friend, Ted, and his dad, Gene, the only friends I had, except for Jack, of course. "But Uncle, summer will come, and we can do the rodeos again. I'll ride the ponies. I'll try real hard. I'll win."

"It's not enough, Bria, not enough. Money was tight when your mother was sending us your keep; now, the situation is impossible. We asked Jess and Frank for help. Frank says they don't have the money to spare, but they're willing to take you, give you a home."

"No! Not Jess!" I screamed. She had strange, scared children, quick hands and weird speech that sounded as if she had snot in her throat. "Em, the way things were, em, done in Edinborough." The last word rolled out of her mouth with a buzz. Even Aunt Peg, who loved everyone, didn't like her.

Aunt Peg had tears rolling down her face. "I know this is hard, hard for us, too. We'll take you over the summers. You can still do the rodeos. We've loved you since you were born. You're like one of our own."

"But I'm not." I had to accept the truth, no matter how bitter.

Clearly, this was a done deal and, unless I conjured up a good argument right now, I was doomed to life with Jess and Frank. I had a flash. "We could ask Jack and Mary for help."

"No." Uncle was definite.

"Auntie, why not?"

"No. You're my sister's child and I'm sending you to our brother and his wife. We keep our business in our own family, Bria. We're not going to air our troubles to strangers in Chicago, people we've never met."

"But Uncle, Jack and Mary are family."

"Not really. I'd understand them taking the baby, should it come to that. She is their blood after all, but you're not."

Auntie wiped her eyes. "We'd manage to keep you alone somehow, but babies need so many things. And we decided it would be wrong to split you up like Jess—" She stopped, flustered.

I understood. They wanted the baby but not me. I got the message. "No, you're right. Even if they don't want me, I have to be there to look after Tara."

"Who said you weren't wanted?" Auntie cried louder. "Did I say that? No. They are willing to give you a home, send you to a good school. Frank can do more for you than we can. You should be grateful."

Grateful? I stopped being grateful the first week. Jess the Mess wanted us all right, to parade us around to all and sundry. "The two children we've had to take in...of course, em, it's been quite an adjustment, you know...em, one does what one has to, family, you see... Frank's youngest sister's girls, such a tragedy, em..." Putting on airs, playing Lady Bountiful. She was ridiculous.

And mean. Fawning over us in public and whacking me on the head whenever I was in reach at home. She punished me for trouble the very first day, and every day since. I used to have two good homes, one where I was special and taken care of and another where I was one of the gang and free to take care of myself. And now, I sat in jail with Jess the Mess as my warden.

The only freedom to be found existed inside my own head, and I escaped in daydreams for hours on end. If Jess peeked into my bedroom, she would see me apparently studying, but I was staring with unseeing eyes at the pages of a book. What she didn't know was I'd travelled far, far away, free and happy.

I thundered at top speed on Chinook, my black and white pinto pony. Above me, the sky was cobalt blue, dotted with cotton ball clouds and beneath us, the prairie wool of tangled dry grass blurred as Chinook's hooves churned little puffs of dust that flew into the air. We sailed over fences and high clumps of sweet clover in our path. The wind blew in my face, fresh and clean. If either of us had chosen to, we would have flown.

Once I dreamed my good friend, Ted, let me ride his horse Ranchhand in a race at one of the rodeos. Instead of running a pony in the children's events, I raced in the arena with the professionals. We hit the track at a full gallop and spun around the first barrel almost parallel to the ground, we came out of the turn so fast. Still flying like the wind, we wrapped the second barrel perfectly and Ranchhand's hooves only skimmed the earth as we tore up to the third. He skidded so hard his front feet left the ground, and he reared and turned in one lunge. Hurtling full force to the finish line, he reared again as I pulled him to a stop. Our time came in, the best anyone had ever seen, and we exited the arena to thunderous applause.

When Ted and his dad and Uncle Dugald all crowded around me, shouting how well I had done and how proud of me they all were, the picture went black, and I opened my eyes to the bleak little room downstairs.

God, I hate it here.

Five:
"We learned logic and problem solving."

1970

I put my journal back in its hiding place up above some wires that ran between the floor joists, a spot I judged to be safest. Jess would never think of looking up there. All she found this time was a letter to Jack, asking him to come and get Tara. A letter I couldn't mail. It was enough.

I was tried, convicted and my sentence handed down. I lived under house arrest, ordered to stay in my room at all times with exception made only for school and chores. This included a complete ban on any and all after school activities.

I shrugged the punishment off. The cloud of impending doom hanging over me had long overshadowed my pleasure in baseball and friends. I was exhausted anyway.

For the first time in my life, I hated school. My teachers complained about me and said I daydreamed, didn't pay attention or do my homework, and they wrote things in my report cards like *Bria doesn't work up to her abilities*. Not that anyone cared or commented. School used to be so easy and fun, and now I couldn't focus on anything. I didn't read much anymore and when I tried, I would fall asleep.

Once the Mess realized she hadn't hurt me with her edict, she staged a midnight raid on my room, waking me from a sound sleep with a resounding slap across my face. She'd found the cache of crackers and peanut butter I'd sneaked down earlier in anticipation of a late night appetite. Looking for more evidence of my thieving ways, she dumped out the drawers of my dresser into a pile on the floor, emptied my closet, and gave orders to clean up before leaving in the morning.

The next day, she announced I had to stay away from Tara, as I was a dirty, sneaky, thieving, rotten, ungrateful and greedy girl, not fit company for an innocent toddler. The only companions left to me were my journal and Kilroy, who had taken to hanging out with me down in my room.

The various layers of me fell away, leaving this scared shell of a girl who wanted nothing more than to stay out of trouble and have some peace and quiet. Jess was breaking me. My brain swelled up in my skull, so full of lies that were secrets and secrets that were lies, I couldn't tell the difference anymore. Inside our house was hell. Outside, was a world of pretence.

"And how is your lovely aunt? Aren't you lucky to live in such a fine home?" people would ask. I would smile beautifully and agree, "Yes indeed, we're so grateful to them for taking us," and, "Yes, they are such good people."

After church on Sundays, we'd stand outside with Jess and Frank greeting everyone, Anne, Linda and I in our fine Sunday dresses, our hair carefully combed and tied in place, all freshly scrubbed like some picture perfect family posed on display. And we lied our faces off. Aunt Jess would smile and smile as people commented on how well behaved we were and what a wonderful mother she must be, such a good Christian to take on two more. Lies. All lies.

The only honest one, little Tara, smiled and loved everyone. Finally the sight of Tara's innocent baby face made me decide. I had to do something.

I spent long hours downstairs in my corner of the basement. Bria the mole, living underground, only coming out to flee to school, hiding from the light of day and digging tunnels of escape in her mind, most of them dead-ends, impractical and impossible, all beyond the reach of a girl of twelve.

We studied logic and problem solving in school. I tried to apply those rules: break down the problem into its component parts and solve each in order. I took out my journal and did just that.

1. Problem: Life around Jess the Mess was impossible. Solution: Go back to Peg's house. Hadn't she said they would manage for me alone?

2. Problem: I couldn't leave Tara with the Mess. She already swatted Tara's diapered little bottom for touching things. In time, she'd move on to face slapping, butt kicking and insanity. *Solution: Get Tara out of her reach.*

3. Problem: Where to take her? Solution: Mary's house. Peg would be good to her, but she wasn't able to afford the two of us. No, Mary was the only answer.

4. Problem: How to get her there? I couldn't simply pack a diaper bag, put her in her stroller and walk to Chicago. I didn't know how to get there, but I did know it was far. *Solution: Get someone who could.*

5. Problem: Who? Solution: Jack, of course.

6. Big problem: I had no way to reach Jack. Solution: The library.

Inspiration hit me like a thunderbolt. My body thrilled with excitement. That was the key—the library! Hadn't Miss Coalbins told us everything we wanted to know would be in the library? Didn't she say we'd be able to find anything, anything at all if we learned how? I had thought the Dewey decimal system stupid and boring, but now it was a godsend. I loved the Dewey decimal system!

7. Next problem: I was grounded. How would I get to the library? Solution: School work. I needed to invent a project that required a visit to the library, but I had to be very, very careful.

***

All afternoon I plotted, schemed, and made my preparations. At suppertime, when summoned to set the table for dinner, I put my plan in motion.

"Auntie Jess," I began, as contritely as possible, "I'm very sorry for the things I said in that letter. I was mad at you and wrote them to feel better but never meant for anyone to read those lies. Please believe me."

"Fine then." She handed me the plates.

"Auntie Jess, I understand you're doing what's best for me. As you say, I'm wild and out of control, and you're right to correct me." I almost gagged on my words. "And I'm trying to do better. I will do better, I promise."

"We'll see." She handed me the cutlery.

I set the utensils out carefully, the way she liked them. Knives went to the right, blade turned in; forks on the left, small one on the outside; spoons above the plate, little one on top and everything perfectly aligned. The napkins had to be rolled-up, tucked through their rings and placed beside the knives. Proper, she called it, because, after all we weren't a family of laborers, were we?

"How's this?"

"Fine."

Supper went as usual: over-cooked meat, mashed potatoes and canned peas served lukewarm and the normal table conversation. "Anne sit up. Linda stop making those disgusting sounds with the food in your mouth. You're turning my stomach. Bria, use the knife properly. Linda, swallow without the gulping. Bria, the fork is not a shovel. Anne, when we chew, our mouths are closed."

Lucky Tara, she got her supper early, by herself, minus the constant attentions of Our Lady of the Proper Table Manners. Frank ate without saying a word. I had to strike before he left the table.

"Auntie Jess, Uncle Frank, I have a problem."

"What is it?" Frank asked.

"I know I deserve to be grounded for being so ungrateful." I hoped I wasn't laying on the penitence too thick. "But I have homework to do this weekend, and I need to go to the library." I pulled the paper I'd prepared earlier out of my pocket. "Here's a list of all the things I'm supposed to look up and get answers to, and I need to show references and how I used the Dewey Decimal system to find them."

I addressed only Frank. "I was wondering, seeing as it's for school, may I please take the bus to the library on Saturday to do this work?" I held my breath, waiting for an answer, too scared to glance at Jess.

Before she had time to say anything, Frank said, "Of course you can. I'm going downtown Saturday morning, and I can drop you off."

Jess glared at me with narrowed eyes. "How long will this take?"

"I don't know. I can catch the bus home if I can have a quarter."

Frank nodded and left to go watch television. Jess pushed her chair back and got up quickly. She was mad. She went over to the coffeepot, poured herself a cup and turned to us. "Bria clear the dishes. Anne you wash. Linda you dry."

"Please may I leave the table?" we chorused as required and got up.

Jess grabbed my arm, spun me around and hissed right in my face, so close I smelled the cigarettes on her breath. "I know you, little lady." Her spit sprayed me. "Full of apologies are you? Butter wouldn't melt in your mouth when you want something. Oh yes, madam, I'm on to you." She stuck her index finger between my eyes. "Watch yourself."

My heart pounded in my chest. I had to be careful, very careful indeed.

***

The following day, Friday, I got up full of excitement and anxiety, ready to move on to the next part of my plan. I dressed, made my bed, checked I hadn't left anything incriminating in my room, and that I'd tucked my journal in the special place in the floor joists, out of sight. I contemplated taking the notebook with me, but decided that was too dangerous. Miss Coalbins might discover it and tell Jess, ruining my plans. Just one more day and it would be safe.

First thing at school, I approached the teacher. "Miss Coalbins, my social studies scribbler is all full. See." I flipped the pages to show her. I'd spent an entire afternoon copying notes from my text. "Please, may I get another?"

"Go ahead."

I went to the back of the class and stood by the stationary locker, pretending to study a picture on the wall until she was busy and not paying attention, opened the door, took out a new scribbler and then reached up to the top shelf where the stack of big brown envelopes sat. I grabbed one, folded it in half with one hand, slipped it inside the scribbler, and scurried back to my desk. As soon as I was sure no one was paying me any notice, I stuffed the envelope into my book bag. Done!

That night I set my alarm clock for 2 a.m. I had barely fallen asleep when the bell rang and I had trouble waking up. A long arm reached out from my pillow and pulled me down in its softness, lulling me once more into dreams. Just as I almost fell back to sleep, I was jolted into sudden consciousness. I had to go forward with my plan.

I slipped out of bed. In my pajamas and bare feet, I crept up the basement stairs, tiptoed to the bathroom without turning on the light and sat on the toilet—my alibi—my ears straining for the sounds of movement upstairs. Any second now, Jess would swoop down, hoping to catch me doing something I shouldn't.

I sat and listened for a long time.

Once I deemed myself safe, I went into the kitchen. Jess's purse sat on the counter. Her cigarettes were inside. She liked to come down at night and smoke them, but tonight the coast was clear, so I fished out her wallet and opened it.

A voice spoke in my head, telling me what to do. *Two ones, three fives, two tens. Which one? Ten is too much and likely missed immediately. A one isn't such a crime, but will it be enough? If I take them both, she'll notice. She has three fives. Yes, one of those.* My body ran like a machine doing what the voice said. The rest of me split in two. Half screamed, *Oh, My God, I'm scared!* The other watched calmly.

I sneaked to my room, stuffed the bill inside my dictionary and jumped into bed, reset my alarm for 8 a.m. and lay quiet trying to get my breathing back under control, listening to my racing heart. "Success," I rejoiced and hugged myself good night with the thought Nancy Drew herself couldn't have done a better job.

Uncle Frank drove me to the downtown library and stopped right in front. As I was about to scramble out, he said, "Just a minute. Here's a quarter for the bus and a dollar in case you get hungry."

He drove off leaving me with my overstuffed book bag in my hand and a word in my mind as I stared at the dollar: nonplussed. I'd found the term in a story once and looked it up in my dictionary. It's a good word.

Inside the library, I felt small in the huge foyer. My footsteps echoed when I walked. A sign on a desk said Assistance, so I addressed the smiling young woman with blond hair like my mum's who sat behind it.

"Hello, my name is Bria Jean Connelly and I'm a student. I'm here to do some research on how to find things in the library and the Dewey Decimal system."

"How may I be of assistance?" She tilted her head to one side and her smile grew brighter.

"Will you show me the place where I can look stuff up?"

"The card catalogue is in the main room on the second floor, stairs to your left." She pointed.

"And if I need help?"

"I'll help you. That's my job." She stood up and put out her hand. "My name is Sue McKenzie. So what are we looking up?"

"I have to find the Dewey Decimal System references for all these." I pulled out the list I'd made for the Mess. I had to do the work. She was quite likely to want to see proof.

"Well this should be easy enough, titles and their authors. Come on, I'll take you up." She was so friendly and helpful.

I followed her up the stairs to the card catalogue. Sue gave me an example and showed me the cards inside as we looked for my first book.

I started working on my list. It was easy. I scribbled down the numbers feverishly, aware of the ticking clock and my need to move on to more important matters. Finished, I trotted back downstairs as quickly as my legs would take me.

Sue had returned to her chair at the desk. "Done already? You work fast."

"Thanks, but now I've got something else to do." I took a deep breath and jumped in. "Where can I find people's addresses?"

"We have local and provincial phone directories."

"No." I interrupted. "For somewhere else."

"Where?"

"Chicago, Illinois."

Sue shook her head. "We wouldn't have those here, sorry."

My heart sank. "You don't?"

"No." She thought for a minute. "But you can get foreign addresses by phone from the operator."

I was so astounded, my mouth dropped open. "How?"

"You dial zero and ask for long distance information. The operator here puts you through to one in Chicago, who finds the number for you."

I wrote down everything she said. "Do you have a phone in the library?"

She pointed. "Public phones are on the wall."

"What's the cost?"

"Nothing for information but you need a nickel to get started. You'll get it back."

The only coin I had was a quarter. "Can I use this?"

She fished around in her pocket. "I have one."

I went to the phone, put in the nickel and dialed zero. A woman's voice said, "Alberta Government Telephones."

"Long distance information, please."

"For what city?"

"Chicago, Illinois." Unconsciously, I put my fingers in my mouth.

"Hang on while I connect you." I waited through a pause and another phone rang. A man with a flat accent like Jack's said, "Bell Telephone, how may I help you?"

"Alberta Government Telephones operator calling for Chicago information. Go ahead party, you are connected." I heard a click and the man's voice came back.

"For what name please?"

"Jack Connelly." I crossed the fingers still in my mouth.

"Address?"

Panic edged my voice. "But I'm calling you to get his address."

"I can get you that through reverse directory. What is the phone number?"

"I don't have that either." I felt trapped on a merry-go-round.

"Without a phone number or address, I'm sorry, I cannot help you."

By now, I was desperate and my voice shrilled when I asked, "Can't you look for Jack Connelly and see if you find one?"

"One? Ma'am, I have two pages of J. Connelly. As I said, without a phone number or address, I cannot help you."

"Oh." My heart stopped beating, but with a new thought, started again. "Wait, wait. How about Mary or Patrick Connelly?"

"I have multiple listings for both. I require an address."

I gave a little sob. "Oh." The line disconnected and I slumped sideways in the chair, deflated. I would need another plan to get Tara away and didn't think I could come up with a new one.

There was a clunk from the useless phone.

Six:
"The nobody nobody wants."

"Bria, are you all right?" Sue reached over my shoulder, flicked open a little drawer and took out her nickel.

"No. They couldn't help me. They said I needed a phone number to get an address and an address to get a phone number." I dropped my head into my hands.

"I don't know what else to tell you. Is it important?"

I raised my eyes and stared at her friendly face. "Yes, it's a matter of family urgency."

She stepped back and eyed me speculatively. "A family urgency requiring the use of the library? Bria, why don't you tell me what you're trying to do?"

Did I have anything left to lose? "I need to find Jack. He has to come and get my baby sister because where we're staying is no good."

"Are you in trouble?" She looked so concerned I decided to trust her.

"Yes. And I'm going to be in a lot more if I don't get hold of him." Hard as I tried not to, my voice quivered and my eyes filled with hot water.

"What do you know about him? Maybe I can still help. For example, where does he live? Does he have a job?" She reached for my shoulder and touched it lightly—a kindness that only increased my tears.

"He lives at his father's house because he's learning to be a lawyer, or at least he did. Now I'm not sure. It's hopeless, and I don't know what I'm going to do." I snuffled loudly trying to clear my streaming nose.

She sat down beside me and handed me a tissue from her pocket. "Well, let's think. Don't give up yet. What's his father's name?"

"John, but that's not going to help. The operator says he has two whole pages of J. Connellys."

"Does he have a job, the father?"

"He's a policeman in Chicago, a captain."

Sue's face lit up in a triumphant smile. "I'll bet we can get an address for the Chicago police department. Will that help?"

"Really?" The soaking tissue was now beyond use, so I wiped off my face with the backs of my hands.

"Really. Let me show you how."

We went back to the card system, and she pulled out the drawer that said Pi to Po. "Here we are: *Police Organizations of North America.* Come on." I followed her brisk steps into the stacks where she ran her finger along the shelf, reading out numbers. "This one." She pulled out a thick, heavy, black book.

"Index. Index. Chicago, page 341. Look, Bria."

There it was:

Chicago Police Department Headquarters
3510 S. Michigan St.
Chicago, Illinois 60601

I pulled the brown envelope out of my book bag. "Do you think if I sent something to Uncle John at this address, he'd get it?"

She considered my question for a moment. "Most likely. They must have some kind of central files to keep everybody's names. I'm sure people write to the police all the time. Mail probably gets sorted every day."

I hesitated, unsure of the right thing to do, and afraid of my journal ending up in the wrong hands. "But I don't want Uncle John to actually read it, only to give it to Jack."

"So you address the envelope to Jack, care of your uncle. Here I'll do it for you." She took my pen. "Okay what's his full name?"

"Who?"

"Jack, silly."

"Jack Connelly." I leaned on the table, weak-kneed in relief and ecstatic to find a solution at last.

"Care of," she spoke as she wrote. "Captain John Connelly, Chicago Police Department at 3510, S. Michigan Ave., Chicago, Illinois, 60601. There." She handed me the envelope. "All ready to go. All you need is postage. Go to the drugstore across the street. They'll tell you how much, and you buy the stamps. You stick them here and drop it in the mailbox in front of the store. And voila! It's gone. Anything else I can help you with, Bria?"

"I need to write a letter."

"Room to your right. Study carrels. Bye."

"Sue, thank you, Sue," I called quietly after her receding back. She waved over her shoulder, ready to move on and rescue someone else. I followed her directions, found the carrels, took out my scratch pad and quickly wrote out the letter I'd composed in my head.

I put the letter and my journal in the envelope, licked the flap and sealed the sticky tab tight. The clerk at the drug store said I should put my address in the corner, so if it got lost, the Post Office could return it to me. I told her, no thanks; it was only going one way, and my heart lightened when I dropped the thick packet in the mailbox.

I ran to Fifth Avenue and asked the driver if this bus was the right one to take me back to north east Crescent Heights. He said, "Sure is." On the bus, I started thinking about the money I had left over—$4.50. Maybe I should throw it away so the Mess wouldn't find out, but that seemed kind of dumb. Better if I kept it hidden in an old sock up in the wires between the floor joists because, I told myself, you can never tell when you might need a bit of money.

The next week dragged by. By Wednesday of the following, I expected Jack daily, but he didn't come, and I grew angry. I knew in my heart I was being unreasonable, but I couldn't help feeling that way. Soon the end of the school year would arrive, and I planned to go to Peg's for July and August to rodeo with Uncle Dugald. I couldn't wait, and not just to get away from here. Now twelve, I met the age requirement for the adult arena at the rodeo, and last summer Ted and his dad had promised they'd let me ride their horse, Ranchhand.

But dare I leave Tara? Just the other day, I heard the Mess yell at the baby. I ran upstairs as quick as my feet would fly, but Tara was fine and Jess said, "What do you want? Get back to your room."

I needed Jack to come soon. I had no fingernails left. I chewed them right down and my fingers bled, but I couldn't stop. On the Friday, I threw up at school, so the office called Jess to get me. Once out in the car, she was mad at me, naturally, but drove me home.

She finished complaining and telling me what an absolute nuisance I was, dragging her and Tara out in the morning, and asked me a favor. "As long as you're here, you can make yourself useful and watch Tara while I go to the store. Won't be more than half an hour. Do you think you can stay out of trouble for thirty minutes?"

Tara fell asleep, so I sat in the living room all alone and enjoyed the situation. I never found myself the only one home. My eyes kept returning to the phone, which seemed to get bigger and brighter sitting there calling me, saying, "Here I am Bria, you know what to do." I picked it up and dialed zero for an operator, asked for Chicago information and the Chicago Police Department Headquarters at 3510 South Michigan Street.

"I have multiple listings: central dispatch, records, Chief's office. Can you be more specific?"

Oh please, I prayed, not another go round. "Uh...I'm trying to reach Captain John Connelly. I can't tell you where he is."

"Shall I give you personnel? I think that's your best bet."

"Okay."

"The number is 312-255-9872."

My pencil broke. I grabbed a crayon. "Thank you."

"You're welcome. Have a good day." The line went dead. I sat for a minute, looking at the number, snatched up the phone and again dialed zero. I was barely aware of my words or the operator's as we crawled through the lengthy process once more.

"Hold on, we are connecting." This lady sang her sentences.

"Personnel," a chirpy woman's voice announced.

"Captain John Connelly, please."

"One moment." I waited impatiently so nervous I jittered, until the chirpy voice came back. "I'm showing no Captain John Connelly in this department."

Desolate, I begged. "Can you tell me where he can be reached?"

"One moment." Through the next pause, a long one, I heard breathing and other operators talking in the background. Scared Jess would come home before I got what I needed, I gnawed on my fingers. Finally, after an age, the voice came back. "I'm showing a Captain John J. Connelly at Southside."

"Yes." I grabbed my crayon. "Can I call him there?"

"One moment." *Don't let her come home now. Hurry, please, hurry.* My fingers bled all over the paper. "The number is 312-972-6661." I scribbled it down.

I had to go through the same process again. This time I asked for Captain John J. Connelly from the start and the operator told the man who answered, she had a "person-to-person" call.

"He's not here right now," said the deep male voice.

"Do you wish to speak to this party?" the operator asked me.

"I guess so." *Damn it!* I swore silently, ready to cry. "When will he be back?"

"He's off today. I'm not sure. I think Monday morning."

"Oh." Monday, I'd be in school.

"Do you want to leave a message?"

I considered the question and decided his suggestion may be the best course of action. After all, I had nothing to lose. "Tell him Bria called. Tell him Jack has to come real soon. It's very, very important."

"Do you want to leave a number, Bria?"

"No." The last thing I needed was for him to speak to Jess. "Just tell him I need Jack and I don't have much time. I'll try to call soon, but I don't think I can on Monday. Just tell him, okay?"

"Don't worry, I'll write it down word for word." A second later he asked, "And Bria?"

"Yes."

"Can I help you?"

"No, thank you. I have to go now."

I hung up as Jess's Chrysler pulled into the driveway, and sucked my bloody fingers clean. I barely had time to stuff the phone numbers in my pocket before she came in the door. I helped her bring in the groceries and put them away. She was pleasant, even thanked me for the help. She could be like that sometimes, almost a real person. She let me change Tara and play with her but by supper she started raging again, so as soon as I put Tara to bed, I disappeared to my room. I stashed the phone number in the same sock as the money in my special hiding place and went back to waiting. I waited a long time.

***

Then time ran out. I had to choose. Would I go to Peg's and leave Tara alone or find enough strength to stay with my sister and give up my summer, the rodeos and my freedom? Jack wasn't coming. He'd forgotten me. If I went to Peg and told her of the goings-on here, would she be able to help me get my little sister to Mary? My fingers were a mess of scabs.

Thursday started like any other day. I got up and left for school, came home afterward and walked into a fresh new hell.

"What's this?" Jess shrieked as I stepped through the door.

Ambushed and befuddled, I asked, "What's what?"

She thrust some papers in my face. "The phone bill."

Oh Christ! I froze like a rabbit in a flashlight. My tongue clung to the roof of my mouth and my throat clamped tight. I couldn't say a thing.

"You sneak! You little bitch!" The Mess worked herself up until she frothed around her lips and spit flew in the air. She terrified me.

Behind the Mess, I saw Linda shaking in the doorway to the kitchen. My voice came back. "Go upstairs, Linda."

Jess screeched. "You don't tell her what to do. You don't tell anyone in this house what to do. Who do you think you are?"

"No one." I spoke quietly, as befits the simple truth.

"Right! No one. Nothing. The nobody nobody wants." Her mouth opened wide. Her eyes narrowed; she turned into a demon. "Your mother took off and abandoned you. Your father—God only knows who he is—doesn't give a damn. Peg was sick of you and shipped you off. No one wants you. You're nothing but trouble. A sneak! A liar! You are a nobody."

I broke inside. I was no longer scared. I yelled, "I am a nobody, but I can tell you one thing true, Jess the Mess. This nobody sure hates your guts!"

Her skin flushed red and her eyes popped out. The veins in her neck throbbed. I saw her arm rise up and watched it descend. Time stopped. Her fist whistled in its arc and I felt the breeze of the blow before it landed on the side of my head. Stars danced before my eyes and I fell. My head hit the table. I tasted blood and crashed to the floor. My elbows and knees hurt. It all happened so slowly.

Another blow thumped my back. She held a glass jug in her hand and it hovered above me, high at an apex, slowly entering a downward curve.

I had no fear. "Go ahead, hit me."

She did, and again, and lifted the jug for another.

I scrambled to my feet, beyond pain, beyond fright, beyond anything but hatred. I grabbed the meat knife off the cutting board and stuck it in her shoulder.

She howled and fell back against the counter, slowly slipping to the floor, screaming and screaming. I felt power surge through me. She was scared of me.

I yelled at her. "Don't you dare hurt my sister!"

I moved to the door. "And leave your own kids alone." I ran downstairs to my room, grabbed the sock with the money and the phone number, got my jacket and raced up the stairs to the kitchen.

She was still on the floor, quiet now, but sobbing. She cringed below me. I looked down at her and felt disgust. "Don't hurt the dog, either. Or I'll come back here and kill you!"

Then I opened the back door and ran.

All the time I ran, I cried. Over and over in my head, I heard "I'm sorry Tara, I'm sorry. I tried, but I have to go. I'm sorry, Tara, I'm sorry."

Seven:
"I have to get to my Aunt's house."

"Where do you folks want to be let off?" asked the truck driver.

Paul waited for me to answer. He'd never been to Strathmore before and had no interest in the place. Currently travelling from Thunder Bay to Vancouver, he'd said seeing as my destination was right on the Trans Canada and he thought a girl might improve his chances of getting a ride, he'd let me hitch with him as far as Strathmore if I wanted.

I did, too scared to put out my thumb by myself.

I pointed. "The Esso."

"You got it." The driver pulled into the parking lot of Bud's Esso Service.

We clambered out of the cab and I yelled, "Thank you."

Paul said, "Peace, man," flashed two fingers at the disappearing truck and gazed around at the gravel lot, the boxy, cinderblock building and the line of pick-up trucks parked outside. "Farmersville. Far out."

The guys inside all stared at Paul when we walked in. I guess he did seem somewhat strange among the locals. Most of them had short hair and wore dark indigo work jeans, plaid shirts and John Deere caps. Paul could have been someone's scarecrow in fancy dress with his ponytail hanging down to his macramé belt, and a string of beads wrapped around his head. If he'd stood like Lady Liberty hoisting a flaming torch, he wouldn't command more attention than his ripped, patched jeans and tie-dyed tee shirt did. For the first time since hooking up with him that morning, I wished he appeared normal. Being so conspicuous left me uncomfortable.

I probably looked no better, but hopefully not as dirty as I felt after sleeping in a culvert the night before. I now had as much ugly orange hair flying around my head all curly and loose as remained in my braid. In my flight from the Mess's house, I hadn't thought of things like hairbrushes and clean underwear.

"Buy me a coffee?" No doubt about it, Paul was a mooch.

I only had $2.25 left, still had to find a way into Buffalo Coulee and I'd already bought him a coffee in Brooks. While he'd busied himself chatting up some dumb, straight-looking, high school girl of a waitress, I'd purchased a donut to eat in the Ladies. I almost died of shock at my reflection in the mirror, the big purple egg of a bruise covering my forehead and the scab that was now my upper lip. I tried to clean myself up, not easy when paper towels and cold water were the only tools I had to work with.

"Two coffees." I climbed up on one of the swivel stools. The old guy behind the counter glanced from me to Paul, poured coffee into take-out cups and told us to drink it outside. I paid and glared right back at him.

"Don't get so mad," Paul said as we sat on the concrete base of a lamppost. "You get used to the shunning, part of being a freak. The music in there was driving me crazy anyway."

"Hank Williams?" I was shocked to the core. "He's great."

"If you say so." He drained his coffee and tossed his crumpled cup in the garbage barrel. "Well, gotta hit the road. Sure you don't want to go to Vancouver?"

"Nah, I have to get to my Aunt's. Bye and thanks." I shook his hand.

"Peace, man." I watched him head for the highway, grateful for his help but glad to be rid of him, too.

I decided to stroll around town a bit, loosen up my stiff, bruised joints while I figured out what to do next. I had new problems. I couldn't remember my auntie's phone number, my back and legs ached where Jess hit me with the jug, and I was hungry again. I wasn't happy.

On 2nd Avenue by the King Eddy Hotel, I heard someone call out my name and I swiveled my head like some radar dish, trying to figure out who and where. I didn't normally go around the King Eddy. It smelled of beer and pee and you never knew when some drunk was going to stagger out and puke, and if there's a fight, you can get knocked down. I half hoped the whole thing amounted to a figment of my imagination, but at the same time, I prayed for someone who could help.

"Bria, over here," shouted my cousin Rob. I couldn't decide if I was happy to meet him or not—he was such a pig. Still, he might be good for a ride home.

He leaned on the tavern door, his beer belly hanging over his belt and that dumb prized silver buckle of his, the size of a saucer strained, ready to slice him open.

"Hey, Rob."

"Bria, what the hell are you doing here? I thought you were off living with Lady Muckity-Muck and her dickless husband?"

"Well, I'm back."

"Did ya enter a prize fight? You look like shit." His eyes raked me over, up and down.

"Gee thanks. I fell off a horse."

"Today?"

"No. Rob, are you going home soon? I need a ride."

"I don't live with the folks anymore. Me and Gary got a place just up the street, over the locksmith's shop. Hey, Gary," he yelled into the tavern. "Come here. Guess who's back in Strathmore and all banged up."

Gary Groves. I held no high opinion of him either. He used to try to get me to take off my pants so he could see what I had down there. As if I would. I'd rather slop hogs than have anything to do with Gary Groves, but the situation called for forbearance. That's another good word: forbearance.

"Hey, Gary," I said when he pushed his fat face out the door.

"Bria, how are ya." He sounded all hearty and happy, so I knew he was half-drunk.

Rob jerked a thumb at me. "She wants a ride to my mum's place."

"You want to take her now? I've got these two guys from Winnipeg ready to rack up the balls. Easy twenty bucks. Can't she wait?" Gary lounged against the door, smoke dangling from his mouth and his cowboy boots crossed at the ankle. Probably thought he looked cool, I decided. Well, he didn't.

"I'm right here. You can ask me directly, you know."

"Touchy, isn't she?" Gary said to Rob just to piss me off.

"Listen Rob, I don't want to spoil your fun, so how about you give me Auntie's phone number—I've forgotten—and I'll call her and tell her I'm here." I felt ready to die; I was so tired and sore.

"She doesn't know?"

"No, I wasn't supposed to come for another few days."

"How'd you get here, then?" Rob rolled himself a smoke, sucked on the end a bit to make it wet and lit up with a flame the size of a blow torch from some fancy silver lighter, probably stolen.

"Hitched." I hoped my daring impressed them.

Gary stared at me all squinty eyed. "No one knows you're here? You ran off, didn't ya?"

"No. I arrived early, that's all." I threw him my best disdainful look.

"Sure." He shot me a knowing one.

I turned to Rob. "Come on, give me her phone number, and I'll be out of your hair."

As always, Gary, the brains of the pair, answered. "We'll get you home, but not right now. We've got a game of pool waiting. After."

"Not you."

"What's wrong with me?" He acted insulted.

"Well for one thing, you're drunk."

I gave him a good view of my back and implored my idiot cousin. "I need to get home, Rob. I'm tired and hungry. Help me, please?"

For a minute, I thought he actually considered taking me, but his eyes left me and met Gary's, receiving some secret signal. "Come on in. Wait for me. One game of pool and I'll take you to Mum."

"I can't go in there! Are you crazy?"

He stomped out his cigarette butt and waved toward the main door. "You can wait in the lobby."

"Okay, but your mum's sure to be mad at you if she finds out you took me inside the King Eddy."

He raised his eyebrows. "Well who's going to tell her? You?"

"Not if you get me home before dark." As far as I understood, we had a done deal. I'd sit in the lobby of the despised King Eddy for a while—how long did a game of pool take?—and then Rob would drive me home. I'd be safe, finally. With all business attended to, I slipped into the coffee shop next door and spent my last $1.75 on a hamburger and a coke.

Two and a half hours later, I still sat on one of the cheap plastic chairs, waiting. The sky turned dark, and I hadn't heard or seen Rob in a long time. Every once in a while, the door to the tavern room opened and some drunk staggered across the lobby to the washroom, giving me a glimpse inside, a chance to try to find Rob. Cigarette smoke, beer smells and noise drifted out until the door closed again.

Once, two men came out and stood and stared at me a while. They wore polyester pants and bright shirts, and both had shiny hair combed back like Elvis, all greasy, and their hard eyes scared me by the way they examined me. Then, without a word, the men turned and went inside.

I waited and waited longer. Gary came out, and for once, I was happy to see him.

"Where's Rob?"

"In there." He jerked his thumb at the tavern door.

"What's he doing?" I couldn't help sounding whiney.

"Having a beer."

"Can you tell him that I need to get home now? Please, Gary?"

"Sure." He turned as if to go, but wheeled back with a new idea. "Why don't you go out and sit in the car? Wait for us."

"I want Rob." I pulled my feet up onto the chair and hugged my legs. "Get him for me."

"I can't. He's passed out. It's gonna be a while before he can drive. You want to sit here all night or do you wanna go to the car, maybe get a little sleep?"

Alarms sounded in my head. My options had grown very limited. Some instinct told me to run and run fast, but the effort was beyond me; I was too tired and sore. "Ok, I'll sit in the car. Where is it?"

"Out back. I'll go get the keys out of Rob's pocket. Wait right here."

He returned jingling keys from his raised hand. "Come on." Together we walked out the rear exit to the alley.

I'd never been there before. The air carried a strange odor, a combination of rotten garbage, urine and stale beer. I looked up at the building, curious, and counted four stories and eight windows each in the upper three, all in a line, some of them open with raggedy curtains blowing out, and a black fire escape zigzagged on the wall.

Busy gawking around, I didn't notice the two men who came out of the shadows. By the time I did, it was too late.

One grabbed me and put his hand over my mouth, pulling my head back against his body. Shock robbed me of thought and strength. I didn't try to struggle, just stared, silent and confounded, as the other gave Gary a wad of money. Then Gary walked away. Before panic had time to enter my mind, something soft and medicinal smelling covered my nose and I tried not to breathe. Then I had to and gagged. The dark night spun around and around and disappeared entirely.

Eight:
"Tell Jack to come soon."

MARY

"She tried to call John?" The room reeled around me. I grabbed the back of the kitchen chair for support. *Why John and not me?*

"Yes," Jack snapped. "She left a message." He sat down, slapped my poor old table with one hand and jumped up again. "'Tell Jack to come soon.'"

"Those children are in trouble."

"Dad and I agree. Detective Bauer got some funny vibes off the call." Jack paced back and forth across my kitchen floor. His troubled energy was contagious, not helpful to my nerves at all.

"Such as?"

"Your guess is as good as mine." He flung out his arms and shrugged. "That's all he had to say. He took the message three weeks ago."

Still dazed, I couldn't think, and tried for some minutes to absorb his words. "Why didn't you tell me sooner?"

"I only found out today." He finally collapsed onto a chair. "Apparently, the call came while Dad was up in Milwaukee. Bauer carries a heavy caseload, and he was understandably busy. As a result, her message gathered dust on his desk all this time. Have you any idea what it's like in the detective's bureau?"

"No, actually I don't." I heard the waspish tone of my voice and tried to soften it. "All I know is a child called the police looking for help and was ignored. She fell through the cracks."

"A lot of things do, Mary." He pointed at the coffee maker. "Please? Anyway, why waste energy assigning blame? It's unfortunate but it happened. Let's move forward from here."

"What do we do?" I was prepared to pack and travel, hire a detective, call the Canadian authorities or run down the street: anything, everything, all at the same time. "Jack, I want her back. I want them both here with me."

He asked the question plaguing my mind as well. "Where's Sandra in all this?"

"God only knows." I walked in circles as I spoke. "Probably off somewhere looking for a new husband and partying it up. Bloody useless excuse for a woman. No thought for anyone but herself."

Jack took me by the shoulders and firmly sat me in a chair. He made the coffee. "Have you ever visited Canada?"

"Canada! I've never been out of Chicago."

"Well start thinking about it, because I think we're going to Alberta, you and me." He gave me a sideways glance. "We'll take a look around. See what's up. Maybe everything is all right, maybe not. Let's not jump to conclusions."

"When?" I mentally picked and packed a wardrobe. What was the weather up there like this time of year? "When can we go?"

"Monday or Tuesday."

"But today's only Thursday."

"Patience." He poured us each a cup of coffee and rummaged around the fridge looking for milk. "We have work to do first."

"Like what?"

"Dad wants to make some phone calls, police stuff, develop contacts. So do I, starting with Aunt Peg." He put the mug in front of me. "Help me out here. When was the last time you tried to call?" He pulled out a yellow legal pad and sat across from me, prepared to take notes.

I had to stop and think. "A week ago. I got the girl, what's her name? Elizabeth. She told me Bria and Tara were still at her aunt's home. The time before, I talked to Peg herself. I asked Peg for the number, said I wanted to talk to Bria."

"What did she say?"

"Her brother and sister-in-law believed Bria was beginning to settle down. They didn't think it a good idea for me to make direct contact with her. I inferred she'd had some difficulties, as she did here at first."

"So you couldn't talk to her. Did you ask any questions?"

I realized I was a fool. "Peg said she recently talked to Bria, and she sounded happy enough. To be truthful, I felt I was getting the old bum's rush."

Jack thought this important. "They wouldn't let you talk to her?"

Worse than a fool, I was a dupe. "But what she said made some sense. When Bria was here with me, she'd be happy in our situation until she talked with her people in Canada, and I'd find her crying, homesick. So many times I wanted to say 'can't you leave her alone for a bit?'"

"But you didn't. You respected her right to enjoy the people she loved, which appears to be more than this aunt does."

"I told them to give the girl our love and to tell her to call us collect whenever she wanted."

Jack leaned back and stared at the ceiling tiles. "How long since you actually spoke to Bria?"

"Months. She's not even aware Pat passed away. Oh God, has that much time passed? I'm ashamed of myself." I looked to him for comfort but found him preoccupied.

"Mary, here's what I want you to do. Get out your phone records and document all the calls back and forth since she left and make notes on things you remember from the conversations." For a second he seemed to be studying my cotton curtains. "When did she go to this aunt?"

Before I found the chance to answer, he added, "And you're not the only one feeling shame."

I chose to ignore his last comment. "I can get my phone bills. And when? They moved a few days before the school year started. Peg said Frank and Jess live in a prosperous neighborhood with good schools. That's why Peg sent them."

"I don't like this at all. We can't even get a phone number or address. The more I think about it the less sense it makes. She goes to this mystery aunt and silence." He smacked the table again. "No, something stinks here. I'm angry with myself because I didn't see earlier."

"Lighten up on yourself, Jack. I remember you studying for the Bar, starting your career, more than a little busy."

"I told her to trust me. We were friends and what did I do? I barely gave her a thought in all these months." He sighed, his expression rueful. "No, I make no excuses for myself."

He got up and tightened his tie. "Time to go back to the office, I'm afraid. Try not to worry."

"We need to find them."

"We will. Dad's got a lead. Bria made the call with operator assistance, person-to-person and there's every chance we can trace it back, one of the things he's doing now." He threw on his jacket. "Lucky for us I'm a cop's son."

I straightened his lapels and pulled his face down to mine. "Call me if you hear anything, anything at all."

"Of course. Now get those records. Give me a shout if you're missing any, and I'll get an order for the phone company to pull them for you. Got it?"

"Yes, Jack."

"Later."

He was gone. I heard the roar of his old car as he pulled from the curb. He should buy a new muffler.

I busied myself looking for all my old phone bills, only to find half of them missing, but the task gave me something to do. I needed to be busy in the deathly quiet and empty house. If it would bring those girls back to me, I'd search out every bill I'd ever received. I made a list of the missing months and called Jack the next morning.

"Mary, make me some lunch. I'll be over at noon. Gotta go."

"Jack! Wait. Any developments?" I heard several voices having a conversation around him and prayed he'd give me a minute.

"Yes."

"What?"

"Noon, Mary. Sorry. Be patient." He hung up.

***

Patience is one virtue I never cultivated. At times, I swear the clocks ran backward. The walls bore down on me as I shuffled mindlessly from one room to the next. I beat myself up. I should have put up some kind of fight, legal standing be damned, and never let that empty shell of a woman take them away.

Lunch sat on the table rapidly cooling by the time Jack's car roared up my driveway. I started on him the minute he stepped in the door. "Well?"

He waved a large brown envelope. "This has been floating around the Chicago Police Department for the past month. Dad only found the thing yesterday at HQ and wouldn't yet if he hadn't gone looking."

He barely pulled up to the table before attacking his lunch, and spoke at rapid-fire speed between bites. "Dad put a rush on the phone thing. He traced back another call to HQ personnel. The idea came to

62

him Bria had somehow found that address, so he went to their office and talked to people." A mouthful in, he swallowed and spoke. "One operator remembered a query from a child, and another thought of this, still sitting in a routing tray."

"It's addressed to you."

"Might have been the problem. Who knows?"

"The flap's open. Did you read it? Can I?"

"Here, give me." He put down his spoon, took the envelope back and pulled out a paper. "What do you think of this?"

I read aloud from Bria's short letter, handwritten in pencil on the kind of unbleached newsprint one gives a child to scribble on. "*Dear Jack, I need you to come and get Tara and take her to Mary's house. She can't stay here. This is not a good place. Please come.* Oh, sweet Jesus." I sat down.

"*We're at 551 7ᵗʰ Street N.W., Medicine Hat, Alberta, Canada.* She was smart enough to send us an address. We can go get them." I was elated.

Jack shook his head. "It won't be that simple. Read on."

"*I'm sending you my journal and I want you to keep it safe for me.*"

"Her journal?"

Jack pulled a school notebook out of the envelope. "Her journal." The cover bore a stamp: Webster Niblock Elementary, and underneath, in red crayon: PROPERTY OF BRIA J. CONNELLY, PRIVATE.

Instead of handing me the book, he slipped it back into the envelope. I asked, "Have you read what she says?"

"Not yet. I merely glanced here and there." Another mouthful of soup went down. "She may have inadvertently sent us exactly what we need."

"I don't understand."

"You will." Everything about him was rushed today. "Read on."

"*Are you still my lawyer? I hope you are my friend even though I haven't written in such a long time. It's not my fault. Please come. I love you, Bria.*" The sweet simplicity of it broke my heart, and I started weeping.

"Yes," Jack said. "Aren't I a shit?" He made an end to the soup and his spoon clinked in the empty bowl. He reached for the sandwich and wolfed it down in five seconds flat.

"Can I read the journal?" I held out my hand, waiting.

"Sorry, need it myself." He smiled a sad smile. "Anyway, don't think she'd want you to. Monday we go. Pick you up at 8 a.m. Gotta go. Thanks for the lunch."

I stared at the door where he'd been ten seconds earlier, thinking I knew little more now than when he'd arrived. Why was he so secretive? I couldn't guess, but a certainty grew in me. Something was very wrong.

***

Somehow I survived our whirlwind trip to Canada. Every morning I woke up in a different place and spent the day trailing along after Jack, pressed to keep up. I marveled at his detailed preparations and meticulous plans. I needed the comfort. For four days we drove here and there, meeting this person and that, and the more we learned, the greater my dread.

We arrived in Calgary in mid-afternoon, rented a car at the airport and without even a break for lunch, we were on the highway. Jack assigned me the job of reading the map where our route was marked out in red ink, no detail forgotten in his groundwork. I suspected I was merely baggage along for the ride, and was grateful for that. I'd lived a quiet little life and pondered my inexperience as I stared out the window at Bria's home.

I never imagined such an immense landscape existed. As far as the eye could see land rolled onward, not flat and not hilly, but undulating—an ocean of gold and tan. Red and white cattle clustered in groups dotted the gold,. Every now and then, a tree rose out of the ground, so rare it demanded attention. Before us, the highway ran on into the distance, a black ribbon, its length measured out by the regularity of the power poles. Behind, the peaks of the distant Rocky Mountains shimmered silver in the afternoon sun. I imagined myself Louis and Clarke all rolled up in one.

I wanted to share this with Jack, but the set of his jaw, his concentration forbade me. He stared straight ahead, both hands on the steering wheel, silent. Then, with such abruptness I jumped, he said, "Strathmore."

It didn't appear to be much, this Strathmore: a few gas stations, a couple of restaurants close to the highway, scattered, without any evidence of a plan. To the left: trees, houses and the tops of some larger buildings. To the right: an officious-looking strip complex surrounded by more trees and ahead, one traffic light. It was red. We stopped.

64

Jack peered past me. "Police station."

I followed his view to the red brick building. A large blue sign, embossed with a crest and "Royal Canadian Mounted Police" stood in front. "Are we going to talk to them?"

"Not yet." That's all he gave me—two words.

I had enough and demanded, "Jack. Talk to me. What are we doing?"

"We're off to see Peg." He drove on.

"If you don't tell me more, I'm going to scream."

He relented. "I'm sorry. I'm not much of a travel companion, too busy in here." He tapped his head.

"Share with me."

"Again?" He gave me a grim smile. "We're going to visit Peg and learn all we can about these people we're up against. I want you to act naturally as this thing unfolds. I want them to see your reactions, unrehearsed."

"Is that why you won't let me read Bria's journal?" I knew it was in his briefcase, and I was dying to learn what had befallen her.

"She was badly treated, Mary, as I've already told you. Bria's entrusted her private journal to my safekeeping, and I'm only going to use what little I need. If she wants you to know more, she can tell you herself." He put one hand over mine for an instant and gave me a gentle squeeze. "Help me find this secondary road, PTH 776."

"What's PTH?"

"Damned if I know. Just keep your eyes peeled."

Jack spied the sign first: Provincial Trunk Highway 776, a gravel road running straight through two vast barbwire fenced fields. Farther along, the route climbed up a large dome shaped hill that struck me as a pimple on a huge, broad face. A small white arrow nailed to a post said 'Buffalo Coulee, 8 mi.'

"That's what we want." We set off at a reduced speed, churning up a storm of dust in our wake. At the crest of the hill, Jack stopped and we sat, two city dwellers staring out into infinity. The only sound in the absolute silence was Jack's muttered "Jesus."

Spread out below us, as pretty as a huge patchwork quilt was a view so immense I could see the curvature of the earth. A cluster of buildings, tiny and insignificant, caught my eye. "That must be the place there, where the road turns and meets a railroad."

I pointed next to the railway tracks at two white tower-like structures, much taller than wide, with sloping shoulders and a narrow steep roof,. "What the hell are those?"

Jack took off his sunglasses and peered down the hill. "Beats me. Let's go find out."

We followed the curving road to the plain below. My eyes were riveted to the strange towers, and as they loomed closer, I read 'Alberta Wheat Pool' in large black letters. Underneath, it said 'Buffalo Coulee'.

"Grain storage would be my guess." Jack pointed past me. "Look: Bria's school."

On my left sat a white building, maybe thirty feet square, surrounded by playground equipment and a playing field. "There can't be more than a single classroom inside."

"Bria once told me she never figured out how someone could sit in one room for nine years and still not learn how to read. I think she had grade six down pat by the end of her second year."

"Except for mathematics." I counted eleven houses scattered on one side of the road. "How will we find Peg's house?"

"Antlers." He regarded me with a serious face: serious except for a twinkle in his eye, as though this should make sense, and drove on.

"What?"

"This is the one." He stopped in front of a two storey, narrow frame house with a porch up front. A hedge bordered the small yard, broken only by an arch covered gateway. He pointed up at a magnificent rack of antlers mounted above the entrance.

"Smart-ass," I said as I got out of the car.

A large and drably dressed woman came through the front door to greet us. "Hello." Her voice was loud and gruff and her accent reminded me of Bria. "You found us."

"Jack Connelly." Jack stuck out his hand. "And Mary Connelly. You must be the famous Auntie Peg."

"Peg MacCleod, pleased to meet you both." The strength and roughness of her red hands surprised me. She was a raw-boned woman with an enormous bosom, taller than me by several inches. Her brown eyes were soft and gentle in her ruddy face, and I found myself liking her.

"Come in, come in. I'll make us some tea." We followed her into the house.

The front door opened on a sitting room, furnished with three couches covered in hand-made Afghans and a coffee table printed and drilled as a cribbage board. A tidy pile of pillows and blankets in a large basket announced clearly this doubled as sleeping space at night.

"Sit down. Please sit." We did.

A teenage girl appeared from a door on the right, fair haired and petite next to her mother. *Pretty, and would be prettier if not for the amount of eye makeup she wears.*

Peg introduced her. "My daughter, Elizabeth."

"Hello, Elizabeth. We spoke on the phone not too long ago."

"I know." She sat down beside me, arms crossed, determined to be included in whatever happened next.

Peg said, "I'll get the tea," apparently ill at ease, and moved quickly through an arch into a dining room, judging by the large table and mismatched chairs. She was back in two seconds, wringing her hands.

"I've got to tell you this right off. Bria's run away and no one has any idea where she is."

Her words hung in the air. I gasped. "No!"

Peg covered her mouth and tears dribbled down each side of her nose. Jack's face showed little change. His eyes seemed to grow under his heavy brows, the only noticeable betrayal of his thoughts. He peered at Peg and calmly asked, "When?"

"Thursday, four days ago. We didn't know ourselves until yesterday."

"Who told you? Aunt Jess?"

"No, the police. The Mounties came looking for her. They said—" she stopped, took out a hankie from a pocket and blew her nose, sucked in a deep breath and calmed herself—"she attacked her Aunt Jess with a knife. I can't believe it. That doesn't sound like Bria."

We sat in shocked silence a moment.

To my surprise Jack said, "Perhaps we should have that tea. Let me help you."

"Here, let me," I offered.

"No." Jack gave me a silent signal. "I'll go."

He guided Peg by the arm and gently walked her to the kitchen. For the next ten minutes or so, as I watched Elizabeth play with the ends of her hair, I listened to their gentle buzz of conversation. First Jack's deep voice—soft and unintelligible—then Peg's—mournful and interspersed with sobs—then Jack's again.

Just when I thought I couldn't stand the tension any longer, that I would leap off the couch, run into the kitchen and demand to be told what was going on, they came back. Jack carried a tray of tea things and Peg a plate of homemade cakes.

Jack sat down and spoke to me. "She ran from her aunt's on Thursday. The aunt is not badly hurt, apparently; it's a superficial wound, only needing a couple of stitches. However, she pressed charges against Bria, and the police are looking for her now. Peg can't think of anywhere she might go but here."

"What about you?" he asked Elizabeth. She shrugged and shook her head.

He poured for all of us. "After our tea, I'm going to drive into Strathmore and talk with the police."

"My husband will accompany you," Peg said. "You'll need someone who knows the place."

"Fine." He passed out cups.

"And me." I reached for my tea.

Jack leaned forward and gave me another of those looks. "I think it better if you stay here. Give you a chance to talk with Peg and Elizabeth." His eyes asked if I understood.

I nodded.

We sipped our tea and sat mute as mannequins. As if commenting on the weather, casual as could be, Jack said, "I have reason to believe Bria was maltreated badly enough that for the past month she's been desperately trying to contact us. Unfortunately, her message came to us too late. Here, something for you to read."

He handed over Bria's letter and Peg fished in one of her pockets, put on some eyeglasses and sat staring at the paper. Finished, she glanced up at Jack. "We didn't know. If we had, believe me, we would have done something."

"No one is blaming you." Jack touched her hand. "Bria loves you. You were always good to her. All I ever heard was Auntie Peg this and Auntie Peg that. You've been a wonderful aunt. Don't blame yourself. All that matters now is to find her."

"We didn't know," Peg repeated. "She's a funny woman, so nervous and—"

"She's a cow!" We all turned to look at Elizabeth who, apparently, had nothing else to say.

I decided I was going to strike up an acquaintance with Elizabeth while Jack was gone, find out as much as possible about this cow.

Jack was back in command. "Now we need to talk about something serious. Peg, the most important thing to Bria was Tara's safety. I've made some inquiries and as far as I found out, no order of guardianship was ever filed for either of these girls. Do you know if Frank and Jess initiated anything like that?"

Peg frowned, perplexed. "No. They're family and we try to care for them as best we can."

"So their mother, Sandra, never made you guardian for the children?"

"No."

He wrote down a few notes on his legal pad. "And over a year has passed since she contacted you?"

"Yes." Peg hung her head and mumbled, "Something's wrong with her. She just up and left them here, and we didn't know what to do." She looked up at Jack, pleadingly. "We did what we thought was best. You can see we have little to give them. Frank and Jess have more."

"I understand." He poured himself another cup of tea. "Now tomorrow, Mary and I are driving to Medicine Hat. We're going to get Tara and bring her back with us. Will you keep her here until we can clear up all the legalities to make Mary her guardian?"

"Of course I'll care for the little girl." Peg seemed comforted by the thought.

"Good. My father and I consider this the best course of action, and of course, we budgeted money for your expenses."

"I'd do my best anyway, but thank you, Jack." She wiped her eyes again. "Bria was right."

"About what?"

"We should have asked you for help. She said so after her mother left. If we had..." She buried her face in her hands and wept. "I'm sorry."

Elizabeth rubbed her mother's shoulders, looking thoughtful. "I don't think Jess will let you take Tara. She's pretty high on herself about being her savior."

Jack snapped his brief case closed. "Yes she will. Now Elizabeth if you'll show me the way, I'd like to phone the police to make sure I'm expected."

Peg pulled herself together. "And I'll call Dugald to come home and go with you. Lizzie stay here."

They went off, leaving Elizabeth and me alone. I slid over, up close to her. "So tell me about this Aunt Jess."

At first, she was shy but a little prodding burst the dam and a torrent of information and opinions came pouring out. Verbosity, I decided, must run in the family.

Later in the evening, Jack and Dugald returned, long after the rest of us had eaten. I started to fade and gratefully accepted Peg's suggestion I sleep in Lizzie's room. My last thought before unconsciousness was of Bria. I was sleeping in the bed she'd called her own.

A knock at the door and Jack's voice "Up, time to get up" roused me out of bed the next morning. I dressed and stumbled into the kitchen to find him on the phone.

"Dad," he mouthed. "Ok, yes. Got it. Call you tonight. And thanks." He passed me a cup of coffee. "Getting some advice. Drink up. We've got to go."

Not yet entirely awake, I grumbled. "I just got up."

"I've been up for hours. I watched Peg light the stove, haul water from outside, make breakfast for the kids and Dugald and me. Now she's in the garden; said she wanted to get the weeds before the day became hot. Can you imagine her life?"

"I'm quite ashamed of myself, actually. I spent so much time wallowing in self-pity lately. Then I come here and realize what a soft, cosseted little life I lead."

Jack mock-punched my chin and left a ten note on the counter. "For the phone. Get your stuff. Let's go meet Jess the Mess and get Tara."

"Jess who?"

He chuckled. "Bria's name for her. Come on, let's get moving. We can talk on the way."

We loaded our bags into the car, and I went to say goodbye to Peg. I found her bent over between rows of green plantings in the back yard. "We're off. Thank you so much, Peg. Try not to worry. Jack and John will do all they can to find her."

She straightened herself out, one hand on the small of her back, and pulled off her gardening gloves to take mine. "If you see her first, please tell her I'm sorry. I didn't know."

My heart went out to her. "I'm sure she understands, but yes I will. Goodbye. Wish us luck." She had already returned to the weeding when I glanced back to wave.

***

I strained my patience until we were all the way to the highway and once again heading east. "So you tell me yours and I'll tell you mine."

Jack pulled his eyes off the road long enough to wink. "You first."

"Well, according to Elizabeth, Aunt Jess's kids are scared stiff of her. She's seen them slapped on many occasions for no apparent cause. Lizzie says her mother will never leave her alone with Jess. Anne, the older daughter behaves much like her mother, quick to hit. Also, and I'm again quoting, the younger girl is a basket case."

"Anything else?"

"According to Peg, Frank is a good fellow, but weak. Peg says he's the only boy in her family of seven, and he's the youngest. My guess: he's used to doing as he's told."

"And?"

"Jess is a nervous, high-strung type with strong ideas on how others should behave and not above creating serious drama. Apparently, and I'm giving you the condensed version here, Jess is a nut case and Frank is a worm." I tapped him on the shoulder. "What's that horrible term you boys use for a man completely under the dominion of a woman?"

"Pussy-whipped?" he offered.

"That's the one. He's pussy-whipped." I looked for hard-earned approbation.

"Well done, Mary." He clicked his tongue. "And did you learn anything about the other members of Peg's family?"

I rattled off the rest of my report. "Rich, the eldest, is a fireman, married with two kids and perfect. The second one, Rob, is having problems settling down says Peg. He's a drunk hanging out around 'grungy' friends, according to Lizzie. The other two, David and Douglas, I met over supper, but honestly, Jack, I don't think they said four words between them."

Jack gave a quick nod. "I met Rob last night."

"You did?"

"Something of a long story, but seeing as you've done so well, I guess I owe you. The RCMP received a report of Bria arriving in Strathmore. A witness saw her at a restaurant in the company of a young hippy type."

"They have those here, too?"

"It's a world phenomenon." Jack pulled out a cigarette. I rolled my window down farther.

"However, according to the proprietor, they parted ways after a cup of coffee. Bria was last seen walking into town. Beyond that, their inquiries lead nowhere." He fiddled with the lighter in the dash. "Dugald thought perhaps she might go to Rob, or met up with him somewhere. After stabbing Jess, she may be frightened, possibly in hiding. We went to his rooms—what a dump—but he said he hadn't seen her." He sounded skeptical.

"I gather you didn't believe him?"

"I got something, call it an instinct, that said he wasn't exactly forthcoming, so I went back to the police and asked that they check on Rob. Apparently, he and his buddy Gary Groves stay on their radar, particularly the buddy—a long history of drunken fights, interference with some of the young native girls off the reserve near here, car theft, typical no goodnik kind of stuff."

I had to ask. "Jack, if she's in Strathmore, why are we driving away?"

"How many people do we know here? What do you propose we do, drive up and down the streets shouting, 'Bria!' as if looking for a lost dog?"

"I suppose not," I conceded.

"No, better we leave the search to the police, decent guys, know their job. And Dad's been talking to them, cop-to-cop. Helps." Jack gave up trying to light the cigarette and threw it out the window. "But the real reason we're going is to do what Bria asked of us. She went to a lot of trouble to get Tara away. No matter her situation right now, we owe it to her to do that, don't you think?"

"I suppose. I'm dying to get the baby, but the thought we may be driving away when Bria needs us…" My heart grew heavy at the thought of her, all alone and frightened.

"Let's do what we can do. And we can get Tara."

"How can you be so sure? Aren't you going to tell me what you're keeping up your sleeve?"

"No, but I guarantee you this: you will hold that baby in your arms by the end of the day. Count on it." He smiled at me. "Now leave me alone, we have a hundred miles to drive."

"I don't see why that should require much thought. The road is straight as an arrow and anything coming can be seen miles away." The power poles and barbed wire fences flashed by in monotonous consistency. The land flattened out to arid barrens of dried clumps of grass and silver sagebrush.

"Look, Jack, antelope!" I yelped, pointing at a herd grazing in the vastness, which only earned me a growly rendition of 'Home, home on the range.'

"For the love of God, don't sing. Your voice is worthy of a bullfrog."

"I'm crushed."

Laughter felt good, like a sunny spell on a rainy day.

I waved at the window. "Isn't this the land God forgot?"

"I find the country beautiful in a way, and you were right, an easy place to drive. Ah, good, we're coming to it now. Medicine Hat 10 miles."

"Hurrah."

On the outskirts of town, Jack stopped for gas and a map of the city. I left the car to stretch my legs and wandered over to a parched area that appeared to end in midair.

He came crunching up behind me and pointed at the welcome sign. "Medicine Hat, the Gas City. Strange name, strange claim."

"Look." I waved at the panorama below.

The city, much bigger than I had anticipated, sprawled along a flat-bottomed valley carved by some slow moving, pea soup of a wide river, its course carving a lazy S. Farther out, great cliffs full of strange stone formations reared a hundred feet up from the plain.

"Mary, watch your step."

I glanced down, realized I stood at the edge of similar cliffs, and moved back several paces. My eye caught a glimpse of bright yellow, a flower tangled in the dry grass. I went over to investigate and found a prickly low growing cactus, its bloom one of the most beautiful things I'd ever seen. Just as I was musing that I needed a little dog so I could say *"Gee, Toto…"* Jack made his own cinematic remark.

"I wouldn't be at all surprised if John Wayne rode out of those hills on a white horse."

He turned and walked back to the car. I followed and we drove off again. He didn't want to arrive at Frank and Jess's until suppertime or, as he put it: he wanted them both present when the shit hit the fan.

In the meantime, we drove over to the school to talk to a Miss Coalbins. Webster Niblock Elementary boasted a dodecagonal - thank you, Jack - gymnasium with two long wings jutting out at right angles. I estimated the school held 500-600 students and thought about the little white schoolhouse in Buffalo Coulee.

I began to appreciate the strain Bria must have endured. In Chicago, at Ave Maria, she had been one of 32 children judged by the sisters to be special enough in some way to benefit from their environment. They had said she was a gifted child, and were happy to accept Bria back, even offered to give her a scholarship. The thought of her in this factory style school pained me. I turned to Jack. "I can't go in. I'll wait here."

"Of course you can but I want to know what you're thinking."

I told him. And had a sudden revelation. "It strikes me Peg would never allow her own children to be alone with Jess, yet she sent Bria to live with her. She knew!"

Nine:
"Jess the Mess gets hers."

He looked saddened for a moment. "You should be a lawyer, old girl. Of course she did. She hoped, don't you see? You've seen how hard her life is. She believed she had no choice and now she's consumed with guilt."

So he'd known all along and accepted it. "How did such a young man get so wise?"

"I'm at the bottom of the pile at the D.A.'s office. I get the dregs. You have no idea what I've seen, and I hope you never do. Now, then…" He rummaged in his briefcase. "I want Bria's journal and her school reports from Ave Maria. Here we are. Bye."

He took three quick steps, pivoted and returned. "Take the keys in the event I parked illegally."

"I don't drive."

"Keep them anyway." He strode into the school office, shouting over his shoulder, "I might be a while."

He was. Even with the windows down, I sweltered. Heat waves shimmered off the asphalt around me. I thought Canada was supposed to be a cold place.

I left the car and sat in the shade of an obviously struggling tree. A buzzer sounded and children poured out—hundreds. School buses came and went. Little groups of boys and girls walked down the long playing fields and disappeared into the streets and alleys. I tried to picture Bria among them.

Jack returned with a scowl on his face and a glance at his watch. "Come on."

"What did you learn?" I asked, practically skipping to keep up.

"Bria's gone from a gifted, articulate student to one who can barely manage a simple declarative sentence, from a happy sociable girl to a recluse." He threw his briefcase into the back seat. "Let's find a place to eat."

After supper, we pulled up in front of a two-story, rectangular house with an ornate portico. Petunias in brick planters bloomed. Cookie cutter beds housed sapling trees, firmly tied to support stakes. A handsome home.

"Let's go do this." Jack strode to the front door and rang the bell. I tripped along behind him.

A young girl—Linda, I guessed —answered. Jack pushed his way in. "I'm Jack Connelly. This is Mary Connelly. We're here to talk to your mom and dad."

"Oh, wait a minute." She turned and called, "Mum," as she left the front room.

Jess appeared in seconds. "Yes?"

I studied her, this woman who had hurt my Bria. Of medium height with dark hair, teased and sprayed into a helmet, wearing a red knit dress that did nothing to hide the fat folds round her waist, and very serviceable black shoes. I saw in her someone who spent a lot of time in front of a mirror, deciding what to wear when.

"Jack Connelly. This is Mary Connelly. We're here to talk to you and your husband. We came all the way from Chicago and we're tired. Won't you ask us in?"

"We're finishing supper, actually," she replied in a Scottish burr.

"We'll wait right here in the sitting room." Before Jess had a chance to say anything, Jack took me by the arm, propelled me into the house and sat me down beside him on a plush velvet couch. "Whenever you're ready, no rush."

"Em, em, certainly." Jess's facial expression left no doubt of her unease. "Em, would you like coffee?"

"Thank you. When you finish your supper." He had the look of a cat that's spotted a saucer of milk.

"Em, yes. Won't be long."

She wasn't. I barely had time to register the color-coordinated and exceedingly clean living room. Within two minutes she was back, Frank in tow with a tray of cups and dainty cakes.

"Em, yes, what can we do for you?"

I noted she spoke, not the tired looking Frank.

"Well." Jack fixed his coffee. "First, Tara leaves with us tonight. We'll be making application to the courts in the near future to appoint Mary here her legal guardian." He glanced up at Jess. "Which you will support. Second, you'll drop the charges against Bria." He surveyed his surroundings with an impish smirk on his face. "What a lovely home you have."

"I don't, em—I don't, em." While his wife fluttered for words, I noticed Frank's eyes brighten and land on Jack with intensity.

Jess finally found her tongue. "Who are you to come in here and make such demands?"

"I'm an attorney. For the moment, I represent Mary Connelly, who is petitioning for control of these children and who, if you do not agree to support this, will press charges of child abuse against you. Isn't that right, Mary?"

"Yes, Jack," I agreed brightly.

"Abuse! How dare you—" she stormed and stuttered and finally found her voice. "How dare you come into this house and make such allegations."

"How dare I, Mrs. Dudley?" Jack's energy radiated from his body, infecting me. Aside from the glint in his eyes, his face remained impassive, his voice low and casual. I began to understand John's pride when he spoke of his son, the DA.

"You can't! You can't just walk in here and demand to take our baby."

Jack continued in a dry and pedantic tone. "You are her aunt through marriage. She is also Mary's niece. She is my godchild. Peg and Dugald are family. She is definitely not your baby. Most importantly, she is Bria's sister, and they belong together in the same household." He raised his voice. "And Bria will not be coming back here, ever."

"She wouldn't be welcome if she tried, after what she did."

"And what did she do? Please inform me. I'd be happy to get a firsthand account." Jack appeared politely interested.

Jess placed one hand on the opposite shoulder, presumably her wound. "She attacked me, stabbed me with a knife. She is a wild girl."

"She's a good girl," I said, despising the woman. "A very good girl."

Jess leaped to her feet, gesturing wildly. Her Scottish accent grew thicker. "I tell you she went wild and stabbed me. She nearly killed me. You have no idea what I had to put up with, sneaking, stealing and most of all lying. She's a terrible liar. Whatever the stories she told you— abuse! Ridiculous. Tell them Frank."

Frank remained silent and Jess sat down, glaring at him.

Jack leaned forward, eyes glittering. He wasn't a cat after milk; he'd found a mouse. "I believe she acted in self defense. Isn't that the truth?"

"What are you insinuating?"

"I'm stating you abused Bria from the moment she came under your control. Have you anything to say?" He turned to Frank.

"I'm listening."

I thought there might be more to the man than I'd thought. He certainly seemed content sitting in his chair, watching his wife twist on the line.

Jack opened his briefcase and took out Bria's letter. "Read this." He passed the page to Frank then sat back, drinking his coffee. I didn't dare pick mine up; my hands were shaking so badly.

"I'll have that back now, thank you, Mr. Dudley." He replaced the letter in a folder, pulled out the notebook and held it in front of Jess. "Do you know what this is?"

"No, how could I?"

"It's Bria's journal. Now I hold enough samples of Bria's handwriting to authenticate this as hers, so don't waste your breath arguing that point. Miss Coalbins at the school recognized Bria's style. Nice lady, inexperienced, naive perhaps. We had an interesting conversation. Do you know what this says?"

"How should I? But let me tell you—" her face drained of color —"she fabricated many lies. Why, she even wrote wild stories about me in school. You can't believe anything she says. I tell you, she's a liar."

"She is not," I said.

"Let's take a look and see, shall we? Let's start with...hum, here we go. *I'm missing my address book. I was sure I put it in my box, but I can't find it anywhere.* I believe you took it away from her." He stared at Jess a moment.

He flipped through the thickly written pages. "And here's another, *I wanted to tell Peg I didn't want to stay here, but she stood there the whole time I was on the phone so how could I? Or why does she dump out all my stuff when she goes through my drawers? What is she looking for?"*

He opened to a page marked by a yellow sticky note. "This bit here is one of my favorites. *When I'm not in school, I'm to stay in my room. I'm not even allowed to spend time with Tara at all because I'm such a dirty, sneaky, thieving, ungrateful girl, and I'm not good enough to be around her.* Shall I tell you what I see here? You deliberately placed yourself between Bria and anyone she loved, even tried to take away her love for her sister."

His voice rose in strength. "You isolated her to get her under your control, and you abused her. Why? Because you could."

"I did not! Frank! Are you going to stay quiet and let them say these preposterous things about me?" Her voice reached a pitch an octave higher than before.

He peered at her over his glasses. "I'm listening."

Jess jumped from her chair and stood in front of Jack. "I never abused that girl. Out of the goodness of my heart, for charity's sake, I took her in. How dare you!"

Jack stared at her calmly. "Are you thinking of slapping me? Let me remind you I'm not a little girl. I'm an attorney, here on legal business. Sit down please."

Jess sat.

"Now you say you didn't abuse her. Let's read on. *Tara tried running today. She looked so funny. Her body was running faster than her legs. I put out my hands to catch her. Come on, Tara. She flopped down on her diaper and started to cry. Jess ran over to me. 'You little bitch, you did that on purpose,' she said and slapped my face.*"

"She pushed the baby down. She was always hurting her. I couldn't trust her. I —"

Jack cut her sputtering off. "Let me get this straight. She's a twelve-year-old girl who may or may not have acted in an inappropriate manner with her baby sister. Instead of teaching her what's right and setting an example of how one should treat those smaller and weaker, you called her a bitch and hit her in the face. Is this your idea of good parenting? I call it abuse."

Jack's voice rose above her denials. "But I'm not finished, not by a long shot. *Today another tantrum. She found a pot someplace. She lost her mind, started screaming at us kids for stealing food. Yes, I've taken food a few times. I had to. Jess and this crazy thing about us and food! We can't just help ourselves to anything to eat if we're hungry.* She couldn't eat when she was hungry? She felt compelled to steal food. Really?"

"She...I had to control...You can't let children eat whatever and whenever...eat us out of house and home... For her own good," Jess sputtered and finally managed a full sentence. "She was getting fat."

"Bria?" I was astounded. The Bria I remembered bounced around on stick legs, waving spaghetti arms.

"And then," Jack cut off what could have become a damn good cat-fight, "when you discovered the girls had made something for themselves, you confronted them with a used cooking pot that had to be hidden for some reason. For interest sake, what kind of cookware will I find in your kitchen? Stainless steel? Enamel? Cast iron? How heavy was the pot you held in your hand that day? Do you remember this, Mrs. Dudley? "

His voice was icy and accusing as he read. "'*Three little thieving liars, that's what I have here. No one will tell me the truth? Fine.' And just like that, the pot crashed on the crown of my head, then Linda's, then Anne's. The shock blinded me for a bit, and ran all the way down my spine. I heard Linda screaming. 'Don't. It was Anne.' Anne was crying 'No, no,' and ran upstairs. I went back to my room, not far enough; I heard Anne get her punishment...* You pursued the older girl up the stairs and beat her. If that's not abuse, I am not a criminal attorney who hears stories of abuse every day."

Jack's voice rose just as I was about to scream my outrage at the woman, jump up and pluck out every one of her shellacked hairs.

"I've gone through this journal and come up with a number of criminal charges that might be filed against you. You can then look forward to all this coming out in public because I will ensure that it does. I'll also initiate any and all actions necessary to make certain your own two children are taken from you and a full investigation ensues. Do you want that?"

No answer. She stared straight ahead, shaking hands and a quivering chin her only movement.

"So you will agree to give us Tara tonight, right now."

She still made no response.

"Tomorrow first thing you'll go to the police and withdraw this ridiculous complaint against Bria."

She jolted back to life. "I will not! Who would believe you, or her?" Jess frantically tried to whip up a new head of steam. "I enjoy a good reputation. People know—"

I cut her off. "I think you'll be surprised at what your reputation is. I spoke to some who know you, who will most assuredly believe every word of this terrible, sad journal." I astounded myself with my anger. "I do because I know Bria. Personally, I think you're very sick and should seek help for the sake of your children who also have a reputation—for being very frightened and unhappy. No, you poor excuse for a woman, anyone who's spent time with you will believe it." Jack shot me an admiring glance.

"This is blackmail." Jess was now reduced to whining.

Jack flashed an unpleasant smile. "The correct term is extortion. Would you like to call the police? The RCMP's description of Bria's condition when she arrived in Strathmore, a very good one, includes the bruises and cut mouth. I'm sure they'd be interested in knowing how that happened."

He pointed a finger at her. "Call them. We can all sit around and read the journal together. Unfortunately, that would also mean Tara, and possibly your daughters, will end up enmeshed in the courts. So everybody's best interests are served if you go and pack some things for Tara and bring her to us now."

Jess sat mute and mulish.

Jack sighed and leaned back. "Frank, you say you've been listening. Listen to this. *Today Frank was told to beat the dog. Like always, Frank did as she said. What a sorry excuse for a man! Won't stand up for his kids, not even for a poor old dog. I never before saw a man who got bossed around so much.*"

"And here she makes excuses for you. *Most of the time Frank wasn't at home. Maybe he didn't know what was going on. I knew for sure his kids would never say anything. They'd be too scared of what she'd do. Maybe he would help us if he knew. Maybe I should tell him. Then I remembered, he did beat the dog.* So Frank, what's it going to be?"

Frank sat staring at his feet. He looked so big and awkward in his chair, I felt sorry for him. He spoke without lifting his head. "Take the child. I should never have allowed them to be brought here in the first place.

"Jess, come." She didn't move, frozen. "I said come. Get her ready to travel."

Five minutes later, Frank carried a sleepy Tara into the room and placed her in my arms. Heavens, she'd gotten so big! She was lovely.

He put a packed bag at my feet. "Here's a few of her things." He turned to Jack. "Where shall I send the rest?"

"Send them to Peg. When the time comes, I expect you to offer assistance, such as this affidavit that I'll leave with you. It states your opinion that Mrs. Mary Connelly will provide the best possible situation for these children. Your signature, Mr. Dudley, and not one word from your wife. Can I have your promise on that?"

"Yes. I do believe that would be best." He met Jack's eyes for the first time.

"And the charges against Bria?"

"What should I do?"

Jack reached once more into his brief case. "Take this to the RCMP office. I took the liberty of filling it out for you. You state your wife overreacted over a small family matter that went awry. Bria didn't mean to use the knife; it was horseplay and accidental."

He pointed to the bottom of the page. "All Mrs. Dudley needs to do is sign here in their presence. They are forewarned and expecting you."

He picked up the bag packed for Tara. "I'll be notified when it's done. Now we'll be going. Say thank you to your wife for the coffee."

Frank shuffled his feet and went to open the door for us. "Please tell Bria I'm sorry."

"Yes. Everyone is sorry, now. I wish I could do as you ask, but Bria is missing and has been for five, no six days now. Good night."

"Mr. Dudley," I said as I carried Tara out the door, "please, get some help for your wife—and your daughters, too."

***

"I don't believe it, Jack," I exclaimed, once we were in the car and on the move. "You were amazing." My exhilaration from the fight and my joy at holding Tara at last overcame my deep sorrow at all I'd learned in that unhappy house.

"Why thank you, ma'am. So were you." Now that the showdown was over, he relaxed, back to being my easy-going friend.

Tara sat in my lap, quiet and suspicious, still half asleep. I stroked her chubby face. "Hello, little darling." I smiled at her. She studied me, frowning and then, having passed judgment, beamed back at me and said clearly, "Tara wants a cookie."

"Here I worried about bottles and baby food. She's grown so much. She might be hungry. I didn't think to ask when she ate. What shall we do?"

"Same as for any other old friend, take her to a restaurant."

"You can't be hungry again."

He grinned. "I could eat."

"And then what, drive all the way to Peg's tonight, with a baby in the car?"

"No, we get a motel room and some sleep."

"Good." I was beyond tired and still shaking from the tension of the confrontation. I let him arrange the rest of the evening and settled back to enjoy having Tara in my arms.

A couple of hours later, with Tara tucked into bed beside me, asleep like a little angel, I looked over at Jack getting comfortable in the other bed. "Thank you for all you did tonight, but there's something bothering me terribly."

"What?"

"Can you think of anything we can do for those two unhappy girls?"

He sighed. "One of the most important things I've learned over the past year is this: you can do only what you can do, and put the rest out of your mind. Hopefully, by confronting Frank on the truth of the matter we opened his eyes, and he will make some changes."

He lay his head back on the pillow and addressed the ceiling. "As for her? She beggars the imagination. I wonder what her young life was like. How did she get this way? "

"It's no excuse."

"No, merely a reason." He reached over to turn out the light and became a disembodied voice in the dark. "In my younger days, I used to have fantasies like this."

"Like what?" I asked half asleep.

"Being in a motel room with you." He laughed softly.

"Jack Connelly, what a thing to say! I'm your aunt."

He chuckled again, still enjoying his joke. "Teenage gonads don't take those things into account. Good night."

"Good night, you rotten boy." I had trouble falling asleep. Despite my joy at having Tara safe beside me, my mind was preoccupied with Bria. I didn't need to ask; I knew Jack thought something bad had happened to her.

Ten:
"Jesus loves the little children..."

Bria

They push me into a room.

I see bright lights, hot against a shiny surface, a bed in the middle, a black sheet. Two stand behind me, one in the corner working some kind of camera. They wear masks that cover their faces from mid brow to nose.

Hands shove me.

I fall forward onto the bed. Fast as I can, I get to my knees and whirl around, staring at them. My heart thuds so hard in my chest, I hear nothing else.

I look down at my body. I wear stupid clothes, a see-through bra top across my little breasts. A tiny, shiny skirt on my skinny hips barely covers my bum.

Why? What is happening?

My eyes flit to the whirring camera. I stare into it as though the lens holds some answers, unaware of the masked one behind. *What do they want of me?*

I know. I know what they are going to do. I know, but I don't know, can't believe.

Jesus, help me. I stare up at the two. Long, lean bodies wear only jeans slung low on straight hips. One undoes his belt. They don't speak. I cry. "Please, please." My voice is a whisper, hardly louder than the chatter of my teeth. I shake so hard I want to be sick. *Jesus, help me.*

One moves behind me. I watch the other. Yellow hair, short and curly covers his forehead, black mask, blue eyes. Bright. He slides off his belt and tosses it to the floor. For a moment, I am relieved. He is not going to beat me with it.

He unzips his fly, slithers his jeans down. I glimpse something purple-brown in his crotch, jutting up and out. He strokes the thing, and it jumps and jerks as he does so.

Two hands reach toward me, big hands on thick wrists, arms covered in a mat of yellow hairs, dark blue serpents winding up to elbows. The hands press into my chest and roughly push me down.

I fall, legs bent painfully under me. He reaches out, grabs my ankles and yanks my legs out straight. From behind me, other hands snake out, grab my wrists and pull my arms over my head. I gasp, "No, no, no," with each breath.

My top is ripped off, the skirt stripped away. I am naked, bare before them. I try to wrest free, buck my body, squirm, but hands hold my arms tight and pin them down. The other wrenches my legs up and out. They stretch me taught. I scream, high and thin. "No, no, no."

They are so strong. I beg. "Please."

The one at my feet crawls up between my legs and looms above on his extended arms, eyes boring down on me, cold blue in a black mask. Hard. An electric shock of dread stabs me. I pray. *Lord Jesus, save me from those dead eyes, empty, no soul, no mercy.* I understand, and fear pours through my veins in a cold flood.

I am nothing. My tears and pleas are useless. I am nothing, less than nothing, a lump of flesh. He will do anything he wants to me. Bria no longer exists. She is gone and I am nothing. I give up my struggle.

The eyes lock onto mine for an endless moment, and he lunges forward. I am ripped in half as something foreign forces its way into my body. Tearing and hot thick wetness, searing pain in my belly and deep in my bowels as this thing barges farther. My mouth gapes open in a soundless scream. I cannot breathe, cannot find air. I teeter on the edge of blackness and want to go, but my lungs suck in a huge inhalation and a strange rattling noise escapes my throat.

I gaze up at the blue eyes in the black mask high above me and down over the thick chest to the abdomen touching my lower body. It pulls up and away from me. The thing on which I am impaled slides out of me, covered in blood. Another gush of hot liquid and searing heat as it slams back into me. *Jesus, Jesus, please save me.*

Somehow, I am in Sunday school singing in my high clear voice. "Jesus loves the little children, all the children of the world. Red and yellow, black and white, they are precious in his sight. Jesus loves the little children of the world." I sing silently, over and over, with the slap, slap of flesh on flesh keeping time.

I pray for Jesus to save me, but receive no saving, only blow after blow from this thing inside me until I no longer beg Him to save me, but to take me to His loving embrace.

I find no mercy, not in heaven, not on earth. I do not die but remain pinned to the bed by my wrists. The rest of my body rocks up and back in union with his thrusts and lunges and the alien hardness pulps my screaming insides.

Finally, it ends. He slides out of me, raises upright on his knees still between my splayed legs, his blood-streaked thing in his fretting hand. I close my eyes to the sight as something warm and wet splashes onto my face. Some lands on my mouth, salty and sour.

My wrists are released. I slowly pull down my aching arms and cover my wet cheeks. I breathe raggedly into my elbow. *I am nothing.*

They talk to each other, a jumble of harsh male voices. "You want a go?" "In that? Fuck, what a mess. You really did a number on her." "I think she pissed herself. No way, I'll do the other one." "I popped that cherry good. Hey, did you get a shot of that?" "Yeah, I got it all." "No man, I mean this – the blood." "Relax, I'll process the film tonight. You'll see." "Better be there. Didn't do all that work for nothing." "Don't worry. Let's get a beer." "What about her." "She's going no place. Take the camera. Lock the door."

Eleven:
"First thing I need to tell you, I am safe now."

Bria

August 15, 1970

    Hello journal, I haven't talked to you in a long time. I missed you. First thing I need to tell you is I'm safe now, at least according to the people here. I don't mind I'm locked in this room. I can sleep. The bed's a little hard, but clean and with a sink on the wall beside me I can wash whenever I want. No more peeing in a bucket, not when my own toilet, one just for me, sits right in front of me. No one is allowed to be here but me. All I do is sleep. I think I sleep whole days away. I'm not sure.

    A woman came to talk to me today. She said she was my social worker, and we'd get to know each other over the next while. In the meantime, was there anything I needed or wanted? I told her I'd like to write my journal. She thought this a good idea. I can keep the paper, but may only use the pen in my room and must give it back when I'm finished. They also promised my papers were mine and no one would read them.

    I'm instructed to stay in my room for now but soon I'll be allowed to go out into the common area, Anna told me. I don't want to.

    I am happy to write in my journal again, even though I know it's not talking to God like Sister Marta said, because I called Him and I called Him and He didn't come to help me. I have nothing to say to God anymore.

August 23, 1970

    I had to go back to the hospital today. Mrs. Friesen, my social worker, came to take me. She explained I was to undergo a pelvic exam, but not to be afraid; she would stay with me. It wasn't a pleasant thing but not too bad. She lied. She said a check-up is important if you menstruate and any kind of sexual activity has taken place and asked did I understand. I answered yes, but I didn't.

The hospital was huge. Mrs. Friesen took me to a little room and told me to change into this stupid gown thing made from fabric like old sheets. She stood outside the door while I did. Then we sat in the corridor, and she gave me a book that showed me how the female body looks inside. Did I know what the uterus was? Well of course, I do, I told her.

I thought the next part horrible. I had to lie on my back with my feet up in silver stirrups while they put a metal instrument called a speculum inside me. That hurt and the doctor said try and relax. She tried to be kind, explained what she did and why. Mrs. Friesen held my hand. I stared at the ceiling and wished the whole thing over.

Afterward, Doctor Lorrie and Mrs. Friesen talked together in the hall, glancing at me while they did, and Mrs. Friesen came and sat beside me and the doctor explained things. They wanted me to have a procedure called a D&C. I asked why, but neither gave me a straight answer, only appeared uncomfortable, so I sensed something was up. I didn't care.

I stopped listening, seeing as they refused to tell me the truth, but the doctor put her hand on my shoulder and told me a girl can get many problems from sexual intercourse, and this procedure is necessary to ensure my future health. I would be sedated and not even aware of what happened.

Good. So long as I don't know, they can do whatever they want.

August 28 1970

Today Mrs. Friesen came and brought someone with her, Miss Loepky, from the Crown Prosecutors Office. I thought her a very nice person, young, friendly and she talked to me like I was grown-up. She works in the office that is asking the court to punish the men who did this to me.

She asked if I wanted to help her. I told her I didn't care. Anyway, what could I do? She wondered would I talk to her about some of the things that happened to me, maybe not right now, but when I was ready. I don't have to if I don't want to, but Mrs. Friesen thought it would be a good idea. She suggested I write my memories in my journal. No, I don't think I will.

September 12, 1970

Mrs. Friesen took me out into the yard. The sun was warm on my skin. We discussed my feelings for a bit, then she asked, 'Who is Jack?' You could have knocked me over with a feather. Jack. For the first time I remembered Tara, and asked Mrs. Friesen, 'Did Jack take her?' Did she know? She promised she would find out for me.

She had many more questions. How did I feel toward Tara? I love her; she's my sister. Had I ever been angry at her? A strange thing to ask, I thought. Why be mad at a little baby? Mrs. Friesen said, 'Boy, it must have been hard to look after her.' I told her yes, she made a lot of work for my Auntie and me, but at the Mess's I wasn't allowed to care for her, and now I really, really needed to know if Tara was okay. I wish I'd never left her.

Did I want to talk to Jack? For some reason I got scared. I asked if anyone told Jack what happened to me. She seemed surprised. Would it be a bad thing? I kept my mouth shut, but I don't want anyone to know— not even me.

I would like to talk to Jack. She'll pass that on. I told her Jack was my lawyer and explained about the dollar and the secrets and privilege.

Mrs. Friesen is easy to talk to and never says an idea is bad or wrong, and when I don't want to tell something, she switches the subject without comment. I see her every day, sometimes just for five minutes, sometimes longer.

September 18, 1970

Miss Loepky came with Mrs. Friesen today. She asked how I was doing and said everyone was so proud of me for the progress I made. Thanks, but I don't get why. All I do is sleep, eat, write in my journal and talk to Mrs. Friesen and Anna, who comes by to check on me sometimes. I said I'd add her to my list of people I'm willing to see, if she promised to talk about only the subjects I choose, and no trying to force or trick me to do otherwise. She said fine.

Miss Loepky had some things to explain to me. I am a ward of the office of the Public Trustee. In other words, the Province of Manitoba is responsible for me and I was sent to this place under an order of protection, which means I'm not here because I did anything wrong, only so the Province can keep me safe. I am glad to be safe and I told her that.

She asked if I would talk about Debbie, and that made me jumpy. I hadn't thought about Debbie in a long time.

I put down my pen. My eyes were so full of tears, I was unable to write and the memory of the conversation came rushing up into me. I had stated with complete certainty, "I don't want to talk about her." But no sooner did the words spill out of my mouth than I asked, "Is Debbie here, too?"

Miss Loepky said, "No, she isn't."

"Didn't you find her?" The little room closed in on me. I had trouble catching my breath.

"We did."

"Where is she then?"

Miss Loepky stayed quiet while Mrs. Friesen took my hands in hers. "I'm sorry, Bria. Debbie is dead."

I lost all my air, as if someone punched me in the stomach. My ears roared with the sound of my heartbeat, and my eyes saw nothing. For a few minutes, I sat in my chair, breathing hard, and started to cry. Mrs. Friesen gave me Kleenex and held my hands.

"It's not my fault," I whispered. "I tried to get her to come with me, but she couldn't climb out the window. She was sick."

"Of course not," Mrs. Friesen insisted. "None of this was your fault. You must believe that."

I tried my best to take comfort from her words, but I couldn't. Once out the window, I had meant to run as fast as I could to find help, but I was too scared. I ran down an alley and hid inside a garbage bin for a long time before I found the courage to run into a restaurant. For almost a day, I thought.

"You had a perfectly normal reaction," Mrs. Friesen said. "To try to save yourself is human instinct."

Miss Loepky said only, "Thank you. And when you're better we'll talk again."

September 22, 1970
Miss Loepky came today, this time by herself. Jack has petitioned to visit me. Because I'm twelve, I'm allowed to say yes or no, and she will represent my wishes to the court. I do want to see Jack.

Mrs. Friesen has spoken to Jack and he wanted me to know Tara is with Peg, and Jack is arranging for her to go to Mary.

I'm happy to hear this news. Mary will be good to her and Pat is such a gentle man; Tara will have a fine home.

October 7, 1970
Jack arrives tomorrow at ten o'clock and I'm to meet him in the visitor room. Anna, the worker who checks on me sometimes, will need to be there – the rules, but she says she'll bring a good book and not to pay her any attention at all.
I don't understand why I'm so nervous, perhaps because it's been so long. I wonder if he'll still like me.

I woke before the sun came up. Anticipation had me up most of the night, that and an upset stomach. I read my journals all together for the first time. The early pages seem written by someone much younger than I, reminding me of my mother and how she, too, lived a period when all she wanted to do was sleep her life away. Now I had an idea of what she'd gone through and felt pity for her. I hoped to get a chance to tell her that one day.

Mrs. Friesen and I talked about her a lot. She thinks people can get to feel so bad, they convince themselves you're better off without them. Didn't I think if my mother had been able to talk to someone, she would have been able to process and deal with her trauma? I knew what she really meant; *I* should talk about *my* trauma.

She wants me to spend more time out of my room and meet some of the others in this wing. Anna told me they were all there on protection orders, like me. I might come out one day soon.

***

Anna came to get me and take me to Jack. As we walked down the hallway, a feeling impossible to understand grabbed me and I grew afraid. I glanced at my reflection in a window as we passed. I wore clothes given to me, but they weren't the kind I would pick for myself. In a skirt hanging halfway down my calves and a button up cardigan, the long sleeves rolled up to my elbows, I looked like a skinny kid wearing her mother's old things.

For some reason, I began to feel dreadfully ashamed. As soon as Anna opened the door to the little visiting room and his face appeared, full of a tremulous smile and inquiring eyes, I started to cry. I couldn't stop.

"Bria, so good to see you." He acted like I wasn't crying at all. He took one step to the doorway and gathered me in a strong hug. I went limp in his arms, crushed up to his body.

Anna made a funny cough, so he let go, grasped my hand and led me to the chairs. I grabbed a Kleenex from the box on the table and covered my face. Anna pulled it away, gave my shoulder a squeeze, sat down in the corner and started reading her book.

I stared at her while I said, "How are you, Jack?"

"Good, good, much better for seeing you." His voice was hoarse, and he cleared his throat. "How are you?"

"Okay." I couldn't look at him.

"Good." He coughed a little. "Mary sends her love. She sent you a letter. They'll give it to you later."

"Thank you." I stared at my hands.

Jack reached over and touched them lightly, with two fingers. "Bria, I'm sorry."

"For what?" I whispered.

"For not being there when you needed me."

"It's okay."

"No, it's not, but thank you. I'm glad you forgive me."

"I do," I murmured.

"Are we still friends?"

"I guess."

We sat in silence for a while, me staring at my hands and Jack touching them ever so lightly.

He started talking to the top of my head. "Mary and I went looking for you. We drove all over the place, to Peg's house, to Strathmore, to Medicine Hat. I didn't like Jess at all, but I do like Peg and Dugald very much. They love you, Bria."

I sat and listened.

"When we heard you'd been found, Mary and I went to Buffalo Coulee, saw Tara and we all had a party because you were safe. Your families love you, Bria. We all pray you get better and come to us."

I didn't say anything. I couldn't. I was choking.

"Bria. Is that what you want? To go home?"

He breathed loudly, and it seemed to catch in his throat. In a soft voice, he asked, "Bria, can you look at me?"

I shook my head.

"Why not?"

"It's not my fault I'm here."

"I know that. Please try."

"Can I go now?"

He swallowed and spoke in a hoarse whisper. "Sure, whatever you want. Can I come and see you tomorrow?"

"Yes."

"Same time, same place?"

"Yes." I got up to go without looking at him at all.

Anna got up and touched Jack's shoulder. "Don't worry, this is normal."

Twelve:
"If I am a bird caught by a cat..."

She took me to my room where I threw myself on my bed and cried until I fell asleep. Paul, the evening guy, woke me for supper, but I wasn't hungry and didn't eat. About to go back to sleep when Mrs. Friesen came in, I pulled myself up in surprise and sat on the edge of my bed.

"Good evening, Bria. How was your visit today?" She sounded same as always, brisk and businesslike.

"Fine," I said.

She peered at me through her thick glasses. "Anna said you were upset."

"Not really."

"She thought so. Maybe she's wrong." She pulled a pencil out of her grey hair, worn as always tied in a knot at the back of her head. "You don't have to see Jack again if you don't want to, if he leaves you unhappy."

I shrugged. "I'm unhappy anyway, so what difference does it make?"

She was writing on the clipboard that hangs outside my door. "A lot if you don't want to see him."

"I do. I just didn't know what to say."

"I thought he was your good friend."

"He is." I hugged my knees to my chest. "But I'm afraid to talk to him."

"Why? What are you feeling when you see Jack?"

"Too full of things."

"What things?"

"Things I don't want to talk about. He always makes me tell him things I don't want to." I struggled to explain, as much to myself as to her.

She thought for a minute and asked, "Didn't you say you felt better when you told Jack about your stepfather's violence?"

"Yes. But that was different."

"How?"

"I don't know. It just was." My fingers found their way to my mouth. "I don't want him to think about me like that."

Just as I knew she would, she asked, "Like what?"

"Nothing." I shouted at her. "I don't want him to think me a nothing."

I ran away into my head but there I found the Mess screaming, *The nobody nobody wants*. I heard Gerry yell while he hit me, *you fucking little bastard*. My mother, on the couch moaned, *Get lost, go away and leave me alone*. I found those men who made me the nothing anything can be done to, and the doctors who talked of my parts as though I wasn't right in front of them. I started to cry. "I'm no one. I'm nothing."

Mrs. Friesen sat quiet until I stopped. "Can you explain what that means?"

"No," I said as I always did but my mouth ran on anyway. "When things are done to you, you're nothing. When you do things yourself, you are *something*. I used to be a something."

"Can you describe yourself at a time when you felt you were something?"

"I was once brave." I told her my tale of the library and the phone, about all my schemes and plans, but not how I stole the money.

In the same calm voice she always used, she asked, "Where is that girl now?"

"Gone."

"I don't think she is." She peered straight into my face. "She's inside you wanting to come out and live again."

Her words scared me, and my fear filled me with rage. "She should stay dead. Look at what happened to me because of her." I started shouting. "She didn't want to live at the Mess's house. She thought she had it *so* bad there, but I know better. If I had just stayed where I was supposed to, none of this would have happened. Everything is her fault. I hate her."

Mrs. Friesen didn't say anything until I was quiet and calm again. "Weren't you hurt at the Mess's house?"

"Yes, but it wasn't that bad. I wasn't getting hurt that much."

She disagreed. "You didn't think so then, not if you made all those plans and worked so hard to get away."

"That was before I learned how bad things could be. Anyway, I was supposed to look after Tara, not run away and leave her there. And all that happened to me because I did wrong." I couldn't look at her now. I talked to my hands.

Mrs. Friesen leaned over, lifted my chin with her fingers and spoke to my face. "Do you think you deserved to be hurt?"

"Maybe." I searched for the truth. "Why else would it happen?"

Out of the blue, taking me completely by surprise, she asked, "Does a bird deserve to be caught by a cat?"

"What?" I thought she was nuts. "Of course not. The cat is simply doing what a cat does, and the bird was in the wrong place."

She raised her eyebrows at me in that way she has. It means *think about it.*

She went to the door. "I hope you enjoy a better visit tomorrow. In the meantime, I have a letter for you. I'm sorry it's open but all mail is read in this place. I'll talk to you tomorrow. Good night."

***

I sat with the envelope in my hands for a long time—hours, I think. My window grew dark and I still hadn't made up my mind. I wanted to read Mary's message, but doing so seemed such a momentous decision.

If I'd been a bird caught by a cat, at least I was a bird that flew away. That wasn't a nothing. It was more than could be said for Debbie. I pulled out the letter and read.

October 3, 1970
My dearest Bria,
I can't tell you how happy I am to be able to write to you at last. I prayed for you every day, and thank God, you are alive. Soon, I promise, as soon as possible you will be here with Tara and me.

You have no idea how hard Jack has worked for you. You should have seen him bring down the Mess. I kept wishing you were there. Like all bullies, when faced with someone strong, she has no spine. Within ten minutes, she was done. Your journal, darling, gave us the ammunition. You are such a clever girl.

I expect Tara here next week. I can't wait. She is growing so fast! And she's a real talker, like you. I do worry sometimes about the effect of so many changes for her, but I'm sure she will recover. She is such a happy little girl. Nothing seems to bother her much. I tell you this because I know how important her well-being is to you. She will soon be here, and we will both wait for you.

I think you are the bravest girl I ever met. I love you and want to give you the home you deserve. Please get well and come to us. God bless.

Love, Mary

I read the letter a hundred times. After a while, I opened the door to my room and walked down the hall to the common area. It was time to venture out. I stared at the TV screen, unable to understand a thing. The other kids looked at me, some of them spoke, but I didn't see, hear or say anything. I thought.

Anna came to my room the next morning carrying a grand selection of clothes for me to wear. Jeans, and my choice of tee shirts: one in plain red, one white with blue stripes, one black with "Jack Daniels" in white letters.

"Where did these come from?"

She waved her hand around the hallway. "Oh, the kids here donated items when I explained you needed clothes."

That surprised me. I had yet to speak to anyone.

Thirteen:
"...I am a bird that flew away."

I chose the red. The Mess popped up in my head saying, "Girls with red hair should never, ever wear red." *Fuck you, Jess.* Red was my favorite color.

I strode to the visitor's room ahead of Anna, who complained she was too fat to keep up with me—which she was, but I loved every square inch of her.

Before we got to the door, I stopped. "This time I'm going to give him a hug and I don't want you to cough or anything, okay? I don't care if it's against your rules. Today we use my rules."

Her broad face broke into a big grin. "Well, well, listen to you. I guess I'll get something in my eye and not see a thing."

I pulled open the door. Jack sat at the table but stood in surprise when I came in. I looked him in the face, walked over, put my arms around his middle and pressed into him. His arms enwrapped me, and we hugged for at least a minute, the first time I'd touched someone in what seemed like forever.

I let him go. "Physical contact isn't allowed, but I wanted to anyway. Sometimes rules don't count."

"You seem better." His eyes were shifting back and forth across my face, as though he thought this a trick and any minute I'd run away.

"Yes, I am and I'm sorry for yesterday. Some days are good and others not." I pointed to the chairs. "Let's sit down."

We got comfortable across from each other at the table and I attempted to share what I had on my mind. "Jack, I don't want you to be sorry. You don't need my forgiveness. None of this was your fault."

"Thank you," he said, his forehead furrowing, and a quizzical expression in his eyes, as though he was waiting impatiently for an explanation.

"I blamed myself for what happened. As if I did something wrong and got my just desserts. I've been so afraid."

"Afraid of what?"

"If I come out, if I start deciding for myself, I'll make a mistake and bad things will happen to me."

He misunderstood. "We're all going to try hard to make sure nothing bad happens to you again."

"But you can't. Mrs. Friesen says life is full of worry, but we can't hide from the possibility. All we can do is learn from our misadventures as much as we can. We must believe we're strong enough to survive and go on."

"I think that's true."

"And most of all, understand we're not punished because we're bad." I had another thought. "Sister Marta used to say the worst things happen to saints. Right?"

Jack smiled. "Right."

"We're not to blame for things that are done to us."

"I know that's so."

"So you can see it wasn't your fault?"

"Yes."

"Good."

His dark eyes fixed on mine, and I stared into them. "Jack, I want to talk to you; I do, but you scare me a little. Please understand I'm not ready to tell you some things. Maybe one day I will, but not now. So here are the rules: if I say I don't want to talk about something, you need to leave me alone. Can you do that?"

"I can," he said firmly, as if giving a solemn promise. "What would you like to discuss?"

"Tara."

He relaxed and grew expansive. "Well, Tara is doing well. She's with Peg, as you already know. We send money so no need to worry. When I leave Winnipeg, soon I'm afraid, I meet Mary in Calgary. We have a hearing scheduled before the court and Mary will become Tara's legal guardian."

"Good." Relief swept through me, but I still had a worry. "How is she, Jack? Did Jess hurt her?"

"Oh, she's wonderful. Mary visits her as often as possible. She and Peg are close friends now, so little Tara enjoys a lot of love. I brought some pictures of her. They'll give them to you later and you can see for yourself. By the end of the week, she'll be in Chicago in her new home with Mary."

"I'm happy for her."

"As for your other question, I can't say whether Jess hurt her. If she did, it doesn't seem to affect her, and she's so young she won't remember."

"Thank you for all you've done." I asked the question burning my brain. "Can you and Mary do the same for me?"

"I don't know yet. Up until now, we waited for you to get better." He hesitated, as though wondering if he should go on.

I sat quietly while he made up his mind.

He glanced over at Anna, who buried her face in her book. After some thought, he said, "I inquired as to your actual legal position. Did you know you are a ward of the province?"

"Yes. Miss Loepky told me."

"Who is Miss Loepky?"

"She works at the Crown Prosecutor's office."

"Oh. A prosecutor, like me. Tell me, Bria, what does she suggest you do?"

Alarm. Why does he suddenly look so intense? The thought ripped into my brain, a new voice, and it startled me.

"She says she's helping me, but all she really wants is for me to tell her things. She says her office needs my help to punish the men who hurt me." I asked him, "Do you think I should?"

Why is he so worried? Again, the outside voice blared like a loudspeaker in my head. I concentrated and listened to Jack.

"Before I answer your question, it seems to me we need to find you a lawyer—one who will represent you and only you, and not another agenda. We need to protect you and your best interests first."

"Why? What for?" My words reached my ears from far away.

"I'll find out this afternoon. Now, about whether you should or should not cooperate with the prosecutors, I think that question can wait until you have representation."

Jack is your lawyer. I heard the voice and repeated the message. "But aren't you my lawyer?"

"No, I can't be —only your friend and advisor."

"Then advise me." My words dripped from my mouth one by one, sluggish and slow.

"I think you should cooperate with the prosecutor."

If you tell, you have to look. The clock on the wall ticked so loud, clear as a bass drum. *You have to look. Look!*

I told the voice, "I don't want to. I don't think I can. I can't even think about it."

Jack swallowed so hard I heard the movement of his throat clear as the clock. He asked, "Did this Miss Loepky explain the status of this case?"

You have to look. Go and look. Come with me to the place you don't want to see. Let yourself fall. Don't be afraid. My mouth said, "No."

"Would you like me to tell you what I know?" He glanced at Anna. "Is this all right?"

She nodded.

You are frightened, but you must go. The clock has stopped; time does not exist. This is but a dream, foggy, dark, spinning—a whirlwind. Let yourself go. Leave the fear behind. The insistent voice overwhelmed my resistance. The mist enveloped me. I let go and jumped.

Out of the twilight of this new world, a truth beams out. "Tell me, Jack."

Everything is slow. The air sparkles. I divide in two. I fly up and watch while half of me sits and listens. He speaks.

"We know you met Rob and Gary Groves in Strathmore, and you asked him for help. Instead, Rob got himself completely drunk. Gary's plan, I think."

Pictures flutter in my head: Rob wisecracking about my injuries, Rob choosing to play pool, betraying me. Half says, "Rob is a piece of shit, a drunken piece of shit. My own family and he left me with Gary Groves." *The other half is afraid. Mary says not to use such language. Is Jack mad?*

But Jack is nodding. "That's right. Be angry. Rob should have protected you. If it makes you feel any better, his father went after him and gave him what for. Dugald is impressive when enraged. Lucky for Gary the police found him before Dugald did."

I don't comprehend. My mouth asks, "You were there?"

"I certainly was. I talked to Gary myself at the police station. I wanted to wring his neck."

Half wants to know. "Gary, what did he do? He took me to the car to wait, and I can't remember." *Other half swims into a fog, deep and dark.*

Half hears. "He sold you to two men. Men he'd never met before. "

"Sold me?" *Out of the shadows, Gary appears and walks away with the money. He disappears into the tavern.* "He sold me?"

"Yes, *sold you* for two hundred dollars. The police arrested him weeks ago. So we know that's true."

A voice sings, I am not a nothing. I am not to be sold. I am a bird. "Two men?" *I float in grey space and mouth says,* "Jack, I can't remember."

In his eyes, I find sadness and love. I drink it and hear, "Those two men haven't been found yet, but we know they brought you here to Winnipeg and sold you again."

My mind searches. Dim and confused flashes jumble up: the hard floor of a van, jostling and bumping, another body, mewling sounds, headache and nausea.

"Those men, they owned me?" *A harsh voice shouts: Shut up back there. A hand reaches out. Hits. The music gets louder.*

"Bria, are you all right?" *He pulls me back.*

I flutter down to him. "Yes. I'm trying to remember. It's wrong."

"What they did is a crime." *His big hands touch my crusted ones. His voice is soft.* "They took you to a house. Do you recall?"

Scenes flicker in my head. Carried over someone's shoulder, male voices, I am dropped on a floor. Another body falls beside me—Debbie. Time passes in the dark. We whisper and cry. Door opens. I am dragged out by my arm, thrown in a tub of water. A voice says get dressed. They are stupid clothes. Hands push me into a brightly lit room and...No!

I stop the film. "I don't want to talk about that."

"Okay, don't talk, just listen." *His fingers dance on my hands. Eyes look at eyes. Ears hear mouth.* "I'm a criminal prosecutor. I hear sordid stories about people doing revolting things to other people all the time. Will it help if I tell you I know what happened to you, at least in general terms?"

"Oh." *Eyes fall. I stare at my scabbed and bleeding fingers.*

His hands grip mine. "Don't hang your head. Look at me."

I cannot. I am somewhere else: another room, a bed, an old man with old hands holding out money. My keeper takes the money and leaves. The old hands touch me, poking and prodding, prying open my mouth...No!

His voice persists. "Come on, my sweet girl. I know what a victim is: someone innocent of any wrongdoing. That's you. I'm simply glad you're alive. Don't tell me anything unless you want to. Come on now."

I listen. I look.

"Good girl. I'm so proud of you. You lived through that. You kept your head and got yourself free. You fought back and now here you are in front of me. Bria, for a while, I was afraid I'd never see you again."

"Me too." *I am here. I am safe. Jack had come after all.*

"Okay now? Can I tell you more? I think you need to know."

I nod yes. I must know. I have to look.

"There was a house, where you and other girls were kept."

Only one other. "Debbie. Mrs. Friesen says she's dead."

Debbie drops to the floor. She falls like a sack. She lies unmoving, blood and feces on her thighs. She smells bad. She moans and cries for her mummy. I am afraid. I don't know what to do. I leave her alone.

Jack calls me. He wants me back here in this room. He is speaking. "She's dead but you are not. Right now, that's all that matters."

Mouth says, "I guess."

"You guess? I can't think of anything worse than finding out you were dead. Speaking selfishly of course, I am so happy it wasn't you. Aren't you?"

"Yes." *I am a bird. I flew away.*

"Can I tell you more?"

"Yes."

"You escaped from that house. You ran into a restaurant and the police came. You went to a hospital."

The bird flies. The bird knows. The garbage, the smell, the fear—my whole world. I crouch in the alley, covered and hidden. A day, I think; it is dark again when I leave. I am in the Chinese restaurant. A lady screams, "Oh my God!" I am naked. The police come, red and blue lights, and later, an ambulance. I cannot speak.

The bird hears. "You were sick but you were able to tell the police about Debbie."

The bird is surprised. "Did I?"

"Yes, brave girl, you did. By the time the police found that house, they were gone but left behind lots of evidence of what happened there. The police started searching."

"For Debbie?"

"Yes. For those men. For any of the other's that went there. A big investigation."

"Where was Debbie?" *Poor sick little Debbie. She was only eight.*

"They found her weeks later. She was dead. They killed her, Bria, a girl like you. When they thought they might get caught, they killed her to hide what they were doing."

The bird remembers. Debbie lies on her mattress. She is sick. Her bad smell is everywhere. She can't get up, can't reach the window. She says go, go and get help. Help me, Bria. She can't fly.

"Bria, here—a tissue. Go ahead and cry." He handed me a Kleenex, and I wiped my watery face.

The bird seeks absolution. "Jack, if I didn't run away do you think they would still have killed Debbie?"

And receives it. "I think if you hadn't run away they would have killed you both. You saved yourself and you tried to save Debbie. No one could have done more." *Little bird understands, not my fault.*

Now Bria's eyes see. The window, the grate and in my hand a dime dropped by some man and with it, I turn the screws one by one. Days, I think. I climb the pipes again and out, up, onto the street. Run. I'm sorry, Debbie. I tried but now I have to go.

I tell him my truth. "I wish it had never happened."

"I know." *His hands squeeze mine, and he tells me his.* "But it did happen. The things they did to you and Debbie, those are very bad crimes. Killing Debbie was the worst crime there is. They didn't get away."

He is happy, says the voice. Why, when it's already done, bird asks. History can't change, but still, as he wishes, Bria asks, "They didn't?"

"No. First, the police caught one. That one told about the others, who told about others and so on. The investigation found other girls and other houses in other places."

So many birds. How many flew?

His face is sad but his eyes smile at me. "Think about that. I understand there have been arrests in four different cities and more are pending, and girls are getting help now. All because you were brave and strong and saved yourself. I'm proud of you."

"I thought it was just Debbie and me." *The images return. This time I let them.*

I see the dark room with the high small window far from the floor; I find the pipes. I visit the two mattresses, the bucket for pee. There is no water for washing. Only when they say, only when they come for us, can we wash. A wash means another man. When I have seen, I fly away.

I tell him. "It was awful in there, Jack."

"Do you want to tell me?"

"No." *I will the flickering pictures to stop. It is done. I am here with Jack, safe now.*

"Fine with me. Are you all right to talk some more?"

"Yes. What's going to happen to me now?" *Can I fly far away from here, away from the little room and the noise of the others? I want to go home.*

"I wish I could say definitely this or that, but I can't. Before I do anything, I need you to tell me what you want."

"I want to go and live with Mary and Tara. I want to go to school. I want my life back and I want to choose for myself." *Mary, I am her favorite. Special. She wants me to be her little girl. I want Mary.*

He is happy with me. "Good. Glad to hear it. First things first. I need to get you a lawyer. Then I'll think and come up with a plan. As soon as I have one, I'll let you know."

"Is it complicated?"

"Yes."

"Why?"

He's reluctant to say. "Can it wait until I look into things?"

Make him tell. "No. I need to know now."

"We're in a delicate situation, you and me. I propose to take you to Chicago, but there's a glitch. You're important to the prosecutors here as a witness."

"Why?"

"You put Debbie alive and in that house. You can tell a jury what was done to her. You don't think every kid who comes in here gets what you're getting, do you?"

"Don't they?" *At night, I hear them. They cry. They shout. Sometimes they scream.*

"I doubt it. They're working hard to help you get better because they want you to testify. Look at things from the Crown Prosecutor's point of view. Their job is to try to prove these wicked people are guilty and made to pay for their crimes."

"Like you do." *He knows about the birds.*

"Yes. Maybe I can help you." *He smiles. I know him. He is leading me somewhere.* "You're a smart girl, Bria, but do you appreciate what it means that Chicago is in one country and you're here in another?"

He means flags and pledges there and "O Canada" here. "I understand about countries and governments. I'm the one who went to school in both places."

"That's true." *He is pleased with my answer and smiles a moment.* "Haven't you questioned why the prosecutor's office is sending Miss Loepky every day? Do you think that after investing all this time and effort to get you ready to testify, they'll be happy to see you go to another country?"

I understand. There is a price. "What are we going to do, Jack?"

With that question, time started again. The air returned to normal. The clock ticked. The voice stopped. *Goodbye. It's over now. You looked.* I came together, back in one piece, and saw Anna in her corner, content and attentive, not knowing I'd been gone and what I had seen.

Jack had no idea either. "I don't have all the details worked out yet, but I'll start by trying to become your guardian. You can tell Miss Loepky. Say I'm applying as guardian in loco parentis. Do you want me to write that down?"

He looked around, searching for something to write with and asked Anna, "Pen?" She shook her head.

I explained for her. "We can't have pens in this room—too dangerous for us unstable types. Don't worry, I can remember. And you already told me what it means."

"Okay. Anna here can remind you if you forget. And don't agree to anything, anything at all, unless you're allowed to talk with me or the lawyer I'm going to find. Do you promise?"

"Yes."

"One more thing, Bria." He stopped and searched my face. "I must ask if, when the time comes, you think you'll be able to testify. It will affect whatever strategy I choose."

"What would *you* do?"

"I can't make this choice for you."

"I didn't ask you to. I asked what you would do."

He started out speaking softly, only to me. "If I had lived through what you have, how would I feel?" His voice changed as though he addressed a room full of people. "I think I'd be mad. If men had stolen me, sold me like livestock, hurt me in terrible ways, rented me out to make money off me, I'd want to stand up in court, tell everyone what they did and demand justice." He summed up his argument. "Not just for me, but for Debbie and all the other girls."

The fear rushed at me. I needed all my strength not to fly back into that strange, timeless world of shadow. I studied him and understood with a flush of dread that was what he wanted me to do.

"I can't. I don't want to talk about these things in front of a bunch of people, Jack. I don't. I can't. When you say it, it doesn't sound so bad— just words—but when I think it...I can't explain." I wrapped my arms around myself. I wanted to plead, 'don't ask me to do this.'

But he did ask. "Bria, you don't have to say what it was like or how you felt. That isn't evidence. All you have to do is tell what they did, in clear, cold words." His eyes latched on to mine, holding me so I couldn't fly away, and his hands held my scabbed fingers down on the table and I was unable to chew on them. "You asked me to advise you. I think it would be a very good idea for you to do this. Certainly you'll find it hard but I want you to try."

I gave him what he wanted. "Will you help me?"

"Of course, in any way I can." We sat like that, connected for a while, until he said, "I must go if I'm to find you a lawyer, get on a plane and meet Mary in Calgary tomorrow. I wish we had more time." He was on his feet, preparing to leave.

"I understand. Anyway, thank you. You helped me a lot today, Jack. You have no idea how much."

"I'm glad, and Bria?" He turned back from the door.

"What?"

"Happy Birthday. In two more days, you'll be thirteen."

"I forgot. And in four days, how old will you be?"

"Twenty-six. Goodbye, stay well. Mary says God bless."

Fourteen:
"My lawyer should ask me what I want so say."

October 22, 1970

I'm not alone in my own room anymore. I have a roommate, Amy. I'm in a group home now. Mrs. Friesen said life would be better for me here.

Some of the girls go out for school and for weekends, but not me. Candace explained they worried for my security. I don't mind. I don't know anybody in Winnipeg, so where would I go?

Candace is my new lawyer. I can call her Candace, but never Candy because her last name is Barr, and she got enough teasing in school. She's tall with dark hair and she always dresses beautifully. Sometimes she comes and takes me places, like a café downtown where we talk. I saw the Legislative Building and the Golden Boy on top.

Most days, we go to her office after lunch. We're working on my sworn statement. Candace thinks there may be some issue, with me being younger than 14, as to whether I can swear an oath or not, but we should proceed under the assumption I will. She talks like that.

My sworn statement will be turned over to the Crown, and once they read it, they'll decide if I should speak in court. I don't have to give all the gory details, just the facts. We're not writing a novel; we're making a legal document. It's enough to say I was raped, without saying how bad it was so I don't find the task so awful. We work in little bits over days.

Most of the time we only work for a while, until she says, 'Let's take a break,' and I hang out in her office. I sometimes do some filing. At first she didn't want me to but when I showed her I understood how the files should be, she said go ahead. Someone had to do something. There are papers stacked up all over the place.

Candace agreed and said so far her legal career hadn't paid enough to get much help. I told her not to worry. Her files are exactly like the Dewey decimal system. She laughed.

Amy is out for the weekend staying with a lady who's going to be her foster parent. Amy says she's quite nice, not married, so it will be only the two of them. She hopes she gets to live there.

She's worried about how she'll be once she's out. She says she can't follow the rules when she's free, even if she wants to. She's scared she'll start running again if she's not locked up. I asked how that could be. She can't tell me. It's just the way she is.

November 3, 1970

Candace took me to her office today and Miss Loepky came unexpectedly. They had an argument. Miss Loepky said her people needed me to go to their place to prepare, but Candace said the sworn statement should be enough for their purposes and her client was not inclined to offer more. The Crown's case was not her concern. My welfare was.

I wanted to know if Miss Loepky had any idea how long it will be before they want me to testify. Candace shook her head at me, which made me kind of mad.

She said I should let my lawyer speak for me. I said my lawyer should ask me what I want to say. She would take this under consideration in the future, but for now I must hold my tongue. I thought I'd asked a pertinent question.

Candace told Miss Loepky to excuse us and took me to the other room. She explained she had to lay out the groundwork, to do things in the way best for me and for now that meant showing them I did not have to testify, that there were valid legal arguments for me not to. Then we would say yes I will, but on our terms, which included me getting out of the system and back to living in the real world.

I said sorry if I spoiled her plan, but I thought she should tell me these things ahead of time. I told her I was sick of people talking and acting as if I had nothing to do with my own life. I am thirteen, for crying out loud.

I don't think we're getting along too well. I wish I could talk to Jack.

Amy's back again. The foster home didn't last a week. The first Saturday she took off. I asked her why, but she shrugged and said she couldn't live straight. I wanted to know where she went, and she told me Portage and Main, drinking and smoking. Where did you sleep? That's never a problem. She always found some guy who'd give her a bed in trade.

In trade for what, I wanted to know. Sex, she said in such a way to let me know she thought I was stupid. I didn't believe any girl liked that, and I told her so. Sex was what you have to do, she explained, like a payment. Then you get somewhere to sleep and sometimes food to eat.

I thought she would be better off to stay in the foster home. She said no. The place was too nice. Isn't that strange?

November 8, 1970

The girls here are mostly older than me, around fifteen or sixteen. Most of them are nice and just like girls anywhere. One got mad at me and told me I thought I was special. I said no, I didn't, but she was a bitch. She left me alone after that. Even so, the truth is, among these girls, I am special. None of them has anyone fighting for their lives.

There's Nora; she's fourteen. She lived on the street for a year, got arrested and ended up here. Before, she had a home in a small place called Pine Dock, way up north. She came to the city with her sister, but the sister went to jail for something, leaving Nora all by herself. Then she got a boyfriend, but she had to work. I figured she couldn't be more than thirteen at the time, so I asked her, what kind of work. She laughed at me and said the only kind there is.

Two of the others said sex was no big deal. It pays good. And besides, what else can you do? I asked if they wanted to. Wanting had nothing to do with anything.

Sex happened to me, I told them, but some men forced me and they took the money. I didn't think I could ever do that by choice. I hated it.

Theresa asked would I rather starve. I thought so and she laughed at me. Try it.

Some of the others were in care because their families don't want them, and some were waiting for foster homes. Everyone had a story and I think everyone of those girls has been raped and hurt—one of them by her own dad.

They were friendly, talked to me about things and shared their makeup and magazines. We watched TV and played cards. I thought of Mary and how good she is. I wondered what she might think of our conversations. Would she understand?

I got a letter from Jack today. He says events are moving along. Finding my adoption papers took time and held things up. He needs them to prove an American adopted me, but why that's important is beyond me.

He will try to visit me soon and in the meantime, please cooperate with my lawyer. She must have told him what I did. Strange, Jack told me lawyers aren't supposed to repeat what you say.

December 12, 1970
Hello, journal. Guess what? Candace is coming to get me to take me to court. Jack will be there. We're having a hearing today about Jack being my guardian and me going to Chicago. I only found out last night. Candace is bringing over some new clothes for me. I couldn't sleep, too much to get ready. When I come back, I'll tell you what happened.

The outfit Candace brought for me was wonderful, like nothing I ever had before: a skirt in pale blue that came to my knees, with a white shirt and a matching jacket, pantyhose, new underwear and shiny black slip on shoes.

To tell you the truth, they pinched a bit but I sure did like the way my feet looked. What a disappointment when I had to put my old donated coat over the pretty outfit, and carry the new shoes while I scuffed outside in my hand-me-down snow boots.

We drove to the court building and went inside. Candace searched on a big board to find out which room was ours, and we took an elevator to the fifth floor. When we got off, the first face I found was Jack's. He was waiting in the hallway, and not only him, but Mary too.

"Here she is!" Mary ran over and threw her arms around me, soaking my cheeks with her tears. "Oh, at last."

"Where's Tara? Who's looking after Tara?"

"Jack's mother." She wiped her eyes with a tissue. "You're so grown up."

"Thank you."

Jack came to us and winked at me as he took Mary's arm. "Come on, old girl, you promised: no tears. Bria, you look very nice."

"Thank you."

"Nervous?"

"No."

He smiled and said we had to excuse him and went over to talk with Candace.

I heard a voice behind me. "Hello, Bria." I whirled around and saw Mrs. Friesen. Jack, Mary, Candace and now Mrs. Friesen—all come to help me. I felt I might cry, like Mary was, still.

Mary

I couldn't believe what my eyes beheld, our girl so grown up and full of life. I thought of the phone call from Jack after he'd visited her for the first time, when he'd described her as broken and had wept. And those bleak progress reports from this Mrs. Friesen: the early ones. I compared the girl who was almost a young woman in front of me to what I'd imagined we'd find.

Bria's arms crept around my neck, and she hugged me. "Don't cry, Mary. I'm okay now." When I stopped my foolish tears, she kissed my cheek again and joined Jack and Candace. She gave them no chance to hold a conversation without including her.

I turned to Mrs. Friesen, her kind eyes strangely huge behind her thick glasses, and took her hand. "Thank you. It's a miracle!"

"The young own wonderful recuperative powers. Good to meet you at last and I wish you success in these proceedings." She had a marvelous, rich, deep voice.

"Thank you." She was such a dignified woman. It must be heart-wrenching, having to deal with shattered young lives, but I realized when I looked at Bria, however difficult Mrs. Friesen's work, she reaped wonderful rewards.

Bria was embroiled in a heated argument with her lawyer.

"I think I may have a challenging job ahead of me," I told Mrs. Friesen. "May I call you from time to time?"

She smiled and handed me some cards. "I'd enjoy nothing more. Now, Mrs. Connelly, I think we may go in."

Jack took my arm and together we walked into the courtroom.

We entered a simple room, much smaller than I expected with white walls offset by light oak paneling. A judge's raised desk, also in light oak, sat front and center before two Canadian flags draped on either side of a crest. Above hung a portrait of Queen Elizabeth.

A long oak table abutted the judge's desk, and we arranged ourselves around the three sides. Bria and Candace took the end facing the judge. Mrs. Friesen sat opposite us, joined by a heavyset younger woman who, I realized, Bria recognized. She waved to her and in a stage whisper said, "Hi, Anna!"

A woman robed in black with a red sash came in, and we all rose as ordered, until she motioned with a sweep of her hand for us to sit. She took some papers from one of the clerks and addressed the small gathering.

"We are here to determine the proposed guardianship of the Child, Bria Jean Connelly. Is this the Child in question?"

Bria stood, despite Candace's attempts to stop her. "Yes, I am." Candace whispered in her ear and, with a guilty start, Bria added, "Your Honor," and sat down.

Candace presented herself as counsel for the minor child.

Jack introduced himself as the petitioner, appearing, he said, "Pro Se."

It began: reports from Mrs. Friesen, then Anna. Candace spoke at length about the best interest of the child and finally, the judge called on Jack to speak.

He stood. "Your Honor, I'd like to address your expressed concerns over my youth. I've known Bria since she was three years old and my sole desire is to provide her protection and guidance. Her day-to-day home will be with Mrs. Connelly, who stands as guardian in loco parentis for Bria's sister. Mrs. Connelly and I believe the sisters should live together.

"I ask Your Honor overlook my deficiencies in maturity as more experienced and qualified individuals offer their assistance. In this petition, I'm supported not only by Mrs. Connelly, but also by my parents—Rose and John Connelly—as attested by their affidavits, copies of which are in your packet." He sat down.

The judge began to gather papers from various corners of her desk. "I require time to deliberate. We will—Yes?"

I followed her gaze to Bria. She had her hand up in the air, like a pupil in school who had sudden need of a toilet. Candace was glaring at her and Jack had his fist over his mouth, but he was smiling.

"Do you wish to address the court?"

"Yes, Your Honor."

"You may do so."

"Just a minute, Your Honor." She pulled a piece of lined paper from her pocket and stood. "Your Honor, I don't wish to be impertinent. Maybe I don't know how things are done, but it seems to me someone ought to ask me what I want. All my life, Your Honor, I've had to do what the adults in my life thought I should and it really hasn't turned out that good, Your Honor. I think you should hear what I have to say, Your

Honor."

I wondered how many 'Your Honors' could be crammed into one exchange.

We all looked at 'Your Honor.' Her face was impassive. "You may address me as to your wishes."

"I want to go to live with Mary, and Jack has been my good friend for years. No one helps me to figure out what I should do like he does. The happiest time I remember was at Mary's house. I attended Ave Maria school. I liked it, and they want me back. I haven't been to school in months and that's where I want to go. My little sister is there. Since my mum went away, I'm all the real family she has left and my mum would expect me to help my Aunt Mary look after her.

"Mostly, I want to go because they love me, and they'll give me a chance to grow up. Please, Your Honor let me go to Mary's house in Chicago." She sat down, stood again, added, "Thank you, Your Honor," and sat once more.

Her Honor stared at Bria for several minutes. "Well spoken, Miss Connelly. Very eloquent. Now I would like some time to review all this information and I'll return and render my decision. Shall we say one hour?"

We spent that hour waiting in the hallway. Bria was subdued, sitting beside me quietly and studious in avoiding Candace.

"I thought your speech was very good. You were so brave to speak up like that. I don't think I could. I was so nervous I couldn't understand a thing."

She gave a fleeting little smile and went back to gnawing her fingers. I took her poor raw hand in mine. "You don't want to do that." She grasped it tightly and sagged against me, her head on my shoulder.

Down the hall, Jack and Candace sat on a bench, engrossed in a serious discussion. I realized they were preparing for the next hearing, and I said a quiet prayer. "Please let the judge see our girl needs to go home. Please give her the wisdom to do what's right. Amen." It wasn't until Bria murmured, "Amen," that I realized I'd spoken aloud.

Bria

I knew Candace wouldn't let me speak. No matter how many times I asked or what arguments I thought up, she said, "It's not appropriate." So

I did anyway. I wanted to go live with Mary so badly, it was eating me up.

I wished the judge would hurry up and say whether or not she'd let me, but when the clerk came and told us time to go in, I filled up with dread. Careful to sit with Mary and Jack, not Candace, who was still mad at me, I let Mary hold my hand. She gripped so tight it hurt, and I felt her shaking.

The judge came in and we all had to stand up again. I studied her face to see if I could tell what she was going to do, but I couldn't. I willed her to let me go, concentrating with all my might, until I became aware she was staring back at me.

"This is a difficult case. On the one hand, I must weigh the responsibility entrusted in us toward a ward of the Province of Manitoba, in particular as this relates to issues of placement outside our jurisdiction."

My heart sank.

"However, on the other, we are charged to act above all in the best interest of the child. I have no doubt that Mr. Connelly's motives for this petition address those best interests, in spite of his youth. I note he has taken great care in his preparations and developed a strong support network in order to meet his obligations to the Child, in particular his choice of Mrs. Connelly as primary caregiver, who will provide a loving and stable home environment."

I held my breath.

"Further, I reviewed the reports from Mrs. Friesen of CFS and her recommendation the Child be returned to her extended family, with whom it is apparent she enjoys good relations and strong affection."

Mrs. Friesen nodded.

"Last, but not least, I considered the impassioned plea of the Child, herself."

I shot a triumphant glare at Candace.

"It is therefore my ruling that the Child, Bria Jean Connelly, shall be placed under guardianship of John Connelly, Jr. of Chicago, Illinois in the United States of America, and that he shall act *in loco parentis* in all matters relating to the future welfare of the Child."

I almost peed my pants.

"This order shall overrule the order of protection placed by the Office of the Public Trustee of the Province of Manitoba, and shall come into effect immediately, and shall remain in place until the Child does reach majority at eighteen years of age."

Jack smiled but Mary was crying again. Confused, I turned to Jack. "Am I going to Chicago?" He nodded and put his finger to his lips.

"Miss Connelly, do you understand what this entails?"

I stood up. "I think so, Your Honor."

"While you will live with Mrs. Connelly, John Connelly will act as your parent. He is responsible for any decisions regarding your health, welfare and education. Good luck to you, and to you all."

I said, "Thank you, your honor," and sat down in my chair.

"Miss Barr?"

Candace rose.

"I understand you now proceed to QB 5 in relation to the Crown's petition. The clerk has taken my orders to Judge Vernon, copies of which are available to you in my chambers. That is all." And she left.

Mrs. Friesen stood before me. "Congratulations, Bria. I wish you all the best."

"Thank you." I watched her leave. I wanted to run after her and tell her I loved her and thank you for helping me, but I knew I shouldn't. Mrs. Friesen didn't invite intimacies like touching. She just talked and listened.

Fifteen:
"He says I deserve justice."

Jack said Mary should take me to lunch and he and Candace were going to meet with the Crown, to "nip this in the bud, if possible," which I didn't understand. Then he asked Mary, "You're absolutely sure?"

Yet again, they had plans that excluded me. Instead of pitching a fit then and there, I figured I'd weasel it out of Mary.

Mary

Bria trotted along beside me, chattering a mile a minute about all the wonderful things we would do once we got to Chicago. I didn't have the heart to tell her it wasn't yet a sure thing. The day was bitterly cold, beyond anything I'd ever experienced. Within seconds, Bria's cheeks turned cherry red and frost sat on her eyebrows and the curls around her face. Barely able to draw breath in the frigid air, I wondered how she managed to talk so much.

We gladly entered the first café we came across and sat down in a booth to thaw out. My feet, so cold they were numb, began to tingle with pain. *How did anyone live in such a climate?* I gratefully received a cup of hot coffee from the waitress. Bria ordered a cheeseburger and Coke. I selected a salad and made a note to myself to work on her dietary choices once we got her settled in. *If* we got her settled in.

"Mary, can I call you Mary now? I'm not a little kid anymore. I'm thirteen and Auntie Mary sounds so babyish. Can I?"

"Yes, you may, but make sure you do remember I'm your aunt."

In a tactic worthy of Jack, she got right to the point. "Mary, what's going on?"

I tried to fend her off. "We're having a nice lunch."

"No." Her face became a black scowl. "What are Candace and Jack doing? What does he want to nip in the bud? And what must you be absolutely sure of?"

"Can't we wait until Jack can explain?"

"No. He's busy. You tell me. Somebody should."

I tried to plead ignorance. "I don't think I can. Jack's plans can be complicated."

"Look, Mary." She spoke as though I was the child. "I'm already aware the Crown wants me here to testify at the trial. Candace says it's probably a long time away, and if I stay, I'll have to go into foster care, and I don't want to do that. I want to go with you."

"Then you know as much as I do."

"No, not true." She slammed her coke down on the table. "It's me they're over there talking about, and my life they're deciding. I'm the one who'll be stuck in foster care. Be fair. Tell me."

She was right, but how to explain the maneuvering, the strategy, the planning and plain machinations behind today's events? "Jack and Candace are meeting the prosecutor to try and make an agreement."

"What kind?"

"To ensure you'll return to testify so you can live with me in Chicago."

"I already told Candace to tell them I promise to come back." Her scowl deepened, and her mouth and jaw tightened. "Didn't she do that?"

"She may have. I don't know. Somehow I don't think the word of a young girl is enough." I reached for my fork to start my salad, but Bria put her hand on mine and stalled me.

"Can't Jack promise?"

"Jack had no grounds to do anything until he was your guardian and that only happened this morning."

"Can't he promise them now?"

"I think that's what he's doing."

She sat staring at me and ignored her lunch. "So why is everybody so worried?"

I sighed. "The prosecutors don't want you to go to Chicago, beyond their reach. They intend to continue the protection order because you're a child witness and the trial is so important. A judge wants to hear both sides this afternoon. And that's everything I know." I crammed the fork full of greens into my mouth.

She was incensed. "Why didn't Candace tell me?"

"We've had no time. Things sat around going nowhere and all of a sudden, here we are."

"And if they don't agree?" She was implacable.

"If not, the next judge will decide if you can go."

"You think he will?"

"You should be asking this of Jack."

Her eyebrows slid together as she pulled a fierce face. "Well, I would if he was here. He's not; you are."

I surrendered. "We think the judge will be on our side now Jack's your guardian. That was the key. Now you're no longer a ward of the province, a judge is unlikely to rule you can't live with your own family so you can be called as a witness."

I watched her fit all the pieces of the puzzle together. "What's Jack going to do if a promise isn't enough and the judge decides I have to stay?"

"Don't worry."

Her scowl told me she wouldn't give up. "But – what if? "

"Jack has a final plan. He'll offer to post what they call a bond, something he gives the court to hold until he does what he promises."

My fork made it halfway to my mouth before she asked, "What will he give them?"

"Money."

"What money? Where did it come from?"

"From me, I can get the money."

Bria's expression swiftly relaxed and her shoulders loosened back into a normal posture. "Is that what you had to be absolutely sure of? I thought maybe it was about me, taking me."

My heart did a flip in my rib cage. "No – never. I've always been absolutely sure I wanted to take you. I've been so lonely since you left, especially since Pat passed away. Now I have Tara and soon you, a full house and a family to love. I need you as much as you need me."

She sat digesting my words if not her lunch. "Is a bond a lot of money?"

"I don't know how much they want, but within reason, we'll get it."

"How?"

"I'll mortgage my house, which means—"

"I know what a mortgage is. And if I don't come back?"

"I guess I'd lose the money," I said as lightly as I would comment on a pair of new shoes.

She flashed a broad grin, completely at odds with the hard glint in her eyes. "Don't worry, I'll come back. Jack and I agree it's the right thing for me to do. He says I deserve justice. Me? I just want to fuck the bastards over."

I'm sure my mouth was hanging open. "Well, I can certainly understand why you might want to do that."

"Somehow, I don't think you do." She picked up her burger and inhaled the rest.

Bria

Poor Mary, she wasn't dressed for the cold. We walked as fast as her frozen feet allowed back to the court building. Her breath came out in little puffs of steam and her face was almost purple. I yanked open the door for her. "Let's get in and warm you up."

"Oh Mother of God, how cold is it?"

I pointed through the window to an electric sign on a building across the street: Time 1:46 Temp -46 C.

"What is that in Fahrenheit?"

"They meet at -40," I explained. "Damn cold."

We stepped into the small entryway between two sets of doors. A blast of hot air blew down on us from the ceiling. "Are you warmer now, Mary?" I opened the next door, and we entered the marble-floored foyer.

"I may never be warm again." She pulled her coat around her, hugging herself, rubbed at her arms and stamped her feet. "If my frozen blood starts moving, I'll survive."

"The feeling will pass." I was trembling with impatience. "Come on, let's go look for Jack."

"We're supposed to wait in the foyer."

"No way." I had to find them before they screwed things up without me.

"Bria, we don't even know which room." Mary stared longingly at the upholstered benches along the wall.

"Yes, we do." I ran off and beckoned her to follow. "The first judge said QB 5 and Judge Vernon. There's a big board over there that lists all the judges and courts. Come on." I waved her forward. "Here! I found them. Court of Queen's Bench, Hon. Judge D. Vernon, Dec. 12, room 55. Fifth floor, Mary, come on—please."

"Bria, we should—"

I pushed the button for the elevator. The bell dinged; the door opened; I popped in and held the car until Mary arrived, still talking.

"I don't think this is a good idea."

"I do." I punched the button for five. "Don't worry, if they're mad, I'll tell them everything's all my fault, and I forced you."

"That's fair, as it's the truth." She exhaled, irritated with me, and leaned against the wall.

The upward motion stopped and the door slid open. I was out in a flash, searching about. "Look." I pointed at a sign. "Follow the arrow. This way."

We found room 55 and huddled outside, listening. "That doesn't sound like court, just regular talking. Let's go." I shoved open the door and walked in.

The discussion stopped. They stared at me: Candace and Jack, Miss Loepky and a grey-haired, goateed man I'd never met. For a second, I wanted to flap my smart mouth. "Haven't you ever seen a girl before?" But I didn't.

Jack spoke first. "Bria, what are doing here?"

Candace was next. "Bria, please wait for us outside. Mrs. Connelly, can you take her out?"

I moved away so Mary couldn't.

Miss Loepky rose, a welcoming smile on her face. "Hello Bria, how are you? I want you to meet Mr. Duchenes from my office. Maurice, this is Bria Connelly."

I glanced at them all in turn, but spoke only to Jack. "What's going on?"

"Everything is fine, nothing to worry about. Come over here." I went and stood beside him. He motioned me into a chair behind him, turned his chair around and whispered. "We've reached an agreement and now we're waiting for the judge to tell him."

"Am I going to Chicago?" My heart rattled, it beat so hard.

"Yes, you are, first thing tomorrow morning."

"Oh, good." I was so relieved I thought I'd cry. "Did you have to give them Mary's money?"

Jack glanced at Mary, sitting by the back wall. "No."

"Do I testify?"

"Yes."

"So you don't need me to tell the judge I want to?"

He mouthed "No," a smile sparkling in his eyes. "You can tell them." He jerked his head at the other side of the room.

I got up and walked over to their table. "Hello, Miss Loepky."

"You're looking well. Say hello to Mr. Duchenes, the prosecutor in charge of this case."

Mr. Duchenes stood up and put out his hand for me to shake. "Hello, Bria, pleased to meet you."

"Thank you. I came to tell you I do want to testify. I'll come back. You don't need to keep me here."

"So I understand from your counsel. I look forward to talking to you. I'll get in touch with Miss Barr when the time arrives. And let me say, I think you're a very courageous young lady."

"Thank you."

Candace moved behind me and put her hands on my shoulders, turning me around. "Come on now, Bria. There's nothing to see or do in here for you."

She took me back to Mary, and we walked out to the hallway and hugged, giggling like two small girls.

I was out and free to go on with my life.

Sixteen:
"She's not a child and she's not a woman."

1973
Mary

Bria did testify. Jack spent hours helping her practice. He posed questions and listened to her stammered responses with all the patience of a saint. At first, she would burst into tears, choke up and lose her ability to speak but Jack, dogged and insistent, repeated her answers and suggested other words until, by the time they were ready to leave for Canada, she was able to relate the most unspeakable acts in clear clinical terms. She used terms like penis and vagina with the detachment of a medical examiner. I don't think I would do as well.

I wasn't supposed to hear; Bria and Jack sat in her room behind a firmly closed door, but snatches of their conversation spilled out into the apartment. What I did catch curdled my blood. I never let on to her I knew, easier for me that way.

When they returned, Jack boasted she'd handled the trial like a champion, collapsed in tears once and needed a recess, but he thought her breakdown impressed the jury all the more. Even though the trial resulted in a conviction, Jack wasn't at all satisfied. Canadian criminal law was inadequate for the crime, or in his words, the Canadians were softies. I'm sure a sentence of hung, drawn and quartered wouldn't have been enough.

For some reason, I believed Jack had himself made guardian of Bria for strictly legal reasons and her care and education would be left to me. I couldn't have been more wrong.

He took her to baseball games, swimming, skating and whatever else she might enjoy, encouraged her ever-shifting interests—the latest passion, her drama classes—and brought her books he thought she would like. He tutored her in mathematics and American civics and debated the politics of the day as though speaking to a contemporary, even discussed his work with her and asked for her input. He made her the center of his existence.

I became uneasy observing the situation. It didn't seem right, a girl of fifteen so closely bonded to a young man of only twenty-eight. I couldn't say why. Call the feeling some sixth sense. The first time I tried to talk to Jack, he dismissed me with an offhand, "She's just a kid."

When I pressed him, he said, "She's already been rejected by two fathers. She needs male attention."

We were long overdue for a face off. Last week he invited her out to Grass Lake and not only spent the weekend alone with her, as had become their habit, but took her to an adult party. According to Bria, he introduced her around and helped her make conversation. Was this fifteen-year-old girl his date for the evening?

I sat him down at the table in my small kitchen, gave him coffee and a piece of carrot cake and tackled him. "Don't you understand, she's not a woman and she's not a child? Fifteen is a tough age."

"She enjoyed herself and so did I. She handles herself well. My friends liked her." He stared at me, genuinely perplexed. "What's the problem?"

"Oh Jack. Young girls love with a grand passion. I fear she misunderstood your intentions." She had come home, starry-eyed and happy with herself at having pleased Jack by her ability to act the adult. Her euphoria had lasted for days.

"Bria knows what's what," he stated matter-of-factly.

"You're sure?" I searched his face. "I'm not."

"If you've got something to say, spit it out." His thick black brows drew closer to his hardened eyes.

He thought me intimidated; he was wrong. "It's not right for you to spend so much time with her. She lives in a different world than you. She's a girl. There's too much potential for pain for Bria; that's my big concern." Then something I meant only as a thought slipped out. "It's not only the nature of your behavior toward her—"

"What exactly do you mean?" The frown was gone, replaced by an outraged glower.

"Plain speaking? She's in love with you and you encourage it, not a healthy situation." There it was out and sitting on the table.

He glared. "Not healthy? Why?"

"It just isn't." *How could someone so smart be so blind?* "You're not her father. You're not her brother, not even a cousin, strictly speaking. You're a young man who showers her with attention, turning her head." I hunted for the right words to explain my emotional worries. "She should be spending time with children her own age, not traipsing out to the lake country, attending cocktail parties and nights alone in the company of a grown man only thirteen years her senior."

Jack dismissed me with an angry snort. "She seems happy. And I'd like to think you know me well enough not to entertain the thought I'd take a mere girl, one I've known since she was a baby, this *child* to my bed."

I sat quietly, waiting for him to calm himself. "That's not what I'm saying. I think you're letting her get too close to you."

"Mary, the way I see it, the best thing for Bria right now is to be able to love a man and to do so in a spirit of trust." He leaned over to peer into my face and spoke in earnest fervor. "Look, she's already experienced the darker side of men. I hope she's learning a man can be gentle and decent, and she can be loved for the person she is. I want to build her up, help her feel good about herself."

He looked at me, seeking agreement. He didn't find it. "Very lofty, Jack, but wasn't it you who told me teenage gonads don't take much else into consideration?"

"Boys are boys."

"And girls are girls, not so different, other than they start at a younger age." I pointed at him, heated in spite of myself. "Are you being deliberately obtuse?"

"And what did I learn from you, Mary? Despite my involuntary adolescent urges, I formed a trusted friendship with a woman, one that's enriched my life in so many ways." He reached over to kiss my cheek. "That's what I want to give Bria."

Saddened, I asked, "And you believe this is what she wants?"

"Perhaps not yet. Even so, it's what she needs." He was so sure of himself.

"I don't think the situation's that simple, nor do I believe in your altruistic motives. This is all for Bria. Hogwash!" I knew in my heart Jack enjoyed her adulation. He reveled in being her knight in shining armor. "Speak the truth, man. Why?"

To my surprise, he didn't respond in anger, but sat quietly, collecting his thoughts. "You weren't present when Mrs. Friesen and I discussed all this. She said a close relationship with me could be beneficial for her."

I wanted to shake him and scream, but kept my voice calm. "I think if Mrs. Friesen were here, she'd tell you Bria needs to live as a normal teenage girl. True, in many ways she's mature for her age, but the bare truth is she's still a child."

"I think I understand why you're worried." He leaned forward, sure of his persuasive ability. "Mrs. Friesen and I had a number of talks. She explained the effects of sexual abuse in young girls, warned me Bria would act seductively, to expect it, so I was ready and laid down the law the moment the first hint came up." He held up his hands. "You don't have to worry. I took care to make sure she understands."

I wanted to laugh at him, at his complacent certainty in the power of his words, but simply commented, "So it did come up."

"Yes, in the early days. And I made very clear exactly what our relationship was to be." He sat back, self-satisfied.

"Enlighten me. Explain your feelings for her."

"I do love her, Mary. I mean to protect her and give her a chance to grow up. I want her to feel good about herself and heal." He paused then added, "And I admire her spirit, her mind, her courage and how full of life she is."

And her strong haunches and pretty round bottom, I contributed mentally. It was not Bria who labored under a delusion. I'd seen his eyes follow her around. I tried another course. "How is that lovely Leslie I met at our lunch a couple of weeks ago?"

"Gone—back to New York."

"Tell me something, Jack. Why do you never introduce your lady friends to Bria?"

The smugness left his face and bewildered annoyance took its place. "Oh, will you let it go? Please!" He shot out of his chair. "I grant you, you're right in one aspect. I'm a man and, as a man, I can't help but notice she's a pretty girl going about the business of growing up. Sure, sometimes when she walks by in those tight jeans she likes, my thoughts aren't of the purest variety. However, those are just thoughts."

He gathered his discarded coat and tie and put them on. "Do you honestly think me capable of such a betrayal? I'm the one held her hands and saw her weeping, broken and shamed. I would never hurt my girl that way—never. I do know right from wrong."

He slammed the door on the way out, loud enough to wake Tara, before I found the chance to tell him he totally misunderstood me. I had failed. What he didn't understand was, with all the best intentions, he was stealing the little left of Bria's childhood.

***

I went to get Tara from her bed. This one at least was mine, my sweet baby girl and all the decisions regarding her growth mine to make. She'd be allowed to remain a child for as long as she needed and when the time came for schooling, I would never allow Tara to follow the course plotted for Bria.

Bria was to transfer to a college on the Loyola campus, to a pilot project there. Jack thought this a wonderful opportunity, and was full of pride at her invitation to take part, and with a scholarship as well. On a university campus before her sixteenth birthday, rubbing shoulders with students who were eighteen, nineteen and even in their early twenties? How could she remain a child?

Only *I* saw her relaxed and being herself. At home, she became the young girl she was, played with her sister, giggled over silly stories, watched cartoons, sat on the floor coloring with crayons. At night, I held her when she cuddled up to me on the couch, and we watched movies together.

I tried my luck with Jack's father, John. "She's still just a girl and Jack doesn't see it."

"Jack's doing what he thinks is right." John, a good man but not a reflective one, adored his first-born son, his pride and joy. When he thought of Bria, well, she was nothing more than another reason to be proud of Jack. Jack could do no wrong. John offered no help at all.

The truth of the matter was John and Bria didn't take to each other.

Like many policemen, John expected obedience and compliance, particularly in children. It was obvious to everyone Bria took great delight in giving him neither. She was adept at bringing out his less admirable qualities: his bigotry, intolerance and, above all, his temper. If not for Jack and his father's grudging deference to him, Bria would have felt his wrath on many occasions.

I chided her often for her lack of respect and plain bad manners. I had, this minute, finished doing so again.

Completely unrepentant as usual, she demanded, "Why's he always over here?"

"He's not. He drops in sometimes to visit." I picked up Tara's toys

127

and returned them to their basket. "And he likes to play with Tara."

"He comes to see you. He only plays with Tara 'cause you like it." Her face twinkled with the wicked little smile of a tease.

I stopped the meaningless chores and faced her. "What exactly do you mean by that, Miss Bria?"

"He likes you. And you like him, don't you?"

"Well of course I do, he's family. We've known each other a long time."

She laughed at me and shook her head. "No, more than that. He *likes* you."

"I don't know what ideas are floating around in your brain, but understand this; I was a wife for almost twenty years to his brother, and he's a married man with five sons." I tried to put a determined stop to her romantic foolishness.

She shrugged and to my growing dismay said, "So? He likes you a lot. Anyway, your husband's dead."

"Thank you for reminding me. However, John's still married and to a woman who is very much alive." I collected the rest of the toys.

Bria hunkered down on the floor, helping. "Some marriage. Aunt Rose spends all her time with Nana Meg, and Mickey told me she took Jack's room after he moved out. That really pissed him off because Mickey thought he'd get it and not have to share with Kevin anymore." She nudged me with her elbow. "So they don't even sleep together."

"Don't say pissed off, it's vulgar." I smacked her bottom lightly. "That is far more information than I need, and if you're playing some kind of matchmaker, forget it. He's my brother-in-law and that's that." I waved her away.

"Glad to hear it." She sounded like Jack. "You could do way better."

"What?"

"Honestly, Mary, you're a pretty woman, you're smart; you're good to people. You could do better than Uncle John."

I lost patience with her foolishness. "Well for your information, first: I'm not looking and, second: John is a good man, and I've never met one better. Simply because you don't take to him doesn't mean others can't."

"As I said, you like him too." She grinned.

"Stop it. And go and finish your packing. You leave for Canada tomorrow."

She left the room like the Cheshire cat—grin last. Damn her! The thought she'd planted wouldn't leave my mind.

Seventeen:
"The schizophrenic life I lead."

Bria

At the age of almost sixteen, I faced a new problem: I'd been living a double life for the past three years, and all my lies were about to catch up with me.

I banged my head against the window as I shifted, trying to find a comfortable position. Difficult, since the economy seat at the back of the plane was so cramped. I pulled down the table in front of me, spread out my journal and wrote.

August 31, 1973
I never set out to be deceitful. The whole fraud happened a bit at a time. My crime grew with each lie of omission and every deliberate fabrication, one on top of the other until I'd made a mountain. I'm a liar. And if one is entitled to boast about such things, a good one.

I swear, I never meant to be. It started as an act of kindness, or so I told myself at the time. I lied to Mary, good-hearted, trusting Mary, simply so she wouldn't worry so much. I lied to Jack, my protector and my best friend, because he had the power to stop me, and I won't be stopped.

The first question out of their mouths was sure to be "Why?" and what explanation had I to give them? This was something I wanted to do so badly I couldn't risk asking permission for fear of refusal. If they refused, I'd have no option except to disobey, far worse than not telling at all. I charged straight ahead on a full head of steam, doing what I thought right for me. Once I made that decision, the lies and deception were just a natural result.

Anyway, the truth of the matter was this: in Canada, I operated pretty much at my own devices and lived by my own choices. Funny, I was taught at my Chicago school that the United States was the land of liberty, but for me all the freedom was in Canada, all the rules in the U.S. I led two lives, as different as night and day. I picked up my pen again to explore this new thought.

Does anyone understand the strange schizophrenic life I lead? For eight months, I'm an American Irish Catholic parochial student named Bria Jean and for the other four, I'm a Canadian Scottish Presbyterian cowgirl known as BeeJay. Little wonder I keep my two lives separate.

Again I stopped. This wasn't helpful, not helpful at all. Jack might think the paragraph clever, perhaps amusing, but not explanatory in the slightest. The lies would be the big issue, not my wonderful adventurous and successful summers, and I'd better have a damned good response at hand.

Even Ted had been astounded at my ability to lie, and I knew for a fact he lied a lot, especially to girls. As his best buddy, I didn't say anything when I heard him denying the existence of one girl to another and thought they probably deserved no better, being so stupid and gullible.

He had walked into the kitchen at his dad's place and caught me on the phone spinning a long line of lies to Mary. I turned around and saw him listening with his mouth hanging open.

"What the hell are you up to, telling your folks all that bullshit?"

"No business of yours," I told him and stared him square in the eyes. "You're only four years older than me. You don't get to tell me what to do."

"We've been friends since you were a skinny kid. Last thing I expected – to find you're a liar. Listening to you now makes me wonder how much bullshit you feed me."

"I don't believe you. Think of the lies you tell all those pretty girls. Who are you to look down on me?" I stuck my face out at him, leading with my chin.

Quick as a minnow, he leaned forward and kissed my lips. Six inches from my nose, so his two beautiful brown eyes looked right into mine, he said, "So I spin tall tales to some silly girls I meet for one night. They know and don't care, only out for a bit of fun. I don't lie to you, though."

I backed up, kind of shaken, confused and a bit fearful. Ted had no knowledge of my history, and I wanted to keep it that way. And I sure didn't want him to kiss me either, moving in so fast and startling me. He was likely to try again. So full of himself and his good looks, he thought all the girls dying to have him. I wasn't about to be one of his scores.

"Well maybe you do lie to me, and maybe you don't. You tell lot's of lies, Ted Lassiter, so why would I be the exception?"

Ted pulled at his blond hair, something he always did when he thought. Lucky for his hairline, he didn't think too often. For once, he beat me to the last word.

"Seems to me you proved my point. Hearing someone tell a whole lot of lies does make them hard to believe, but I can promise you one thing: I don't lie to my friends. Don't think that's something you can say."

Chagrin at not having a witty comeback and humiliation at finding myself bested by the slow-witted Ted struck me speechless. Not even Jack could leave me wordless like he did that night.

A few weeks later, in Coeur d'Alene, Idaho, he surprised me again. He sneaked me into a party where people were drinking and, though piles of other girls wanted to dance, flirted and swished all around him, he danced with me all night.

Later, we climbed up into the stock trailer's feed storage loft and he taught me how to kiss. I had to learn from someone, and with his experience, he was bound to be an expert. In the aromatic folds of green alfalfa and sacks of grain, he showed me how to use lips and tongue to please someone. The kissing suited me fine, but when he grabbed at me and ground into my belly, I pushed him away and started crying.

He sat up so quickly, he banged his head on the roof. "Fuck!" He immediately pulled me up beside him and plucked the straws and leaves out of my hair. "I'm sorry, Bria. I didn't mean to go on like that. I should have thought. Young as you are; you're still a virgin."

His misunderstanding only made me cry more but I never gave up. With time, persistence and practice, I improved, became a first-rate kisser and Ted left our love life at kissing. Yeah, and when he thought I'd gone to sleep in my bunk like a good little girl, he sneaked out again.

Later, back in Buffalo Coulee, I told Lizzie and she said, "He's nineteen. All nineteen- year-old guys are horny toads," as if that explained anything.

***

After a long spell of contemplation, during which I meant to beat myself up for the liar I was, a truth surfaced and began to nibble at my thoughts. Under all the assumed remorse and self-castigation, I found anger. Why? No matter how I strained my brain the question remained unanswered.

I flipped absentmindedly through my notebook and a loose sheet of paper fluttered out, a journal page from three years ago. It must have fallen out of one of my books and been somehow tucked into this one.

December 13, 1970

What is wrong with adults? They always think they know best, and never ever want to listen to your side of things. Take Mary, for example. I love her to bits, but with her, it's always 'this isn't right and that isn't right,' like she has the only copy of some sacred rulebook. She just won't listen to what I think at all. Especially anything concerning Jack!

Every day I receive a new version of the same old sermon: why I shouldn't sleep at Jack's apartment or go with him to his place at the lake, or why I shouldn't hug him so much. Young girls have no business hanging on the arm of single grown men, she says.

I don't understand why she's so worried. Jack isn't about to do anything to me. He made his opinion on the subject crystal clear the time I kissed him on the mouth. You'd of thought I'd infected him with poisonous venom the way he grabbed my shoulders and pushed me away.

I laughed aloud reading this. I remembered his embarrassment and my own, but a kiss had seemed such a natural thing to do. He was always kind and gentle to me, so why not? I thought all men wanted young girls and I needed to please him so much.

He'd taken me skating. I showed him my hockey moves and in an attempt to impress him by my crosscheck abilities, I crashed into his husky body at full speed and we both went careening off the pond into a pile of snow.

"You crazy girl." He pulled me up and brushed the snow off me.

I stretched up and kissed him on the mouth. I pressed my body to his, about to wrap my arms around his neck when his hands grabbed my shoulders. With startling speed, I found myself at arm's length staring at shocked black eyes. He looked like he wished for longer limbs.

"No, no, no way." He was offended, though I didn't have a clue why.

Scared, I got mouthy. "What's the big deal?"

He grew dark and serious. "You're thirteen and I'm your guardian." He spoke as though climbing stairs. "You – don't – do – that."

"I only wanted to kiss you." I offered a nonchalant shrug.

"If you want to kiss me, you kiss me here." He touched his cheek.

"Sor-ree." I tried to pull away, but he held me tight.

"No, you listen. You're a young girl and I'm a grown man. Men don't do that with girls." He let me go so suddenly I almost fell over.

"Some men do." I spit out the words in malice, flooded by a rush of conflicting emotions.

He regarded me with sadness. "Well, I'd sure hate to think I was one of them. I wouldn't like myself much."

"What, you don't like girls?"

"I like women, Bria, grown-up women."

Still in smartass mode, I said, "Oh, I'm too skinny and flat-chested for you."

"No, too young." His voice was firm. "Got it?"

I couldn't back down. "I told you once before; girls grow up."

"Yes, you'll grow up," he agreed. "But I'll always be too old for you."

I turned to skate away, but he grabbed my arm and forced me to face him. "This is an end to it."

I shouted, "Don't worry. It will never happen again. *Never!*" and skidded off, unable to fathom his reaction and my sudden shame and remorse. I couldn't look at him.

After that, I was very careful.

With time, I learned his rules without his even having to tell me. A hug was acceptable so long as you pressed only your upper body against him. A kiss? Yes, but on his cheek. He deemed side-to-side contact permissible but no front-to-front and certainly never any touching on my part.

He allowed me to lie beside him on the old bed in the porch at his lake place and even let the length of my side rest against his, but no more.

The first time he took me to Grass Lake was the Memorial Day holiday. "A country girl like you must miss the wide open spaces. Want to come to the lake this weekend?"

"Yes," I answered, more interested in spending three days with Jack than seeing Illinois' great outdoors.

Mary wasn't happy. She made her feelings clear both to me and to Jack, but we went anyway.

I loved the place. Jack's hideaway consisted of the loft above the boathouse of a big house owned by some friend of his. With lots of trees and a big lake surrounded in grassy shores, I imagined we'd arrived at our own private paradise. At night, we listened to the laughter of loons and legions of croaking frogs.

The place boasted only one big room inside, but best of all, a spacious screened porch sat directly over the water, facing west. We sat out there and watched the sun go down or tracked the thunderstorms that rushed in, towering all the way up to heaven. An old bed filled one side of the porch, covered in a couple of plaid woolen blankets.

Jack liked to sleep in the fresh air, and I had to go inside, but in the evenings, he allowed me to lie beside him and talk. If it got cold, I had to get my own blanket and wrap myself up; I was definitely never, ever permitted to get under the bedclothes with him.

Sometimes I would snuggle up to him, warm and close, and he'd put an arm around my shoulders, holding me. He liked me to talk to him.

I'd natter my fool mouth off. Often, his hand started caressing my neck and his thumb slipped under the neckline of my shirt. I would lie absolutely still, afraid to move in case he realized what he was doing. If he had, I knew he'd stop. I told him anything he wanted to hear.

At times, he asked me things about school, like why I did poorly in some subjects when he knew I was smart. I gave him the only answer I could think of: I thought mathematics and science boring and couldn't focus on them, but look how well I was doing in English and Social Studies, History and Art. Wasn't that enough?

And drama! I loved my drama classes best of all. He said he certainly understood why I would, but perhaps I should leave off practicing those arts quite so often.

Other times we'd talk about what I wanted to do in life, and I'd tell him my half-formed ideas. Sometimes we discussed Mary and why did I fight with her so much. I said we just do. Mostly, he let me say whatever I felt like, and I did my best, anything to keep his hand stroking my neck. I became Scheherazade.

After my testimony at the trial, we never again talked about that time. Jack said I could anytime I wished. I didn't.

Only once did he ever mention it, when I announced some months back I had no desire to marry and wanted nothing to do with guys. He said there's a big difference between being raped and making love with someone I cared about and when I grew old enough I would find that out. I hoped I would find out with Jack, but knew better than to speak of it.

I understood this was an interlude, possibly a gift from Jack to me. I settled for having my neckline touched and took secret delight in the little quivers and longings his fingers produced.

***

In my mind, the lake place was our private sanctuary, but on one visit last month, I found a black bra that only in my wildest dreams would I ever have the equipage to fill, and seethed with jealousy, torturing myself, imagining what might have transpired.

I picked up the seamy evidence, held the lacey thing between my thumb and forefinger and asked, "Where'd this come from?" He grabbed it out of my hand, stuffed it in a drawer and mumbled something about none of my business what he did on his own time.

After a long taste of my silent treatment, he relented and said "the item" belonged to Leslie, and she had gone back to New York. "Unfortunately," he added. A little later, he said, "I met Leslie while she was in town on business. I've got to tell you, Bria, I liked her a lot. However, her work is in New York and mine is here. I have you and the family to think about so…" He shrugged.

Good, I thought but said, "Too bad."

"Yes, certainly is," he repeated, all wistful and I realized he was truly regretful over what could have been.

For the first time, I considered Jack as someone beyond the Jack and Bria universe I had created in my imagination. I was uncomfortable but tried to give him the appearance of interested sympathy. "Is she nice?"

"You'd like her, Bria, honestly you would."

I seriously doubted it, but didn't voice that opinion. "Maybe she'll come back."

"Maybe."

Why, I wanted to ask, did you bring her to our place? Instead, I acted interested. "Did she like it here?"

"Well, probably not a whole lot. It's a far cry from what she's used to, you know. She's a defense lawyer in Manhattan and this is a touch rustic in comparison to her city digs." Then he laughed at some private memory "But shabby as the place is, it's a shade richer than my apartment, don't you think?"

I had to agree. Jack's apartment was a study in early Salvation Army thrift store. His couch had seen better days, probably at the turn of the century, and if two people sat on it, they ended up in each other's laps in the middle.

The only saving grace to the dump was location – close to my school. I had a key and strict instructions to go there every day after classes to do my homework and wait for Jack or Uncle John to pick me up and take me home. I wasn't allowed to ride the bus after dark.

I tidied things up and did Jack's shopping for him with the money he left on the table. I tried to make sure he had fresh fruit, bread and milk. If I didn't, the only thing in his fridge would be leftover Chinese food and beer. Most evenings I cooked something for him and left it on the stove for him to warm up. Lucky he liked mac and cheese or chili or soup, the entire repertoire of dishes I knew how to make.

I kept a few clothes in the closet, and if it was snowing heavily, which seemed to be every other day in Chicago, or he or John couldn't get there until late, I slept on the saggy old couch: another thing that raised Mary's hackles. She railed at both Jack and Uncle John, her objections growing stronger the older I got, but we had a practical arrangement that continued in spite of her misgivings.

I tried to talk to her. I told her Jack would never do anything wrong or indecent with me, but she just looked at me and said it wasn't Jack she was concerned about. She said, "You can't keep hanging on to Jack like that. He's a man and you're just a slip of a girl."

"He's my best friend," I told her, "and my guardian. It's not like you think." But it was. It was and she knew it.

***

Uncle John told her not to worry; I heard him one evening while I studied in my room, and he drank coffee with her in the kitchen.

"Jack's a level-headed boy. He won't let things get out of hand. Anyway, she's off to Canada for the summer. She'll lose her schoolgirl crush while she's away, find herself some good-looking young cowhand and have herself a romance. That'll put poor old Jack in his proper place."

Annoyed they were talking about me behind my back, I quickly developed a thirst that required a trip to the kitchen. Uncle John sat at the table with Tara on his knee, helping her color in a coloring book. Tara grinned and said, "Hi, Bee," and I said, "Hi, Tara-Lara."

I grumbled a hello, how are you to Uncle John, wondering why he spent so much time at our place these days.

Both he and Mary eyed me in the guilty way people do when they've just been talking about you, so I went and got my glass of water. As if I wasn't in the room, Mary said to Uncle John, "I don't like her going off to Canada. Did they take good care of her when she lived with them? No."

"Mary, I'm right here. You can talk to me directly."

"I could, but I'm not. I'm speaking to your Uncle John. I've given up talking to you or Jack."

"I was fine last summer and the summer before, so I will be this summer too." In her eyes, when not asleep in my bed down the hall, I must be in some terrible peril. "Besides, I'm almost sixteen. I'm grown up now. I'll be fine."

Uncle John smirked and Mary rolled her eyes. "You're fifteen. Why are you in such a hurry to grow up?"

"So you won't worry about me," I said and kissed her cheek.

I'd be going to Alberta for the summer, no matter how Mary worried. She knew it too. She and Jack had argued the first time I went, two years ago. He'd said it was his decision to make, and I was entitled – that was the word he used – entitled to keep my ties to my family and country.

I was glad Jack made the decision because if Mary had, I would have hurt her when I found a way to go anyway. Nothing and no one could take those summers from me, but things hadn't come to that.

May fifteenth, after my last day at Ave Maria, Jack drove me to the airport and put me on the flight to Calgary without much protest on Mary's part at all. Now here at the end of the summer, I was flying to Chicago, not from Calgary but from Laramie, Wyoming, six days early and no one would meet me at the airport.

The plane made its ear-torturing slow descent into O'Hare. One heavy bounce and we landed, the traffic so busy we sat out on the tarmac for twenty minutes before taxiing up to the gate. Of course everyone jumped out of their seats, reaching over each other to the overhead bins, jostling and contorting in a rush to gather their belongings and deplane. I was in no hurry. I sat in my seat and waited until the aisle cleared, said "Thank you," to the flight crew and followed the crowd down to baggage claim.

Once I had my bag, I went outside, got into a taxi and gave the driver Jack's address. Forty-five minutes and $15 dollars later, I let myself in with my key. Jack wasn't home yet, so I made a cup of coffee and waited for him. To my surprise, I fell asleep, and the sound of a key and the click of the lock as the door opened woke me.

"Bria! What the hell?"

"Hi, Jack. I have to talk to you."

Eighteen:
"For God's sake, don't leave me alone with her."

Mary

"Jack, what a surprise to be hearing from you so early in the morning." In the middle of making coffee, I spooned grounds into the basket, holding the phone to my ear with my shoulder. "What's up?"

"Are you free this evening?"

"Well, I'm not sure. Let me check my social calendar. I may have a soiree at the Playboy Mansion. I can't remember offhand. Oh, right, that's not for tonight. Of course I'm free this evening." I put the basket into the coffee machine.

"We need to talk. Can I come by around seven or so, after Tara's gone to bed?"

"Seven? Yes, that'll be fine." I would expect him at nine. I filled the carafe at the kitchen sink. "What is it we need to talk about?"

"Can't you wait?"

"No. Tell me."

"Bria."

I set the full carafe on the counter in case what came next caused me to drop and break it. "Have you heard from her? Is something wrong?"

"Yes to the first. No to the second. Third, I simply want to talk to you."

"Jack, don't be so cagey. Is she in trouble? Is she hurt?"

"No trouble, not hurt. She's quite safe." He hesitated. "Actually, she was sitting in my apartment when I got home last night. I left her there asleep and came to work. She simply wants me to talk to you before she sees you."

What? Then a terrible thought. "Is she pregnant?"

"Mary! Stop this. I told you no trouble and she's certainly not knocked up. She came to my place last night with a situation and asked me to explain it to you. And I will. Tonight."

"Well, why can't she tell me herself? Does she think I won't understand? Is she afraid I won't listen? I'll get upset or something?"

"I can't imagine why she might think that." He left a moment of silence, probably wanted to make sure I got it. "Look, I'm at work—supremely busy. This isn't the time and the telephone isn't the way. Listen carefully: there is nothing, absolutely nothing wrong with Bria. She's been up to something." I heard him tell someone he needed a minute. "Nothing bad. Got it?"

"But Jack—"

"Wait. Tonight. Gotta go. And Mary, don't go calling her and trying to pry anything out of her. Wait." He hung up.

I went about my usual day, getting Tara up, fed, bathed and dressed. We spent the morning grocery shopping and visited the park. At one, I took her to her kindergarten class and treated myself to a visit to the Espresso Connection Coffee House. I sat alone and sipped a coffee for two and a half hours of contemplation.

I was angry. *Why haven't I earned her complete trust?* After all, for three years now, I've stood behind her, supported and protected her, no matter what I may have personally felt about her choices. I accepted she would never be the usual young girl, carefree and involved in the normal silly pastimes of teenagers. If I had the power to take all her past hurts onto myself, I would gladly do so.

Yet she went to Jack to run interference between us. I chided myself for my pettiness, but I still couldn't work my way past the betrayal. We did quarrel a lot. Bria fought tooth and nail against any form of control or restriction. She often told me I should trust her more, but how can I if she isn't honest with me?

I had fought the sisters at Ave Maria when they put her name forward for this International Baccalaureate, but only because I don't believe she's ready. I still find rocks in Bria's coat pockets, and I've seen her practicing her shot with tin cans in the yard. A child who needs to arm herself should not be sent to a downtown campus.

Jack decided, after politely listening to all my objections, that of course Bria would enter the program. He believes she could never get the kind of education she requires any other way. A normal high school matriculation was out of the question, he said. So he won the day.

Bria has a disturbing way of seeing the world and is prone to passions. Lately, it's been hookers—streetwalkers. I've always thought of them simply as prostitutes, but she calls them sex trade workers and exploited women. She said she is going to do a study of the profession for a future paper.

I've seen her over at the Seven Eleven on 68th, standing around talking to those girls—the ones in black leather skirts, scooped out tops and knee-high boots, with the perpetual cigarettes and a stream of fuck this, that and you pouring out of their mouths.

Jack says to leave her be; she's all right.

Did I suggest this might not be an appropriate subject to write about at a parochial school? Well, yes, I did, and for my pains, she informed me in the most condescending tones she was preparing for a college term paper, a long-term project and I wasn't to worry. She said, "They're just girls and women like anywhere else."

One night she and John almost came to blows over the subject.

John had stopped by, as was his habit, for a chat and coffee minutes before Jack delivered Bria home. John had had a rough day and described a scene of chaos at the station house following one of those periodical crackdowns on South Side streetwalkers, most underage and addicted.

"Little hookers, baby whores and cocksuckers," he called them.

A second later Bria charged into the room.

"Don't say that! What do you know about anything anyway?" She assumed a pose, one hand on a jutted hip, the other outstretched in a gesture of the classic orator. God bless those drama classes.

"I know those girls. I lived with them. Hell, Uncle John, I *was* one! Yes, I was forced, but so are they. Don't you understand? They aren't doing this because they want to; they have to."

John sat speechless before this performance, probably as taken aback by her passion as I was.

"Most of those girls know nothing else. Jesus Christ! They're just trying to stay alive like everybody else. Can't you see that?" She threw up her hands. "Oh, you *cop!*"

His face flushed purple as he stared at her. "Don't you speak to me like that, my girl."

My little kitchen thrummed with tension.

Without a word, Jack grabbed Bria by the arm and walked her right out the back door.

I went to the window and peered out into the twilight gloom to see what passed between them.

Bria pushed Jack away. "How dare you!" She sounded much like that horrible aunt of hers. "If I have something to say, I'm going to say it! And if you have a problem, too bad, Jack Connelly."

"Fine," he shouted, the first time I'd heard him raise his voice to her. "Say your piece to me, not him."

"Why, are you scared of him? Scared he might break my nose?" she taunted, and I wanted to run out and slap her.

"Yes," he said quietly.

Bria's posture and manner changed instantly. She had the grace to look embarrassed and hung her head. "I'm sorry."

Jack walked her toward the house. "I'm asking this as a favor. I want you to go back and give him one of your famous overblown apologies. After you've done that, we're going to the park and talk about this. There are things I need to explain to you."

I turned to John and told him, in no uncertain terms, "They're coming in. John, you keep a lid on it or go home and don't come back. You hear?"

"I hear." Thank God, he was once more in control of himself. I wasn't about to have any of his shenanigans from the old days.

Bria stalked into the room, not an iota of the penitent about her. "Uncle John, I'm sorry for disrespecting you. I didn't mean to. I have something to say. Those poor girls don't deserve your disdain either."

"Apology accepted."

That would have been an end to the scene, had Bria the sense God gave a squirrel, but no, she was determined to change his mind on the matter.

"Honestly, some of the girls tell me the police aren't very nice to them, to put it politely."

"What girls? And why would you be talking to them?" John had very fixed ideas on what fifteen-year-old daughters named Connelly should and should not do.

The cheeky little bitch said, "Well, I'm certainly not going to tell you. You'll order me to stop, and I don't want to. It's research."

"Research? What are doing talking to hookers?"

"Learning." Bria's pale, pointy little face was downright mulish.

"And what might you be learning?" John's color was rising again.

"That those girls have a hard enough life. Most have little education and no chance to do anything else. Some are all screwed up before they're even ten." She held up one hand, counting off points on her fingers as she made them. "They deal with customers who can do whatever they want to them, pimps who take most of what they earn, and society despises them. And when one ends up dead, no one cares."

She pointed an accusing finger at John, who was suddenly the poster boy for his profession. "The police, who should help them stay safe, like everybody else, don't. Some cops extort free services, others information, and then round them up like stray dogs, sometimes just to improve stupid arrest statistics."

Finally, she dropped all her attitude and apologized. "Anyway, Uncle John, I'm sorry if you thought me impudent."

John didn't say anything. He sat there bristling, his mouth a grim straight line.

Jack grasped her hand and pulled her to the door. "We'll take that walk now." As they descended the back steps, his voice wafted back into the kitchen. "Great apology, Bria, just terrific."

I tried to smooth over the situation. "John, she's young and passionate."

"She might find something more suitable to be passionate about. Is Jack aware of what she's doing—talking to hookers on the street?"

"Apparently so."

"She's only fifteen, a little girl."

How irritating to hear my own words that had fallen on deaf ears for so long thrown back at me. I wanted to scream, "I told you so." I didn't; no, instead I found myself defending the pair.

"She wants to study sociology and this is her pet project. She's only free to pursue her research in the afternoon and early evening, and she's never alone."

He was unbending in his opinions. "Still, it's simply not decent—a young schoolgirl like her exposed to this. I'll set him straight, encouraging such a thing. And why would she be interested in hookers?"

"Jack says it was her proposal to write this paper and her essays on what she hopes to do in the future that got her into this program, in spite of her age." Although I had objected, I spoke with pride.

"I thought the new place some kind of high school." He ran his hand through his silver hair, thinking. "It isn't?"

We had discussed all this at the time, or perhaps I should say I spoke and assumed he listened. "Bria would never be able to do normal high school, John. She's too far behind on some things, and so far ahead in others."

He still shook his head. Surprising, considering his stiff-necked ways. "But Mary, it's not right."

I called up the ultimate authority, the church. "The Jesuits are big on social service, always have been. If they're for her going ahead, maybe there's something to it."

"Well, I suppose. It is a Catholic campus. Still, I don't know." He was wavering.

"The opportunity certainly put some fire in Bria's life; she's become so dedicated. And if it makes you feel any better, I phoned Mrs. Friesen in Winnipeg and—"

"Who?" His bushy eyebrows flew halfway to his scalp.

Even though I'd already explained all about Mrs. Friesen at least a half dozen times, I patiently did so again. "She's pleased for Bria. She thinks the project might help her put some things in perspective."

John was not convinced. "I don't like her out there. Aw hell, I'm only an old cop; what do I know? Tell her not to discuss this with Rose, will you? She would never understand."

I thought he looked suddenly tired and old.

"These days, she's not interested in anything more than the church and her duty to her sick mother. Me and the boys, we're on our own. She'd be distressed by this."

Of course I promised him I'd talk to Bria and asked if I could be of any help.

He said I already helped more than I knew, and pulled himself out of the chair to leave.

All this happened a week before Bria left for three and a half months. I prayed she hadn't done any research on her own. *Am I really so unreasonable to be worried about what she's been up to? When I think of all she does right under my nose...*

***

Jack arrived at seven-thirty, as close to punctual as I'd ever known him to be.

Tara lay in bed not yet asleep, talking a mile a minute to her toys, dreaming up some five-year-old style theatre for them. I ushered Jack into the kitchen and asked him to keep his voice down.

"Join me?" I poured myself a tot from the bottle of Johnny Walker's

I kept in the cupboard for those especially difficult days.

"Good idea." He rubbed his temples. He looked fatigued.

"Tough day?"

"Busy, and I didn't get much sleep last night. I sat up talking with Bria until the wee hours."

"Am I permitted now to ask about what?"

"I'm sorry. I appreciate this is hard for you, but I think you're about to be amazed. I was." He sat smiling at me, not in any hurry to share his amazement.

"Well, get to it." I put my hands on my hips and started tapping one foot.

"Right. Here goes." He deliberately took his time sipping and savoring his drink. I wanted to hit him, but kept quiet.

With a half strangled chuckle he asked, "Do you remember, even when she was a little girl, Bria talked about riding ponies at the local rodeos?"

"Yes."

"Apparently back then she rode one of her neighbor's ponies at some kind of track, around three barrels in a clover leaf pattern. Each contestant takes a turn and the one with the best time wins. Sounds simple, doesn't it?" He was mute awhile, waiting for a response.

"If you say so."

"Everything was all very casual in the beginning, nothing official, possibly even illegal. Each entry costs a few dollars, with the races held in the afternoon. The winner takes the pot. That's the basic gist of the game as far as I can see—a children's event at small town rodeos."

How annoying. All this work-up to what? That Bria spent her summers competing in some Wild West sport. "How can this possibly be illegal? It sounds pretty innocent to me."

With a perfectly straight face he said, "Oh, the part where Dugald makes book on her."

"Surely not."

"Oh yes, quiet old Dugald bet on the outcome and apparently she won often enough that he made a tidy little sum off her. She did say once or twice they lost her winnings from the day before but overall, she's pretty good at this."

"He had her racing horses, and he bet on her?" Jack was right; I was amazed. Amazed at the audacity of the man, using Bria to make money.

Jack poured himself another drink and shot me a sly smile. "Indeed

146

he did. She says she's been riding horses since she could walk and racing since she was seven or eight. At age four, Dugald took her to stock sales and for a fee, those trying to sell pleasure mounts would have her ride the horse into the auction ring. Look." He handed me a photograph.

It was a small black and white of Bria, maybe a year after she first came into our lives, dressed up in a little girl party dress, complete with flounces and a sash and two large white bows in her hair. What made the picture so arresting was the tiny child perched up high on the big black horse, her chubby legs stuck straight out to the sides, barely clearing the breadth of the beast's back. She held the reins without another person near, and had the biggest smile plastered on her face.

"Jack! That's..." I struggled for the right word and came up with Bria's favorite. "That's exploitation."

"Bria sees things differently, more a point of pride to think she helped out financially."

"So, she works on a farm—that she told me—and she races horses for fun. Why all the secrecy? Why not share this with us?"

"I imagine she thought we'd be opposed. After all, you've been so against her going at all and made no secret of it. She didn't want to give you the ammunition, I guess."

"I don't approve of children working." I waved my finger back and forth. "Didn't we send her off each summer with money in her pocket to pay for her food and expenses? There was no reason for Peg and Dugald to put her out to work. Seems to me Dugald took advantage of the girl. Did he profit off his own daughter, too?"

This time he wagged *his* finger. "You're missing the point. Bria wasn't sent out to work, although apparently in the MacCleod household, anyone who is capable of earning does."

As soon as he finished, I jumped in. "No, Jack, you're the one missing the point. You said Dugald took the money, the money she earned. That isn't right."

"Yes, I agree with you, but he drove her around to the rodeos, made sure she was safe and acted as her manager. He probably felt he earned it. Remember, Mary, they're poor. If it makes you feel better, Bria told me that two years ago she agreed with Dugald on a fifty-fifty split." He chuckled. "She threatened him with my intervention—as her lawyer."

"I don't find that amusing, at all. It just proves my point. Dugald took advantage of her."

Jack's face turned serious. "He did, and worse. As a minor child,

Bria couldn't open a bank account on her own, so she had Peg open one for her and her winnings from the rodeos went into it. She arrived last year to find her savings looted."

"No." I was appalled. Bria loved and trusted her uncle.

"She was angry, but accepting when Peg told her some tale of hardship." He toyed with the ice in his glass, clinking it around and around. "She wanted to use the money to pay her own entries and expenses."

"Son of a bitch!" I exploded. "Poverty is no excuse for stealing from a child."

"My thoughts exactly." He smiled again. "But I haven't come to the good part yet."

"Do tell."

"You don't think Bria would let lack of funds stop her, do you? Last year, the first she competed in official rodeo events—she was fourteen—she needed a better horse. According to her, she can ride anything."

He picked up his empty glass and eyed the emptiness pointedly. "But the training of the horse is every bit as important as the skill of the rider. No way had Bria the resources to get one of her own. Apparently a good barrel racer is an expensive proposition."

He stopped and went up to the counter. "Can I make coffee?"

"Go ahead, but keep talking."

"Enter two new characters, some friends of Dugald from Great Falls, Montana. Bria met them years ago. Lassiter is the name, Gene and Ted Lassiter, father and son who rodeo on both sides of the border." He pointed at me with the carafe. "It seems Bria keeps correspondence with Ted. Another thing we didn't know."

For the first time since he started this saga, he appeared annoyed.

"The summer before last, Ted bought a new horse and offered to let her ride the old one, even went so far to as to haul the animal up to Buffalo Coulee. I suspect there's more to this relationship than rodeo buddies."

I held up my hands for him to stop. I had an important question. "How old is this boy? If he's old enough to be driving from Montana to Alberta, he's obviously too old for a fifteen-year-old girl."

"I didn't ask," Jack switched on the coffee maker. "But I'm informed he goes to college in Bozeman: Agriculture at Montana State."

"Don't you think he's a little mature for Bria?"

"This year Bria attends college on the campus of Loyola University.

There's more to maturity than years, Mary. What would you suggest I do —forbid the relationship? We both know that wouldn't work."

The fridge slammed shut as he pulled out the cream. I almost yelled, "Don't take your ire out on the appliances."

He went on. "Nor would I feel right about doing so. Bria deserves her freedom; she's not a stupid or flighty girl. She can take care of herself. You can't still believe you're dealing with a child."

"Yes I do, because I am, no matter what she does, how grown up her accomplishments," I insisted, so tired of this argument I sounded shrill.

Jack sighed, his signal he thought me unreasonable. "Well, this child of ours has come home with more money in her hand than I make in a year."

"What?"

"Yes, Mary, $20,000 earned, and she's too young to open her own bank account."

"She earned that much? Where is the money?"

"She had this Ted fellow safeguard her last year's winnings. She trusts him, it seems, and he didn't let her down. She has a bank savings-book from an account in Great Falls in both her and Ted's names that shows slightly over $7,000."

"She has another in Strathmore in her and Mr. Albert Lawson's name, the rancher she works for and who keeps her horse. He's also her good friend. This one holds around $1,900 Canadian. You want one of these?" He held up a cup of coffee.

"No, thanks." I didn't think my stomach would accept any at the moment.

"The rest is in a grubby brown envelope full of checks, yet uncashed. She wants my help to manage this money and a few other problems. I intend to do so. I'll open a bank account for her, get her money in one place in her own name, pay out her expenses to the Lassiters and others, including a percentage to Dugald she insists on." He paused, thinking. "I'll have to set up investments for her."

He was happily making plans for his prodigy.

"Unbelievable."

"Oh, it gets better." He laughed and shrugged in helpless acceptance. "Last year, her first on the Canadian rodeo circuit, she finished with the tenth highest overall rating. This year she came in sixth in Alberta and eleventh in Montana."

He laughed again. "Oh yes, she's working both sides of the border, and we had no idea. But I'm still not finished. Get this, Mary; she says she'd rank higher if she had a better horse."

It was too much to take in. "What does one of these horses cost?"

"Far more than I can afford, but – ta-da!" He whipped a piece of paper from his shirt pocket. "Solution found. A rancher in Wyoming wants her to ride one of his top horses. She and Gene Lassiter met with him in Laramie."

"And?"

"And now we come to the reason for this sudden confession of the facts. Bria can't do anything without my consent and signature. Up to now, she's had old Dugald sign for her."

I flushed hot with anger. "She knows better, Jack."

"She only got away with all this because so far her escapades were all small time. This isn't."

"She should have told us everything from the start."

"She said she feared we would try and stop her. That I believe."

He turned grave and caught my eye. "The extent of her duplicity bothers me. Can you guess how she gets away with competing on the Montana circuit? She claims the Lassiter residence as her own. Think about it: two separate countries, registration and entries on two different circuits, and no one checks—a fifteen-year-old girl. Amazing."

"You sound almost proud of her."

"I'm not. I don't like being played." He refreshed his cup and slammed it down abruptly, slopping coffee on the counter. "Why do I know now? It's all become so complicated, she doesn't have a clue how to handle the business end. She needs me to sort everything out for her."

He went back to the table and dropped another bomb. "She asked me to go to Laramie, meet with Mr. Keyes and help her. She wants to try out his horse."

"And you're going to go, in spite of the lies?"

"Of course I am. Mary, this might well set her up for the future. She can pay for whatever education she wants, not rely on scholarships and loans. I would be terribly remiss as her guardian if I didn't."

"What do you know about rodeos?"

"Absolutely nothing, but Bria does. I did study contracts in law school, and I'm a smart guy. I'll be able to make sure she's protected. All the information in the world is a phone call away and if we need any kind of specialized counsel in the matter, I'll simply seek out the knowledge. First, I'm going to contact this Gene Lassiter and talk with him. Make a start."

"This is all too much, too sudden for me. I don't have an opinion and, even if I did, it's obvious the two of you will go ahead anyway."

Then a thought struck me. "When has she had time for all this? She's called me every week and told me all kinds of stories about what she was doing."

"Me, too." He sighed and rubbed his tired face with his hands. "Nothing but lies. The truth is she's been on the road with Dugald and the Lassiters all summer. She called you from wherever she happened to be and told you what she thought you'd be happy to hear. Wrong, I know. For whatever it's worth, she feels badly for deceiving us."

All of my bitterness from earlier in the day returned. "Why did she have to lie to me?"

Jack shrugged. "You should ask her. I'm not making excuses for her behavior in this regard at all. She's wrong and she knows it."

"At least she hasn't been chasing down and interviewing prostitutes all summer. We can be grateful for that." I needed a laugh.

So it seems, did Jack. "I wouldn't be so sure. These rodeos usually happen along with state fairs and carnival shows; more than a few hookers hang out there."

The humor was short lived, and I voiced the terrible thought that had been haunting me all day. "Oh, sweet Jesus, Jack, she's beyond me. I'm really starting to think I've taken on more than I'm equipped to handle."

"Don't say that. She loves you and you give her a solid foundation for her life. She needs you, and besides, you know you'd be miserable without her."

He flung out his arms, mock alarm on his face. "For God's sake, don't leave me alone with her."

Nineteen:
"Bent on seduction."

Bria

The day after I turned sixteen, I was back on a plane heading west. Jack sat beside me. A whole week in his company stretched out before me, an opportunity even more enticing than our reason for going: a business trip to Laramie, Wyoming to meet Mr. Delmar Keyes at his ranch. Jack thought he came to act as my lawyer, but I hoped for something beyond his professional assistance. Surely, once he saw me in *my* world, when he recognized my success—I was a celebrity in the eyes of some, certainly an equal, and an adult—away from Chicago where everyone still considered me a schoolgirl, he'd understand I was no child. I was a woman now, albeit a young one.

Assuming things went well with Mr. Keyes, we'd go on to Billings, Montana for a three-day rodeo. Jack said he'd never been to one before, so for once I'd know more than he did, and I'd show him around, be his teacher for a change.

I expected to meet my new horse later today, an arrangement leaving me only four days to work with him before he was loaded into a trailer for a seven hour, 430 mile trip. Then I would get half a day to practice prior to the race. I was nervous.

I had the window seat, but the sky was too cloudy to permit more than the occasional glimpse of the patchwork of fields, hills and rivers below us. Jack's shoulders kept me pinned close to the wall. As usual, he had his nose stuck in some files.

I had intended to catch up on my reading assignments for my American Writers of the Twentieth Century course. The current book was *The Web and the Rock* by Thomas Wolfe. My facilitator had waxed poetic on "such literary genius." I didn't like the style much and, not in the right frame of mind to slog on, I found myself reading Jack's file over his arm.

He used a yellow highlighter on a report written in police-speak: an interview of a victim's mother. She denied everyone access to the child —a girl of thirteen—raped, beaten and left for dead, and would not cooperate with the police investigation or the prosecutors.

"Tough one." I reached over and tapped his paper.

"What do you think? Is this mother trying to protect her daughter, or is she just afraid to know all that happened? I often wonder."

"Maybe the girl's not ready yet. It takes time."

Jack's black eyes stared into mine, only six inches away. He spoke in a soft, careful manner. "What does, Bee?"

"To acknowledge, even to yourself let alone someone else, the violence done to you." I forced the words out through a tight throat. I shifted my sight to the report and pointed to one sentence. "She is only thirteen. Is she getting some help – a professional like Mrs. Friesen to talk to?"

"Not that I'm aware of. The mother hopes it will all go away."

"Uh-uh," I said, much more vehement than I intended to be. "She's in denial and ignoring her daughter's state won't work. It will never go away—never."

He turned his head so quickly; I thought he was startled. "Is that so for you?"

I drew back, hard up against the window. My stomach did a flip-flop. "Well yeah. It can't be undone. Accept and move on, as Mrs. Friesen taught me."

Jack returned to his file, but a few seconds later, he nudged me with his elbow and whispered. "I wish Mrs. Friesen was here. We need the girl's testimony, but we can't force her—not a child this age."

"So you know the culprit?"

"Yes, he's been arrested." He turned and stared at me, watching my reactions. "A conviction without the victim's testimony is difficult, perhaps impossible. The sad thing is we know but can't prove in court he's raped before, and will again. Each incident is worse. He targets young girls and almost killed this one. Impotence in the face of a monster is very frustrating."

"Uh-huh," I said, uncomfortable with the subject. I went back to Tom Wolfe, or tried. With my mind occupied elsewhere, the words were nothing but blobs of ink. "Jack, I was thinking what this must be like for the mother. You have a little baby girl, and you take care of her and love her and watch her grow for years. One day – whoosh—some son of a bitch snatches her up and uses her as though she's just a thing. Her mother must be incredibly mad, even a little crazy."

He nodded. "I'm sure, but who's right: the mother who wants to spare her daughter, or the prosecutor who needs her to talk in order to stop a monster? One who will assuredly do this again and ruin another young life?"

I thought of Miss Loepky for the first time in years and stifled a desire to vomit. "Wow, that's a heavy question."

"Yeah." He stared down at his legs, deep in contemplation a moment, and then regarded me with his brow furrowed and his lips tight. "I want to hear your opinion."

"Okay. You need to change the language you use. You said 'ruin a young life.'" My stomach settled as I chose my words. "The trauma doesn't have to become her whole existence, you know? Ruined means forever: can't be fixed."

"Point taken. Thank you." He continued to direct his level stare into my eyes. "Go on, give me the rest of your answer. What's right?"

"In my opinion, she should testify. But that has nothing to do with your question, though." For a moment, I felt myself slipping into the shadows, fought the fear and grabbed on to Jack's face as an anchor. "When someone is raped—like this girl—she finds not responding to the rapist's point of view almost impossible; she's only good for the use he has for her. That's the worst part. She's left with a new frightening understanding of the nature of the world, and how vulnerable she is." It was surprisingly painful to say this out loud, even to Jack.

"Go on," he urged.

I nodded but held up my hand to say, 'give me a second.'

When ready, I told him, "Being overpowered, used in a manner so personal, so intimate, it takes something important away from you—your sense of self. You're a person with thoughts and feelings and plans, and then you're nothing."

Jack was quiet for a few seconds. "In your opinion, is that what the girl's feeling now?"

"You're powerless when things are done to you and all the stuff that comes after only makes the impression worse." I pushed hard up to the wall of the plane and stared out the window.

Jack leaned over and spoke in my ear. "I think I understand what you're talking about: police, doctors, questions. When will she start to get better?"

"As soon as she gets mad. If you find a way to fight back, you get strong again." I turned to face him. "Is this making sense to you?"

"Yes. Thank you." He leaned down and kissed my forehead. "Have I told you how lucky I am you're in my life?"

"I love you, too."

His big hand curled around mine and squeezed gently, before returning to the file. A few minutes later, he asked, "Bee, would you be willing to talk to this mother and daughter?"

"You're kidding." I laughed. "I'm no Mrs. Friesen."

"If I set up a meeting, will you share your own experience and all you've just told me?"

"I don't know." I returned to the window and the non-existent view.

"Think about it. I don't need an answer right now." His lips touched my ear as he whispered, "And if you don't want to, that's perfectly fine with me."

"I'll let you know." I spoke to the window.

My mind no longer held anything else. True, I was no Mrs. Friesen, but I remembered our conversations, and I still had my journals. Perhaps I should read them; I hadn't in a long time.

"Jack? Suppose I did talk to her, wouldn't that be another way of fighting back?"

"Yes, I think so."

"I've decided; I will." I already had a plan. "But I insist the meeting be just them and me."

"Why?"

"So we could all sit around and be victims together. Your or some cop's presence might seem like a set up, an attempt to get them to do what you want. Don't you think so?"

"I'll take your idea under advisement and let you know."

"Okay. Can I ask a question?"

"Shoot."

"You see people who do these crimes every day. How many rapists have you met?"

He jerked his head up, surprised and stared at me. "A few, quite a few. Why?"

"Do you ask them why they do what they do?"

"I don't think we'll ever know, and I'm not trying to slide out of your question. It's a good one, but the truth is, I honestly don't have an answer."

Just as I was conjuring up another subject to get his attention, he said, "And I don't care. All I want to do is punish the bastards, make them the powerless ones, get them off the streets, and stop them."

"Don't they do it just to get sex?"

"I believe their motive is more about hurting someone." Again, I lost him to the file.

I wanted him to put his damn work away and spend time with me. "I read an article once stating pornography was a good thing, that it gave people a way to divert their sex drive in harmless ways. Do you agree?"

"I've heard that, but I have my doubts. What do you think?"

Success. "The writer was wrong. I was thinking about the film those men made in Winnipeg and—" My own words astonished me and my belly began to roil again. I sucked in a deep breath. "The kind of person who finds pleasure watching such a thing is likely to get a taste to do it themselves. If you see someone eat a hamburger, you get hungry for one too. You can't get the satisfaction of eating a hamburger just watching it being eaten, can you?"

"No. I think you're right." He lowered his voice further. "Bria, this is an interesting conversation but the woman next to me is starting to look at me sideways."

"Shame on her for eavesdropping. We're practically whispering. Her ears must be straining like a rabbits." I raised my voice to its normal pitch. "And do you think prostitutes perform a necessary service in that respect?"

Jack had a hard time keeping a straight face. "What respect would that be?"

"Any desire involved in the transaction is likely one-sided at best. I think sex workers keep the streets safer for the rest of us. We should honor them."

"Let's start a National Prostitutes Appreciation day. I'll write my congressman tomorrow."

"What a great idea!"

The woman, brassy haired and heavyset got out of her seat, gave Jack a disapproving glare and walked down the aisle toward the toilet. We both burst out laughing.

Jack leaned over. "You're a wicked, wicked girl."

"You're my role model in all things." Our play drove away all my nerves, and I settled again, proud I'd given him the gift of laughter. He was a man who didn't laugh enough.

***

The plane touched down and taxied to the gate. We found our way to the baggage claim and retrieved our bags and my saddle, my dearest possession, the only purchase I'd made from the money I'd earned. I paid six hundred dollars—a fortune. We lugged all our stuff over to the car rental booth, and finally out into the fresh air and our adventure.

The land around Laramie could easily be mistaken for Medicine Hat, Alberta—vast and empty. After three quarters of an hour of endless barbwire and a lesson from Jack on map reading, we pulled onto a gravel road and under a gate that said Lazy K Ranch.

Most imposing was a long, low ranch style house, large enough to accommodate a family of fifteen, surrounded by the tallest cottonwoods I'd ever seen. About two hundred feet from the house stood the largest, most modern stable imaginable. The air hummed with the steady buzz of air conditioning and ventilation. I stared, willing this horse, my betrothed, to appear.

He didn't. Instead, two men approached. One was Mr. Keyes: white haired, large, pot-bellied and florid. The other I'd never met before but recognized by type: an old cowboy, lean, weathered and bandy legged. They walked up to the car as we got out.

I hurried over to Jack and took charge. "Hello, Mr. Keyes, nice to see you again. This is Jack Connelly, my lawyer."

"Call me Del." Mr. Keyes accepted Jack's hand and pumped it heartily.

"Well hey, Bria," he said, taking mine. "Meet Walter, my stable manager. Walter, this is Jack and Bria Connelly from Chicago."

I couldn't have a cowboy like Walter think I came out of somewhere as unlikely as Chicago. "Actually, I'm from Alberta. I race there and in Montana. Hello, Walter."

"Pleased to meet you, ma'am." He lifted his hat and nodded, as courtly as a Renaissance gentleman.

"Walter here raised and trained this horse. And let me tell you, little lady, it's his decision, not mine, whether you ride him or not." Mr. Keyes had a deep drawly bass, more Texas than Wyoming.

"Can I see him? What's his name?" I asked, eagerness sticking out all over in spite of my intention to be cool and professional. I had traveled in jeans and riding boots, ready for this moment.

"Don't you want to rest, get something to drink first?" Mr. Keyes waved toward the house.

"We've done nothing but rest and drink the whole way here." Belatedly, I thought of Jack. "Unless you do."

He looked like he was trying not to laugh. "No, I'm fine."

For a moment, I retreated, unsure, but certain I'd made a gaff; what other possible explanations existed for his amusement? I dismissed the thought and concentrated on something more pressing. I shared my problem with Walter. "I could use a bathroom, though."

"This way." He pointed to the stable.

Jack walked at my right side, Del at my left. Del grasped my shoulder. "The horse's name is Sunson. When you see him, you'll know why. I think you'll like him."

I wanted with all my soul to shrug his hand off, resenting the possessiveness of the gesture and repelled by his presumption, but I managed to control the muscles in my back, and parked my tongue firmly between my teeth.

We crunched our way through the dry grass and waved away the grasshoppers whirring up and out before our passage.

Walter stopped at a double-door entrance and opened a man-sized door to the right. "Straight on back to the end and turn left."

I entered the cool, horsey smelling building. The lines of box stalls to either side of the barn had to contain a dozen horses. I made my way down the central passage and studied the inquisitive heads that popped over the solid gates and nickered softly as I passed. By their quality, I estimated at least a million dollars worth of horseflesh in the barn.

On my way back, I stopped at a bin by the door and grabbed a handful of alfalfa crunchies. I rejoined the men to find Walter missing. About to ask why, I heard the thunk-thunk of a shod horse approaching and turned to see a medium-sized sorrel stallion.

"Oh, my God!" I whispered. I'm sure my lust shone out of me like sunbeams. I wanted to turn to Jack and say, "Give him whatever he wants but please, please let me ride him."

***

In the late afternoon sun, he blazed the exact color of new brass. His chest was wide and deep, his shoulders thick and strongly set on well-boned front legs. Around 15 hands high, not overly tall, closely coupled,

158

almost square in stocky strength, he was built to turn quickly. His rear end screamed power. His hindquarters rippled with definition and his hocks angled perfectly, thickly boned and laced with tendons. Whatever he lacked in stride would be more than made up for in thrust.

He arched his solid neck and turned his long, aristocratic face to examine me.

I loved him. I walked toward him, set on seduction. "Hello, Sunson, beautiful boy." I stood in front of him, a supplicant before a local god, hand outstretched offering him a crunchy. He accepted my tribute and while he munched contentedly, I made so bold as to touch his face and stroke the long line from his eyes to his velvety muzzle. His nostrils flared at my presumption. He jerked his head high, regarding me from his lofty view.

I reached up and tickled him between his nostrils, all the time singing his praises. His soft agile lips pulled up from his long teeth and with the gentleness of a loving dog, he fondled my fingers.

In a quick move, he lowered his head into my armpit and inhaled deeply of my scent, then exhaled with a deep huff-huff. He dropped even lower, and with his nimble mouth pushed up my sweatshirt and tickled my belly with his whiskery nose, sucking in my smell and blowing it out in a moist windy rush.

When he'd had enough, he pulled back and stared at me a moment, then nudged my hand for another crunchy. I was acceptable.

I rewarded him with a treat and moved closer, off to his left. I ran my hands down his thick neck, using my finger nails to scratch through his hair and continued up over his withers and across his wide back. His skin twitched and shivered beneath my fingers. From time to time, he turned his head and stared at me, saying plain as day, "I don't know who the hell you are, but don't stop." I spoke to him softly, sweetly.

He let me touch him all over, even pick up his hoofs and check them. I moved down to his rump, scratching his side all the time. His posture relaxed and he leaned into me, presenting me with areas he wanted attended. When my hands stroked his rump, his left rear foot lifted off the ground as if asking me to check it for him. I did. I passed behind him, lifted his tail and checked for foul feces or recent diarrhea. Throughout the examination, he stood quiet. He was the picture of health.

I wanted to ride him so badly I was sick with longing.

Walter stood off to the right, holding the halter rope. I asked, "Could you get me a headstall, please? I'll walk him while you're gone."

Without a word, he handed me the lead.

Sunson followed me around the stable yard, his chin hanging over my shoulder, snuffling into me, looking for more treats, but he would have to wait. I walked very slowly and then quickly until we were trotting in small circles. I stopped and gave him what he wanted—a crunchy. By the time Walter came back, Sunson was following me around like a lap dog.

Walter handed me the headstall.

I checked the bit, a simple snaffle. "Soft mouthed?"

"Yep."

"Leg trained?"

Walter grinned. "Only if he thinks you're right."

"Can I ride him now?"

We both looked at Del and Jack sitting on a bench, beer in hand. I yelled, "Can I try him out?"

Del nodded.

I slipped Sunson's bit into his mouth and pulled his headstall over his ears. He accepted it with no sign of displeasure.

Walter asked, "You have your own saddle, or do you want to use one of ours?"

"No saddle."

This first ride together had to be an intimate one. I wanted to feel every movement of every muscle, and I admit I was intent on showing off. With one jump, I lay on my belly across his back, swung one leg over and shuffled up until I sat closely behind his withers.

Walter passed me the lines. "He's going to want to run at first, so keep a strong hand. Let him know you mean business and he settles down."

I nodded my understanding.

He led us over to the training ring, opened the gate, let us loose and closed it behind us.

Del and Jack were at the fence, watching. I wanted to be alone with this horse and decided I had to ignore their presence.

Sunson responded to the line across his neck and turned left. I walked him at a leisurely pace around the ring. He pulled at the lines, trying to take control, so I kept taut pressure on his mouth. He complied grudgingly. As soon as I felt his pent up muscles relax and he stopped jerking his head, I gave him some slack and nudged him with my heels to a trot.

The ride was as bone jarring as expected. Once around the ring at that gait was enough. I squeezed my knees, prodding him into a slow canter, rhythmic and easy, as comfortable as a rocking chair, and we circled several times. He was well behaved but sneaky, edging up in speed. I corrected him each time.

I took him through tight figure eights around two of the barrels. To my delight, at the apex of every turn when signaled with my knee, he obediently changed his lead leg. I had to hand it to Walter; this horse was superbly trained.

Once we started the cloverleaf using all three barrels, I had a hard time holding him back. He knew what this was about and fought my control, wanting to break into racing speed. Twice I had to pull him out of the pattern and bring him to a complete stop.

His mouth worked overtime as he attempted to take the bit with his teeth. Without the stability of a saddle, my level of control was restricted, and I returned him to canter around the ring until he calmed.

I loved his eagerness.

On the next cloverleaf, he did as I asked, slowly loping, circling the three barrels and down the straight stem, allowing me the choice of approach angles and turns. We practiced for over an hour. I marveled at his strength, how I could feel his haunches gathering and flexing behind me, how his shoulders bunched and rippled in front of my legs. With each circuit, he surrendered more control.

Finally, I gave him what he wanted and pulled him to a complete stop, facing the first barrel. "Give me a signal," I yelled to Walter.

Walter drew a whistle on a chain from his pocket. "Holler when you're ready."

Sunson quivered in anticipation beneath me. I adjusted my seat and my legs gripped the girth of his ribs. I held the lines in both hands at the sides of his neck and yelled. "Ready."

Two or three long seconds passed: Walter, testing my control of the horse. I heard the shrill blast, squeezed Sunson's ribs, dug in my heels, and loosened the lines.

"Go!" His hindquarters surged. We rocketed forward. I had been shot from a cannon.

At the first barrel, his weight shifted to the front, braking for the turn. As my legs passed, I reined hard to the right, signaling him to change lead. He pivoted, almost unseating me and turned so sharply my leg banged into the padded drum. I couldn't believe his agility.

We were off again, accelerating in bounds. Again, a speedy gathering of strength to wrap the second barrel, but this time I gave him more clearance and the barrel remained untouched.

Up to the third at top speed, a good execution and for the finale, a thundering run down the stem and Sunson skidded to a halt in front of our audience.

I slipped off his back and stood on my own, shaking, exhausted and sweat-soaked legs. "Mr. Keyes, I love this horse. I can do a good job with him."

Del looked at Walter. Walter nodded. "She can ride."

Del turned to Jack. "We should talk."

Jack leaned over the top railing and whispered into my ear. "I had no idea. Is this what you want, Bria?"

"Yes."

Jack and Del sauntered back to the bench and a fresh cold beer, leaving Walter and me alone. I smiled at his lined and leathery face. "Walter, he's an incredible horse. You've done a terrific job. Will you help me train with him?"

Walter's smile made a desert landscape of his skin. "We'll start working tomorrow morning. Now I'll get him cooled off and put to bed." He reached to take the lines from my hand.

"I'll do it." I always looked after my own horse. Grooming was a bonding thing.

Walter waved me away. "Tomorrow, you start tomorrow."

I walked back to the house with Del and Jack on legs that didn't want to obey me. My jeans were soaked in horse sweat and covered in hair and the flies showed as much interest in me as they had in my mount. "I need a shower."

"We're in there." Jack pointed toward one of three small bungalows set off to the side of the big ranch house. He spoke to Del. "Will you excuse us? We can meet with you later, at your convenience. Name the time."

"Supper's at seven, drinks at six thirty," was his word thrifty reply. He turned to walk away and shouted over his shoulder. "Annie looks forward to meeting you."

Twenty:

"Are you sure we haven't wandered into a Hollywood set?"

Jack and I made our way to the smallest bungalow, a simple house of two bedrooms, two bathrooms and one main room that doubled as sitting room and kitchen with walls of knotty pine. A table and two benches, saloon style, made an eating area next to the kitchen equipment, and easy chairs in plaid, well stuffed and comfy, sat before a small fireplace faced in natural stone. I liked the homey little place a lot.

At six-thirty, clean and appropriately dressed for dinner, I presented myself to Jack. I wore the new dress Mary had helped me pick out, plain black with a low neck—a grown up dress. Her silver locket containing a snip of Tara's hair for luck hung around my neck. I had let my freshly washed copper hair loose, and it curled and waved past my face and draped my back.

"Jesus, Bria, you're beautiful." Jack's shocked expression said everything. His eyes traveled up and down my body, but I didn't mind.

I caught my reflection in the full-length mirror mounted by the door. I was certainly no Leslie of the D cup, black lace demi-bra, but I wasn't so shabby either. All the curves were new.

I laughed at Jack, who still appeared stunned. "I'm getting used to it myself. Sometimes I look in the mirror and ask whose body this is."

He ripped his eyes away, embarrassed.

I took pity on him. "Get over it," I said as I grasped his arm. "I'm hungry. I hope it's a good dinner."

"Well, ma'am, let's go find out." We laughed at his ridiculous cowboy drawl, and by the time we reached the house, we were comfortable with each other again.

I suffered a pang of nerves when a Mexican woman in a maid's uniform let us in. Once inside, I was even more unsure of myself. The room was sumptuous in a country way, richly appointed and decorated with western art.

"Look, Jack, that's a Charles M. Russell." I pointed to a painting of a cowboy, his legs extended forward, spurs raking the shoulders of a bucking bronco. The bronc was high in the air, bent almost double in his efforts to lose his rider. Aunt Peg had a calendar print of it scotch-taped to the kitchen wall. This one was oil on weathered wood and the size of a school blackboard. "Can it be the original?"

I espied another. A famous bronze statue of a windswept and blanket-wrapped Indian and his equally tormented pony sat on a side table. It stood four feet tall and gleamed dully in the subdued lighting. "Jesus."

My eyes roamed the huge room. Over a blazing fireplace, a prong horned antelope gazed down on us through dead glass eyeballs. Heavy, brass-tacked leather couches draped in richly colored Navaho saddle blankets formed a three-sided square around a solid pine cocktail table. A cowhide rug covered a small fraction of the planked wooden floor—a surreal scene.

I looked to Jack for reassurance. He murmured, "Are you sure we haven't wandered onto a Hollywood set?"

I laughed and relaxed a bit.

We were still standing around gaping when Del and a plump, cheerful looking woman with grey hair entered. Del said, "Annie, this is the little lady who's about to make Sunson famous, and her lawyer. Bria and Jack, my wife Annie."

Jack offered his hand. "Pleased to meet you, Annie. What a beautiful room."

I followed suit. "Thank you for your hospitality."

Annie's face lit up with a warm smile. "We like it." Her fingers, heavily ringed, waved over to the couches. "Won't you sit down?"

"What's your pleasure?" Del slid open the glass doors of a tall armoire. Inside were rows and rows of bottles. He must have had every type of drink ever distilled in there.

Jack said he'd prefer a beer and Del opened a small fridge hidden in the lower part of the cabinet. "Anything in particular? Bud? Corona? Heineken?"

Jack picked Corona.

"Bria?"

Was he asking me? I glanced at Jack before answering. "I don't partake of alcohol, Del."

Annie rescued me. "Lemonade, ice tea or perhaps a coke?"

I opened my mouth to answer, but she called out "Yolanda!"

The uniformed Mexican woman returned and Annie arched her thin eyebrows at me expectantly.

A few seconds ticked past while I figured out I was to give her my request. "Ice tea, please."

"Tell me about yourself, Bria." Annie slid to the corner of the couch close to me.

I sat blinking like an idiot, and finally pulled myself together enough to ask, "What do you want to know?"

"Del says you ride like a Cossack. How long have you been racing?"

"Since I was a child."

"How old were you when you first won?" She had a friendly smile and pale blue eyes framed in lines that smiled too. I thought of a word for her: gracious.

I heard myself telling her all about the rodeos of Alberta, my babyhood at the horse fairs and the work I did watching cattle.

By the time Jack and Del finished debating the merits of various football teams, she'd led me on to some of my first impressions of life at Loyola and my hopes of a degree in Sociology. When I told her about my study of street prostitutes and the paper I planned to write, she didn't blink. She wanted to understand and asked searching and intelligent questions.

She was lovely. I'd be satisfied to be like her in my later years.

Even though Jack appeared to be engrossed in their chat, I was aware he kept an eye and an ear on me. I hoped he was proud of me, and that he noted how adult both my conversation and behavior were.

Yolanda came in and announced supper was ready. Annie gave my hand a squeeze as we got up. "We're going to be good friends, I can tell."

I said I hoped so.

Dinner was excellent. A spicy chicken stew Yolanda called Poblano Mole—aromatic and rich—yellow rice and black beans with fresh tomatoes and green chilies all excited my inexperienced taste buds. What a wonderful change from meat and potatoes. The feast was followed by creamy custard and thick, strong coffee. I sat back, thinking I'd ride their horse free if they'd supply me with meals like this one for a few years.

I said, "Thank you," to Annie and, "Gracias," to Yolanda, who smiled and murmured "De nada," as she picked up our dishes.

Annie sighed as she stood. "Let's go get comfortable, and you can tell me more about this project of yours—so interesting—while the boys can go and have their talk." She walked back toward the fireplace and those luxurious leather couches.

I lingered behind for a second. "Jack, shouldn't I come with you?"

Strange to my mind, Del answered. "Sit tight, little lady. No point to lawyers at all if you have to sit through all the dull preliminary stuff."

Jack said, "Not to worry. Nothing will be decided without your say so. Got it?"

"Got it." The situation called for acquiescence, a good word but not one of my favorites. I joined Annie.

She patted the seat beside her. "Come on, sugar, sit down and tell me more about those poor girls."

***

Much later, Jack and I strolled back to our little bungalow. He smelled like brandy and cigar smoke and seemed quite pleased with himself.

I poked him lightly in his ribs. "Well?"

"Well, what?" He arranged his face into a caricature of innocent bewilderment.

I thought about kicking him. "Jack, don't."

"Point one, this is important so listen." He looked down at me to ensure I was. "Del is a charming man and a fair one, I think, but above all, he is a shrewd businessman with a first-rate mind. Don't let any of that hokum-oakum stuff fool you. He's a very smart man."

"I wasn't about to treat him like an idiot. Nor was I planning on being disrespectful."

Jack blew out a sigh and with a voice dripping in exaggerated patience said, "Just keep that in mind whenever you talk to him, Bria."

"Are you warning me that he may try to exploit me?"

Jack whistled another irritated sigh, and I demanded, "What?"

"You read too much leftist literature. Certainly, he hopes to, but not the way you're thinking. No, he will use you to his own advantage, but to yours as well."

"Stop talking in riddles. Tell me clearly and plainly what he plans for me."

"In a minute, I have something to say first." He stopped walking and put his hands on my shoulders. "Bria, I want you to be careful around him. Don't get flirty. Try not to be alone with him."

I was startled. "Oh, you mean—"

"He'd like to slip your pretty sixteen-year-old ass into his bed. Yes."

The thought gave me the creeps. "I shouldn't do this?"

"You should. I just want you to watch yourself around him. 'Forewarned is forearmed' is the appropriate cliché."

We started walking again. Jack pointed to a wooden picnic table under a large cottonwood next to our house, and we sat on one bench, side by side. A breeze rustled the leaves and the air shrilled with the music of the night crickets.

"I've been thinking we should insist on an allowance for a chaperone to travel with you. You're still a minor and that would be reasonable." His voice was soft and tentative.

So much for impressing Jack with my maturity. "A babysitter?"

Jack laughed. "I'm afraid so, but we'll find someone you like, someone who can share in all this fun, a companion."

I didn't protest at all. I was too busy. My mind obsessed on a gross image: grappling with the beer bellied, red-faced Del, having him try what old men liked to do to young girls. If not for the lure of that beautiful horse, I might have given up the idea and asked Jack to take me home.

Jack broke the silence. "You've gone quiet. What're you thinking?"

"You don't want to know."

He reached over my shoulders and pulled me close. "Yes, I do."

"Jack, do you truly think Del would try to have sex with me?"

"In a heartbeat." His voice softened. "I'm not saying he'd rape you. I'm sure he wouldn't. He adores his wife and she likes you."

"Still, pretty unpleasant if it did come up." I shivered and rubbed my arms. "He might be mad or embarrassed because I tell him no, and take all this away from me just when things were getting good."

"Then I would happily sue him on your behalf and get enough money for you to buy that horse and a ranch to keep him on." We laughed together, and I began to feel better.

Jack turned serious again. "I didn't mean to scare you. You're a smart girl. Make sure he never has the opportunity to bring the possibility up, and if he tries, you tell him you're underage, his employee and no means no. Comport yourself professionally."

"Understood." I said. "Move on. Aside from my ass, what does he want?"

"First, here's a little background." He pretended not to notice my huff of impatience. "Del made himself a fortune in oil and real estate in Texas and Annie was born there. Happy with his millions, they moved to Laramie and Del set up as a gentleman rancher. He likes the idea of being a big time horse breeder, but he's not an accepted part of the rodeo world. He'd like to be. That's where you come in."

"How?"

"He wants you because you're a damn good horsewoman—his words, also because you're pretty and will attract a lot of attention—my interpretation. You're to ride his horses and represent the Lazy K ranch and make a name for Sunson, help earn him a breeding career. You'll have promotional duties."

"Like what?"

"Compete under his brand. Take part in rodeo publicity. Public appearances." He laughed softly. "Maybe enter for Rodeo Queen—his wife's idea."

My toes curled up inside my shoes. "No! I don't want to."

"What?"

"Be a rodeo queen. Come on, Jack, a beauty contest, me?"

"According to Del, there's a lot more to it." He held up a hand and counted off points on his fingers. "You have to be an excellent rider, uphold the ethics of rodeo—whatever they are—and be an ambassador for the sport. You'd win a scholarship." He put his outspread hand in front of my face. "Why wouldn't you be proud of that?"

"It seems, well, like a beauty contest to me. Have you ever seen those women? Not a plain one in the bunch, let me tell you. Me? I haven't a clue how to put on makeup."

"From what I saw tonight, sweet girl, you do fine in the beauty department, and other necessary skills can be learned, although I find you gorgeous just the way you are."

"Thanks." I acted offhand but was enormously pleased.

"Seriously, Bria, think on the opportunity," he urged. "Del is offering to have you educated in those aspects, poise and handling yourself before media and makeup too, I imagine."

"I'll consider it." I'd already made up my mind. "What do I get for all this?"

"A personal services contract that will, in the next year or two, pay you a salary bigger than mine, plus some of the prize money and bonuses when you win and your ranking goes up." He reached over, put a finger under my chin and turned my face toward his. "Del won't talk hard numbers until he sees how you do in Billings."

"Oh crap!" I shrank; I was so unnerved. "Is he expecting me to dazzle when I'm up on a new horse that has never been in a real competition?"

"No, he is not." Jack patted my back. "He and Walter are looking at potential right now. They're planning for next year, and you should, too. Don't be in such a hurry."

I began to calm down, until Jack gave my shoulder a squeeze. "But, Bria, if you do dazzle this weekend, it will improve our negotiating strength."

I jabbed him in the ribs with my elbow. "Think you can pile any more pressure on this race on Saturday?"

"Hey!" He tugged at my hair in revenge then became the mentor again. "Ignore it. Do your best. Leave Del to me and I'll do my best, too."

I yawned. "One more thing and I'm going to sleep."

"Shoot."

"All this will require time, a lot. I can't just zoom out here the day before a rodeo, saddle up Sunson and compete; I have to work him regularly. Now you're talking publicity and makeup courses. What about school?"

"I've given some thought to the problem. A lot of the study you're doing in this program can be done anywhere if you have the books. Perhaps the companion we plan to find can be someone who can tutor you. We'll come up with a solution."

"You're sure?"

"The I.B. dean is prepared to be flexible." He chuckled. "Mr. Finch seemed a little blown away by professional rodeo riding, probably not something he encounters every day."

"Not judging by the people I've met so far," I agreed. "Do you think I can do it?"

"Yes, I do. I'm not saying this won't slow you down, but you only just turned sixteen. You've got piles of time." He added under his breath, "Maybe Mary's right. That might not be such a bad thing."

I was astounded to hear his admission after all the months of debate between the two, but chose to ignore the comment. I had another worry. "The expenses: paid companions who are tutors, plane fares, lots of them. Will the job be worthwhile if our costs are so high?"

"Depends on the kind of money Del's willing to pay."

We walked the few feet to our front door. Jack opened it, stood back to let me enter. As I did he added, "And that will depend on how you do over the next few days."

"Yeah." I was tired.

"Good night, Jack." I kissed his cheek and whispered in his ear. "Thanks for everything."

He put his hands on my upper arms and gently but firmly moved me away from him. "Good night, Bria."

***

The next morning I rose early, long before Jack. I found the refrigerator stocked with brown eggs, milk, orange juice, bread and two thick slabs of smoked ham. After my breakfast, I left a birthday card on the table and went out to the stables.

Walter said, "Morning," and slapped a battered straw cowboy hat on his head. "Let's get to work."

So we did.

I led Sunson out from his stall, tied him to the hitching post and brushed him until he gleamed. I examined his feet, looking for chips, small pebbles or any sign of injury, checked his shoes and washed out the sensitive tissues inside the horny hoof. With that done, I doused him in fly repellent.

Next, I turned my attention to the tack. After cleaning the bit, I slipped the headstall over his head, blanketed him, placed my saddle on his back and cinched him up tight. Walter appeared at my side, checked everything I had done, and chuckled. He thrust his knee into Sunson's ribs; the horse exhaled and the saddle was suddenly loose. "Tricky bugger," Walter grumbled, tightened the cinch and grunted his approval.

He pointed to the training ring. "Warm him up."

I worked and reworked figure eights and clover leafs, never allowing him to move beyond a canter. Today Sunson gave me control without a fight. Two hours of drill work and he didn't break a sweat.

"Hey!" Walter hopped down from the fence and approached. "We're going to focus on your barrel approaches. Our boy's already shown you he turns on a dime. If you hit the turn just right, you can shave off a second. Let me show you."

He reached for Sunson's lines and walked us to the first barrel.

"When you get to here," he said, pointing at the space behind the saddle in relation to the padded drum. "He'll clear his turn close and tight without over shooting. Come at it at a lope and let's see."

We did, once, twice and over and over again.

Each time, Walter found some fault: too early, too late; no need to pull at his mouth; push your leg forward; tell him what you want; swing your weight with him not against. The instructions fell from his lips like hail. By lunchtime, my back and legs screamed and I despaired of ever doing it right.

To my surprise, Walter clapped my leg. "Good work."

I unsaddled Sunson, washed him with a sponge and warm water, brushed him, reapplied the fly repellent and turned him out into the cool-off pen. I cleaned the tack and put it away. Then and only then was I free to find some lunch.

I trudged back to our bungalow and found Jack working on a file, more files and books piled all around him. I plunked myself down in a chair and tugged off my boots.

"Oh my God." I collapsed onto the table. "What time is it?"

"Two. Hungry?"

"Two?" I groaned. "I have to be back at four. Oh, wow. And yes, I'm starving."

"There's your lunch." A tray sat on the small counter.

I pulled up the cover to find eggs smothered in tomatoes on two tortillas, and a side of left over beans. I tasted and swooned. Delicious. "Jack, I think you should marry Yolanda. Then I'll live with you forever."

"Sounds like a good deal on all sides." He bent back to his files. His black curly hair hung over his face and even without seeing him, I knew he was deep in concentration.

I ate in silence and after washing my plate, decided to lie down. "Jack? Wake me at three thirty?"

"Sure thing."

"And Jack?"

He looked up. "Yes?"

"Happy Birthday."

"Thanks." He looked down.

I barely reached my bed and fell instantly asleep. All too soon, Jack woke me. Time to get up and go back to work.

From four until seven, Sunson and I rode around those barrels in slow motion, trying to find the right combination of moves and shave a few precious hundredths of a second off the maneuver. Walter barked orders and instructions every inch of the way. Both horse and rider worked hard.

After I'd taken care of Sunson, I hauled my aching body back home. Jack's files littered the table but I found no sign of him, so I showered, put on my pajamas, fell into bed and slept until he shook me awake. He brought me my dinner, spicy chili, rich and aromatic, thick and full of chunks of tender steak—succulent, but I barely had energy to chew.

Jack told me Annie had invited him into Laramie and shown him around town. They had a wonderful time, he said and agreed; she was a lovely woman.

"She asked me to tell you Walter thinks you're doing just fine. He's impressed by how hard you're working. He told Del the two of you— you and the horse that is—will make a solid team. Feel better?"

"Yep. Thanks." I yawned and stretched out my aching back. "I'm too tired to talk. I want to go to sleep."

I woke in the morning and worked another arduous day, same with Tuesday and Wednesday. Thursday dawned and it was time for Sunson to go to Billings.

Walter and his helper would drive him. It was my job to groom him, check and pack all his tack, load him into his luxurious trailer and bid him a safe trip. Walter promised to take good care of him until I arrived.

Jack, I, Del, and Annie planned to fly out the next morning in a small plane, something I was nervous about.

I went looking for Jack and found him talking to Annie, who was full of plans for me. "How would you like to go into Laramie and do a little shopping?"

I had hoped to spend the day with Jack, but he and Del had arranged an afternoon of golf. I didn't know Jack played, never would have guessed.

"That would be nice," I told Annie, to be polite, although I wasn't big on shopping and had no money.

"Wonderful, we'll enjoy a girls' day out. Go get changed and we'll be off. You've certainly earned some fun."

Downhearted, I walked back to the bungalow, hoping Jack received the signal I mentally beamed to him. Surprisingly enough, it worked. Just as I was coming out of the shower, I heard the door open and close. "I'll be out in a minute."

"Take your time."

Twenty-one:
"Put a shine on the little filly and pimp her out."

But I *was* out in a minute, dressed in my better jeans and a red-checkered shirt. I pulled a black leather belt through the loopholes as I ran out to the main room.

"Are you really playing golf?"

"Yes, but I made it clear I stink at it."

"Why are you doing that?"

"Men like Del talk business over a game, so off we go. I have this feeling we'll probably spend more time in the bar than on the green. I hope so; I'm better at beer drinking than golf."

"Oh, it's business and beer," I said, pulling my face into a skeptical sneer. "I didn't know those two things went together."

"Nobody likes a smart mouth. You should try and remember that." He pointed to the couch. "Sit down a minute, will you?"

I sat obediently, like a well-trained Labrador.

Jack swung around one of the kitchen chairs and sat in front of me. "You're doing well, Bria. Walter is full of your praises and, according to Del, anything better than not bad is a high tribute from Walter."

"Wow, news to me. All he ever says is 'not like that, like this, do it over.'"

Jack chuckled. "Annie wants you dressed to impress in Billings. Her heart's desire is to go shopping for whatever a girl needs for these affairs."

"I have them all with me: jeans, white shirt, decent boots and black hat. I don't need clothes."

"Well, Annie believes you do, so why not surrender and let her buy what she wants? It will make her feel good." He smiled and winked. "She means this as a reward. She watched you work and left very impressed with you. So is Del."

"I didn't see anybody."

"No? Not surprising, I've been down there too, and Walter kept you busy."

"What does working hard have to do with buying me clothes?"

"Don't ask me, but my advice to you is let Annie buy what she wants. Consider this a sign they're happy with you and Del is serious about giving you the job. Why would he care what kind of image you presented if he had no intention to hire you?"

"Okay, if you say so." What difference did clothes make? This was rodeo, not a fashion show.

"So get on out there, go with Annie and have a good time. I thought girls liked shopping."

I whirled back to him from the door. "I'm different."

"Go on, get."

I discovered it was easy to have fun with Annie. We sat in the soft leather bucket seats of her new-smelling Cadillac as it sailed down the road while she asked questions of me. We'd driven halfway to town before I realized we always talked about me, and I learned nothing of her.

"Do you have kids, Annie?"

"I do: one son and two daughters and five grandchildren."

"Where are they?"

"My first daughter, Coral, is in Dallas with her husband and two children. My son Baker is in Los Angeles and has a wife and three sons. My youngest, Cheryl, is gallivanting around Europe at the moment, finding herself. She's been looking for about five years now." She laughed.

"Do you get to visit them?" I hoped she wouldn't consider the question too nosey.

Annie let loose her wonderful happy chortle. "Not as often as I'd like, but that's the way of life. Every mother raises her chicks to watch them fly away."

We pulled into the Roper's Supply Company parking lot. Annie barely had the car in park, and she lunged out the door. "We'll start here. They have the best selection. Let's go."

Inside, the smell of new leather assailed our noses. On one wall, the entire length of the store, shelves full of boots ranged from the floor to the pressed tin ceiling and the other side displayed saddles and assorted tack. Racks of Western clothes jammed the center without evidence of plan or order. There was barely room to walk between them, or any discernible straight path from one end to the other.

"Come over here." Annie wound her way through the maze at a brisk pace, scanned the offerings lined up against the wall and selected a pair of intricately tooled sienna boots. "Like these? What's your size?"

"Eight. But—" I held the boot she passed me. It was leather, soft, beautifully worked and monotone, nothing garish. I examined the heel and sole: well built and angled forward, then glimpsed the price tag, $135.00.

I gasped. "They're certainly lovely, but awfully expensive."

She laughed again. "Sunson deserves the best. That's why he's getting you. Try them on."

I rolled up my suddenly shabby jeans, slipped my foot into the boot and stood up. Soft as butter, they molded to my feet. "Feels good."

"Try the other one. Walk." I did as I was told. They were perfect.

"Now, these." She passed me another pair, reddish brown on the foot, gold on the leg, tooled in a floral pattern. $164.00!

"What?"

"Try them."

I did and loved the fit, like old worn gloves, but thought the price ridiculous. "I prefer the first pair."

"Let's get both, and we'd better find some field boots for practice." She speed-walked over to the other end of the boot department and was back, quarry in hand, before I'd had time to tug the others off.

"I have some, Annie."

She shook her head. "I saw you rubbing your feet and holding them under the pump the other day. You need new ones."

"No, I—"

"Try these. I'll be back in a minute."

I tried on the boots, dazed, glanced up from my task and almost giggled at the sight before me.

Annie marched forward, purpose evident in every stride, with a cart pushed by a helper, a pale, skinny young man. She swept her hand at the two boxes of riding boots, and he put them in the cart.

She pointed at my feet. "How are those?"

"Good." Luxuriously padded, made of soft quilted canvas thickly soled and with strong heels at the perfect slant for riding, good wasn't the right word. Heavenly was.

"Wonderful." Annie waved at the clerk to help me pull them off, crooked her finger for me to follow and trotted off so quickly, I padded after her in my sock feet.

"Now hats," she announced.

"I own a hat."

"A good hat, practical, and you can use it for practice." She turned and touched my nose. "You should always wear a hat, Bria. Your pretty face is getting all sunburned. We'll take care of that later."

I followed her like a pet dog over to the hats. Jack had advised me to let her do as she wanted, but I'd never met anyone who could spend $450.00 in five minutes as she did. What if Del was mad at her for it *and* mad at me and Jack thought I was greedy?

I had to ask. "Annie, why are you spending so much money on me?"

"Del wants you to look your best out in the arena on Sunson. You represent us, our ranch and our horses. Think of yourself as a model in a magazine, and anyway, sugar, this is just so much fun, isn't it? Relax."

She put her hand on my back and propelled me down the aisle. "We were about to find a new hat."

"I usually wear a black one."

"Black is good and matches your saddle. We're going to dress that up, too, with silver, I think. So, let's try this one."

She pulled down a Stetson, tested the roll to its brim and popped it on my head. "With a silver and turquoise band, I think." She looked at me speculatively. "Yes, and with that lovely hair of yours, let's try a white one too. Two hats, one black and one white."

She laughed her happy chuckle again. "One day the good guy, the next the bad. A feather band in gold and black for the white one, I think."

She had to be the most business-minded shopper I'd ever met. I followed her around for half an hour while she held various snap down shirts against me, constantly debating the colors relative to my hair and Sunson's. She had me try on jeans in every possible color. At the end of the marathon, our helper pushed a heaping cart.

She added three pairs of dangly silver and stone earrings and I pointed out I didn't have pierced ears.

"We'll take care of that later." Her words scared me.

When we arrived at the cash register, the man behind it beamed. "Mrs. Keyes, how lovely to see you. How are you?" He practically pissed himself fawning over her. I guess so for a sale of $2,023.25.

"Hungry?" Annie asked when we loaded the purchases into the car.

"Are you?" Appetite was the furthest thing from my mind. I still reeled in shock. Mary could outfit me for school for a whole year on a tenth of what we'd just spent.

"I do think we should eat before moving on."

"Ok, let's eat." I surrendered and turned myself over to her, nervously wondering about "moving on."

We went to a fancy restaurant where all the waiters knew Annie and hustled, making sure her wine glass never emptied and her napkin didn't hit the floor. I barely tasted my food, still half scared at what we'd done.

Annie finished her meal with gusto and leaned forward, peering at me.

"I'm admiring your lovely skin and coloring. And that hair! We're off to the beauty parlor next. We're going to make you absolutely gorgeous."

I bowed to the inevitable and found myself reclining in a chair while a woman peered through a magnifying glass at my face. She massaged cream into my skin and cleaned the stuff off with a steamy towel. I swooned, melting and half-asleep by the time she finished, until she started pulling out my eyebrows.

Annie sat beside her, listening and nodding while the cosmetician talked about cleanser and toners, moisturizers and foundation. She kept asking me if I understood.

I nodded, but Annie still insisted she write it all down for me.

I was just starting to think all the attention pretty pleasant when the woman came back, holding a long needle in her hand. She squeezed my earlobe between two wet cotton balls, stretched the flesh out taut and jabbed the point through. No sooner had I caught my breath and the other one was done. She slipped two small silver hoops through the new holes. "You must clean them twice a day with alcohol."

Before I could recover, Annie whisked me off to the hair consultant, another woman with the most startling fire-engine red coiffure I'd ever seen. She undid my braid and brushed my hair until it gleamed like Sunson. "We need a good conditioner, and this—" she held up a fistful of my hair, "needs to be thinned. The ends are brittle, have to come off."

Annie stood up from her chair and barked like some drill sergeant. "Just the ends. Her hair is too lovely to cut. Bria, when you ride, I want you to leave your hair loose behind you."

"But it will get all tangled," I whined. I rarely let my hair out of its braid. The results were simply too painful to deal with.

The consultant said, "We've got a product that will help, a detangler."

Annie nodded and another bottle landed in our bag.

Then she flew into action, and two hours later, shampooed, conditioned, trimmed and thinned; my hair flowed out from my head in long copper waves. My newly plucked eyebrows rose in surprise. "Hey, it looks good."

"Sure does. Now for your face." Annie ran me over to a brightly lit counter, seated me on a high swivel chair before a mirror, and a woman in a white lab coat examined my face yet again. She and Annie held a conference above my head.

"With these green eyes, I think a dusting of gold over the lids." A light as a snowflake touch slid across my eyelids and when I opened them, my eyes appeared bigger, deeper and more intense.

"Charcoal mascara, I think."

I struggled to keep my eyes open while this stranger brushed out my lashes several times.

"She's young and doesn't need much for the skin, a little blush under the cheekbones." A ticklish circular swipe swept my cheeks.

"And pink for the lips, definitely rose." A tube of lipstick appeared under my eyes and slicked my lips in short vigorous strokes.

"Look."

I stared at the stranger in the mirror. Her pale freckled skin glistened. Her green eyes jumped out of her face and her mouth plumped out, soft and luscious. She looked a lot like a fiery edition of my beautiful mother in her best days.

"Annie, I'll never be able to do this myself."

"Don't worry, sugar, I'll help you. You'll learn."

"Thank you," I said, remembering my manners and followed her, limp with astonishment as another two hundred dollars changed hands. I left with a burgeoning bag of hair and skin products and makeup.

I thought the day finished, but Annie had other plans. "Life's not all horses and arenas. You need some party clothes. Del and I love to entertain."

The Cadillac floated out of the parking lot and into traffic. We stopped in front of The Dress Barn.

Inside, Annie hustled here and there, selecting possible candidates for me. I found one, low cut, with shoulder straps that crossed over in back, mid calf length, of a slinky jersey fabric in the softest tangerine, almost like a creamsicle. I wanted it.

Annie noticed. "You like that one?"

"Yes." Never before in my life had I felt covetous of clothing.

"Take it with you, but try it on last. These three first."

I examined the dresses she'd selected for me. One, an emerald green, I wouldn't wear, ever. Jess the Mess always forced me to wear green, "the only shade suitable for such unfortunate coloration."

"Not this one. But the others I'll try."

"Sure thing. Off you go." Without a trace of argument, she returned the dress to the racks.

I didn't mind the other two and dutifully modeled them for Annie.

She circled me, examining me up and down. "Um-hmm."

I wondered was that good or bad, but gave those dresses little thought. All I wanted was the creamsicle dress, and I waited impatiently for Annie to finish her evaluation. Finally, she waved me off.

Something happened when I put on the orange dress; I underwent a transformation. My bra peeked above the daring cut, so I took it off and stood before the mirror admiring myself. The long cut and flowing fabric hugged every curve of my body, long, lean and shapely – elegant—and the orange color made me into a glowing coal. No one could consider me a girl; in this dress, I definitely became a woman.

I stepped outside to show Annie.

"Can I get this one, please? I'll pay you back." I held my breath.

Annie appeared surprised at first and then contemplative. "You look like a million dollars. Yes, definitely that one and the turquoise, I think. You already have a decent black dress."

I couldn't bear to take the orange dress off. "Can I wear this home?"

"In your bare feet? Or were you planning on wearing boots with that?" She chuckled at me. "We need shoes. Beige or gold espadrilles, I think. I saw some over there, with ties that come up the ankles. Perfect. Oh, you're such a doll."

I gathered up my clothes from the change room and followed her to get the shoes. Three pair, assorted panties, two bras—unpadded I insisted —hosiery and some gewgaws to put in my hair.

Finally, we were done, loaded down like fairground merchants and ready to go home. The bags and boxes on the backseat of the Cadillac piled up to the roof, and I sank into the soft leather seat, exhausted. Shopping was more work than shoveling out a barn, I decided.

***

Annie was quiet until we pulled out onto the highway. "You're going to give your young man quite a surprise."

"What?" My face flushed into high color.

"Jack. He'll be surprised, to say the least."

"Annie, he's my guardian and I'm too young for him."

Annie laughed loud and long. "Sugar, I'm twenty years younger than Del. Didn't stop him. I wasn't much older than you are now when I first caught his fancy. Been with him ever since. No regrets."

"Really?" I said in surprise and never gave a thought to how rude I sounded.

"I'm not saying our life is perfect." Another wonderful laugh and then her voice changed, and in an intimate way she confided, "He has a roving eye, if you get what I mean. You come to me if he gets frisky with you. He can get like that, especially if he's drinking, but he's harmless, more bark than bite these days. Understand me?"

"Yes." I didn't know what else to say and squirmed around in my seat.

She clicked her tongue and winked at me. "But we've always been happy together. I'm a lucky woman."

We pulled up the driveway and into the capacious garage, almost as big as the stables. I noticed she had a doodad in the car and when she touched it, the doors opened and closed all by themselves. Was there any end to these luxuries?

"Here we are home. Jack's most likely up at the house with Del. Go show him your pretty self." She waved me away when I moved to help carry in all the purchases. "Jimmy will get the bags and take them down to your bungalow, and I'll come by in the morning and help you pack."

She beckoned me to follow her. "Hurry up, now. Yolanda will have supper ready soon."

We found Jack and Del sitting before a fire, drinks in hand. Jack had a yellow legal pad on his knee, which fell to the floor as he stood abruptly. The astounded expression on his face more than made up for the day's ordeals.

"Oh, we had such a fun day," Annie crowed as she walked over to Del and kissed him. "Hello, darling, I could sure use a drink."

"Hi Jack," I said, unfathomably nervous. "Hello Del."

"Well, don't you just look like the fine end to a beautiful day?" Del checked me over, brazen interest glinting in his eyes, and I tried not to shiver under his gaze.

"Thank you." I went and sat beside Jack. He still hadn't said anything.

"Look." I pulled back my hair and showed him my ears. "Pierced."

"You look lovely." He spoke in a quiet, subdued voice.

"Thanks. We shopped and went to a beauty salon. I've never done that before."

"You look lovely," he repeated. He seemed a little sad, and I didn't understand why.

We ate another wonderful meal. Annie still happy and voluble after a few drinks, talked and talked and even Del grew expansive. He told me the history of the fine horses behind Sunson, and he was glad the horse and I worked so well. Then, bless him, he said I shouldn't worry too much about tomorrow's race; it was little more than an introduction for Sunson and as long as we both learned from the event, how we did didn't matter too much.

I thanked him and assured him I would do my best, and I thought we had a pretty good chance of making a decent showing.

Jack remained quiet.

***

Later, back at our bungalow I asked, "What's wrong?"

"Why do you ask?"

"You haven't said two words all night, and please don't answer a question with a question." I waited for an explanation and got none. "Did something happen? Is Del unhappy with me about the shopping? All Annie's idea, not mine."

"Nothing is wrong and as far as I'm aware, Del is ecstatic, and clearly, Annie is in love with you." He waved his hand at the mountain of bags on the floor.

"Okay." I waited from him to say something, anything, but he stayed quiet.

"I'm going to go to bed," I announced, uncomfortable with his blues when I didn't know the cause. "But first I need to clean this stuff off my face, if I can find the right bottle." I rummaged through the bags. "My God, Jack, I felt like a Barbie doll today. I did as you said—let her do

182

what she wanted." I pirouetted for him.

He rewarded me with one of his half-smiles. "I hope you had fun."

"I did in a weird kind of way." I went to kiss his cheek good night.

He stood and gave me an intense glance as I approached, and when I kissed him, he rubbed his cheek against mine. His stubbly beard scraped my skin. He pulled himself upright and, with a set expression, said quietly, "Good night, Bria. Get a sound sleep. We have a big day tomorrow."

Fifteen minutes later, I went to the main room, back to being me, with a washed face, in pajamas and my hair back in its braid. "I think I know what's bothering you.

He sat at the table, his head resting on one hand, staring out into space. He straightened up. "What?"

"You know this is a great opportunity for me; at the same time you don't approve of all you see going on."

"Which is?"

"You're disgusted, aren't you?" I shared my own feelings. "You're helping me pimp myself out."

"Bria, honestly! Pimping?"

"That's how it feels. Shine the little filly up and put her out there."

He gave me a thoughtful look. "How far are you willing to go?"

"Only so far as I'm not pushed to do something I don't want to do."

"Glad to hear it." His smile returned. "When I saw you tonight, I became afraid for you. I'd hate to see your head turned around by this lifestyle. I much prefer you the way you are."

I wanted to comfort him somehow. "Annie's good people. I like her." I surveyed all the shopping bags. "She's coming to help me pack in the morning. Good, I've already forgotten what goes with what." I shared an amusing thought. "Hey, Jack, wherever I'm going, at least I'm going in grand style."

"I suppose you are."

I flipped through all the new things I'd learned that day, searching for something interesting to tell him. "By the way, did you know she's been with Del since her teens and he's twenty years older?"

"Aha," he said, like Sherlock Holmes. "What do you construe from that?"

I tried out my oblique message. "That some women know what they want at an early age."

"Maybe so." Smiling a strange little smile, he suggested, "Or perhaps he's a man with a taste for teenage girls. Go to bed, Bria."

"Okay. Cheer up, please."

I stuck my head out of my bedroom door. "And Jack, I know the clothes stay here when I go back home, but the skin care stuff has to go with me everywhere. Isn't that funny? Who's going to notice my complexion as I race around the barrels? Good night."

Twenty-two:
"Jack says... "

The rodeo ground in Billings boasted a moderate turn-out. The venue hadn't drawn a lot of entries, especially for the rough stock events, and only seventeen riders in barrel racing. Walter said that was common for the fall rodeos, mostly contestants trying to improve their ranking before the end of the year. It was not the usual high grade of competition.

The crowds didn't amount to much. Without the fairground hoopla, the rides, games and freak shows, this rodeo was all business.

I took Jack all around, showed him the stock chutes, the clocks, the judge's box and explained how things worked. We were sauntering over to the barns to check on Sunson when I heard a familiar voice call out from behind us.

"Hey, Bria."

I turned around and discovered the last person I wanted to see come walking toward me. Lean and tall, blond and good-looking: he of the summer necking sessions, my good friend Ted Lassiter. I wished I could whisk Jack away to some remote corner and Ted to another.

Trapped, I put on my glad-to-see-ya face, smiled and shouted, "Hey Ted. How's it going?"

I decided to make the best of things. What better opportunity to show Jack I was no longer a little girl than to introduce him to the other man in my life? "Excuse me." I left Jack, ran over, threw my arms around Ted's neck, planted a kiss right on his mouth and enjoyed his strong hug, front to front. Ted didn't have rules. None.

"Come meet Jack."

Each man took the other's measure as we approached. I wouldn't have been surprised if they started circling, sniffing butts; they looked so much like two dogs meeting for the first time.

"Jack this is Ted. Ted this is Jack."

A long uncomfortable moment passed before Jack stuck out his hand. "Pleased to meet you."

"Likewise."

They clasped hands, moved them up and down a couple of times, dropped them and stood staring at each other.

I found myself babbling. "Jack, I've known Ted almost as long as I've known you; didn't I tell you? Oh yes, we go way back. Ted loaned me my first horse and last year, I traveled with him and his Dad all over Montana and into Idaho. Ted, where's your dad?"

"Over there." He pointed at a group of men and shouted, "Dad!"

Gene joined us. He was tall like his son, but heavier and grey haired. He offered his hand to Jack. "Gene Lassiter."

"Pleased to meet you at last and thanks for your help."

They started talking like two old friends, which puzzled me a little. Then Gene invited Jack to come meet some of the others, and they walked off, leaving Ted and me alone.

I watched Jack join the group of men. He looked so out of his element in his khaki chinos, Chicago White Sox tee shirt, beige windbreaker and loafers; he might as well have had Eastern Dude printed all over him.

I turned to Ted. "I've got to go check on Sunson and I'm scheduled to practice soon. Want to see him?"

"Sure." His smile lit up his face and for the millionth time I was awed by his pretty, good looks, but I pushed the thought back and remembered he knew it and was insufferably conceited. Still, he was a good friend, and I wanted to share my new love with him. "He's gorgeous, Ted. Wait until you see him in action."

"Fast?"

"Yes and hot." I tried not to dwell on how his soft brown eyes smiled at me from out of his tanned face. "I'm a little scared of how he's going to react to the arena and all."

"Walter will get him steady," he reassured me.

"You know Walter?" I asked in surprise.

He laughed, his expression a little bewildered. "Bria, everyone does. Walter Krauss, eleven times World Champion and in the Cowboy Hall of Fame. No one told ya?"

"No." I was training with a star, how amazing. "Do you know Del and Annie too?"

"Dad does. He says Del's a wannabe, but knows his horseflesh, and he's spent enough money to get good blood. That's Dad; if a guy loves well-bred horses, he must be okay."

He put his arm around my waist. "They treat ya right?"

We walked on, our hips bumping until we got in step. "Yeah, I guess so."

I explained, more to keep my mind off how Ted's head turned to appraise every female—human and equine—we passed, than to impart information. "Everything's happening so fast. Nothing's been completely decided yet, but they spent a lot of money on me already, so they must like me for the job."

Ted's eyes caught mine. "You watch yourself. These high rollers are different from plain old working people like us."

"Jack said the same thing."

This didn't please him one bit although, for the life of me, I couldn't figure out why.

"So the great Jack isn't happy either?"

Again, my pale skin burned hot and I pulled down the brim of my hat to hide it. "Yes and no. And don't talk about him like that."

I chewed on my peeve for a while, walked in silence and spit it out, along with my thoughts on my new opportunity. "But here's the thing, Ted, I'd be stupid not to try and do this. And I'm not stupid. Jack says I could be set up for the future but I have to remember who I am. Jack says as long as I keep my head together, I'll be fine. Jack says—"

"Jack says," he mimicked in a high falsetto.

I stepped back from him and gave him a good scowl. "If you're going to be like that, go away."

"No," he said, pulling me back. "I want to see this horse."

We led Sunson out of the stock barn into the corral. I snapped a long lunge line on him and put him through his paces, watching his movements as he circled around me, but found no apparent lameness or favoring of any leg. He hadn't been hurt during his trip.

"Isn't he beautiful?" I shouted to Ted, who leaned on the fence.

"He's flashy. Looks strong. That short body, he must give you a hell of a choppy ride."

"True, but he moves like the wind and turns like a dancer."

Ted joined me in the center of the circle. "He's a pretty horse, Bria. I admire him a lot, and I wish you good luck." He ran the back of his knuckles across my face. "And you're a pretty girl. Later?"

"Don't know," I said, squirming under his gaze. "I think I should stay with Jack. He says I have to act like a professional and no fooling around."

"Jack says… I bet he does. No problem, see ya."

He spun on his heel and walked away, lifting his hat and giving a sweeping bow to a brunette woman leading a dappled gray gelding. No problem, indeed. Tomcats could take lessons from Ted Lassiter.

I tied Sunson to a hitch and he lifted his head high, nostrils flaring, savoring the breeze. Looking for a mare in estrus, I decided, and hoped he wouldn't find one. He was going to be a handful without the added excitement, all nerves in the unfamiliar setting. I prayed he'd be more settled by seven when our first event started.

***

He wasn't. He fidgeted, quivered and stamped as we waited for our call. All the cantering and pattern practice had not been enough to work the fire out of his system.

I sat on his back dressed in my new finery, white hat tonight, hair hanging loose down my back as instructed. Annie could come over later and help me brush the tangles out, I grumbled. A slight breeze wafted under the number pinned to my back, lifting my hair with it.

I turned Sunson around in a tight circle to relieve his tension and mine. Waiting.

"Eight up!" The ring announcer called.

I moved Sunson a good distance away, started him in a canter and entered the chute. The front gate sprang open, and I urged him on. By the time we hit the arena, we ran at a full gallop.

Out of the corner of my eye, I saw the white flag sweep down. We were on the clock. At top speed, we took the first barrel. I swung him hard around, throwing my weight into the turn with him. Good.

His hindquarters pumped rhythmically. I focused on the second. Everything else was a blur. Going into the approach, Sunson jerked his head forward, taking control and we lost precious moments as he fought me and took the turn wide.

I headed him into the straightaway to the third, and he settled down, concentrating again on the job at hand. Our approach and turn were perfect. I batted him hard on the rump as he started into the stem, trying to make up for those wasted hundredths of a second. The flag swept again as we crossed the finish.

I cantered him around, waiting for my time: 15.36 seconds. Tears blinded me as I exited. On a horse like this, I should have done better.

Walter met me outside and gripped Sunson's lines.

I couldn't wait to explain. "I lost him on the second barrel. I'm sorry."

He patted my leg. "The first barrel was pretty good. The third was very good. I'm proud of you."

"But we should have been better." I kicked my right foot free from the stirrup, swung my leg over and dismounted.

Walter ran his hands down Sunson's legs, talking to me while he did. "It's his first time. He's all hot and bothered. You performed better than I thought you would."

I searched his weathered face. "We weren't too bad?"

"Not bad at all."

Walter told me to go find Jack, Del and Annie in the grandstand, one of the boxes of course. He would look after Sunson. "Go on, have some fun. Let me take care of our pig-headed boy."

I followed his directions and found the three, way up high in a private room, all glassed in front to protect them from the dust and grit of rodeo.

"Good ride," Del said. "Damn good ride. So far, you're third."

"I won't be for long, Del. There're some real good riders coming up." I tried to look him straight in the face. "We should have done better. He fought me at the second barrel, and I lost him for a sec. But tomorrow we'll improve, I promise."

"I'm not complaining." He reached out to touch me, but I drew back, pretending I hadn't noticed.

"You looked real good out there, sugar," Annie said. "Beautiful."

I stared at her in bemused confusion for a moment. Beautiful? I remembered to say, "Thanks."

Jack held out a welcoming arm. "Are you all right, Bria?"

"I should have done better." I flopped down beside him. He swung the arm around me and gave me a squeeze.

At the end of the evening, I came in fifth out of seventeen. Once upon a time, I would have been happy with that, but on this horse and considering everything riding on the outcome, I felt I'd let everyone down. And no one could tell me otherwise.

Later, in our motel room Jack asked, "You said you and Ted had been friends a long time."

"Since I was eight or nine. I don't remember exactly." I didn't want to discuss Ted with Jack, and hoped he would drop it.

But no, he didn't. "And that's all you are? I got the idea you were more than friendly."

Might as well cut to the chase, I thought. "Are you asking me, am I having sex with him?"

"Yes, I suppose I am."

I narrowed my eyes to tell him he'd crossed a barrier. "I'm going to quote a very wise man I know. What I do on my own time is my business." I had no idea why, but I felt perverse.

"Well, consider this," he said, back to being the adult full of instruction and unasked for advice. "You're underage. He isn't. I'm your guardian and that makes it my business."

"Wrong!" I punctuated my remark with a stomp on the floor. "I don't have to tell you everything, Jack Connelly. What I do and with who is my private life. And seeing as I'm not doing it with you—" Damn! My face burned red hot – "it doesn't concern you in the slightest."

He pulled himself up to his fullest height, drew in his eyebrows and tilted his head until he peered down his nose at me. "Considering you'll run to me if you get into trouble, I think it does."

"Really!" I put both hands on my hips and stuck out my chin. "For the record, I am not now, and never have had voluntary sex, nor do I particularly want to, and certainly not with Ted. He's got a new girl at every rodeo. Who wants a guy like that?" Faced with Jack's obstinate expression, I relented, but only a little. "He's my friend and I love him. We fooled around a couple of times. Happy now?"

He was not. In the same dry manner he'd say define *race ipso loquator*, he said, "Define 'fooling around.'"

"I have to?" I laughed at him. "Didn't you ever fool around with a girl, Jack?"

"The only kind of fooling around I know is the kind that gets you ready for sex," he said in a pedantic tone and added, "to warm up to it."

"Well I didn't warm up to it," I shouted and then my stupid mouth ran on. "Maybe there's something wrong with me, but I don't warm up at all."

I stamped my feet, angry at him and angrier at myself. "So there. *Now* are you happy?"

"Good night, Bria." He turned to leave the room and go back to his adjoining one.

I couldn't let the day end this way. I hated the lonely feelings that swept over me whenever we fought, and I didn't mind apologizing, even when I knew in my heart I was right.

"Jack?"

He stood framed in the doorway. He wasn't mad, just upset for some reason and maybe tired. I could tell by the way he said, "Yes?"

"I'm sorry. I wish I understood what gets into me these days. Mary says I've become a firecracker with a short fuse."

He smiled. "Don't worry, sweet girl. I have a thick skin. And I remember how I felt at sixteen: not a pretty time."

His comparison angered me all over again. The sixteen-year-old boys of my acquaintance—Mickey, for example – acted like kids, *were* kids, and I was far more mature. He'd handed me an insult, but I shoved that thought down as soon as it rose and concentrated on the positive. At least he had accepted the apology and tried to understand. Not his fault he couldn't, being male and all.

Feeling a little bold, I asked a question I'd long wondered about. "How old were you when you first had sex?"

He stared at me a moment and then answered, "Twenty-one."

"Kind of a late bloomer weren't you?"

His eyebrows flew up and his gaze wandered over to the mirror. To his own reflection, he said, "Girls didn't exactly flock around me. I'm more Abraham Lincoln than Robert Redford, a pretty homely guy, in case you hadn't noticed."

"Wrong again." I wanted to run over and give him a hug. "All I see is Jack. And I think you're beautiful."

He sounded sad when he said, "Thank you, Bria. And good night."

He closed the door between our rooms and I got ready for sleep. I spent almost an hour detangling, brushing and braiding my hair, and I decided we had to find some compromise on this hair-flying-in-the-breeze fetish of Annie's. At least she would be pleased had she known I remembered to clean my face with her potions and lotions.

Twenty-three:
"The little lady has a head for business."

The next afternoon, Sunson behaved himself and relaxed. No more nervous stomping about the wait, only excited restlessness. When the loudspeaker called us up, he bolted through the chute, set on running.

We had no problem at the first two barrels, coming out of the second at a cose angle to the ground. He straightened up in two bounds and approached the last, braked for the turn, adjusted his lead, threw himself around in one single leap and tore off down the stem with everything he had. We finished with a very respectable 15.06 seconds and placed third.

"Well done. Way to go," Del and Annie yelled, thrilled. Walter said our run wasn't at all bad, which I took to mean great. Jack hugged me to his side and gave me an "Atta girl."

On Sunday afternoon, we roared through the pattern, executing turns so close my leg brushed the barrel. Thank God it didn't move, not even a wobble. No way could we afford the five-second penalty. Sunson ran with all his heart. He was a true competitor now, and he loved his job. He gave me a new personal best time 15.00 seconds exactly. We placed first.

I returned to an ecstatic Del and Annie. Annie threw her arms around me, jumping up and down in glee. "We did it! We won!" she whooped and insisted on opening a bottle of champagne.

I had some. Aside from the fizzles and bubbles that made the stuff hard to swallow without hiccups, and the sour taste, it wasn't bad, but I preferred Coke.

Jack beamed at me, threw me a thumbs up and a wink. He pulled me aside and whispered, "You're amazing. Well done."

Del insisted on taking us all to a steak house, so we piled into Annie's rented Buick and drove to the Ranchman's, a dimly lit place with red upholstered booths and candles in red glass jars on every table. We had barely sat down when a pretty waitress came for the drink order.

The drinks arrived and Del turned to Jack. "Give me that paper."

Jack pulled some papers out of his inner jacket pocket, unfolded and smoothed them out on the table in front of me. He pointed to the first clause. It was mostly about who was what and known-hereinafter-as: legal speak.

He skipped the next two clauses and turned the page. "Read this."

"Services rendered for consideration..." I slogged through the heavy dry language and understood I was not to appear in any rodeo anywhere except as a representative of Lazy K Ranch Inc., nor to ride in any public event any horse other than that dictated by Lazy K Ranch Inc.

I must always comport myself in a manner to bring credit to the Lazy K. Intoxication, drug use or moral improprieties, whatever they may be, were expressly forbidden. There was a sub clause explaining what would happen in such a case, which I interpreted to mean I'd be out on my ass.

Further, I read I would always maintain adequate grooming, personal hygiene and dress as directed by Lazy K Ranch Inc. And I would not cut my hair. What, I wondered, did my hair have to do with anything?

I gazed up at Jack, my brain full of question marks.

"Do you understand all this?"

"Yes."

"Good," he said. "Now read this part."

I followed his finger to the next clause.

I was to present myself at Lazy K Ranch fourteen days before any scheduled rodeo event. I would make myself available to public appearances when requested, under which Jack had written in red pen, except when in conflict with my education. I was to make myself available for social occasions deemed to the benefit of Lazy K Ranch. I promised never to make derogatory comments about Lazy K Ranch, its owners, employees or stock handling practices. I nodded.

"Now here." I was to request a change of circuit from Montana to Mountain State Circuit of the W.P.R.A. I was to maintain my card status with the W.P.R.A. and I was never to violate their code of ethics. Any fines or penalties assessed to me would come from my own pocket. Lazy K. Ranch would pay annual dues and entry fees.

"Okay."

"This," Jack said, running his finger along another convoluted paragraph, "says housing, clothing, food and medical insurance will be provided by the Lazy K Ranch whenever you are representing them in any way and includes travel expenses to and from rodeo events, public appearances or training. You also agree you will ride in a minimum of 15 rodeos each year within the Mountain State Circuit. Got it?"

"Got it," I answered, a little annoyed that none of the details had been discussed with me.

"The next paragraph, Bria," he began, and I understood from his tone I was about to hear something important, "states the representatives of Lazy K Ranch Inc recognize you are a minor. While you are involved in their business, they will act as my surrogates concerning your guardianship, except for any legal issues, contracts and matters related to education. On these, only my approval and signature are acceptable." His eyebrows drew together over his nose. "Do you understand?"

"Yes, Jack." I tried to sound contrite and wondered if he would ever forgive me for the fraudulent use of Dugald's signature last summer. I had attempted to convince him I thought Dugald was my guardian when in Canada, but he didn't buy it and suggested if I was going to make up excuses at least try to use one commensurate with my intelligence.

"Now then," Jack said and turned to another page. "Look this over."

The following remuneration and consideration in each category as previously defined herein:

Annual salary _____ to be paid in twelve equal installments on the thirtieth of each month. **Travel allowance** to be construed as standard coach fare to and from Lazy K Ranch to be paid by_____ **Educational subsidy and tutorship**_____ annually to be paid in twelve equal installments on the thirtieth of each month. **Bonuses**, as defined in 9.2 to be paid as follows_____ **Disbursement of prize moneys won**_____ (%) Bria Jean Connelly _____(%) Lazy K Ranch Inc. All monies to be paid to John J. Connelly, Esq. and held in trust for the minor child, Bria Jean Connelly. All checks to be made payable to John J. Connelly, Esq. trust acct# 79864. Lazy K Ranch Inc. will maintain an accounting of same, which will be made available for audit by John J. Connelly, Esq. or his appointed agent. This agreement will remain in effect for twelve months from signing and is subject to renegotiation at that date.

This page Jack passed over to Del and handed him a pen.

Del sat back in his chair, puffed on his cigar, sipped at his Jack Daniels and glanced at Jack's inscrutable lawyer's face. His exhaled smoke drifted up and his eyes followed it as though waiting on inspiration from God.

I chewed my nails until Annie looked up, noticed and slapped my hand.

Del snatched the page forward, threw his left arm around like a wall, scribbled a few moments and passed it back to Jack, who set the completed section between us, so we could both read.

Jack looked at me with no change of expression, and I took his cue and kept my face neutral. He picked up the pen, changed a few numbers, and the paper passed back and forth several times. Finally, it stopped and Jack placed it in front of me.

Annual salary *$12,000* to be paid in twelve equal installments on the thirtieth of each month. **Travel allowance** to be construed as standard coach fare to and from Lazy K Ranch to be paid *by Lazy K Ranch Inc.* **Educational subsidy and tutorship** *$12,000* annually to be paid in twelve equal installments on the thirtieth of each month. **Bonuses**, as defined in 9.2 to be paid as follows *$200 for each 1st place finish, $500 if National Finals placement in 1974, $1,500 if in top three nationally, $5,000 if first place nationally.* **Disbursement of prize moneys won** *60* (%) Bria Jean Connelly *40* (%) Lazy K Ranch Inc. All monies to be paid to John J. Connelly, Esq. and held in trust for the minor child, Bria Jean Connelly…

Jack raised one heavy black eyebrow. *Yes?*

Yes, yes, yes! I signaled back with both my carefully groomed ones. They were offering me a fortune!

Jack said, "We have an agreement."

Annie whooped up a "Woo hoo!"

"Welcome aboard, Bria." Del smiled and gave me his hand.

I accepted his, and he crushed mine in one of those macho handshakes men like to give. "Thank you."

I attended to the matters no one had discussed with me, and should have. "I want to make one request."

"What?" Jack and Del asked in unison.

"I want to be known as BeeJay, B. J. Connelly, so for business and all, call me BeeJay."

"Sure thing, BeeJay," Del drawled.

"And one more question," I enjoyed being in charge at last.

Del said, "Go ahead."

Jack said, "Shoot."

"Well, seeing as we all signed on this date, doesn't today count as a first place finish?" I asked.

"And you're two hundred dollars richer as of right now." Del roared his amusement in a hearty guffaw. "I knew this little lady had a head for business. Let's get another drink."

I'd never seen Jack as he was at that dinner: loquacious, prone to laughter and unsteady on his feet, but he did better than Del, who had to be helped out to the car by Annie. We put the two men together in the back. I told Annie though I didn't have a license yet, I knew how to drive and probably was the best person to do so.

Once in the driver's seat, I needed a while to get familiar with the vehicle, never having been in a Buick before, let alone driven one, and it was the first automatic transmission I ever encountered, very different from Uncle Dugald's old Chevy truck. I almost sent everyone through the windshield when I tried the brakes, but my passengers were all too inebriated to protest.

I drove from the restaurant to Del and Annie's hotel and then to ours. I was careful to follow all the rules and watched my speed, not wanting to be stopped by the police with no license and a half-drunk Jack in the back seat.

I felt restless and asked Jack if he wanted to go for a walk in the park across the street. He thought my suggestion a good idea. Clear his head, he said, obviously still in high spirits.

Twenty-four:
"*Worst of all you lie to yourself.*"

We walked to the small lake in the center. Huge cottonwoods hung out over the water, their leaves yellow now in October. It was a cool night and he slung an arm across my shoulders.

I still buzzed inside and babbled, full of excitement and happiness. He let me ramble on until I ran out of words. I stopped walking and turned him to face me.

"Jack, I can't thank you enough. Thank you. Thank you."

I put my hands on his shoulders and stretched up to kiss his cheek. My cheek skimmed his beard shadow, thick and dark as always by the end of the day. Somehow, when my lips touched his cheek, one of us moved and his mouth landed on mine, softly at first then, as if something gave way inside of him, harder. His arms went around me and pulled me tight against him. Oh God, the kiss lasted a long time.

Numbed by shock at first, I relaxed and kissed him back, using all the skills I'd learned over the summer. Was this not where I'd hoped and schemed to be? I passed beyond thought and hung on to him with every ounce of strength I owned. I was warming up. Yes, I was. His erection pulsed against my belly and I pressed into it. I was hot. My heart thudded in my ears. My groin ached and grew wet. And suddenly, abruptly, unbelievably, it all ended.

His arms no longer encircled me. His hands on my shoulders pushed me away. I resisted and pulled tighter, moaning into his neck. I gazed at his face.

He turned away, staring up into the sky. In the light of the street lamp, his face was all angles and stricken. His mouth moved. "Oh, Christ."

Then, "No, Bria. Stop."

I let him push me back, scared. I had the horrible thought things could never be the same between us, not now, not after we'd stepped across the line, and our true feelings lay out in the open. I had to find a way to make everything right.

"Jack." I whispered, placed a hand on his jaw and pressed his face until he looked at me. "Let's walk around the lake. Come on, we're all right now. It was some kind of madness, but it's gone."

He let me pull him back onto the sidewalk. I linked my arm through his and led him as I would a horse. He walked in silence for several minutes. "I'm sorry, Bria. I have no business behaving like that with you."

"Seems to me I was right there with you; no apology needed."

I let silence rule for another moment and said quietly, "Jack, I know you. You're the best man I've ever met or probably ever will. I love you and you love me."

He said nothing so I tried again. "You'd never hurt me. I trust you."

I started getting a little prickly about the silent treatment and attempted to explain the special circumstances that, in my mind, made everything okay. "I've always lived a life I'm too young for. You think it's been easy? In some ways, I'm older than you."

His voice was hard. "You're sixteen. I'm twenty-nine and your guardian. This is morally wrong and against the law."

I wanted to joke. I wanted us to laugh and make the fantastic kiss small, unimportant and amusing. "Ah, the law. Right, I have to be seventeen. I guess you'd hate to end up prosecuting yourself."

Instead of laughing, he dismissed me with a heated, "I'm not in the mood for a smartass routine."

Why was he changing into some uptight, self-loathing idiot? One stupid kiss wasn't such a big deal. "So? Just because you're caught up in all this guilt, I can't enjoy a bit of humor?"

He laughed bitterly. "Why not? I suppose it is absurd."

"Thanks a heap. Good to hear your opinion of my desirability." I searched his face for some hint of amusement. "Give yourself a break. It's only human."

I received no reply, so I stepped right in front of him and poked him in the chest. "You listen to me, Jack. I told you years ago, girls grow up and as things turned out, I had to be fast at it. If you didn't know me and met me out one night, and learned I attended Loyola, currently working on a paper in sociology, worked as a professional rodeo racer earning good money, and I love to go to parties out at the lake country, you wouldn't feel bad about wanting me at all."

He grabbed my hand and held it away from himself. "Possibly so, if you lied about your age, but I do know you, and you're only sixteen.

"Yes, but let me tell you something. I've been menstruating for five years now and my hormones are functioning fine."

"I'll keep that in mind." He sounded miserable.

"And thanks for showing me. I was beginning to be concerned about my lack of —*warmth.* Seriously, thank you." I thought he would find that funny and lighten up.

His voice sharpened, even more impatient. "Do you have to say everything that comes into your mind?"

I took his arm and started walking again. I laughed as if all was fine and spoke flippantly. "Pretty much. Wasn't it you who said I shouldn't keep a lot of secrets? And seeing as you're obviously still my lawyer, you can't tell anybody."

He finally gave me a short laugh, one that ended abruptly.

Something in his attitude chilled my blood. I clung to his arm, panic in my heart. "We'll always be friends, won't we, Jack?"

He pulled out of my grasp, took my hands and spoke from two feet away. "Yes, always friends and I'm still your guardian and lawyer but this has to be an end to—" He stopped, swallowed and peered down his nose at me. "I think you understand me. Back off."

"What?" I froze motionless, stunned and betrayed. I'd followed the rules, always so careful never to put one toe across the line. "Me? You started it."

"I'm not so sure about that." His eyes glared down on me, a hard, angry glint in the lamplight. "But I'm definitely finishing it. Now."

"You don't have to be so—" In my outrage, my vocabulary deserted me, and I couldn't find a suitable term for how he was acting.

"Bria, find someone your own age to practice your arts on. Stop flirting with a grown man."

My jaw clenched so tight with anger I could hardly speak. My voice vibrated with rage. "I already got the message. And thanks for the advice. Mary will be happy to hear it." *You're no better than your dad, laying down the law and refusing to talk about it anymore. Son of a bitch.* I stood staring at him, trying to figure out what was really happening.

His desire came as no surprise to me. I'd known it for years, right from the beginning when he took me to Chicago. Men wanted girls. Why else would he have done it? I wasn't like Tara, his own blood, and he didn't owe me anything. I thought he took me to Mary to keep me safe until I was old enough for his tastes, and here I was, ready.

My confusion turned into fury.

A chasm yawned before me. *You! Your eyes follow me around and have for years. I walk away and feel them on my ass. You feast your sight on my breasts in a wet bathing suit. I go without a bra because you like it. You do. I know you do. Your eyes tell me so. They covet. Now, you self-righteous bastard, you tell me to back off?*

I remembered all our shared intimacies, how he sought out my company and spent all his free time with me. I read widely just to find interesting things to tell him. I tried so hard to be what he wanted, to behave as he suggested, and I followed all his stupid rules. It shamed me that I'd centered my life on him.

Ferocity rose up in me, took me over. I raised both fists and pounded him on the chest as hard as I could. "You son of a bitch, you're a liar, and worst of all, you lie to yourself."

He grabbed my wrists, pinned them against me and wrapped his arms around me. He held me close. "I'm sorry, so sorry."

I thrust him away, pulled back from him. "Stop being so fucking sorry. You don't even know what you're sorry for."

The red-hot rage rebounded through my blood, until I glimpsed his mournful face and the heat drained instantly, leaving cold terror in its place. If Jack made up the core of my world, how would I go on without him? The thought left me limp with dread, but strangely calm.

As if nothing had happened, I took his arm, and we continued walking around the lake. I didn't say anything and he walked staring at his feet, deep in thought. Finally, he looked up and said he'd been stupid, and I agreed, but doubted we were talking about the same stupidity. "But I still love you, anyway."

My words, meant to comfort, caused him more unease. "I love you, too but not that way—"

"Bull shit." I cut off his lies.

"Listen to me." He held me by my shoulders at arm's length and the intensity of his gaze bored into me. "I can't. Understand?"

"No."

He sighed in exasperation. "You will, one day."

"When I'm older, you mean." I rolled my eyes to let him know what I thought of his reasoning. "I'm sure tired of hearing that one."

"Too bad." He dropped his arms and walked toward the motel at a brisker pace.

Striding along beside him, aware he wanted nothing more than to be alone, away from me, my calm evaporated. I couldn't let things stay as they were, mad, unhappy and our future so uncertain. I needed him to laugh with me as we always did, so I wouldn't be so frightened and lonely. I ransacked my mind, looking for something clever.

"Someone my own age, you said. Who of my acquaintances is my age? Hey, didn't your little brother Mickey just turn sixteen the month before me? Yeah, that's what I'll do. Go hit on Mickey."

He glared at me and walked to his room without speaking.

Pissed off again, I added, "Though I doubt he kisses like you do," and slammed my door a good one.

Twenty-five:
"Park your libido in the car."

Mary

"We're having lunch today, Jack, and unless you're prepared to have me thrown bodily from your office, you'd better rearrange your schedule. I'll wait right here while you do so."

He snapped his head up and sat upright. "Is this a hijacking?"

"Call it what you want. We're having lunch." I anchored my feet firmly to the floor in front of him.

He indicated the ringing phones, dozens of conversations and the clacking typewriters. "Mary, look around you. I'm busy. How about I meet you tonight?"

"No. Lunch. Call out for something if you want. We need to talk. I assume places with more privacy than this cubicle exist somewhere." I crossed my arms.

He sighed and gave up. "Give me half an hour. Tom!"

A young man barely old enough to be a high school graduate popped his head over the screen. "Yes?"

"Book an interview room for me, will you? And take Mrs. Connelly with you and organize something to eat. Half an hour, Mary. Tom keeps a wonderful selection of menus you can choose from."

I followed young Tom to the open common area and sat in a chair to the side of his workspace. His desk formed a one-quarter section of an island. His island was one of a dozen. There were no screens for the plebs.

He handed me a fistful of restaurant menus to peruse, picked up his phone and started a rapid-fire set of questions to an unknown party on the other end. Just one more voice in the cacophony around me.

I sorted through them. Pizza, pizza, barbeque, deli, burgers—these young ADA's must own the worst clogged arteries in the country. Chinese, hooray! I circled my selections and passed the menu back to him. He used his pencil to dial the number and quickly and efficiently placed the order.

"Mrs. Connelly, I booked a room for Jack. Wouldn't you prefer to wait there?"

I'd rather stay where I was; all the activity was fascinating, but said, "Yes, thanks." He led me out of the busy office, down a corridor and opened the door to a small room containing a table and six chairs.

I sat and waited. Close to an hour later Jack arrived, a bagful of lukewarm Chinese food in hand.

"Sorry for the delay," he said, closing the door behind him. "I told you I was busy. Now what 's up? "

I went straight for his throat. "I'm here to ask you what's going on between you and Bria."

"Nothing." He busied himself unpacking the food cartons, and wouldn't meet my eyes.

"She's been back for over a month and you haven't seen her once. She's moody and blue and won't tell me why. What happened in Wyoming? I need to know."

"Nothing terrible." He looked uncomfortable and certainly was not forthcoming.

I jumped to my own conclusions. "You slept with her."

"Oh, for God's sake. No, I did not." He sat silent a minute, looking somewhere beyond me. "But I wanted to. And she wanted me to."

"So something did happen." I sat waiting for the details.

"Just a kiss. Our last night, after she won and signed her contract, we were celebrating. I had too much to drink. A kiss, no more." He flashed his crooked smile from a troubled face. "But it was one hell of a kiss."

I said nothing, just stared at the man I'd known since he'd been a boy. It worked.

"The whole trip was unreal. Suddenly, she was this beautiful woman, made up and dressed up, holding her own with these business people. You should see her on a horse. Christ, it blew me away."

"And?"

"I let things get out of hand. That's all. I put a stop to it right away." He shrugged as if to say that's all.

"In fine fashion, I'm sure. What did you say to her?"

"She was too young and I was her guardian. I said better she find someone her own age."

I laughed at him. He was so absurd. "If you wanted to stop it, you should have thought about that three years ago. Where did you think you were heading?"

"Okay, so you told me so. Do you feel better?"

"No. You have no imagination at all. You showered her with attention and affection well beyond the scope of a guardian, and then dumped her because you finally realized what you'd done, this stupid game you played with her."

His face grew hard and I found myself staring at the aggressive courtroom warrior. "Tell me, Mary, what kind of game are you playing with my father?"

"That won't work, Jack. I've known you too long to fall for your tactics. Whatever I'm doing with your father, we're two mature adults and it is, frankly, none of your business. We're talking about a sixteen-year-old girl, one you're responsible for—over my protests, I might add."

"I haven't dumped her. I'm working on finding a tutor to travel with her. I'm taking care of her business interests. I'm looking for an agent to take care of all this. I haven't the time or background for what she needs."

"You're handing her over to others and backing off. I'm telling you, you can't." I put my hands on the table, moved toward him and let my words hang in the air.

"I'm not." If he leaned back any farther, his chair would go over.

"You are." I was now six inches away. "You've gone from being her best friend to some distant business manager."

"I thought some time to cool off a good idea."

"For her or for you?" I was so angry with him I quivered.

"Okay, for both of us. It shook me, Mary, how close I came to... You're right and I was wrong. I blamed her and it was as much my doing. I suppose I should talk to her and tell her that."

"No, I don't think so." I backed away. "You should come over for dinner and pick up where you left off before any of this happened. Talk to her about school. Talk to her about prostitutes, whatever. Show her you're still her friend. And one last thing."

"What?" He turned a rueful and relieved face toward me.

"Take your own advice and find someone your own age."

He reached into his inner pocket and showed me some airplane tickets. "Already working on that. I'm off to New York for four days."

He was going to see Leslie, the beautifully dressed mature woman I'd met last year. I wanted to say, Jack, someone your *own* age, please, not mine, but didn't. I didn't let up on him either. "Make sure Bria knows."

"Got it." He raised his hands. "Are we done?"

"I guess so." I pointed my outstretched finger at him. "Dinner with us tonight, no excuses. And park your libido in your car."

I picked up my purse and put on my coat. Just before I left, I surveyed the table of uneaten food and my old friend Jack, looking abashed. I shook my head and opened the door.

"One last thing," he said.

I turned. "What?"

"Bria offered to talk to a witness of ours, a girl, a victim. Do you think that would be a good idea?"

I didn't think so. I thought Bria had had quite enough of crime and punishment and stupid young men, but instead, I said, "Don't ask me. Ask her tonight."

"I will. And Mary, thanks."

"Anytime. I'll straighten you out yet, Jack Connelly. You'll be a fine man one day. Now I'm going to go home and work on Bria. Enjoy the food."

"Good bye." He opened some of the cartons and started eating his lunch.

He was prompt in arrival – a wonder. I met him at the front door and I'd never seen a more visibly nervous Jack. I took a good deal of pleasure from the sight. "Come in." I accepted the proffered bottle of wine wrapped in a brown paper bag.

He followed me down the hall to the living room. What was the first thing he saw? The "beautiful woman, made-up and dressed-up" sitting on the floor in front of the TV, coloring a picture with her sister. She looked twelve.

She jumped to her feet, embarrassed, and brushed off the knees of her jeans. "I didn't know you were coming over." Then she glared at me.

"A surprise," I said, airily and left them alone while I finished dinner.

By the time I put the food on the table, they were laughing and talking, same as always. Bria acted her usual cheeky-funny self and he laughed and egged her on, only embarrassed when I caught his eye.

Message received, I thought, with satisfaction, *and now that he sees her for the girl she is, he'll back off and seek his enjoyment elsewhere—even if it is with a woman closer to my age than his—and finally act like a guardian, fool of a man.*

No sooner had I finished the thought than he asked, "Do you remember that witness we discussed, the thirteen-year-old girl?" and my comfort evaporated.

"Yes," Bria said, her eagerness as apparent as the shine on her hair.

"Are you still willing to talk to her?"

Twenty-six:
"Picking up the pieces is all we can do."

Bria

I found a place on Jack's old couch stable enough to let me sit and write, put my papers in the clipboard and propped them on my raised knees. In my neatest handwriting, I transcribed from my scribbled notes to a proper report, where I did my best to copy both the form and language Mrs. Friesen used.

She had sent me redacted copies of professional reports, with a stern injunction to use no real names or addresses, anything giving a clue to the victim's identity.

"I've never read the laws of Illinois, but I imagine they're not too different from here. Privacy is of paramount importance in these cases."

I was so scared of what I was about to do, hearing her voice on the telephone comforted me. "Jack already has her name. He's taking me to her home." I tangled my fingers in my hair as I twirled a shank round and round in my hand. I stopped and settled for chewing my pencil instead.

Mrs. Friesen's voice became serious. "Don't give him any details of your interview. If you insist on attempting to reach her, you must do so for the benefit of the girl, not to help Jack in his case. I want to hear you say you understand this."

"I do. I won't tell Jack anything. I promise."

"I'm going to reiterate my reservations. Connecting with a victim is a delicate task, and a difficult one, but having said that, I'll do my best to assist you. Give me the details of the case as you know them, and we'll see what we can do to prepare you."

I gave her the information I had collected. Most of the facts came from a report forwarded by Victim Services, by the last worker thrown out of the Pinelli's place.

Jane Doe #1, rape victim, age 13 and Mother Doe, estimated in late twenties. Father is not in residence, location unknown.

Current Status: Jane Doe #1 has received no counseling in the three months following the attack; medical treatment ongoing for pelvic inflammatory condition, is unable to attend school or return to normal social life, housebound, only interpersonal relations with mother.

"Oh dear, her isolation and lack of intervention disturbs me considerably. We start with the premise there are two victims of this crime, the girl and her mother. On your first visit, look around, note their condition and surroundings."

"I should just sit and look at them?"

"Of course not. Introduce yourself and the special qualifications you possess."

"What are those?" I asked, graduating from the pencil to my fingernails.

"Your history, share it. There's comfort in knowing you're not alone in the universe."

The thought made me sick with anxiety but I prepared as best I could and by the time Jack came to drive me, I was as ready as I would likely ever be.

I spent no more than an hour that afternoon in the disheveled and tiny two-bedroom apartment: a box-like main room of depressing cinder block walls and a small square window looking over the neighboring building—equally squalid. Similar windows and occasional moving shadows in a blank concrete wall were the only view.

One corner housed a tiny kitchenette, a fridge and stove, perhaps three feet of countertop and four cupboards, two above and two below. The sink was heaped full of unwashed dishes. A battered couch littered with magazines, throw pillows and a couple of blankets; a matching armchair; a television and a small dinette with two chairs were the only furnishings in the room. A crate covered by a towel served as a coffee table. The dismal scene glared, too brightly lit by a fluorescent overhead fixture.

Everything was dusty and littered and smelled of despair and heartache. I stood in the doorway looking around me, taking the miserable scene in while Ms. Pinelli hurriedly picked things up from one place only to throw them down in another. She finally gave up, turned to me and shrugged. "Don't mind the mess."

I didn't and walked over to the table and cleared a spot for my notebook. "Please come and sit down. No need to tidy for me."

Ms. Pinelli sat across from me and gave me a helpless look. "I work nights. I'm a baker over at the supermarket on Main. I sleep in the day and with Lisa the way she is, nothing gets done." Her eyes got a little hard. "I know how things are supposed to be."

She was young, much younger than I expected, and careworn. I thought I should proceed carefully. "I understand life can be difficult, and I'm not here to make judgments. I only came to speak with you."

"That prosecutor sent you. He wants Lisa to talk, to tell him what happened. She can't, so don't waste your time."

"That prosecutor is my guardian, and he thought I may be able to help you and Lisa. He's a good man."

Ms. Pinelli blew out a huff of air in disbelief. "For months the cops and those lawyers have been pushing me. They only care about their case, not us. What can a girl like you do for us? You couldn't possibly understand."

My answer was delayed by the opening of one of the two doors in the far wall of the main room. Her daughter came out. She was only beginning her development into puberty, with messy shoulder-length dark hair, dressed in pajama bottoms and a sweatshirt. Her face still showed shadows of old bruises. Her eyes were vacant and non-responsive.

"Hello, Lisa," I said. "My name is Bria."

Her head jerked in my direction, and I thought she registered my presence for a moment, but curled up on the couch, wrapped herself in a blanket and lay with her back to me, staring at the wall, making shadow play with her fingers.

"Ms. Pinelli, I want to answer your question." I raised my voice, hoping Lisa would hear. I swallowed hard and as I had rehearsed, ventured into the most difficult part of my speech. "I do understand. I was twelve years old when I was abducted and taken far from my home. Men raped me and filmed themselves in the act. For the next several weeks, they rented me out, and others raped me many times over."

She stared at me. Lisa's finger play ceased. I wanted to go on but couldn't. My heart pounded in my chest and my body prickled with sweat. I labored to calm myself. It took several minutes.

Quietly, Ms. Pinelli got up from her chair and came back carrying a glass of water for me.

"Thank you. Even four years later, I have difficulty talking about my past. The only reason I'm here and able to do so is because I had help.

Mr. Connelly, my guardian, thought if I came and told you, I might be of assistance."

"You poor girl. I'm sorry for what I said." She spoke kindly but her eyes went from concerned to hard again. "Is this some kind of trick?"

I wondered how life had made her so suspicious. "I wouldn't be a party to trickery. Nothing I learn here will be repeated to the law, I promise. I'm studying sociology and I intend to go to law school. I plan to work helping girls like your daughter, and I'll try to be entirely professional."

She wouldn't be easily won over, and I was thinking about how to get to her and make her understand Lisa needed help when I noticed tears on her worn, tired face as she looked at her daughter. "You see how she is? What can be done? She won't talk to anyone. It's been months now, and she's no better. I thought time healed all wounds but she gets worse each day."

I wanted to cry with her at first, but remembered Mrs. Friesen and how she never showed her feelings. Her neutrality always made talking easier. I reached deep inside myself, using every art I had learned in my drama classes and took on a role. I became Mrs. Friesen. "I'm going to leave you with some copies of the journals I kept at the time. I was a lot like Lisa; I slept my days away and refused to face what happened. You read them. There's hope."

My hands shook so badly, I had trouble opening my briefcase but did manage to fish out a dozen pages I'd selected from the hundreds I'd written and handed them to her. I studied Lisa, who lay still, facing the wall and found myself floating back to a place I didn't want to visit. I wanted nothing more than to get out of the sad place.

"I'll leave now and call you later when you've had a chance to think. I can tell you, you need to do something for her. This depression will never go away on its own. She needs to accept what has happened and go on. If I can help her do that, I will."

I stood up and walked to the door. "Goodbye. I'll call you tomorrow."

***

I ran down the four flights of stairs, out into the street and over to Jack's car where he waited for me. Naturally, he had his nose buried in a file.

"Hey, here you are. How did it go?"

"Okay," I said, still trembling.

"Are you all right, Bria?" He put an arm around my shoulders. "Maybe this wasn't such a good idea."

"No, they need help. It's just hard." I finally let myself cry. Safe under Jack's arm, I let out my grief for the poor girl upstairs, for me and for the horrible state of the world. I finished and felt better for the relief. "Can you take me to your place? I want to call Mrs. Friesen and think on all this. Do some work."

"Are you sure?"

I told him I was and explained I couldn't tell him anything, and he should trust me and not ask questions—professionalism and all. I thought he understood and forgave him for the half-smile he wore, one I almost classified as a smirk.

A few hours later, Mrs. Friesen found the time to return my frantic message. The moment I heard her comforting voice, I wailed, "You were right; I'm well out of my depth here. I don't know what to do for them, but someone has to do something, and I'm all they have, at least for the moment. If I can convince the mom to seek professional help, I've done some good."

Her quiet dry voice told me to calm down and instructed me to describe the situation. After I had, she asked, "How did Jane Doe react to your presence and what you had to say?"

"She didn't; she sat staring off into space. I don't even know if she heard."

"She did. She's locked up inside herself right now, afraid to come out. Don't you remember, Bria?"

I curled up into myself and listened to a tiny voice say, "Yes."

"Then you know what's going on."

"But Mrs. Friesen, you're so right in everything you said. This is a delicate job, and I'm no professional like you. What conceited idea made me think I could handle something like this?"

"Stop berating yourself. You're not a professional, true, but you've been in her situation. I still maintain reservations but considering all you've told me, you would do better to try and fail than do nothing at all. You may not get through, but she'll hear you and, even years from now, remember your words."

I listened, contemplated her opinion and decided I would try. "Will you help me?"

"Yes, and I'll tell you why. You're still my patient and no matter what occurs with Miss Doe and her mother, I think the attempt will be of benefit to you."

"How so?"

"Remember something, Bria. We don't deal with our trauma once and call ourselves cured. Emotions have a tendency to come back and haunt us, sometimes when we least expect it. We must go through the process again and again."

"You sound as though I'm not as well as I feel," I said in more than a little pique.

"I think you're doing very well, perhaps too well. Our experiences always affect us, often in ways we don't recognize. Only later do we begin to appreciate why we do what we do, sometimes too late. Do you understand what I'm telling you?"

"Maybe. I'm not sure." I offered my usual evasion, but before she told me to think about it as she always did, I said, "You're saying I may do things based on past experience, unknowingly. Possibly things I'll regret."

"You've made a good start. The rest will come to you in time. I have faith in you, Bria."

I basked in her rare compliment. "Thank you, Mrs. Friesen."

"In the meantime, continue to visit Miss Doe. Don't push to get to the trauma itself. Ask her questions about her life, befriend her and learn what other factors may have led to this severe reaction to the attack."

In a casual way, as if speaking to a colleague, she added, "Puzzling, I've seen rape victims who just shrug the experience off and say, 'well it happened but it's over now.' Others shut down. There are always underlying issues. Understand?"

"I think so."

"Let's set up a time for you to call me on a weekly basis, say each Tuesday evening at 7 p.m. Does that suit?"

"Yes. Thank you. Goodbye."

I hung up the phone. She thought me capable, and if she thought so,

I probably was. I hauled out the rest of my journals from Jack's storage space in the basement and searched for the descriptions of my talks with Mrs. Friesen, and my responses at the time. They lay spread around me when I fell asleep.

I woke up later to the sound of Jack's voice on the phone to Mary, explaining I was sleeping and would spend the night. I heard her outraged voice clearly, and wondered why she got so upset, more so since we'd come back from Wyoming. I had told her nothing about what had happened there.

The next morning was a Saturday, but Jack was already out and at his office, as usual. I was full of schemes and plans and, after calling Mary to let her know I was fine and unravaged, I got right to work.

For a start, I needed a plan to get Lisa talking, not about the attack, but speaking at all. I wondered what she did with her time, all alone in the apartment while her mother slept days. She watched TV no doubt. I could suggest doing that together, and once she seemed comfortable, ask questions about the show and her life at school, her friends. A place to start. I pulled out a notebook and jotted down a list of safe subjects.

I called Ms. Pinelli. "Hi, it's Bria Connelly. Is this a good time to talk?"

"As good a time as any." Her speech was flat and lifeless. I wrote that down.

"Did you have a chance to look over those journals I left you?"

"Yes."

"Do you have any questions, any thoughts?"

"You came a long way." After a long pause, in a slightly more lively voice she asked, "Do you think my daughter will get better?"

"Maybe, I can't promise anything. May I come over sometime and spend some time alone with her? We'll watch TV and I'll be just another girl, a friend. I won't talk about the rape or anything. Having a friend may help, don't you agree?"

"Wouldn't hurt." She took a deep, shuddering breath and sniffled. "You promise you won't try and make her talk about that? She doesn't want to, not even to me. She cries and screams whenever I try."

"I promise for now. I'll be someone to spend time with, that's all, but sooner or later, she'll have to talk about the rape. She can't hide forever."

Ms. Pinelli sounded weary and terribly sad. "I guess it'll be all right. I don't know what else to do. My poor baby."

March 7, 1974
Journal 28, Jane Doe #1
Four months since the subject first spoke of the attack. She is now confident.

I started the entry but put down my pen. Jane Doe, Lisa, was ready to talk with law enforcement, but I was worried. She was anxious to the point of being sick, and categorically refused to allow her mother at the interview.

In retrospect, I hadn't needed much brainpower to figure out her current mind-set. She'd been doing something she shouldn't and now believed herself responsible for all that befell her; she was pickling in guilt. Her mother was hurt, feeling rejected and, as a result, angry and jealous of me. I walked on eggshells, trying to balance the two of them without getting involved. That would be so easy; they'd happily suck me in.

When I tried to explain to Ms. Pinelli how a victim might suffer guilt after such an experience, she cut me off.

"She went to take out the trash and he grabbed her. How could anyone call her guilty?"

Lisa had shut down again. Many questions popped into my mind, but I couldn't ask them, not with the two in the same room. I had to wait another week to ask Lisa, "Does your mom expect you to do the housework after she goes to work at midnight?"

"No." Lisa didn't see the next question coming, which surprised me.

"I was wondering, seeing as Mom doesn't think it strange you took out the garbage so late. You were, weren't you?"

"No." Lisa's eyes went blank and she turned off.

A few days later, I brought the subject up again. "What do you usually do when your mother's at work and you're not asleep?"

"Watch TV."

"Do you ever sneak out?" I smiled at her. "I would."

"Sometimes I go to my friends'."

"At night? I'd be scared, but then I'd never get the opportunity. How old are your friends that they get to stay up so late?"

She shrugged. "Some are older, some younger." She turned on the TV and watched in rapt attention. Our conversation was finished for another day.

More weeks went by and I was already talking with Carol, the young ADA Jack had introduced me to, preparing for Lisa to come in and talk to her. Allocution, they call it. I thought Carol a good choice for the job—professional and clinical, unlikely to gush out compassion. I knew from my own experience, nothing sets off a crying jag like pity.

Lisa was adamant that she was ready and equally stubborn about her mother not attending. I knew something was amiss but not what, so I called Mrs. Friesen.

"Be prepared for an adverse reaction," she said. "If necessary, perhaps you can reschedule the first interview at their home."

"That would be worse. Li—I mean Jane Doe won't talk at all in front of her mother. Remember, I thought she lied about the circumstances. Now I'm certain, but I'm unable to get her to tell me the truth."

"She must be truthful with her mother and get this burden off her mind. Make that paramount in your objectives." Mrs. Friesen made it sound so easy.

The day of the allocution dawned, and I woke up ill at ease, but tried to push the bleak thoughts away and prepare. I called a cab to ride over to the Pinelli's, fetched Lisa, who miraculously was ready and waiting, and we went downtown. I made sure to ask the cab for a receipt, as instructed, so Jack's office would pay me back.

She held up surprisingly well until Carol placed photographs of six men on the table and asked, "Is the man who attacked you here?"

Lisa blanched white as fleece and trembled but managed to lift one hand and place a finger on a photograph of a thirty something, bookish-looking man. Then she turned and vomited on the floor.

I put my arms around her and supported her as we left the room to the janitor and moved to another. Carol ran off, leaving us alone. After ten minutes or so, she was back with a glass of water.

Jack accompanied her and held the photograph in his hand. He asked, "Are you sure, positively sure, this is the man who attacked and raped you?"

Still hanging on to me, Lisa nodded in a definite affirmative.

I whispered in her ear, "You have to say it."

"Yes, I'm sure." The words seemed to bring her some relief. She straightened up, took several deep breaths and her voice grew stronger. "That's him. I'll never forget."

Jack motioned to a man in uniform. "Get a warrant and arrest this man."

I stared at him in surprise. "I thought you already arrested him."

"We had to release him. No choice. Not enough evidence to indict and convict—until now."

He patted Lisa's shoulder. "Thank you. You're a brave girl. We can punish him now, and he won't be able to hurt anyone else." He looked at me. "And thank you, Bria."

He left and talked with Carol out in the hall, came back and asked Lisa, "We need you to formally identify him in a line-up. Will you do that?"

This brought on another small panic attack but this time, thankfully, no vomiting. She spoke only to me. "I can't. I don't want to face him."

"Yes you do," I told her. "He won't see you. He won't know you're there. Right, Jack?"

Jack nodded. "Right."

I did my best to give Lisa the truth I'd learned. "You want to look at him and say to yourself, 'it's your turn to suffer now.' Believe me, I promise that will feel good."

She thought about this and wiped the tears off her face. "Only if you come with me."

"I will," I promised.

Jack said, "We'll set it up for tomorrow. I'll call your mother and tell her what's going on. We'll send a car to your apartment for the two of you and your advocate can meet you here. Okay?"

That started a new batch of tears. "Don't call my mother."

Jack sent an alarmed glance at me and back to Lisa. "I'm sorry, but I must. You're still a minor and so is Bria."

Lisa gave a strangled little scream that echoed down the long hallway. A couple of heads popped out from behind shut doors, looked around and disappeared again.

I took her hand. "Jack, can we use this room for a minute or two?"

As soon as the door closed, I turned to address her with as much firm insistence as I owned. "Listen, now is the time to tell your mother the truth."

Lisa paled again, shook her head and started shaking. "I can't. She'll be so mad."

"She might be mad for a minute or two, but she'll get over it." At least I hoped she would. My assumption was based on what Mary would do, but I put the thought away. "You can't go on worrying she's going to find out. Tell her. You'll feel better."

"I won't. Then she'll know." Lisa sat on the corner of the table wrapped up in her arms.

"Know what? That you did something stupid, like all kids do."

"No. She'll blame me," she cried, rocking herself. "If I was good, none of this would have happened."

For a second, I flew back in time to a place better left behind. I found Mrs. Friesen there, sitting in the background, telling me what to say. "Because you're not good enough, you deserved to get raped and beaten up."

Through dry-eyed sobs, she whimpered, "Maybe. I feel like I did."

I sat beside her on the table. "Tell me, what were you doing out so late at night?"

"Sneaking around. I'm not supposed to see Luke. He's sixteen and too old for me, and Mom says I'm too young. She's going to think the whole thing's my fault." She was sobbing out six months of guilt and remorse.

"You were simply in the wrong place at the wrong time. Okay, so you went out sneaking around with some boy. So what?"

In a shrill childish voice, she shouted, "But I shouldn't have been there."

"A woman I respect very much once asked me, does a bird deserve to be caught by a cat, simply because it wandered into the cat's back yard?"

"What a stupid question." She stared at me as though I was a great disappointment, probably out of my mind, and returned to rocking back and forth.

"No, it isn't." I was perplexed, disappointed the magic question hadn't set off new understanding, but glad she was at least no longer crying. "Tell Mom the truth. I bet she did some sneaking around in her life."

"My mom?" Lisa pulled away from me, puzzled, as if I'd spoken gibberish.

"Yeah. Do the math. She couldn't have been more than seventeen or eighteen when she had you. There was sneaking with boys involved somewhere, I guarantee it."

"Huh, my mother sneaking around," she said and began high-pitched, fast laughter that made the hair on my arms stand up.

"How else do you think she knows so much about it?" I laughed along with her, and she lowered her pitch to match mine.

"Will you help me?"

"No." I put my arm across her shoulders and spoke directly to her face. "She's your mother and I think she'll be happy you're talking to her at last."

Lisa sat studying her own feet as they swung back and forth under the table, then raised her head to look at me. "How did you get to know so much?"

"The hard way." I smiled to let her know her secret wasn't so terrible, and even though she didn't smile back, I knew we had crossed the river now and that, in time, she'd go back to living. "And tomorrow I'll come with you and your mom. We'll nail that son of a bitch to the wall, right?" I raised a clenched fist.

"Right." She returned the salute.

***

Later, Jack took me out to a Japanese restaurant. He wanted to try something new everyone was talking about: sushi. I personally thought the idea of eating raw fish was disgusting and best left to the Inuit up in the arctic, but to please him, I was willing to try. I was pleasantly surprised.

"Hey, this is good. What's this one?" I flicked at the colorful bundle with my chopsticks.

"Haven't a clue. Try it." He slipped something suspiciously like an octopus part into his mouth.

"Jack, the name you called me today, an advocate. Is that what I am?"

"Yes it is." His answer came out all muddled as his teeth worked on the fish. He put his napkin up to his mouth and discreetly spit it out. "Yuck, didn't like that one. Yes, that's what you are, and a damn good one at that. I think you may have found your calling in life."

"I don't know. It's so hard. There has to be something more than just picking up the pieces."

"Bria, in this world, picking up the pieces is all we can do."

Twenty-seven:
"So busy getting to know your delightful young ward."

1976
Bria

I was on a plane to Laramie, humming "Back in the Saddle Again" in my head while I tackled *Sleeping Murder,* twelfth in the series featuring Miss Jane Marple. The ability to do these two things simultaneously disproved Jack's contention that my continuing addiction to mystery novels would rot my mind.

Sunson and I were working toward our second World Championship, and he was famous. He had studded twice and Walter now trained his beautiful yearling filly I'd named Sunshine.

While not enjoying equal fame, I'd earned a lot of money, had a sports agent and a financial consultant, signed my own contracts and no longer had to travel under the embarrassing encumbrance of a babysitter. Now officially an adult at eighteen, my life was entirely my own, and for the most part, a roaring success.

My education hummed along. I graduated with my I.B., published my first paper, <u>Street Prostitution: a Study in Social and Economic Marginalization</u> and celebrated heartily when accepted as a third year undergraduate in Sociology at Loyola Marymount. Currently, I was up to my ears in research for my next paper: <u>Child Victims: Trauma and the Justice System.</u> Thanks to Jack and his colleagues, not to mention the proliferation of predators targeting children, I had an abundance of material.

Earlier in the year, a situation arose leaving me flabbergasted, although I'll admit to some secret satisfaction the fate often predicted for me afflicted the predictor. Mary announced, at the age of forty-three, she was pregnant for the first time. She would not agree to an abortion and

John was pissed off. So much so, she quickly found life only two doors down from John, Rose and the boys impossible and sold her house.

I withdrew some money out of investments and together we purchased a 640-acre farm close to the village of Chestermere, twenty minutes outside of Calgary, for $43,600 Canadian. The home was shabby, but the lure of a fabulous view of the Rockies and enough trees around to give a sense of shelter decided for us. Mary and Tara moved in right away, and I acted as sponsor for Canadian immigration. We bought a dog: a mastiff puppy named Tess.

I rented a broom-closet containing a single bed, a desk and a wardrobe incapable of storing a week's necessary clothing, in a student residence close to campus, and spent as little time as possible there behind a locked door. Some of those students were nuts. Mostly, I hung out at Jack's apartment. In fact, I lived with him—unofficially. If not for the risk of calling attention to my status, I would have asked him if I could buy a bed and move it in, the sofa being so beat up. Lucky for me, my spine still held a claim to youthful flexibility, but even so, I often awoke to stiff muscles.

Also, the year boasted another first; I had sex, such as it was. Ted said he loved me enough that he'd willingly give up his tomcat ways. I admit to a lukewarm reaction, but what the hell, for everything comes a time. I went to the Women's Health Center to get contraceptives, but Ted said I didn't need to; a case of mumps in puberty had rendered the problem moot. I guess sterility made him pretty much the perfect boyfriend for me, but considering all his other girls, I insisted he use condoms anyway. What do they say? The leopard doesn't change his spots.

But the biggest event of all? Jack finally found a serious girl friend: Leslie. Yes, the same woman who'd invaded my private paradise out at the lake, the one from New York. The one with the black lace bra. Mary and I secretly called her Messlie in honor of her striking resemblance to Jess, and neither of us was happy about his choice. Not jealousy on my side, I swear. I worked hard at learning to love Jack as my close, trusted friend and not as I wanted him to be. At least, I succeeded in acting the part and kept my warmer desires to myself. I had to, or lose him completely, and I couldn't stand the thought.

Leslie didn't buy my act, though. From the moment we first met on my seventeenth birthday, I received her message telepathically; she resented me.

Jack and I always celebrated our birthdays together and had since my thirteenth, but for this occasion, he brought Leslie along. I was to meet them at a fancy restaurant, and took unusual pains with my appearance. One of the few times I used any of the cosmetics Annie bought for me. I chose my creamsicle dress, the only one truly mine.

Jack wore a brand new suit that fit him, one Leslie picked out for his birthday, and he sported a new haircut—his normal shaggy curls but styled.

"Isn't he handsome in decent clothes," she gushed.

He looked like Jack.

After the formal introductions, when we still bothered to be polite for his sake, he had to take a telephone call. "Excuse me, ladies, I'll be right back."

"So you're Jack's little Bria? How happy to meet you. Jack speaks of you all the time." Her voice spoke to a child of ten. Her eyes measured my womanhood.

I returned the examination: good legs, nice cheekbones, professional makeup job, expertly dyed blond hair and boobs a Jersey cow would be proud to own. Even I recognized the clothes as couturier. What did she want with Jack? "Hello, how are you?"

Just then the maitre d' showed us to our table. He pulled out our chairs, pushed them back with us in them, flicked our napkins out of the stemmed glasses and laid them on our laps. Lucky for me, Annie also had a taste for establishments offering decent cuisine and slavish attention, so I knew how to behave.

After a few moments of silent contemplation, Leslie's fixed smile began to move. "I understand you're a rodeo star: how exotic."

"You live in Manhattan and keep a house in Nantucket—equally exotic to me."

Before I could ask her about life in her part of the world, she said, "Yes. I suppose it would be."

As I tried to decide if her tone was as waspish as I suspected, she added, "Jack says you're a student at Loyola."

How does one make conversation out of bald statements and no questions, I wondered, and lo and behold! She asked one. "Awfully young for that aren't you?" Her tone struck me as being a little snotty.

"I'm an I.B. student: college not university," I explained in my most gracious manner. Just to prove I knew how to converse, I inquired, "Jack told me you met through work. You're a lawyer?"

"Yes, criminal defense." She leaned forward, elbows on the table, displaying her perfectly manicured fingers. "Today I successfully interviewed with Barnwell, Getz here in Chicago. We're celebrating."

Yes, we are, you cow – Jack's and my birthdays. "You're moving to Chicago?" I inquired sweetly, through a warm smile, so she wouldn't know how much I already hated the idea.

"Yes, I am. I thought I might try a change of scene for a while." She smiled even brighter.

Determined to be happy for Jack, though I did think she could be nicer, I posed a polite question. "How do you like Chicago?"

"It's not Manhattan."

No joke. The smart mouth living between my ears said, *that's why we call it Chicago*, but I managed to keep this flippancy from flying out my lips.

Leslie smoothed the lapels of her gorgeous dove grey suit, and looked at me with a defiant glint of steel. "I'll feel better once we find an apartment and get out of the hotel."

She put extra emphasis on the "we," so I picked up on my cue. "We? Do you have kids?"

"No, silly girl." She eyed me as one cat does another. "Jack and I, we're looking for an apartment."

Unfortuitously for him, Jack chose that moment to appear at our table. I played naive. My voice pure silk, I asked, "Hey, Jack. You're moving?"

He flushed deeply and glanced at Leslie. "Thinking about it."

"Can I keep your old apartment? I can afford the rent and I need a place to work."

"*If* I move, you can have first dibs." He picked up a menu and studied the night's offerings with interest: his signal the subject was dead.

I was more than willing to bury the corpse and tackle him later, but Leslie wanted the body alive.

"If? Of course you're moving, darling." She reached out, stroked his face and purred at him. "I found us the perfect place. You'll love it. Marvelous."

Nauseated but not beyond torturing Jack a little, I threw my two bits in the pot. "Of course you're moving, Jack. It's a done deal."

Jack remained shielded by his menu and said nothing.

"And I'll take all the old furniture off your hands. You wouldn't have any use for that old stuff, would you, Leslie?" I was pretty sure she'd never been to the apartment. *I'd* never invite a Leslie there.

Her eyes narrowed a little. She saw through my ingénue routine. "I haven't thought. Possibly not."

"Clearly, you've never seen the place, or 'possibly' wouldn't enter into your mind. It only makes sense for me to take the apartment, Jack. This way I don't have to move out all my stuff."

Leslie's smile froze on her face.

Jack rotated his eyes sideways and surveyed me over the top of the menu. He didn't look at all amused, and I was mad enough not to care.

He put down his barricade. "Ladies, have we decided?"

"I haven't had time." Leslie glanced at us both coldly. "So busy getting to know your delightful young ward." She snapped open the menu and disappeared behind her handheld screen.

"Hey, Jack, are you up to bending the law just a little and giving me some wine?"

"No." His hard eyes stared at me steadily.

"Fine then, I'll drink water." I'd be afraid to give me wine too, the mood I was in. He owed me enough respect to tell me himself, the son of a bitch. I wanted to yell at him and demand he explain where he supposed I was to go. However unofficial, his place was my home too. I glared right back.

Seemingly unaware of the undercurrents flowing between us, Leslie emerged from behind her menu and forged ahead. "Bria, what are your plans for the future? Jack tells me you're quite the serious student."

With a voice coated in syrup, I answered. "Yes, well he helped me every step of the way, so he gets a lot of the credit. My plans? A degree in sociology and then law school. Jack says I must do law school. I plan to work in child protection."

"You're so ambitious for one so *young*. Tell me, which school do you have your eye on?" Her tone was as bright and shiny as a first day kindergarten teacher.

"I'm not even an accepted undergraduate yet," I explained, in the hopes of reminding Jack of my situation. "I'll stick with Loyola. I'm comfortable in the place, and they run a decent law school, good enough for Jack." Strictly for etiquette's sake, I returned the serve. "Where did you attend?"

"Columbia."

"Oh, what year did you graduate?"

Jack kicked me under the table, so with a buttery tone I apologized. "Oh, excuse me. That was too personal a question, wasn't it? Sorry."

Poor Jack. Torn between two bitches. And it got worse, much worse.

***

He did move into a new apartment with Leslie. It ended up like a picture from a magazine once Leslie finished decorating—all the latest colors and styles in a downtown tower close to the lake. I didn't spend much time there; not that I wasn't invited on a regular basis, but conversation with Leslie always had a competitive edge. Who could throw the most barbs?

Once I went to a house in the suburbs for a barbeque thrown by one of the partners at Leslie's law firm. She took me to meet our host and introduced me as, "Jack's young ward, Bria"

Before I could even say a "Pleased to make your acquaintance" and get to know the man, Leslie leaped in. "The young people are probably out back by the pool. Why don't you go join them, Bria, darling?"

Bria, darling stomped past Jack. "Where are you going?"

"To find the young people."

Out at the pool I found a few pimply-faced kids, maybe of my years but ages younger than me. I went back into the house and phoned one of my friends to come pick me up.

They were going clubbing, Keri said. Did I have my fake ID? Was I dressed for it?

"Bring me some clothes, the trampiest ones you own."

"Bria, I don't own any trampy clothes, thank you."

"Do your best."

I sat by the pool for eons. The young people stared at me as though I was a visitor from outer space. I stared back.

Jack finally came looking for me. "What's up?"

"Absolutely nothing."

"Why don't you come meet these nice people? You might find them interesting."

"I've been uninvited."

He threw up his hands in disgust and stalked away.

Keri and Michelle arrived, in their early twenties, gorgeous and dressed for the hunt. I met my tricked-out friends in front, changed in Keri's car, grooving to 'Dancing Queen' on the stereo.

I invited the girls in while I informed Jack as to my plans. Michelle sang, "Shake, shake, shake, shake your booty," and we warmed up our pelvic muscles gyrating our way to the patio.

The rumble of conversation ceased as the three glittering disco queens entered. I sashayed over to Jack in a pair of ridiculous platform high heels and passed him a bit of paper.

"Where I'll be tonight. Address and phone number but probably not till later. Much later. Good night."

"I'll pick you up tomorrow." He had his poker-perfect blank mask on.

Nonchalant as hell, as if I did this all the time, I arched my eyebrows and asked, "Breakfast, lunch or supper?"

"Breakfast, definitely breakfast." His face remained illegible.

I had the satisfaction of seeing the despairing look Leslie slung at him as I left.

The stereo blared, "Play that funky music, white boy," loud enough to entertain the whole neighborhood as Keri's Pinto backed down the driveway.

Twenty-eight:
"It's high time you moved on."

And then it happened—the showdown.

The next day, I stopped by their apartment to give Jack the final draft of my first paper. I wanted his opinion on my efforts, three years' work finished, done, complete. He wasn't home.

Leslie was, with a knife in her hand. "Come into the kitchen and watch me make a salad. I hoped for an occasion to talk to you."

I eyed the blade and decided I was stronger than she was and faced no real danger. I could take her down in a heartbeat and would probably enjoy doing so.

"What about?"

"You and Jack." The knife pointed to the bar stool at the counter. "Sit."

I stood. "Go ahead. Talk."

"I don't like how you behave toward Jack."

"Oh? In what respect?"

"I see how you're soaking your panties over him." She chopped briskly at a cucumber. I thought her actions an allegory of ill-bodings for Jack. She glanced up for an instant, malice on her beautiful face. "We're getting married. He's going to be my husband, and it's high time you moved on."

I tried to tell her the truth. "You don't know anything about me and Jack."

"You wear him around your little finger. This love-sick behavior has to stop." Three more chops and the cucumber lay in thin slices.

I tried again. "Are you sure Jack wants me to go, or doesn't he have any say?"

"He wants to get married—to me. Stop getting in the way." The sharp knife stabbed into a ripe, round tomato—my turn.

"I'm not. If Jack's desire is to marry you, that's his business. You want me to say I'm happy about it?" I stuck out my chin. "Here: I'm fucking ecstatic."

The diced tomatoes slopped into the bowl with sufficient force to puree them. "Enough!" she shouted. "You've made it damned obvious you don't like me."

"Because you don't like me," I retorted, but remembered Jack and how much I owed to his kindness and help. "I own up to acting the cheap bitch, but you've been up in first class as far as bitchiness goes. Admit it. As to my friendship with Jack, do you think that's your decision?"

"Yes." Chop. Chop. Four fresh green onions turned into confetti.

"Then I'm truly sorry for Jack. He thinks he's getting a wife. He's not. I know who you are. I've met you before."

"What do you mean?" Now the knife pointed at me.

"I had to live with a woman like you a long time ago. She was so insecure she thought she should control everyone around her, make all decisions, and isolate them from the people they love."

"What are you talking about?" Chop, chop—slam. Some purple-leafed vegetable I couldn't name lay in small bits on the wooden chopping block.

"You don't love Jack, not for who he is. You think you'll make him over into what you want."

She pulled out a bottle with a fancy label; extra virgin olive oil gurgled and bubbled across the salad. "I'm not going to stand by and watch you render a fool of my husband and me. Have you any idea how ridiculous he looks, running after a little girl with a bad case of the hots?"

"Jack loves me, so he can't love you. What a tiny, cold stone for a heart you must have."

Freshly ground pepper scattered from the wooden mill, a miniature piano leg.

"I'm not going to compete with a girl. It's you or me. You need to go."

"I wish I did like you; I could be happy for him. I'll go away, Leslie, but you're making Jack pay a mighty high price, don't you think?"

She rinsed fresh basil under the water. "I'm worth it."

"Does he agree? I hope you were up front about what he must give up to marry you. And who's next? His Aunt Mary, his father, any of his friends who don't meet your rarefied standards?"

The large aromatic leaves turned into ribbons.

"I understand he's helped you, but you need to put an end to this schoolgirl crush of yours. Let him go. Let him live his own life. Get one of your own. Get out of ours."

She sprinkled the delicate ribbons over the contents of the bowl.

"Jack loves me for being me and has for as long as I can remember. It's going to pain me to leave him, but he'll hurt as much, maybe more."

She tossed the salad with wooden spoons, a picture perfect mélange in a thick walnut bowl. "He'll get over it. We're going to make a life and I don't see any room in it for you."

"Don't worry; I'll take my young self out of the picture. Go ahead. Play with him. Fix him up. Good luck."

I reached forward, put two fingers under the bowl and toppled her creation onto the floor.

I slammed through the swinging door into the living room and found Jack, grey-faced, eyes hard and mouth a thin line. We stared at each other as "You little bitch!" flew out from the kitchen.

I tried to walk past him but he grabbed my arm. "Sorry, Jack. Please let me go."

"Will you wait for me? I need to talk to Leslie, then I'll drive you to your apartment."

"Better I just go." I grabbed my paper and carried it under my arm and out the door.

***

Later that night, as I lounged on the couch dressed in old pajamas, comforting myself with some ice cream, I heard a knock. "Jack, what are you doing here?"

"I came to check if you were all right. I want to talk to you."

"I think Leslie adequately expressed her feelings. What else is left? No, that's not true. There is something I should say. Come in."

He walked into the comfortable and familiar mess. "I'm sorry for the things Leslie said. Believe me, losing you is not what I want."

"I'm sure you are and I know you don't, but Leslie isn't regretful at all. If she was, she'd be here." I stuffed one last spoonful of ice cream into my mouth and tried to act as though nothing was wrong.

"I don't think she can. Bee—" he used his pet name for me, as thought the endearment helped his argument – "take some responsibility here. You haven't been fair to her."

"Ha!" I said. "She hasn't tried to get to know me one bit. All she cares about is my age and my looks, and can't get past appearances. I'm a younger woman and you love me—a threat." I finished off sadly, "She doesn't have a clue about us. Maybe she does care for you, Jack. I don't think so."

He stood, didn't even take off his coat. "I hope she does. We're getting married."

I curled back on the couch and stared up at him. "Why? I know it's a rude question."

He shrugged and as though I'd asked something very stupid, announced, "For all the usual reasons. I want a wife and a family."

"Kids with Leslie? Better hurry up."

His voice grew sharp. "Bria, stop this."

"Can't help myself." I searched inside for some honesty and handed him the best I found. "Believe me, I am sorry. I thought when you married someone, she and I would be friends and I'd be Auntie to your children. I never imagined having no Jack at all."

He grabbed one of the old kitchen chairs and sat down. "It doesn't need to be this way."

"It does." I wasn't being mean or childish. I knew for a fact, marriage to Leslie meant no Jack for me. "Can I ask you something?"

"Shoot."

"Did you think this through? You're not the family guy type. You, who never leaves work before ten without an urgent summons, and even then, you're rarely on time."

He leaned forward and searched my face. "Don't you think I'd be a good father?"

"Yes—an excellent one. I can vouch for that."

"But?"

I tried to make him see what I did, looming, waiting for him on the horizon. "Leslie is no Mary. Somehow, I can't imagine you arriving from work at six sharp each evening with a 'Honey, I'm home,' and all the little Connellys bound up to you, yelling, 'Daddy, Daddy.' Out in the kitchen is Leslie, happy and contented putting supper on the table for her beloved family. Not a likely portrait."

"You watch too much television." He tried to suppress a trace of a smile, and his condescension pissed me off.

"Possibly."

"Marriage isn't a TV show."

"Nor a magazine ad, Jack." I shot his barb right back at him and ignored the flicker of annoyance crossing his face.

I held my hands over my ears to forestall any comment and gave him my final nugget of wisdom. "I'd think when you ask a man why he's getting married he'd say because I love the woman and wish to share my life with her. Not I want a wife and family."

He stood up, hands stuffed in his pockets, his face grave and determined. "I know what I'm doing."

I hauled my body off the couch, pulled open the door and gave him my scripted speech. "All I can say is I wish you nothing but joy and success. I love you, Jack and always will. Because of you, I'm alive and able to take care of myself. Thank you, for everything. If you ever need me, you know where I'll be. Now I think you should go back to Leslie." I thought that as well spoken as anything on my favorite PBS dramas.

"Bria, don't—"

Like a puppy with imploring eyes, he silently pleaded, but I hardened my heart and did what had to be done. "Jack, you heard Leslie. If you want to marry her, you have to give me up. Go and get married. I hope you're happy; you deserve to be."

"I don't think—"

"I do. How about a hug for old time's sake? Come on, I promise not to let you kiss me."

And just like that, I set Jack free. No more annoying, big mouthed, little kid to look after.

I installed an answering machine and refused to return any of his phone calls.

I held no grudges, and tried not to blame him for leaving me alone. The girls back at Seven Oaks clued me in to the facts of life years ago: you only get help to the age of eighteen and then, ready or not, you're on your own. Jack gave me the gift of self-reliance, and in all honesty, was it his fault when, like everything else, independence came to me a little early?

A mere two months later, they married. Although invited, I did not attend the wedding.

Twenty-nine:
"God forbid! Sneaking, and with someone else's husband."

Annie brimmed over with consolation. "That man sure will be sorry when he wakes up and smells the coffee. Cheer up, the bloom fades quickly on old roses, and he'll be divorced in a few years and back on the market, up for grabs."

Strangely enough, I found her string of clichés comforting. "I don't mind so much he's married, Annie, but marrying *her*! I don't understand. A smart man like Jack, you'd think he'd see what he's getting into."

"He's thinking with the wrong head. They all do."

Hardly a comforting image. "Let's drop the subject and talk about something more fascinating: scheduling."

"August 15, the date for the Wyoming State Fair and Rodeo— definitely a biggie. We need the entry in by July 28th. Are you still sure you won't do the Miss Rodeo Wyoming contest?" That was Annie's idea of organization; we filled in all the things she wanted to do and worked around those.

"Positive," I said as I had every year, and pointedly added, "I'm going to be far too busy this season for that."

"Up to you, but it sure would be fun." She let out a heaving sigh of longing and dissatisfaction.

"For you maybe. You only hired me for my hair; the color matches your horse."

"Enjoy youth while you can." She rattled the ice cubes in her empty glass and went up to the patio bar.

"Have another cocktail, Annie."

I heard liquid glugging behind me. "Already got one. Where were we? August."

"Why are we talking about August when we haven't done June and July?"

"I want to make sure the Wyoming State Fair is a must do. August belongs to us." Her silver charm bracelet tinkled as she tapped the August planning sheet with her ringed fingers.

I pulled out July and waved the page around. "We're going to the Calgary Stampede in July. That's as big as rodeo gets."

"Dallas is bigger. Del loves Dallas. Make sure you write those dates in. Another must." She gave a hearty guffaw at God only knows what.

I summoned the little patience I had and reminded myself with whom I was dealing. "That's November; think June and July. I need to be in Alberta. It's high time for Sunson to get international recognition, and considering the eight rodeos I can do, the trip will hardly be a waste. Anyone who does well in Calgary is a star."

Annie swirled the contents of her cocktail glass and announced, "You'll be there and so will Sunson. And guess what, sugar? So will I. I'm coming with you."

You and Queen Elizabeth, I thought to myself, and jolted to attention as I realized she was serious. "Huh? That's kind of you, but Annie, our house is a bit rustic, not the lifestyle you're used to."

"Does the place have plumbing, a phone, electricity? Then it's a heap better than the one I grew up in. You think me a snob. You wound me." She clutched her chest.

I tried to explain the absolute improbability of our leaky two-storey farmhouse and my hard working family as a suitable environment for her. She couldn't be serious. "Mary is wonderful. She'll love you. And my Aunt Peg is the salt of the earth, but you wouldn't find much fun. My aunts aren't great partiers or shoppers either."

She *was* serious. "Your Mary will need help and I haven't had my hands on a baby in ages. This way you can give more time to Sunson. Besides, life gets dull around here without you."

What remained to say but, "I love you, Annie. Thanks."

"I love you too, sugar."

She left me to fill in all the forms, the waivers and proof of medical insurance. I hated paperwork. More, I hated I had committed myself to a crazy schedule, booked so heavily in clusters of rodeos that my travel plans were as busy as some delivery driver's route. Somewhere in between, I had to squeeze in my reading, attend lectures, take exams and write a paper.

For the first time, I had to do everything without Jack's help. So be it. I had a family to support and a new baby on the way.

Mary

I'm as big as a hot air balloon. Ten minutes is my limit for standing and after five, I have to use my hands to help my abdominal muscles. My ankles are twice the normal size. I can't sleep. There *is* no comfortable position. Someone put my hips on a rack and stretched them beyond imagination, and my baby likes to play with my lower ribs. Pregnancy is a young woman's job and I am not young.

My days now are languorous ones, spent shuffling from one reclining spot to another, where I doze. All my life I yearned for a baby and now, at a time when I should have been waiting for grandchildren, my long-ago forsaken dream is reality. Not as I expected, with no father in the picture. This baby's sire wanted him killed, demanded it. To hell with him. A life is worth more than a reputation.

I was sure the little one was a boy. John sired nothing but, and he felt like a boy—rough and active, probably a pro wrestler by the activity. My belly wobbled from one side to the other, and I pulled open my robe to watch. Definitely a pair of heels pushing just under my ribs. Dr. Bartlett said he was head-down, low and ready any day now. I hoped so.

I had to pee again. I hauled my bulk up, got my feet on the floor and stood. *Oh God! I didn't make it. I've wet the carpet and myself. Only it's not urine.* "Tara!"

She ran into the room, eyes big as saucers when she saw the puddle at my feet. "What? What's wrong?"

"It's time. Go get Bria. She's down at the barn with Annie. Get them."

She flew from the room. Two minutes later Bria, Annie and Tara fluttered around me.

"Get me some clean clothes and my suitcase. It's beside my bed. Tara, honey, can you get a towel or two and soak this up. Annie, help me over to the chair. I'm scared to move."

The girls scattered like frightened chicks to their tasks.

"Come on, sugar." Annie held my arm, put her hand on my back and eased me away from the wet.

"Slow down," she yelled at a sprinting Bria. "We've got heaps of time yet."

"Hang on a minute." Annie's hand slipped under my baggy robe and pulled down my soaked panties, reached for one of the towels in Tara's hands and gently dried me off. "Now, you just make yourself comfortable here. Any pains yet?"

"No."

"Good. No need to rush." .

Bria dashed back, suitcase in one hand and a tent of a dress in the other. She'd forgotten underwear. "One second."

"Take ten, sugar. Mary's fine. Simmer down. Tara, give me those. I'll clean this up. You go get a nice cup of coffee for Mary, good girl."

She took calm control of us, and I gratefully gave myself into her care. "Thank you, Annie."

"You relax. The first one always takes its time. I was in labor for a day and a half with Baker."

"That's not heartening."

She stroked my hair and grasped my hand. "Nothing's ever as bad as you fear. Don't you worry; as soon as you hold this baby in your arms, you'll forget all about the hard road to get him here."

"I'm frightened. I'm too old for this." I grasped her hand tight, grateful for her calm good humor, and jumped as a band of tension squeezed from my back to my front. "Oh."

"Nonsense, I know a woman who had a baby later in life than you," Annie said, one hand on my belly, her eyes on the clock.

I suspected she was handling me, but went along with her line. "How old was she?"

"Can't rightly recall. How old are you?" Our laughter calmed me down.

Bria was back, breathless. "I'll go get the truck."

"No, sugar, not yet. Let's sit around and talk a bit. The show hasn't started yet." Annie patted the seat beside her and lounged back in exaggerated relaxation.

"I'll get the damn truck anyway." Bria searched in all the wrong places for the keys. A few mumbled obscenities wafted through the air, until she pulled the keys out of the bowl where they were normally kept. She was off, with my underwear still in her hand.

Annie laughed her contagious chuckle. "I think I'd better come with you. That girl is wound up."

"Much as I agree, I can't do that to Bria. She's read every book written on childbirth, gone with me to the doctor, came to those classes. I won't."

"Let me talk to her," she offered, her eyes suddenly turning to the kitchen door. "Here's your coffee. Thank you, Tara."

Tara entered the room, delicately balancing a tray. "Auntie, are you okay?"

"Yes, sweetheart, nothing to worry about."

"Can I do anything?" she asked, shyly casting her eyes around and shuffling her feet.

Annie answered for me. "Tell you what, sugar, you leave your auntie to me and go finish those cookies you were making. We're all in need of a snack."

I thought Tara grateful for a reason to depart and silently thanked Annie for her quick thinking. Now if she could only do something for my older girl, who announced her return by the slamming of the screen door. In a second, she stood before us in the room, breathing hard

"Bria, will you give me those underpants still in your hand? Annie, can you help me get them on?" I stood up. The chair was soaked. Annie folded a blanket from the back of the sofa and set the pad under me.

Casually, as though making normal conversation, she asked, "Bria, don't you think I should go with your aunt? I've had three babies and know what's coming better than you."

"No. I can do this. I want to help Mary." Her expression when she turned to me broke my heart. "I'm ready after all those classes as your coach."

Annie put on a thick Southern drawl. "What do you know about birthing babies?"

Bria answered in kind. "Don't you worry, Miss Scarlett, I know everything 'bout birthing babies." In her own accent she added, "I've pulled calves out of cows, piglets out of sows, foals out of mares and puppies out of bitches. How different can it be?"

"Loads, but let's ask Mary. She's the one giving birth."

I wanted Annie but I chose Bria. The third contraction squeezed me tight, and I almost changed my mind.

"Three." Annie checked her watch. "Let's wait for the next."

Twenty minutes later, another, not too bad—a squeeze that held for a minute and passed.

Annie announced, "That's four, lots of time yet."

"Mary, you're supposed to walk around, remember." Bria had the Lamaze book in her hand and began reading instructions to me.

"Forget it. I'm fine sitting in this chair. Bria, find something to do other than stare at me. Go check if Tara's set fire to the kitchen yet."

"No. I'm happy right here, staring."

"Cheeky." A pain and fifteen minutes later, another.

Tara brought in a plate of fresh peanut butter cookies and as I reached forward to take one, my body tensed in the grasp of a contraction, stronger and longer than the last. "I think we should go."

Bria leapt from her chair. "Okay. Come on. Suitcase is in the truck. Truck is outside the door. Let's go."

Annie laughed. "Easy girl. You make sure and call us. Tara and I will be right by the phone, won't we, Tara?"

Tara was in tears. "Good luck, Auntie. I love you."

They waved as we headed out the driveway. Annie had her arm around Tara, holding her close, stroking her dark hair.

Bria drove like a bat out of hell, speeding down the highway toward Calgary. In the city, she cursed at slower drivers and fumed at red lights.

"Slow down. I want to get to the hospital alive—Oh, God!" The strongest contraction yet gripped me and stripped me of any self-control.

Bria searched both ways at the intersection and eased forward through a red light, hand on the horn. Praying for deliverance, preferably in one piece, my heart slowed only when we arrived at Grace Hospital. She stopped the truck right at the front doors, ran around the cab, opened my door and walked me in.

"She's in labor," she shouted at the women behind the desk, plopped me in a chair and ran out to park. She was back, breathing hard, before we'd started filling in the forms.

I was admitted. Written at the top of my chart, in bright red ink were some dire words: Stat: Mature maternity patient, first pregnancy, followed by three asterisks. Interpretation: too old.

***

Fourteen long hours later, I lay on a table in a surgical room. Masked and robed, Bria held one hand, her anxious eyes peering over the gauze. My own gazed at the mirror set up to reflect my exposed crotch. I'd never seen that part of myself in such detail.

Dr. Bartlett stood between my legs. "On the next contraction, push. We're almost there."

It came. I pushed. I pushed so hard I blacked out for a second.

Nothing.

"One more time, Mary. Push."

I bore down with all my strength. Over the doctor's shoulder, my reflected vagina bulged out, red and straining and still nothing.

I screamed. "I can't! I'm too old!"

"Need an assist here." She took something from the nurse, something of bright stainless steel.

She glanced at Bria. "Leave the room for a moment."

"No."

"I think you should."

"No."

The next pain gathered itself in the small of my back. I groaned, "Let her stay."

I began to bear down. I pulled myself up, half sitting. Something pushed up inside me. My body strained.

Bria worked herself behind me, supported me and urged me on, "Push, Mary. Come on, push!"

I sucked in a lungful of air and with every ounce of life left in me, labored down. Something hard passed from me.

"Here's the head. One more little push, Mary, you can do it."

The rest of my baby slithered out of me.

"I have him, a boy—a beautiful boy."

I had done it. I sagged back against Bria as the doctor's hands placed my son gently on my belly. He hadn't cried. His arms and legs waved frantically about.

Dr. Bartlett was busy tying off his cord.

"Is he all right?"

"He's perfect," she assured me.

Bria slowly let me down to the table. Tears sliding down her face, she looked from me to the baby and back again. "Oh, wow."

"I'm glad it was you with me."

"Me, too."

A nurse took my son away to the side of the room. She washed him and suctioned out his nose. He protested vigorously, wailing a thin, long cry, the most beautiful music in the universe. She weighed him. "Eight pounds, ten ounces." Once she had him wrapped up in a blanket and pulled a cap over his head, she brought him back to me.

I was too weak to hold him so Bria held him close to my face and opened his blanket. I touched him. His little fingers grasped at mine. He had long fingernails. Furry dark hair covered his head. His unfocused eyes, mere coal black sparkles under swollen lids, twitched open and closed, and jerked to the side as soon as light hit them. His scrotum seemed remarkably large for such a tiny body. My baby. My son. Mine.

Later, my son slept, safe in his acrylic bassinet in the nursery, and I rested in my room, aching in every inch of my being and more exhausted than I'd ever imagined possible. Bria sat in a chair beside my bed.

"Mary, what are we going to call him?"

"I'd like to name him after his father but that wouldn't be right. One John Connelly, Jr. in the world is enough," I said.

"I have it on good authority there are two pages of them in the Chicago phone book alone."

"But still, I'd like to—call it revenge if you want. How about Sean? That's Irish for John."

"Nah," Bria said. "Every second kid in our old neighborhood answered to Sean or Kevin."

"Or Michael. What do you think?"

"Hey!" She stood up in excitement. "Ian – still John, but Scottish. Ian Connelly sounds good."

"Ian Patrick Connelly. How do you like that?"

"Perfect. Can we call the question settled? "

"Yes, and you gave him his name."

She bent over and kissed my cheek. "I'd better phone home again. Annie wanted an update once you were pronounced fine and back in your room."

"Will you stop by the nursery and see he's all right? And then, Bria, go home and sleep. I could use some myself."

"I'll see you in the evening. I love you, Mary. And thank you for sharing this with me."

"You're welcome, darling. Now go. I need rest before you bring Tara to meet her new brother. That's who he is, a brother for you girls. Right?"

"Right." She flashed a thumbs-up and left with a breezy, "See ya."

I let myself drift off to sleep.

When I woke up hours later, I felt a little better, stronger, but the area between my legs ached and burned. The tight stitches down there tugged with every movement. The elastic belt holding two thick pads in place cut into the gelatinous tissue I once called my belly, and my breasts were strange, all prickly pressure. I buzzed for attention.

"I want my baby."

"Are you up to it?"

"Yes."

Ten minutes later the nurse returned, wheeling the clear plastic bassinet. Inside, Ian rested comfortably, his miniature legs and arms twitching, his mouth suckling at nothing.

"Do you intend to breast feed?" she asked.

"Of course I do."

"Well, it's early yet. You won't have much to give him, just colostrums at this point, but that's important, gives him your antibodies." She lifted him out of the bassinet and brought him to me. "Want to try?"

As soon as he was against my naked breast, Ian started rooting about. I pushed my nipple down to his searching mouth. He clamped on, jerked his head and lost his prize. We tried again. On the fourth or fifth try, we connected and he locked on and sucked briskly. My body twitched oddly in reaction.

***

I held him asleep at my breast, still marveling at his tiny perfection when Bria and Tara came in. Tara hung back shyly, her dark eyes filled with wonder.

I called her over. "Here he is, Tara, your baby brother. His name is Ian. Come and see him."

"He's so little."

"So were you in the beginning. You barely filled my hands. Do you want to touch him?"

She stroked his fuzzy dark head. "Can I hold him?"

I smiled up at my sweet gentle girl. "Yes, of course you can. You'd better get used to him. I'm counting on your help when we get home."

She sat down in a chair and held out her hands. Bria took Ian from me and as gingerly as though carrying priceless crystal placed him in her sister's arms. "Careful."

Tara glowered. "Yes, Bee, I know. I read in that book you have to support the head. Okay?"

"You don't know everything. You're only eight."

Tara's glare grew stronger. "I'm almost nine."

Bria pushed her exasperated face into Tara's, then ignored her and walked over to the side of my bed. "Mary, Annie's downstairs. She wants to see the baby."

"Why didn't she come up with you?"

"Wanted to give us a private moment, she said."

"What a lady. Well, go and get her." I caught the warning look she shot at her sister. "Tara's doing fine. You won't drop him, will you love?"

"No."

"See? Now off you go." I waved her out the door. I wanted to give Tara a few minutes alone to meet our new baby without her sister's interference.

Annie arrived carrying a huge bouquet of flowers and a tiny teddy bear for Ian. When she examined him lying in Tara's lap, she bubbled with enthusiasm. "Oh, look at him. Isn't he just the most precious thing you ever saw? Except for my own, that is. Can I hold him?"

Tara reluctantly relinquished him to Annie, who sat on the corner of my bed, expertly jostling his body into her arms. "Welcome to the world, little man. You don't know it yet, but you're the luckiest fellow. Look at all these females waiting to spoil you rotten. Lucky, lucky boy."

They passed Ian around, giving everyone a chance to admire him and praise me. By the time the nurse came into the room to take him back, we had all agreed; he was the prettiest and healthiest looking baby boy any of us had seen.

After Ian left, Bria appeared restless, shifting from foot to foot before the window, a sign she needed to get something off her chest. She wasn't asking for my attention, and wouldn't on a day like today, but I sensed she wanted me.

"Annie, why don't you take Tara down to the cafeteria for a bite? Would you?"

"Sure thing," Annie said and left, towing a disgruntled Tara.

"Honestly, Annie, they're always doing this. You can bet the talk's about something that doesn't need my big ears around."

"She's right." I chuckled at my little girl's astute grasp of the situation. "What's wrong, Bria?"

She looked at me over her shoulder. "Nothing at all, just something funny to share with you."

"Good. I could use a small laugh, not a big one though. What is it?"

"This."

She handed me an envelope addressed to Bria, with a return address of the Cook County District Attorney's office. Jack. Some of the sunshine seemed to quit the room. Much as I missed my dear friend, I wanted him to leave Bria alone.

I pulled out an elegant white card, embossed with gold lettering.

Mr. and Mrs. John Connelly
are pleased to announce the birth of their daughter,
Helena Louise
Born May 16, 1976 at Chicago Memorial

Aha! That certainly explains a lot. I decided against sharing this with Bria. Instead, I found something light to say. "Helena Connelly – too many syllables, don't you think?"

"I did the math, Mary. Jack is a moron."

"This explains the rush, but why is he a moron?"

"She got pregnant to make him marry her. She always did strike me as very desperate." She turned back to the window. "Stupid Jack, to fall for such an old trick."

"Jack is a lot of things but stupid isn't one of them. I hope they're happy. We don't like her, Bria, but he obviously sees something in her we don't. He did father a child with her."

She held up her hands as though holding melons. "He always was a tit man."

"Don't be vulgar," I corrected out of habit.

"I wouldn't marry someone who wasn't right for me simply because I was pregnant. I'd have my baby and look after it myself *and* make sure he helped me."

I chose to ignore her barb.

"That's you." I told her. "You and I know Jack well. He's not the kind of man who'd leave his child fatherless. He did the right thing."

"If 'right' means shackling yourself to a harridan. There's other ways to look after a baby."

"If she is, as you say, a harridan—and where do you come up with these words? – he had even more reason to marry and stay close to the child. I'm proud of him. And Bria, like it or not, he may love her."

"I hope so, for his sake."

She got up and turned back to the view of the Rockies.

"There's something else in here, a note. Have you read it? May I?"

Without turning around, she said, "Yes and yes."

May 31, 1976
My Dear Bria,
The enclosed birth announcement is self-explanatory. Fatherhood always did appeal to me and I'm pleased to have a little daughter. A son wouldn't be near as much fun or benefit from all I learned about girls from you.

I hope this finds you, Mary and Tara in good health and spirits. Thank you for the new address and the copy of your paper, which I judge excellent. You deserve highest praise for the work

Won't you talk to me again? I miss you more than I can say. You may write to me at my office, should you decide to take pity on me and pen me a line.

Love, Jack

"You notice, Mary, not one word about his beloved wife. He doesn't say if she survived the experience."

"He probably thought you wouldn't want to hear. So there's one question you can ask him when you answer this note. Is Leslie well and enjoying motherhood?"

She was silent for a moment. "I'm to respond, am I?"

"Of course you are. Jack's been good to you all the days of your life. You don't toss him out like yesterday's garbage because you don't care for his wife."

"I'm not sure I should start up again."

"You don't. It can never be the same as it once was. You sit down, write him a letter and tell him he has a new brother; we're all fine; school is going well; you've met lots of nice prostitutes. Open a door in the spirit of friendship and make sure things stay at that level."

Bria laughed quietly to herself. "And send this missive to his office."

"Yes. Well I don't like that part. It seems sneaky."

She whirled around from the window. "God forbid! Sneaking, and with someone else's husband. Shocking."

"Bria, honest to God, if I wasn't stuck in this bed, I'd smack you."

Thirty:
"Five years is a long time."

1982
Bria

I sat at the rickety old table in my seedy little apartment, reading, highlighting in brilliant yellow, scribbling notes, totally oblivious to the outside world, when the phone rang. Startled, I jumped up, knocking over a pile of books, which set off an avalanche of photocopies toward the floor. I muttered "Shit," and grabbed the still ringing telephone off the cradle. The tangled cord toppled my coffee onto my notes. While reaching for a paper towel, I managed to get the demanding apparatus to my mouth. "Hello?"

"Bria?" A voice from lives past stopped my heart.

"Hello, Jack." I tucked the phone between my cheek and shoulder and ripped several sheets off the roll.

"Mary told me I'd find you here."

"Why did you call Mary?" I mopped at the coffee, now dribbling onto the floor.

"To tell her and you my mother passed away this morning."

"Oh." I stopped mopping. "I mean, I'm sorry. Are you all right?"

"Yes."

"Is your dad?"

"He's not so good."

My mind refused to function. All I could summon was a string of well-worn banalities. "I don't know what to say at a time like this except to ask, is there anything I can do?"

"Come to the house on Saturday around three. Please?"

"Okay."

"Thank you."

Silence strained the line between us. I couldn't think of another thing to say, and waited for him to say good-bye.

Instead, he started talking, "I wanted to say thanks for your letters, as well." Then after an awkward pause, he asked, "How is my baby brother?"

"He's Ian. Please use his name," I snapped and, with the slow realization of how I sounded, made an effort to push away the foggy cloud in my head and soften my voice. "He's five years old, has a big nose and black curly hair. Sound like anyone you know? And also, just like his big brother, he has a will of iron."

"I hope to meet him one day."

"What's stopping you?"

My curt question led to another uncomfortable gap in the conversation. I smacked myself on the forehead and vowed to try and hold my tongue, as Mary often entreated me.

"I will."

"I received your last letter. Congratulations on the promotion, well earned I'm sure. I was sorry to hear Leslie lost her baby, but that was some time ago. I'm not current. Is she better?"

"Yes she is. Thank you for asking."

Before I could think of anything else to say, Jack spoke all in a rush as though uncomfortable and full of something he needed to get off his chest. "This is long overdue, I admit, but I'm sorry about my father, the way he handled Mary and the baby. I believe he thought himself trapped in an impossible situation. He was wrong."

"Don't make excuses for him. In my eyes he's a rotten bastard and one who hasn't sent us a thin dime, but come Saturday, I'll put my grudges aside and present him my sincere condolences, don't worry."

"In your place, I'd haul him into court."

"We're doing fine. I can take care of your brother and his mother. Quid pro quo, if you recall."

"I remember."

"Well then, you understand." Ashamed of my earlier belligerence, I searched for some appropriate words of comfort. "I'm sorry about your mother. She was good to me in her way, always feeding me and trying to save my soul."

"She's been more dead than alive for years. I consider the coronary a blessing, not a tragedy."

"I can't say. I haven't spoken to her for a very long time. But even in my youth, I thought her disconnected from reality. I don't believe she was unhappy, though."

"I hope not. Your words bring me comfort. It's good to talk to you, Bria. Is it possible to come by and speak in person?"

I couldn't help but catch the hopeful tone in his voice, and almost slipped back into my old ways and said yes. With all my heart, I wanted to but, for once, my head ruled. Mary would be proud. "No. I'm studying. I'm sorry."

"Don't be sorry."

I didn't say anything and Jack ended the conversation. "I'll see you on Saturday. We'll get a chance to catch up then."

"Perhaps we will. Good night." Most likely, we won't, I thought. Leslie wouldn't be at all pleased if we crept away to a corner and spoke.

With my coffee soaked notes spread on the counter to dry, I turned my attention to the photocopies lying strewn about, out of order. I scooped the mess up, patted the pages into a pile and dropped them in a box. My mind rattled, and further study tonight was out of the question.

I needed Mary to tell me how to behave on Saturday. This would surely be a tough one.

***

Five years is a long time.

The moment I entered the room, I saw him. He faced away from the door, talking to his brothers, and presented his profile. Gone were the shaggy black curls, his hair now closely cropped and grey at the temples —an improvement. He'd stopped hiding his strong features and showed his face without self-consciousness. While no one would ever call him good-looking, he was manly, very much so. I had to give Leslie credit; she'd smartened him up. He'd be thirty-seven. My God.

The second person I noticed was Uncle John, holding a drink. Judging by the flush on his face and slightly unsteady gait, the glass did not contain ginger ale. He was the first to notice my arrival and greeted me with the exuberance of half-soused drunks.

"Well, look at you. How's our red-haired girl? Damn, you're looking good. I heard you aced law school. Great going."

"Hello, Uncle John. I'm sorry for your loss." As I mumbled the well-worn platitude, I stuck out my hand.

John did not take it. Instead, he threw an arm across my shoulders and tried to hug me against him—the first time he had ever touched me. The smell of whiskey hit my nostrils and I flinched away. He said sibilantly, "Whatsamatter?"

Mary hadn't instructed me about such circumstances. I was at a loss.

From behind, hands landed gently on my shoulders and Jack's voice rescued me. "Come, Bria, say hello to the boys."

Uncle John chuckled heartily as I was led away. Muttering salacious opinions about us, he returned to his group of police buddies.

Mickey, Kevin, Joe and Adam, all grown men now, welcomed me in lukewarm fashion. Kevin had married Annabel from down the street. I used to play rounders with her at the baseball field. Today she had a plump baby in her arms and another in her belly. Joe walked a beat—figures. Kevin taught at an elementary school and had his girlfriend beside him: Kiko, tiny and Japanese. Adam wore a uniform, U.S. Navy. I asked him why, after growing up inland, he would choose that branch of the services. He wanted to see the world. Mickey, the baby, older than me by one month, worked as a bartender but of course, the job was only temporary, until he got his life together.

We caught up. I hadn't heard from or of them in five year's time. Pointedly, not a single one asked about Mary or their smallest brother. Mary and I headed up the lost tribe of the Connellys it appeared.

One person who made no appearance was Leslie.

Jack didn't look happy. Nobody did. The boys, especially those with wives, children or girlfriends, already gave excuses and prepared to leave, glancing at Uncle John as they spoke. It was only five o'clock.

Store bought food, mostly sandwich trays and cartons of potato salad sat untouched on the table. Over in the dining room, the police contentedly exercised their elbows and swapped stories. A buzz of female conversation from the kitchen told me where the wives congregated.

We stood face-to-face and unnoticed, so I asked, "Jack, isn't Leslie here?"

"She couldn't be."

"Is she sick?"

He looked uncomfortable. "No."

John's hearty voice interrupted our quiet conversation. He pointed his finger at us as he roared out, "Watch yourself, Bria. He's an old married man now. Hands off, hot stuff."

My face flamed red hot. For the millionth time, I cursed the pale complexion that exposed my emotions to the world. I wanted the floor to swallow me whole.

Jack jerked his head toward the drinking cops. "Please, Bria, let's get the hell out of here. Let's go to the park."

"Good idea."

I grabbed my windbreaker from the foyer. In their haste to leave, one of the boys or their entourage had knocked it to the floor, leaving footprints. I threw the soiled jacket on anyway.

***

We followed our usual route to the magic park, and so strong was the pull of nostalgia, I almost put my hand in Jack's.

He walked listlessly, like a man under a heavy burden. He looked tired.

"Jack, when did your dad's drinking start?"

He shrugged. "I don't know for sure, only been there for the last few days."

"Mary said he'd quit and would never drink again."

"Mary believed wrongly about a lot of things concerning my father." I thought he sounded angry. "I'm glad she had you to take her away from here."

"Are you?"

"That man ground to dust any woman he got his mitts on." His hands balled into clenched fists hanging at his sides.

"You're thinking of your mother."

"No, my father. Ma gave up a long time ago. Poor woman, even her funeral is all about him." Now I was certain. He was angry.

Without another word, we walked together to the bench canopied by the low hanging branches of a graceful elm tree—our old rendezvous.

"Well here we are at our favorite spot," I said. "Talk to me about your father. What do you want to discuss first? How much you hate him or how much you love him?"

"Neither, tell me about you." He kept his eyes focused on a spot clear across the park.

Something in his attitude left me feeling gentle, so I asked in a soft voice. "What would you like to know?"

"What you've been doing recently. For example, tell me why you were studying the other night."

"For the Bar exam."

He glanced at me for a second, those black eyebrows drawn up in the familiar expression of inquiry. "Why are you writing the Bar here? You live in Canada."

"Some little voice in my head said look, Bria, home may be Canada, but you spend as much time in the States. It wouldn't hurt to be admitted to one American Bar somewhere."

He turned back to gazing across the park. "And you picked Chicago."

"I have contacts in Chicago. I did my internships in social work here and now I'm doing a locum at the Public Defender's office, working with youthful offenders."

"Defense?"

"Have you seen me around your office?" I waited for a comment but got none. "They're just kids, screwed up kids. I like the work, and it's giving me lots of new material. All I do is take case histories, talk to the clients and make recommendations. So now you're up to date."

"I'm a little concerned about the voices in your head."

His attempt at humor only emphasized his air of sadness. He couldn't even look at me.

"Don't be. It's yours."

"Mine?" He perked up a little.

"When I have decisions to make, I often try to imagine your advice. You'll be happy to know these days we agree on almost everything."

My effort earned me a trace of a smile. "I'm proud of you, Bria."

"Thank you, that means a lot." Still the braggart, I added, "Sunson and I now have three World Championships under our belt. We'd be able to boast more, but the last three years were consumed by law school."

"How did you manage? I remember law school as an uphill race with a piano tied to my ass."

"I had to put my foot down hard on Annie and Del. I've been lucky to get in enough rodeos to keep my W.P.R.A. card."

"They agreed?"

"Annie's my good friend, another aunt, one with a lot of whimsies. We've done what we set out to do: made Sunson a star and Del a name in the horseflesh set."

Jack turned to face me fully for the first time. "So the rodeo adventure is over?"

"No. How else am I supposed to pay for my extravagant lifestyle: the drafty old house in Alberta and the shoebox, once your apartment? Lucky for me, the bungalow in Wyoming is a perk."

I smiled at him, a reward for letting me talk to something other than his ear, but his reactions were not as they had been. No attentive eye contact, no sense of connection.

"Bria, you must have a gypsy in your background the way you travel around."

"I suppose anything's possible, my paternity being the big mystery it is, but how many red headed gypsies do you think there might be?"

His mouth remained a sad, tight line.

"Jack, am I losing my touch? I never before had to expend so much effort to get a smile. Amusing you used to be my biggest talent."

For an instant, he was there with me. "I miss you Bria. You left a hole in my life."

"Don't say such things."

We both stared out across the lawn.

A mother towing three small children entered the park. Mom collapsed on one of the benches and sent the kids out to frolic. Their play lasted all of two minutes, and back they came, demanding and whining. The mom, a tired expression evident even at a distance, picked up her shopping and left.

"Did you bring a picture of your little girl, Helena? Is that how it's pronounced, like the capital of Montana or did Leslie add an exotic twist to it?"

"The capital of Montana. Here she is, on her fifth birthday." He handed me a photograph of a little girl sitting on his knee, a Barbie doll in her hand.

"She's lovely, Jack. She has your coloring, same curly black hair and big dark eyes. She's going to be a knockout."

"Thankfully, not my profile. That she got from her mother."

I had to ask. "Why hasn't Leslie come today, or am I too nosy?"

He immediately found that fascinating spot far away again. "She's in New York."

"And Helena?"

"With her."

"Working?"

"She left me eight months ago." He clenched his hands again.

No great surprise, but for Jack's sake, I pretended. "Why?"

"She said I work too much. I'm a drone."

"And the queen bee wants a full-time consort." I exhaled a nasty little laugh that left me instantly ashamed. "I'm sorry. I promised Mary I wouldn't let my cat self out today."

"Go ahead. Don't worry. Anything you can say is mild compared to what I think."

My mind jumped to the Illinois statutes. Family law is subjective, best interest of the child, but still, there are rules.

"She can't just take your daughter and move to another state."

"Well she did and what am I supposed to do? Keep Helena here with me, all alone? How can I look after a five-year-old by myself?"

"Don't surrender. Do you visit her?"

"In New York. I go whenever I can. Something else I need to tell you."

"Shoot."

"Aha. Don't pick up all my quirks." His eyes finally met mine and for an instant, we connected. "I'm moving to New York."

Shaken, I whipped up what self-control I could find and masked my inner reaction. "Wow. Chicago won't be the same without you. Are you and Leslie making up?"

"Don't know. I think we're a lost cause but I need to be close to Helena. I can't leave her alone with her mother." His face tightened. "No, let's not go there."

"What can I say? I'm sorry."

"As long as it isn't 'I told you so,' fine."

"I would never."

"Right," he said, sarcastically, followed by a bitter chuckle.

We both fell silent and sat side by side, deep in our own thoughts.

Leslie had won. Even if she no longer wanted him, she'd found a way to take him from everybody he loved. Did she care for Jack one whit? His whole life was in Chicago.

"What about work, Jack? You wrote you'd received a promotion."

"Yes, but this is a lateral move. I'm going to the District Attorney's office in New York County, Manhattan, the center of the universe, according to Leslie. I'll be a Bureau Chief. I'm a good prosecutor, Bria. I have an excellent record. They snapped me up."

Five years with no contact and now I was sorry. Even when not on speaking terms with him, I felt safe and supported knowing he was one phone call away. He would have come to save me; I knew that. And now he was leaving for good.

"When?"

"I'm traveling back and forth now, cleaning things up here and starting there. I think I'll be permanent in three to four weeks."

"Have you told your father?"

"Last week. I'm living in his house whenever I'm in Chicago, back in my old room, if you can imagine. I couldn't wait to get rid of that damned apartment. I can't afford the rent on my own. Leslie's family is dripping with money, and she has no idea how the rest of us live."

I reached out and put my hand on his. Quick as a trap, his turned over, grasped mine tight and held it. His head hung low, staring at our hands. When he spoke, his voice was hoarse.

"I'm doing this for Helena, all for her. Not having her in my life is unimaginable. Everything I've done has been for her all along, since I first knew Leslie was pregnant. I couldn't let my child grow up without a father, not after knowing you and what that means."

His hands pulled mine up to his face. He kissed my fingers and let go. I almost choked on his pain and honesty. Mary had understood. Several minutes passed before I recovered the ability to speak.

"You'd never leave your own little girl alone. You did the right thing, unlike some I could mention by name."

"This brings us back to my father. I don't want to talk about him. I'm too damned pissed off."

He returned to his brooding.

A teenage couple wrapped up in each other's arms did a swaying waltz over to a bench on the far side of the lawn. For a few minutes we watched them neck.

"Bria, I'm ashamed of myself. I let Leslie drive you away. I worried so much for the child coming, I lost the one I already had, and I let you down. I was damned grateful when you started writing to me."

"Girls grow up. Don't you ever listen?"

He laughed at last and lit a cigarette.

"Happy now? You made me laugh."

"Yes. Now I'm unhappy about something else. Why did you start smoking again? You worked so hard to give it up."

"The last few years … I'm lucky I'm not drinking like my dad."

"Speaking of whom, shouldn't we get back and assess the damages, get that nest of cops out of the house? Tomorrow when he's sober, you can talk to him. Get him to go to a meeting. He'll be all right."

"I hope so. We're friends again?"

"Of course, you're my Jack, finest man I know, always will be. I still love you."

For the first time in five years, he wrapped me in a hug. I was careful to hold only my upper body against his and when I kissed him, I pressed my lips to his cheek.

On the way back to his father's house, I felt lighthearted and enjoyed walking around the old neighborhood with Jack. I thought him in better spirits, too, so I slipped my hand in his and commented on some of the changes, and the state of various houses and yards. I walked and chattered along beside him, and he quietly listened, just like the old days.

We fell back into our old banter when he casually asked me, "How's your love life?"

"Ted, the long tall cowboy from Montana, remember him? We've been at it since you told me no."

"At it? Sounds like the height of romance."

"Nope, merely convenient. I have no desire to live with him, nor he with me. The perfect relationship."

"So cynical. Don't you want to settle down and get married, Bria?"

"No way am I handing over control of my life to someone else and certainly not to Ted."

"Marriage doesn't have to be that way."

"Well aren't you just the prime example? Besides, I already have a wife and family."

He laughed, this time wholeheartedly. "I certainly missed that mouth."

"I'll bet."

Thirty-one:
"No balls."

We opened the door to his father's house, stood in the foyer listening, and heard a couple of male voices, thick and slurry, arguing. We stepped into the living room. The place was a mess. The only ones left, Detective Bauer and Jack's dad, sat at the formal dining table, an open bottle of Scotch between them.

Jack strode over. "Call you a cab, Nick?"

He started picking up bottles and throwing them into a trash bag. When he reached for the Scotch, his Dad's heavy hand clamped down. "Leave that alone."

I went to the kitchen. Obviously the women had left in a hurry. We had work to do. I found a plastic basin under the sink and took it with me to start collecting dishes.

Jack stood at the phone giving out the address, presumably to a cab company.

Over on the dining room side, John grumbled to Nick. "You don't have to go. Don't mind him. He isn't the law around here. I am."

Nick was as stupefied as any bum in the gutter. "S'not a problem, Captain. Time to get home to the old ball and chain."

"Pussy whipped the lot of you and him"—John jerked his thumb at Jack – "he's the worst. No balls."

Jack continued picking up empties and paper plates.

I moved back to the doorway. Drunks. I feared them.

John slugged down a mouthful of whiskey directly from the bottle. "None at all, and now he's running off to New York after that cunt he married. Knocked her up and had to marry her, didn't you?" He glowered at Jack. "Fucking pansy. Oh hell, yes, he can use fancy words. Can't keep his woman though, can you? No balls, that's your problem."

Nick put his hand on John's arm and sloshed out placation. "Come on, Captain."

John shook it off. "No balls! I thought I taught you better. You show a woman who's boss right from the start." He raised his closed fist and waggled threats at Jack.

Jack ignored him, went on picking up.

"Hey, pansy ass, you missed one." John grabbed a paper plate laden with food and flung it in Jack's direction.

Jack threw the mess into the trash bag and didn't look at his dad.

"Running off after a woman, what's wrong with you? Ya should stay here. You listen to me. Stay here. I could make something out of you."

An empty glass flew at Jack. He deflected it with one hand and went on about his task, seemingly oblivious to his father's animosity.

Nick tried to grab John's arm, missed and fell off his chair. His head wobbled as he looked up at me. "Get'im a coffee."

I stayed where I was—rooted.

"Fucking useless son of mine. Should stay here. You could have been something. District Attorney. Senate. Could finally make me proud. No balls. No balls at all."

John tipped the last of the Scotch into his glass and slammed the empty down on the table. "He's useless, no good. Always has been. Always will be. Couldn't keep his woman. Pansy ass."

The bottle hit Jack in the shoulder. He pretended nothing had happened, just went on picking things up.

"I kept my woman." John's voice roared. "She knew what was what. She knew who was boss. No man lets his woman run around on him." He pointed at Jack. "He did. Not me, I'm a man. Kept my woman at home, had any others I wanted too. She didn't tell me what to do. I showed her. I got balls."

He picked up the crystal bowl from the table, hefted the delicate thing, ready to throw at Jack. It was Rose's prize possession.

I ran forward to stop him. "No, don't." Too late.

Nick grabbed John's arm. John wrestled himself away and the bowl hit the wall, smashing into a million pieces.

Nick tried to hold him. "Come on, Captain. You don't wanna do this."

John's bleary eyes swiveled to me. "Hey, Nick. Did you ever meet Jack's little cocksucker?"

He glared at me.

I froze. The smell of whiskey nauseated me.

"Yeah. The pansy got tired of fucking a baby. Thought he was ready for a real woman. Couldn't keep her, though. What're you going to do now, boy? Go back to your baby whore. Here she is, waiting for you."

I backed away until I hit the wall and stood, unable to comprehend. *Is this what he thought of me all these years?*

Jack finally spoke. "Nick, cab's here."

"Maybe I should shtay."

"No." Jack grabbed him by the collar and belt and half carried him to the front door.

Nick stood swaying in the doorframe. "Maybe I should help."

"No. You've helped enough." He dragged him out to the cab and tossed him in the back seat.

The front door slammed. Jack entered the dining room. In four steps, he stood before his father. His fist shot out. It landed square between John's eyes.

John slumped slowly sideways and slid out of the chair and onto the floor, where he lay motionless, the bubbles in the blood seeping out his nose the only sign he lived and breathed.

I broke my paralysis and went to him, got down on one knee and examined him. I couldn't make myself touch him though. His nose, already swollen and deepest red, lay flat and askew on his face.

"Oh God, Jack. What have you done?"

"I hope I broke his nose." He walked over to the phone. "I need an ambulance at 6556 South Laflin. My father is inebriated; he's fallen and hurt himself. No, it's not an emergency. He'll survive. Thank you."

John groaned. I scuttled away from him as he tried to sit up. His eyes blinked open, slits in the swelling bruised flesh.

"What the…? My nose."

Jack stood over him. "An ambulance is on the way. You fell and hit the table."

"I didn't fall. You—"

Jack reached down, grabbed John's shirt and hauled him up on to the chair. His face was cold as frost and his voice sharp. "A gift for my mother. You want another—for me?"

"Oh Christ. My nose, help me."

"See you, Dad. Come on, Bria, let's go."

"Shouldn't we stay, wait for the ambulance?"

"What for?"

***

The calm control abandoned Jack as we approached his car. "You drive."

I got in and started the engine. "Where are we going?"

"I don't know. Wherever you want."

I drove to my apartment and all the way, Jack said not one word. He sat staring straight ahead but I doubted he saw a thing. We parked; I got out and went around to his side. He hadn't moved. I opened his door and took his arm. "Come on, Jack."

I led him into the building and up the three flights of stairs, unlocked the apartment and pulled him in. He was a zombie. I had to lead him to the couch and tell him to sit down. I had only a half bottle of cheap red wine in the place, so I poured him some and turned back to give him the glass.

I found him bent over, elbows on knees, face buried in his hands. His shoulders heaved and he groaned, twisting in spasms. I had never seen Jack cry, couldn't believe he had tears in him. He was always such a rock.

My heart twisted in my rib cage. Slowly and quietly, I lowered myself gently beside him, tugged his hands away from his face and kissed his wet cheeks, embraced him, pulled him to me and rocked him while he poured out a lifetime of grief. His arms grasped me, and he sobbed in gasps that racked his body. I stroked his hair, crooned baby talk in his ear and wept with him.

Once he quieted, I slipped off his jacket and pushed him down, tucked a pillow under his head, pulled off his shoes and covered him with a blanket. I kissed his cheek again. He murmured, "Thank you, baby," and slept within minutes.

I went in my bedroom, closed the door and called Mary.

A couple of hours later, I made leek and potato soup and toasted some two-day-old bread into croutons. I found a half-dried slab of provolone cheese in the fridge so I topped half potatoes with the grated remains, and baked them in the oven. I set a simple table for two, including a glass of the cheap red wine for each of us. When all was ready, I went to wake Jack.

I studied his sleeping face, familiar with every square inch of it. Those features had played a part in all the twists and turns of my life, helping me, saving me and loving me. I reached out two fingers and stroked his long nose, following the bend of the sudden detour to the left. I softly touched his lips on the side of his mouth that didn't work anymore. I remembered the crunching noise when John's face met Jack's knuckles, and pictured a much younger Jack, wondering what sound he'd heard when his father's meaty fist destroyed his nose and jaw. His eyes opened.

"Hi. Feel better?"

"Considerably."

"I made us some supper, not much I'm afraid, but you should eat."

"Anything will be fine. What time is it?"

"Tomorrow is Sunday. Time doesn't matter. Come and eat."

"Yes, ma'am."

We ate. The soup turned out good, better than I'd hoped. Or maybe anything would have been satisfying. I offered him Oreo cookies with instant coffee, the best I had. He accepted.

Neither of us mentioned all that had happened that day.

Finally I said, "I talked to Mary."

His two hands curled around the big mug. He lifted it up to his mouth, took a sip. "You told her?"

"Yes, Jack. I tell Mary *almost* everything."

His eyes roamed the two-room apartment. Not much had changed, except for the addition of some curtains. I wondered what he searched for and was about to ask when he snapped out of it. "Are you going to tell me what she had to say?"

"She said I should bring you home."

He shook his head. "I can't."

"So I told her. She asked me to tell you she loves you and prays for you every day."

"Give her my thanks."

I pointed to the phone. "Thank her yourself. You know the number."

"I will one day. Bria, I should get going. I need to get a motel room or something."

He started to get up, then slumped back in his chair, cradling his head in his hands. "Give me a minute."

"Stay here."

"Good of you, but honestly, I couldn't take a night on that couch. My back is killing me already."

"No. Stay here with me." I reached out and touched his face, letting my fingertips trail along his high cheekbones and down to his uneven jaw. I ran my thumb across his mouth and whispered, "In the morning, if you decide we made a mistake, we can pretend it never happened."

His eyes were two pools of blackness.

"You want me, Jack."

"Yes."

"I'm all grown up, twenty-four, almost twenty-five. I'm not your young girl; I never was. She lives in New York, so don't confuse us. You and I—our love is different. Admit to your real feelings, just this once."

He reached out and caressed my face. "You're so beautiful in every sense of the word, but, Bee, I'm a mess. It wouldn't be right."

"I don't care. Right or wrong is so meaningless. What does it matter? We could take a little time just for us: one night, two nights, a week, whatever works out. At the end, you go to New York and me to Alberta, you to your family and me to mine."

I lifted his hand to my mouth and softly kissed his bruised knuckles. "And we'll still be friends. Always."

I held my breath. I wanted him so much.

"All right."

I got out of my chair, sat on his knee and put my mouth on his. I did all the things Mary told me not to do.

Thirty-two:
"Three and a half weeks."

The next day, we drove over to his father's house to get his stuff. Jack pulled out his key and opened the door. From somewhere inside, we heard John say, "Son?"

Jack didn't answer and climbed straight upstairs to pack.

I went into the garbage littered living room and found John. His nose was a heap of white tape, his eyes swollen, angry red and deep blue. He looked up. "Where's my son?"

"Upstairs, getting his stuff."

He glared at me. "I want to talk to him."

"Not my decision."

His manner and voice changed. He whined. "Bria, tell him I'm sorry. Blame the drink. I'll never let this happen again."

"I'll tell him."

He begged. "Make him believe."

"I don't think I can."

"He's my son."

The wheedling, self-pitying manner stuck in my craw. I yearned to grab him by the shirt and shake him until his brains fell out. I wanted to scream "How could you do that to your own child: smash his face and ruin his looks, tell him he wasn't good enough for anyone." But I didn't.

Instead, I took out the photograph Mary had asked me to give him. "You have six sons, John. You've treated them all badly but Jack was the first and he got the worst. Just to prove I'm not a heartless cocksucking baby whore, I'll leave a picture of your youngest here."

I placed Ian's fifth birthday portrait on the table and walked outside to sit in Jack's car until he had loaded his possessions—four bags.

We drove home to the little apartment we had shared since I'd been a girl of thirteen. Two damaged children together again, helping each other heal our wounds. We had three and a half weeks.

***

He gave me the sweetest, gentlest time of my life.

Jack's smooth and silky caresses, his low voice always telling me how pretty and lovely and sweet smelling I was, and the delicate tracings of my body with his tender hand, ending between my legs and touching ever so softly as he whispered, "Oh, my precious girl," excited me. I came just like that, a new experience. He was so happy about it too. "You look so surprised."

I was. I told him so.

He put his hand over mine and showed me where and how he liked to be touched and then kissed me and told me how good it all was and how well I did it.

If Jack had anything more to teach me in life, I couldn't wait.

He also helped me cram for my exams every evening. The night before I sat, he said I should go to bed at nine o'clock and he would suffer the couch but I told him, "I don't need that kind of sacrifice."

After the exam, we went to an Italian restaurant and had a fabulous meal of veal and steamed mussels, along with a bottle of excellent wine. I wanted to pay but we compromised on sharing. We had a good time.

I even told him my secret fantasy, the one where I find my mother and she does love me and always has. He cuddled me and said he'd tried long ago. Her pension checks from Veterans Affairs remained uncashed for years, and while I might never learn what became of her, if she was well or not, perhaps it was best to leave alone those who don't wish to be found.

Once I wondered out loud if all families were as screwed up as ours. He said he hoped so. He didn't like to think we'd been singled out for punishment. Mrs. Friesen popped into my head and spoke through my mouth. "Only the luck of the draw. Don't question fate. Accept and move on." He liked my answer and we talked more in that vein.

Those three and a half weeks revolved around Bria and Jack. I thought he felt better by the time he left, not so beat up and dejected. He'd write to me soon and let me know how he was. Maybe I'd visit him in New York one day and when I did, he promised to take me to the top of the Empire State. I said I looked forward to the event, but we both knew it would never happen. He kissed me goodbye and thanked me for all I had done for him. He said he loved me, always had and always would.

I told him to take care of himself and to think before he acted.

He laughed. "What a reversal of roles."

The week after Jack left Chicago for New York I completed my locum at the Cook County Public Defender's Office, Youth Offender Division, and gave up my apartment. Chicago held nothing for me anymore. My landlord would forward any important communications.

It was an interlude and possibly a gift from me to Jack.

And if anyone wanted to know, I could attest to the fact Jack did have balls.

***

Well of course, my Accu-Test results read positive, no room for doubt. The pink stripe lit up like a neon tube, and no, the news didn't come as a surprise. Six years of Ted, six years of no need to think about contraceptives meant I never developed the habit. I dove into bed with Jack and when the potential consequences did enter my mind the following morning, a lightning bolt hit me: have a baby. The idea became a yearning, the yearning an obsession, and the obsession a compulsion. An irresistible directive.

When Jack asked me, a hoarse whisper thick with desire, I lied. "Sure I'm on the pill," I told him. "Have been for years." Devoid of any further thought, I went about giving conception a good shot.

My periods, as regular as the monthly bills, didn't show up on schedule. I took the test and certainty slapped me in the face. I was pregnant. For the first time, and woefully belated, I asked myself why.

The worst part had to be telling Mary, strange as that might seem considering her circumstances. Some years back, I had foolishly told her about Ted and the mumps to quiet her concerns of the contraceptive kind, so I couldn't count on her jumping to natural conclusions. Jack and the three weeks in Chicago remained my little secret. Now I had to fess up.

I waited until one morning when we found ourselves alone in the big farm style kitchen. Mary collected the breakfast dishes and I washed the pots and pans. I took a good long look around, enjoying the peace while I could.

From where I stood at the sink, I had a fabulous view of the mountains and the city in the valley, twenty miles to the west. Our yard with its trees, bushes and vegetable garden lay immediately outside.

Everything was finally green again.

I hung the pots and pans on their hooks over the large range, grabbed the wet cloth, wiped the grease spatters from the old round-shouldered refrigerator, and washed down the wooden butcher-block countertops for good measure. I almost forgot my mission in the comfort of these everyday chores.

Fresh water running into the double sink reminded me, and I turned to Mary, telling her all about Bria and Jack's interlude, how special a time we'd enjoyed. "The end result is I'm pregnant." The tale, complete with long-winded explanations, took forever, and all the dishes sparkled, clean and drying in the rack long before my story ended.

Thirty-three:
"You simply must tell him."

"Poor Jack, tired and worn, and you chose then?" Her face was an open accusation.

"Poor Jack, yes."

She rapped the back of my head with her knuckles. "Don't be smart."

"Don't start spouting morality; we've known each other far too long and too well. And keep your hands to yourself."

"Yes, poor Jack. Here he is trying to rebuild his life in a new city and you're about to drop the bomb that he has another child on the way."

"No I'm not and neither are you."

I had never seen her so *shocked*. She stood stock still, open-mouthed, wide-eyed with her hands on her hips. Her head started shaking long before her mouth could say, "You can't do this. He has rights. He's the father."

"I'll tell him one day, I promise. But not today."

"Why? At least let me try and understand."

Help her? I couldn't comprehend myself and, certainly, I was not yet ready to examine the question. When it came to the why, I had nothing to tell her and opted for evasion.

"I'm not getting into a debate with you. This is my decision, and if you go behind my back and blab you'll put one big kink in our friendship."

"I wouldn't. I simply asked why."

"You would. And why? She needs him a lot more than we do."

"Not the why I wanted answered but as you brought it up, which *she* are we talking about – the wife or the daughter?"

"Take your pick. And if you're asking me why I'm pregnant, if you can have a baby, so can I. I help you and you help me."

She reacted as though I had slapped her and stared at me with a hurt expression. That was round one. A few jabs, some light sparring, nothing serious and we retreated to our respective corners to regroup. My corner was my bedroom, and I left Mary to fume and fret alone in the kitchen.

The next morning, I stumbled into her domain, grabbed a cup off the open wooden shelves and as I was about to pour some coffee, she ambushed me.

She stood studying me for a bit. "Bria, I can see fifty without squinting. Another baby, now? You're asking a lot." She came at me from a new angle with the same destination in mind.

I decided to be direct. "Yes it is and I'm asking. Will you help me?"

"Are we to pretend this is my baby and I'm to be mother? I'm a little old for the part."

"Of course not," I said in an offhand way. "Don't be silly. I thought I'd teach my children to call you Nana."

"Then I will be Nana, but Bria, you'll only be twenty-five when the baby comes. Why are you always in such a hurry?"

Her favorite themes: 'slow down Bria you go too fast,' right up there with, 'leave Jack alone.' I was sick of it.

I said the first clever thing that popped into my head. "You can never tell when something may come up and put an end to everything, can you? Better grab your life and live it, I think. Carpe diem."

She huffed at me in disgust. "Nobody likes a smartass. Have you given this any real thought at all? You're still young and here we are in a foreign country and—"

"Whoa there. Much as I love the U.S., Canada is my home." Divert and redeploy; I wasn't ready to answer her questions. I had no answers.

She parried. "Well, you're fresh back, aren't you? Not settled, no job, no immediate prospects of one. Weren't you explaining to me just the other day, it would be another year at least before you get your Canadian accreditation? You pick now to have a baby and from a man who's struggling to deal with his own problems. Yes, my situation is no better. That's not the point." She pointed at me. "What on earth were you thinking?"

I put on a suggestive leer. "I don't remember thinking."

Mary went stone cold quiet for a bit, banged down her cup and shouted. "It was your idea to come here. A fresh start for both of us, you said. We'd be a family. We'd work together and make a new life. I trusted you. I put myself in a situation where I'm dependent on you… because you wanted it. Shame on you for talking to me like that."

I flushed with self-loathing and intended to apologize but some inner demon wouldn't let me. Instead, I hurled the worst words I could find at her.

"So what do you want me to do? Get an abortion?"

I stared at the angriest Mary I'd ever seen. I waited for her to burst into spontaneous flame. Her silence intimidated me, and I was relieved when the storm finally broke.

"I don't recognize you right now. I'm going to town and I'm taking the truck. You're stuck here? Good! Take the time to think things through and when I come back, I'd better find a change of attitude and some answers."

She grabbed up her purse. "And Bria, I don't want one word of this to the others. Not until we work things out. Do you understand me?"

Before I could say anything, the door slammed and the truck moved slowly and carefully down the driveway. I watched her leave and muttered, "Shit." Round two and both of us blooded.

***

What was the big deal? I didn't get it. Wasn't I the wunderkind who aced everything? I had a plan: find a position to expose me to social law, something meaningful and important. Get myself accredited in Alberta. Buy my own horse and rodeo in Alberta to make extra money. Set up my own office so I could work from home and spend as much time as possible with my baby. Simple, right?

All I had to do was organize my thoughts and present them to Mary. *No need to worry*, I'd tell her. *Everything will be fine. I'll get started straight away.*

Sure, I was pregnant, but only just. I had enough time to find a contract position somewhere, anywhere, doing anything related to social law so I qualified for the PLTC—the mandatory prep course for all newbies wanting to be called to the Alberta Bar. It started in October and finished in early January. My due date to give birth was February 13 or 14. Lots of time.

All I needed was a job under a practicing lawyer to act as my principle, and when necessary, I'd take time out until the baby came but surely my boss would understand, and then I'd go back and complete the required twelve months.

When I'm finished articling, Mary, I'd explain, I'll write two exams. One as a solicitor, all the dry stuff: wills, probates, contracts, real estate and corporate practice, the subjects that put me to sleep in law school. I didn't want to work in those areas. I'd rather eat sawdust.

The second exam, the barrister's exam, will lead me where I intend to go: criminal and civil procedures and family practice, an entry into the field of social law. Remember, Mary, I did very well at Loyola Law, and I hold a degree in sociology. The good work earned me references from all kinds of people back in Chicago.

Undoubtedly, I could find a place wanting my unique talents and background. All I needed was a start. Life up to now had fallen in my lap. Why would that change? Mary worried over nothing. I had everything under control.

But stop asking me why I'm pregnant, Mary, because I have no answer for you. Nor could I explain why I wouldn't tell Jack. I believed in my heart I shouldn't, at least not now.

When she returned, I invited her to sit with me out on the deck and enjoy the sunshine and fresh air. After apologizing contritely and sincerely, I laid out my plans.

She was dubious. "Somehow I don't think it's going to be so easy."

"How can you say that? Doesn't my track record speak for itself? I did good work in Chicago, even as a student. People, important people, thought so."

Mary spoke hesitantly, as though wondering if she should say what weighed on her mind. "Doesn't it occur to you your easy success is due to Jack? He opened those doors for you. I don't think you've ever given a thought to how much he did for you. Who do you know here?"

"I can do it myself. All I need is a foot in the door."

"Only if your pregnant belly doesn't get in the way. I don't imagine the Calgary legal world will be so enamored of your credentials to overlook that. You really do live in a dream world, Bria, and you're spoiled. Jack spoiled you, made life too easy for you. We're on our own now."

"We do have reserves put away: investments, mostly real estate. Greg the moneyman put a lot of my money in the market, and property's boomed over the past few years. We're holding enough to last us a while if we live conservatively, and I invested in stocks and equity funds. I don't want to dip into those funds, but if we must, we will."

"Hopefully, we won't. Don't forget, Tara is fourteen. In another four or five years, she'll be ready for college. She has her heart set on veterinary school. What I have left over from the house, I've earmarked for that. I think you'd better talk to this Greg the moneyman, and find out exactly where we stand."

"Okay. Now will you stop worrying? I gave you your answers." I got up to leave.

Mary motioned me back to my seat. "Those aren't the questions I wanted answered. First, you're not an ignorant girl; you know how to take care of yourself, and still you used no protection. Why?"

I gave her my prepared and evasive answer. "For the obvious reason, I want a baby."

"Since when?"

She didn't wait for my response. It was probably written on my face, as she claims many things are. "And why Jack? In spite of his difficulties right now, you went ahead, took him to bed and got yourself a baby. Did you explain your intentions?" She wanted me to answer this time.

I used Jack's favorite tactic: another question. "Tell me, did you ask John?"

"I suppose that's fair. For many years, Pat and I tried for a family and nothing happened. I didn't believe it possible I could conceive, so took no precautions. But you now, that's a different story. You deliberately went about getting pregnant and I want to know why."

I told the truth by way of a shrug and, "Search me." Then I lied. "The idea of a baby has grown in me for a long time. I'll never get one from Ted and Jack was handy." And finally, another truth. "I would rather have Jack's than anyone's."

"I'll accept that much as true." She tried to take my hand but I pulled it back. She looked hurt but went on. "You simply must tell him, Bria. You can't have his child and not let him know. Try and imagine what he'll feel when he does find out – and he will. I wouldn't make book on you staying away from him, not for the rest of your life. Tell him."

"No, I won't. Please stop asking me to. I won't and don't ask why; I can't tell you." My defenses fell down and truth flew out my mouth. "Not why I got pregnant, nor why I can't tell him. Leave it alone."

"You're wrong. I hope one day soon you'll understand how wrong. I'll never agree with you, so don't try to change my mind. If you can't tell me why all this is come about, I suggest you do a bit of soul searching. Until you can answer, we keep it to ourselves. No need to speak to the others, not yet. Promise?"

"I don't understand, but I promise."

***

So ended round three. A draw. With an agreement to disagree, she let the idea grow on her. She complained she was too old, and never did let up about telling Jack, but for the next month we got along reasonably well. Peace reigned on the home front, so I turned all my attention to finding a job.

First, I had to be accepted as a student at law by the Alberta Law Society.

You'd think, since I was almost accredited in Illinois, I'd be a shoe-in. Not so. My non-Canadian academic credentials currently floated around the appropriate authorities at the National Committee on Accreditation, presumably in the process of perusal, examination, evaluation and eventually, I hoped, approval to apply as a transfer applicant. Unlike me, they were in no hurry.

While waiting, I hauled my butt around the legal community of Calgary only to find Chicago was considered as foreign and suspect as Outer Mongolia, and interesting as my social papers were, students in droves pouring out of university in Calgary and Edmonton had educations not quite so exotic.

Greg, my moneyman, said things appeared to be on a downturn. Commodities, pension funds, the Dow, all indicated negative growth. "1983 looks to be a bad year." I could use my interest income, but that was all. He would shift investments around to ensure my protection, or so he avowed.

A week later, he phoned with dire warnings. The bottom had fallen out of the real estate market, not the time to liquidate. I should fund anything extraneous out of current cash flow but not to count on my previous level of interest income as rates had plummeted.

Once I figured out that in the space of a few months our net worth had fallen to less than half what it had been, I redoubled my efforts to find a position.

Mary was right; my pregnant belly got in the way. When lucky enough to talk to some senior associate whose job it was to fend off eager beaver students-at-law like me, any gleam of interest died the moment I mentioned maternity leave.

To make things worse, the one place I'd counted on, the Duty Counsel's office wasn't hiring. They felt the pinch along with everybody else and weren't taking on any new law students at present. Children's protection agencies—ditto. Unemployed social workers littered the sidewalk. In times of recession social programs were the first cut, so I was told.

I couldn't share this with Mary. She worried enough for both of us.

Finally driven to the solo practitioners, those I'd found through research in the law library who had worked on cases I deemed admirable, I did gain some interviews, but most independents couldn't afford to take on an article. About the time a return to Chicago started looking good despite the humiliation, I met Abe Metzger, a bulldog of a man.

An activist with a wide array of interests—aboriginal rights, senior abuse, child neglect and the rehabilitation of those emerging from the clutches of the Justice System—he shared a storefront office with a bail bondsman in an unsavory area of downtown Calgary. At least he gave me the time of day.

My references from the locum in Cook County glowed. Metzger approved. He showed more interest in the work I'd done as an undergrad, my papers on street prostitutes and child victims than my law school results. He asked to keep them.

"Sure."

"This kind of law doesn't pay well. Real estate conveyance pays the bills." He waved around the dingy cluttered place and added, "From home not here."

"I have another source of income. Or I will, after my baby's birth."

"Baby?"

"Yes, expected in mid February," I said with all the confidence of a well-settled woman of means, happy and unconcerned in her maternity.

"Aren't you lucky? And what is it you do that allows you to pursue this underpaid, underappreciated but noble arm of our profession? "

"I ride rodeo: barrel racing. Three World Championships."

His eyes widened. He laughed, throwing back his head and opening his mouth wide, a real belly shaker. "The cowgirl avenger. We need to get you a costume."

"I already own one: jeans, boots and a cowboy hat."

"You'll have to lose the hat when you put on your robes, but you can keep the jeans and boots." He still chuckled. "Does your regalia include a big silver buckle we can use to blind the opposition?"

"Three of them. This sounds promising. Is it?" My heart tap-danced.

"Look around. My practice consists of Jean, combination paralegal, secretary, file clerk, receptionist and all round super woman and me. I can't afford to hire you but—"

"Oh." Hope had been sweet for one brief moment.

"But I'll think on all this and see what I can do for you."

I'd heard that before and felt I wanted to get up and go, but I didn't. I couldn't afford to burn any bridges, no matter how rickety.

"I appreciate your efforts. Seems times are tough all over."

"They are. Oil is down, thanks to those bastards in Ottawa, so real estate is down to a crawl. I'm scraping the bottom myself," he said, swiping some document with liquid paper.

Through the dusty glass, I read the bumper sticker on the Chevy pick-up parked outside. 'Let the Eastern Bastards Freeze in the Dark.'

I got up to leave reluctantly. For a brief moment, I'd thought this interesting man might lead me to my goal. "I understand, and thank you all the same. It was nice to meet you and may I say I respect the work you do."

"Don't give up."

"I won't." Words are cheap; I was close to surrender.

Thirty-four:
"That sounds pretty final!"

Every passing day made it harder to smile for Mary and pretend life was ever so wonderful, and I tried not to take her grumblings too much to heart. She insisted she was too old for another baby but Mary never thought herself capable of anything until you threatened to take it away from her. Then no one could do the job as well as she.

I wished she'd let up about Jack. I simply would not tell him.

"Jack always wanted children. You have no right to take this away from him and your child needs to know his father. You must speak to him."

She delivered her latest outburst along with an envelope addressed to me, and the Office of the New York County District Attorney embossed in the corner.

"Mary, for the millionth time, it's my decision to make. And I'm making another one: let the others in on our little secret. I'm not ashamed of having this baby and I don't intend to hide anymore. Tomorrow is Saturday and everyone is at home. I'll start then."

"You're not even three months along. What's the rush?"

"I want to, that's all."

I left her still shaking her head and dreaming up new arguments, and escaped upstairs to my bedroom and changed out of my business clothes. I shimmied out of pants already a little tight around the waist and pricked myself with the pin I needed to keep my shirt closed over my swollen breasts.

Once comfortable in a pair of old pajamas, I opened Jack's letter. Before unfolding the single sheet inside, I played a little game in my head. Either he's written to tell me he's getting divorced or he's making up with Leslie. I voted for the latter, remembering how upset he'd been over his daughter.

I was right. The letter started beautifully.

Hello, my sweet girl,

I sat down to write a hundred times over, but couldn't find the words for what I needed to say. I was drowning and you saved me. Thank you is nowhere near enough. Our time together was wonderful, and I will always treasure the memory. You are forever in my thoughts and my heart.

Here in New York, I'm the mid-west bumpkin finding my way around, but I am settling in. Apartments are not easy to find or to afford, worse even than Chicago but I finally found one. You would approve; my new digs are the size of a sardine can and furnished from the trash, but serves for a temporary home.

I say temporary because Leslie has once again offered her hand in matrimony. She says the unhappiness of her life in Chicago drove her away, not me. Funny, I thought one of the partners in her law firm caused her sudden desire to leave town, but I may be wrong.

You will think me a fool, but I am inclined toward living with Leslie. She agreed to try for another child, and if that is possible, we should waste no time. Neither of us is as young as we were. Most of all, a reconciliation will allow me to live with Helena and for me, this is the heaviest factor to weigh.

I hope your return to Canada brought you all you hoped, success, happiness and contentment. Enclosed are some business cards, should you ever need to contact me. Love to Mary, Tara and Ian.

Love, Jack

Such a strange formal note, considering our lifelong history, and his news was no more than exactly as I expected when I put him on the plane at O'Hare. Jack would do what he saw as right, always had, and I knew of only one exception: the three and a half weeks with me. This once, he let go and did as he desired.

I thought about him a lot these days and I understood now, he had his own demons to defeat. He was not the perfect man with all the answers, the solid rock of strength my girlish eyes had seen, but a lonely and abused young man who found in me a reflection of his own trials.

He loved me as a little girl, saved me and loved me again as a grown girl, but when I became a woman, he ran from my love right into the web of the glamorous and self-centered Leslie. Foolish man, he should have stayed with me where he belonged.

I still didn't understand what Leslie ever wanted of him. I suspected she saw in his homely damaged face and shy ineptitude around women a final chance for herself, a man who would be entirely devoted to her fading beauty and charm and dance attendance in gratitude. She struck me as that kind of woman.

He hadn't abandoned me, as I had believed at eighteen. After all he had done for me, when he found himself in trouble, I turned my back on him and let him step knowingly into the mire without a friend. I felt nothing but shame for my selfish actions.

I refused to make his situation any worse. He gave up his entire life to love and protect his child because he wanted to do right by her. I was proud of him and respected him more for it. Helena would never be the nobody nobody wants.

I planned to show this note to Mary, and perhaps she might understand and leave me alone. My baby's destiny included love enough here at home without stealing love from someone else.

***

The next morning, I set out like the town crier to spread the news of my pregnancy to everyone.

Tara was thrilled but well, gee, you know, kind of embarrassed. At fourteen, her life was still a fairytale with innocent expectations and happily-ever-afters. Happy for her, I hoped she lasted a few more years unscathed.

We weren't close. The state of our relations bothered me in a guilty kind of way, my fault rather than hers. Once she was safe with Mary and my responsibility accomplished, I had turned my interest to the adult world and Jack.

We often argued about which made better pets, horses or dogs. She claimed to be a dog person and I found her in the porch busy cleaning up after Tess and her five-week-old puppies.

"Hey, Tara. Hey, Tess."

Tess lifted her massive head. Her droopy squinted eyes didn't see well and she sniffed at the air suspiciously until her dim brain caught on. Not the smartest dog on the planet, but don't tell Tara. She loved her mastiffs.

"How are the pups?"

"Great. I'm out here on poop patrol."

273

My sister, who would screech like an owl when she stepped on a dried up cow pie, felt no compunction about picking up urine soaked newsprint and stinky, sloppy puppy do-do.

She had few friends at the moment. Fresh into middle school and terribly unsure of herself, her status probably wasn't improved by her habit of prefacing many remarks with, "Well back in Chicago…" The dogs helped.

"Hey, Tara, guess what? I'm going to have a baby."

"Cool." That was it.

The next day she asked some pointed questions. Apparently, she also knew about Ted and the mumps, information most likely gleaned by skulking around doors and windows with her big ears flapping.

"I don't think it's right you cheated on Ted." She spoke in an air of moral superiority.

I acted entirely perplexed. "Cheated? He's not a test or a sport."

"When someone's your boyfriend you don't fool around with others."

"Ted's not my boyfriend. He's just Ted."

"He's your boyfriend."

"Which means what?"

She put one hand on her hip and shook a finger at me. "Bria, you don't get pregnant by someone else when you have a boyfriend."

"So you're saying a boyfriend owns you, decides what you do and with whom. Not so, at least not for me, nor Ted. No one owns me and I sure as hell don't own him."

Now *she* looked perplexed. "So I suppose your baby's a secret."

"No. You can tell all of junior high if you want. The truth will be evident to everyone soon enough."

She turned her attention back to the pups and dismissed me. "You can be such a pain."

"So can you. Public opinion aside, do you have a problem with another baby in the house?"

"No. It's great, but well, gee, you know, kind of embarrassing."

As a goodwill gesture, I went so far as to scratch Tess's ears and comment on how the puppies had grown. They should, the amount they ate. At least Tara dealt with the other end, not me. I just bought the food.

Ian said, "I hope it's a boy," and turned his attention back to his Junior Erector set.

I called Annie, told her I wouldn't be riding this year and why. She went quiet. At least I now knew what it took to get her that way. I had to hold the phone out at arm's length. "Woo hoo!" Annie also knew about the mumps—and Jack—and Chicago. The thought wouldn't occur to her I'd be anything other than thrilled.

We had a comforting conversation. I brought her up to date on my trials and tribulations, my frustrations and fears. It felt good to share.

The next words out of her mouth were, "I was thinking, seeing as you're not lawyering all over the place, I could use some help. Del has his eye on a girl coming up in the Prairie Circuit and he's thinking of hiring her to ride Sunshine, but Walter is out of commission for a while. Could you work in August and September helping her train? Yolanda will take good care of you. Please. We'll make it worth your while; say, pay out your contract."

What a lady! I thought I'd take her up on the offer, give her August and September. October too, if she wanted me. It would be good money and fun to help this new girl, whoever she was. I didn't envision any more lucrative offers on the horizon.

***

Things settled down. Everyone important to me eventually offered wishes for my happiness and promised support—except Ted. He punched a hole in the wall of our motel room.

"I knew it. As soon as you came back from Chicago all hot to trot. Why him?"

As if I knew nothing about the girl in Idaho Springs, or the wild party he'd had in Cody, or any of the others, I softened the blow for him. I told him a lie, the first of many to follow. "Who else was there? I want a baby and you and Jack are the only two men I know well enough to give me one. That's all."

Then he got nasty, so I did too.

"So how was the great Jack? Did you lie under him like some dead fish?"

"Fantastic, and no, no need."

The door slammed. His truck revved loudly, taking off in a shower of gravel that ricocheted off the door. He never returned, so the next morning I checked out and drove across the border and home.

Several weeks later, he phoned me at the Lazy K. He'd given me and my pregnancy a lot of thought and claimed to understand. Of course

I wanted a baby, he said. Every woman did and he wouldn't hold my going to Jack against me. I left that lie undisturbed, like any sleeping dog. No hard feelings, he assured me, and asked would I meet him halfway in Sheridan?

I agreed and on the weekend, I drove up to join him at the Ramada Inn on the I25. I admit to a little trepidation as I arrived at the motel, found his truck and knocked on the door, but I received a royal welcome when I walked into the bland room.

"Your tits are bigger."

"That's it? Not, 'Bria, I care about you enough to get over it,' or 'I can't and this is goodbye.' Just my tits are bigger."

"I'm only an aggie. Farmers don't need fancy language and I don't have your way with words. Doesn't mean I'm stupid. What I meant to say is you look good, and the tits... well I can't help but notice. Wow."

"They hurt so don't make any plans with them."

He laughed and looked rueful, sat down in the chair, took off his hat and put it on the table. "Want a beer? I got a six pack out in the cooler."

"I'm pregnant, remember, and I don't like beer, as you're aware."

"Sheesh, try to be polite... Look, I got something to say."

I interrupted him. "So do I. Ladies first. I understand you're mad at me and I don't blame you. You don't see things the way I do."

He ran his hands through his hair and flung them out at me. "I love you."

"Yes I believe you do, in your own way, and I love you, too. We've known each other since we were kids and shared a lot of fun. That doesn't mean I can't also love Jack. One has nothing to do with the other and anyway, sooner or later, you'll move on. It's as sure as snow in January."

He frowned and shook his head. "You got a crystal ball?"

"Ted, one day you'll want to settle down with a real partner, one who wants to live on that farm and work with you, share your life. You have to know that will never be me."

"So you hedge your bets."

"I'm no more likely to end up with Jack, raising a pack of little Connellys in some New York apartment. It's not about who I pick. Why should I have to pick anyone at all?"

Ted leaned back in his chair, put his boots up on the bed and in the way of a man who thinks he has the lay of the land asked, "What were you thinking, getting yourself in the family way with a married man?"

"You can't understand."

"Well, educate me then."

"I can't. You don't know what Jack and I lived through together."

He stared at the floor a second, leaned forward and spoke softly. "My dad told me you were raped when you were just a kid. I try to keep that in mind, knowing what happened to you."

"No, you *don't*," I shouted, sickened that he'd learned even that much. I stuffed those feelings down and added quietly, "And I don't want to talk about it."

"But you do with Jack."

"No need, he stood beside me the whole time."

Ted was not a man of words or complicated thought. This was a major effort for him and I loved him for trying. He sat staring at his boots, deep in sad contemplation.

"Ted, we've lived lots of things, too—happy things. With you, I was young and free like any other girl. We had fun and shared so many good times. I didn't carry all the baggage and it's always been easy between us. I needed that."

"Like any other girl? Not you. I tried so hard to make you love me."

"I did and still do. I always will. We know each other so well and have for most of our lives. Why can't that be enough?"

"You're so different from the others and I try to understand but…" His voice trailed off and he sounded forlorn.

For the first time I thought about what loving me must be like for him. In his world a woman followed her man, put his needs before hers, expected marriage and children, a home and a place in the community. He'd been raised to believe this was life and it couldn't be any other way. I knew that.

And it wasn't as though loving me brought him any great satisfaction. I knew that too. Even after all this time, I disappeared during lovemaking, helpless to do otherwise. A switch flipped in my mind at some point, and I flew away, no matter how hard I tried to stay.

I'd thought something might be wrong inside me. It certainly couldn't be Ted, not with all the women who still swarmed around him and had for as long as I remembered. I hadn't asked him to love me like this and couldn't understand why he did. Happy just being his buddy, I thought it unfair of me to let him go on dreaming.

"Ted, why do you want me? I'm not beautiful and I'm aware I'm not exciting in bed. You can have any woman, it seems to me."

"You're different, like I said." Ted opened a second beer and with a face screwed up in concentration, thought for a minute. "You liked me for me. I'm sick of those stupid girls always chasing after me, the good-looking cowboy, just so they could say to their friends, 'I did him.' I can't help how I look."

I was astonished. *Men feel like that, too?* "I thought you liked it. You didn't seem to go out of your way to avoid them."

Ted laughed a little. "When I was younger, I did; couldn't get enough, to tell you the truth. But later I just got tired of the uselessness, the stupidity. I wanted someone special and you are that."

He leaned over and took my hand. "You're so smart and talk about so many things. You showed me a new way of looking at the world and I couldn't believe you were interested in me, wanted to be with me. What am I? A pretty face and a couple of silver buckles and when I'm too old for rodeo, I'll be only a farmer."

"I can't give you what you deserve. I live in another country. I have work to do, and a family to look after, not to mention a baby on the way." I almost cried from shame. I too, had seen Ted as a plaything, a good-looking fellow to prove to the other girls and myself I was normal, just like them.

"I can't give you or any woman what a man should either. I can't make babies for you or grandchildren for my parents. That's up to my brother. But I do love you; I can offer you that much."

I climbed into his lap and laid little baby kisses all over his pretty face. I whispered in his ear. "Love me then."

We got undressed and into bed. As Jack had taught me, I put my hand over his and showed him what I wanted. He held himself back and let me take charge. For the first time, I stayed in my body and didn't fly away from Ted. It was sweet and successful. Afterward he lay beside me, running his hand across my rounding belly.

"I wish it could be mine."

In the warmth of our shared bed, I gave him the gift of a small lie. "So do I. You would give me a pretty baby."

He sat straight up and looked down at me. "I came here to ask you to marry me. I can help you raise your child."

"Please don't," I said, full of panic. "I don't want to get married. If I did, I'd snap you up in a heartbeat, but I don't."

"That sounds pretty final."

"It is." I pulled him down to me and stroked the length of his back.

"Let's just love each other. You can be an uncle to my baby if you want. We're friends first." His muscles relaxed under my hand. When I thought him ready, I said, "About marriage—you're free to go searching and if you find someone right for you, I'll be happy because I love you. Make sure it's a woman I can like so we can be friends. I don't want to lose you completely."

"I don't. I won't."

Happy again, Ted threw his arm across my chest and pulled me close to him, and fell sound asleep in seconds, my beautiful man.

***

Back at the Lazy K, Annie wanted to know all about it. We sat out on the patio, washed in the constant wind of the plains, warmed by the sun and sheltered by the cottonwoods. She fixed orange juice for both of us, vodka in hers.

"So how's Ted. All made up?"

"Everything is fine as can be."

"Is he coming to see us? I miss him, that tight butt of his. He's as pretty to look at as a good blooded stud." She gave him a thumbs-up.

"He'll be around."

"Good. My eyes love him. So how's Becky coming along?"

"Lots of promise."

Becky, Rebecca from South Dakota, rode like a wild thing, reckless and daring, but with training, she'd be a top-grade racer. I drilled her for hours, as Walter had me. Needless to say, she was gorgeous, slim and petite, crowned in blond curls that bobbed in rhythm with Sunshine's gait. She and the young mare made a strong team.

I met her parents, Walt and Lydia Carlson—good people. They engaged me to negotiate her contract with the Lazy K and I did a thorough job, squeezing every drop of sweat possible out of Del. I counseled them to insist on an education fund clause, but they didn't. Unlike me, Becky had no real interest in school. Why should she, when she earned good money like this? She was feckless, but good-natured and dedicated.

One day I took her aside and gave her sound advice concerning Del.

"That old goat? The first time he touches me, I'll break his arm." Her curls practically bristled with affront.

"Find a better way to handle him, Becky. Be professional. Remind him you're underage, his employee and no means no." For a moment, I heard Jack's voice pour from my mouth. "He'll leave you alone. Go talk to Annie if he gets to you. She'll smarten him up."

"She knows?" Her eyes flew open and her tone was indignant.

"Of course she does. She doesn't mind he likes to look. She loves him and wants him to be happy and, for the record, he adores her. They're one of the few happy couples I've met."

"Well they creep me out. She lets him have girls around to ogle. What a pair of pervs."

"Don't judge. Everyone has to find his or her own way in life. The arrangement works for them."

I challenged her to be honest. "And I don't see you turning down this great opportunity over it, do I?"

"No, I'm not stupid. This is the best thing that ever happened to me."

Just as I thought. Pleased with her frankness I threw in some more unsolicited advice. "Exactly. There's always a price to pay for anything. Accept that as truth, and you're halfway to understanding how the world works, especially for girls. Just know your limits."

"It's still creepy."

"No it's harmless. If it wasn't for Del's little hobby, some young cowboy might be on that horse, not you."

She weighed her options and came to the same conclusion I had years ago. "I guess I can deal with the old lech. He's nice to me and so is she."

She bounced off. I watched her, thinking, *sixteen, and still such an innocent. Lucky her.*

I went to the apartment over the stables and knocked on Walter's door. He was recovering from surgery for blood clots in his knee. Like most old cowboys, he'd paid the price for the sport's terrible wear and tear.

"How you doing, Walter?"

"Good. Real good."

But he didn't look good; he looked old and prematurely worn out. I made sure he was comfortable, cracked a cold beer for him and spent half an hour listening to his instructions on how best to train Becky. It was the same old same old, all over again, but he was happy and I let him ramble on. Eleven times World Champion and ensconced in the Cowboy Hall of Fame, he deserved my respect.

I had one last piece of business before I left the Lazy K. Something a little more delicate than the exorbitant price I'd extorted from Del for the knowledge and education I'd given his latest Barbie doll.

I found Annie in the kitchen working on one of her innumerable flower arrangements and chatting up a tempest with Yolanda. After half an hour's small talk and a plate full of spicy pinto beans and tomatoes, I got down to business.

"Annie, the bred chestnut mare, the one Del didn't want to breed?"

"Yes."

"I want first call on the foal when it comes, but I might need a couple of years before I can come up with the money."

Annie turned her head sharply. "You want to buy?"

"I like the mare, and Sunson is the perfect racer. I'd love to buy the foal but I can't pay right now. Things have been a little tight for us lately. Will you consider holding on and selling the horse as a two-year old?"

I walked over to her, close and confidential, and leaned on the gleaming stone counter top.

"And when I come down here and work with Sunson, would you let me work with the foal too? And I'll train any other horse you want, help out, with Walter laid up and all."

"Why don't we put some of the money we're winning on Sunson aside for the foal?"

"Right now, I need every penny I get."

Annie studied me, pursing her lips and chewing on them while she deliberated. "Consider it done. We'll work out the details tomorrow, when I haven't had my lunch yet."

"Understood. God forbid your lunch should slop out of its glass." I eyed her drink and winked at her.

"Well, see, you do understand. You're going alone?" She stopped fiddling with the flowers and cast her eyes down, looking sad.

"I'll still ride Sunson for you, after the baby is ready, of course but eventually, I need to be in Alberta and race up there. BarBeeJay is a good brand for a racer. I made it so. Damn right I want to ride for myself, wouldn't you?"

"Yes. I certainly would."

She had tears in her eyes, poor lonely woman, neglected by her own family. I served as far more than a hired rider for her. "I'll miss you."

I threw my arms around her neck and planted a kiss on her cheek. "No you won't, not a chance. Aren't you my Annie, good woman and best friend?"

"I am." She wiped at her eyes and reached out to pat my belly.

"Sugar, isn't it time you stop tying your jeans together with a shoestring? Go get into something decent and let's go into town and buy you some maternity wear. You can't go on like this."

I knew better than to argue. She still loved to dress me up and I did need the clothes. With Annie in charge, assuredly my new outfits would complement my hair.

On the way into town, she talked about Becky and how she didn't have my zip and no one could be as cute as I was, racing around those barrels on Sunson.

I tried to be fair and pointed out all of Becky's attributes but I was glad I was only to be replaced as a rider and not in Annie's heart.

Just before I left the Lazy K, Mary phoned me, all excited. A letter from the Illinois Bar Association had arrived.

I told her to open it, open it, held my breath and waited. I'd passed.

Thank God. If all else failed, we could always move back to Chicago and I could practice law there. Dual citizenship was a wonderful thing. Border, what border?

I went home with enough cash in my hand to support my yet to be established legal career and us for another little while, at least until well after the baby. I had to remember, one step at a time.

Thirty-five:
"The family tree leans to one side."

Mary

Seeing is believing, and I didn't, not until Bria came home with a bump as big as a bed pillow where her flat belly used to be. We really did have another baby on the way, and that bump grew rapidly.

Nothing else to do but be happy about the expected event. Yes, but I worried at the same time. One evening while we cleaned up the supper things I told Bria I wasn't as young as I'd once been.

She brushed me off with a breezy, "Who is?"

"I'm too old for another baby."

"Yeah, well I remember you screaming, 'I'm too old!' while you gave birth to Ian. I don't intend to just hand you my kid and say, 'here, raise it.' I'll be the mother, and Lizzie already said she'll do day care a few days a week."

Lizzie, the slatternly cousin? Her house was a health hazard and her children ran around in rags. Over my dead body would she hand over our baby to *her*. Of course, I didn't say that. No, I simply said, "No need for day care. And not Lizzie. Her own run around Strathmore like hooligans."

"Well make up your mind."

"I'm not having our children tearing about town in dirty clothes." I mentally added *or without responsible supervision.*

"They're playing. Lizzie's kids are happy."

I laughed at her innocence. "There's more to raising children than keeping them happy."

"Like what? Anyway, this is a stupid conversation, and bad timing."

Bria acted restless and edgy, her signal she had something important to tell me, something difficult. I asked the question she was waiting for. "Why, what's wrong with the time?"

"Remember I went to the doctor last Thursday. She had some

concerns and—"

"Concerns about what? Something wrong with the baby?" I asked, choosing to ignore her sigh of impatience.

"I'll tell you if you'll hold yourself together long enough. The doctor had concerns about an echo she heard and sent me for X-rays."

I was all pins and needles. "And?"

"Nothing. Inconclusive—not surprising, when they expected me to lie on my belly. I felt like a teeter-totter. So she sent me over to Foothills. They have something new over there, an ultrasound machine."

"A what?"

"Ultrasound, apparently it works like sonar. Well, maybe you'd better sit down."

"Why?" *Oh, dear God, was the baby deformed or Bria in danger?*

"I'm not having a baby. I'm having two."

I sat down then—hard. "Oh, sweet Jesus."

I had a little boy just starting school, a sweet and lively little boy; a teenage girl with a bad case of angst; Bria, still a thrill ride and now, two more babies. All I needed was to hang up lace curtains and I'd be the stereotype Irish American woman.

Bria had to work. She was the breadwinner. That meant that I would have those babies most of the day – certainly *not* Lizzie. I was not a young woman and menopause reduced me to an overheated, sweaty and teary caricature who dithered over chicken or steak for dinner. Money was tight. Tara would be ready for college in a few years and Bria didn't have a job.

And we had not one, but two babies on the way.

The irony of life hit me like a downtown bus. I began to laugh and once started, couldn't stop. I gasped for air and finally was able to say, "And to think I was married for nineteen years and despaired of having one."

With a straight face, Bria came out with, "Connelly women breed best outside of marriage."

We howled with laughter. We got giddy. I said, "Two more additions to the branchless Connelly family tree."

"The tree that leans over to one side."

"Aren't we just the picture of the independent feminist?" I asked and poured myself a drink. "Raising two generations of Connelly kids by ourselves."

Bria added, "In a drafty old farmhouse and no child support." She had tears of laughter running down her face.

It was when I said, "I make that three generations if we count Jack," that Bria wet herself.

And as sudden as it started, we sobered up. "Bria, you must call Jack."

"No."

"Listen my girl, you have no idea how wrong you are. He needs to know."

She grew angry, as she did whenever I brought him up. "Mary, respect my decision. Don't you dare pick up that phone and tell him, or John. Yes, I saw last month's phone bill. Why are you calling him?"

"Because we have a son together and he has the right to know about him."

"Fat lot of good it's doing you. He still hasn't sent any help."

I tried to explain. "His choice."

"There's a law against abandoning your child. He shouldn't have that freedom."

"I don't care about law. Maybe John won't come round but my son won't grow up not knowing his father because I decided he shouldn't." I thought I'd made a concrete point, but she didn't.

"No. He'll grow up knowing his father just didn't give a damn. Is that better? I don't think so."

"Jack would never do that. What are you going to tell yours when they ask where their daddy is?"

"You know, I thought I might concentrate on giving birth to them first and worry about all that later."

She left the room in a huff, a very pregnant huff. From laughter to anger in seconds. I had to admit between her pregnancy and my menopause, the hormones in this house ruled the day.

Bria

She never let up. She was too old, worried about money and above all, I should call Jack.

Annie called one night from England – "Surprise, sugar!" – currently with her self-seeking wild child. Cheryl, injured in a car accident, ended up in the care of National Health, so Annie tore over to rescue her. Much as I wished her well and hoped she would reconcile with at least one of her ungrateful children, I was miffed I couldn't talk to her about any of this.

The only ears left to moan into belonged to Ted. His plan was simple: the babies and I were to go and live with him, and I wouldn't need to work at all. Sweet, thank you, but I didn't think so.

Dr. Shalissa Nadoo, my obstetrician, insisted on another ultra sound two weeks before my due date. Afterward, during our consultation, she advised a caesarian birth because the smaller baby's umbilical cord grew in such a way as to cause a dangerous delivery.

Fine with me. After watching Mary give birth, I wasn't exactly looking forward to that part anyway.

I thought I'd be out cold while they cut me open and took out my babies, but no, I lay on a table, wide-awake, holding Mary's hand and staring at a curtain drawn across my waist. I felt a tug or two, but no pain, a strange sensation.

First came the small one, a girl, Sheila May. Sheila because it was the prettiest name I knew, Celtic for music, and May for Mary—five pounds, two ounces. Mary's hand looked huge as she held her to my face. Tiny but full of life, she screamed her outrage at having been ripped from my cozy, warm womb.

The second was a boy. He would be Garret John—seven pounds, four ounces—and he couldn't be bothered to scream. He just lay on the table gazing around, arms flailing, but his ribs pumped up and down, so he was all right.

Fuzzy black hair covered both tiny heads, and later, I discovered their obsidian eyes. They were the most beautiful babies the world had ever seen and Mary agreed with me.

Tara said, "Cute sort of, you know, well, yeah cute," and each of them spent time in the arms of their inarticulate aunt.

Ian checked inside Garret's diaper to make sure he did indeed hold a boy and we hadn't lied to him and, content, cuddled his nephew exclusively.

Peg came in, admired the babies and couldn't resist making a comment about Bria never doing anything by halves. She took Tara and Ian to her home.

Mary stayed at my side around the clock for two days. She trundled the bassinets to and from the nursery, changed their diapers, treated the stubs of both umbilicus with disinfectant and passed them in turn for feeding. She taught me how to breast-feed and pacified one with a soukie while I fed the other.

The nurses brought in a reclining chair for Mary, but who can sleep in a hospital? We spent the wee hours of the mornings talking in whispers, not to disturb the three other new moms on the ward.

"Bria? Are you awake?"

"Of course I am; they just took my blood pressure again."

"I've been thinking—worrying I should say—about money. It's going out faster than we planned. Listen, I know Greg the moneyman said not to liquidate anything, but we're going to need to arrange something. Any thoughts?"

Something about talking in the dark made it easier and tired and feeling inexplicably dejected, I dropped all my pretenses and spoke to Mary from the heart. I hadn't in a long time.

"I'll tell him to sell something. Who cares if we take a loss? Not much point in hanging on to something for the future if the present isn't taken care of, don't you agree?"

"I suppose, makes sense. You'll be home in another day, and we'll talk then. I shouldn't have brought it up here and now, sorry."

"We're not destitute yet and we won't be. We've enough for about six months. I want to stay with the babies for at least that long."

"Of course you do."

The dark calmed me for a time, but something rose up inside. "Mary? You were right about my living in a dream world and being spoiled. I had such big dreams: find a job, outfit an office over the garage, fill it with law books and subscribe to Westlaw, set up so I could research at home. I thought all this would come to me simply because I wanted it."

To my astonishment, I found myself weeping. "Look at me, can't even get a place as a student-at-law. I thought I'd be writing my exams by now. I thought I was so special; all would be easy. Trust me, Mary, you're talking to a humbled Bria, all my shiny plans shattered."

She whispered back to me. "Maybe God wants you to learn something."

"I don't believe in God anymore. I haven't for a long time." A profound confession to put to Mary, so devout she believed He took charge of every little thing. 'God's will' was her favorite expression. I waited for a heated response. I was surprised.

She quietly asked, "Why is that, Bria?"

The tears continued as I sank into a black hole. "When I really needed help there was no answer. I begged and I prayed, but no help came. If there is a God, am I so worthless I was left to that?"

Mary's voice was soft and hoarse. "Didn't He save you in the end? You came out of there and back to us. You didn't do that all by yourself."

"I thought I did in spite of Him. I hated Him for leaving me there."

"Is this the same girl who once believed she had so much power, she could command Him to take Gerry's life? You may believe or not, as is your right. I'll tell you my belief. I think He spared you for a reason and all these hard times are meant to prepare you for that purpose."

I gave no response. My whole soul mourned. A big, dark blanket descended over me and drew me down into a pit of misery.

Mary left her chair, sat on the edge of the bed and gently caressed me. I wept quietly on and on until I wished myself dead, I was so empty. She got up, disappeared into the hallway and returned with a uniformed body in tow.

The nurse took one look at me. "Baby blues, it will pass. Post partum depression is the medical term. I can ask for a sedative if you want one."

"She's nursing her babies," Mary said. "Will it be safe?"

"We have one or two we can use. I'll ask the doctor on call, see what he says." She returned in ten minutes with a syringe in hand. "Roll over. This will fix you up."

Later, still wrapped in that dark blanket, the only difference was I no longer cared enough to cry. My world became detached and unreal to the point of numbness.

Mary felt better though, mistaking my stillness for improvement. She dragged the heavy recliner to the side of the bed and took my hand. "Do you feel better now? Can you sleep?"

"Yes," I lied. "And no, I don't feel like sleep. I don't understand what's wrong with me. I'm scared."

"Tell your Mary."

"I'm not who I thought I was. I used to be so sure of everything. Now I'm not and I don't know what to do next. Maybe we should go back to Chicago where I know people. At least I'm accredited in Illinois."

"You may be surprised to hear this but I like our life here. I never dreamed I'd be a country girl, but I've grown to appreciate the wide-open spaces and love how we can see the city and the mountains from our porch. Besides, if we went back to Chicago, I'd hate John. At least here I can give him the excuse we're far away."

She sat quiet, massaging my fingers. "And if we did, how long do you think it will be before someone tells Jack you have twins with dark hair like his?"

"Oh, we're back to that."

"Can you explain now why you won't tell him he has two beautiful babies?" She squeezed my hands. "Please, won't you try?"

"It will tear him in two. He's trying so hard to be a good man and do the right thing, as always. He never does what he wants. I know in my heart he really should be with me, where he's comfortable and happy, but he sees that as wrong. Maybe because he raised me or because we have the same name. I don't understand it."

I took some time to formulate my ideas, the drug making it difficult. "If he knew about the babies, he would try to do right for everybody, and we'd all lose. He didn't ask me to have them. I took them from him. Do you understand? Am I making sense?"

"Yes, for the first time in a long time. Why did you do that, take those babies from him?"

"I don't know." That was the truth.

The world whirled around. I heard Mary say, "You're wrong and must tell Jack," and the next thing, it was morning.

Mary was gone and I wondered where. I vaguely remembered our conversation in the dark of night, and the shot that had left me with this strange buzzing hangover. I felt even worse and wanted nothing at all but to go back to sleep, into oblivion.

She shuffled into the room, pushing one basinet and pulling the other. "Here's Mummy. Here she is. Let's get some breakfast into your little tummies." So cheerful, I wanted to kill her.

I couldn't understand. I should have been ecstatic with my two perfect babies and was, except for the misery.

The doctor, her eyes scanning my chart, approached my bed. "Better?" I lied and told her fine, thank you. She said she'd discharge me that day and not to worry, the blues would go away soon.

Not soon enough.

***

Two months later, the babies thrived, but the effort to haul my weary ass and engorged breasts out of bed at night to feed and change them was difficult to muster. Two babies. Did they coordinate and need care at the same time? Of course not.

Predictably, Mary appeared in our room seconds after the first squawk, bustling about in her efficiency, ensuring I did everything right. When I stumbled into the kitchen in search of my morning coffee, I found her there, bright as a sparrow in spite of three or four late night feeding sessions, cheerfully making breakfast for Ian and Tara. Too old? My ass. She reveled in her new additions and bloomed.

I wilted. I was a milk machine. Mary cuddled my babies, sang to them, walked the floor soothing them and drove off to town to buy diapers. I fed them; that's all. I sank deeper into lethargy and indifference each day. I let everything go to hell. I bounced two checks.

The checks terminated Mary's patience. "How could you be so careless?"

"I'll fix it."

"How? The household account is empty. Bria, wake up, snap out of it."

I lifted my head off the arm of the couch. "I will. I'm just so tired."

"Have you any idea who you remind of now?" Her blue eye's seemed unusually cold. "Your mother."

She hit a homer. I did something I hadn't done in years: curled up in a ball in the corner of the couch and bawled like a baby.

Mary wrapped her arms around me, stroked my hair and called me her darling girl. "We've got to get you some help."

Thirty-six:
"Jack is my lawyer and will never tell my secrets."

We left the twins with Tara and Ian. A measure of how far gone I was, I made no protest.

We drove to Strathmore. Mary disappeared into the doctor's office for a while, then dragged me in behind her. Dr. Davis checked me over physically, pronounced me nicely recovering from surgery, and then we talked.

She said pregnancy and birth trigger chemical changes producing a profound depression in some individuals. Interesting my mother suffered the same phenomenon, she thought, as medical opinion was such tendencies may be genetic. However, she added, I should not despair, modern pharmacology could help. But I would not be able to continue breast-feeding, not on medication.

My overcast skies blackened because not only was feeding my babies the only enjoyable part of my days, but formula was expensive.

Mary drove over to the bank and prepared all the paperwork to transfer funds into our household account. The only action required of me was my signature. After that, off to the drugstore, where she left me half-comatose in the car and ran in to fill my prescriptions and buy the recommended formula, bottles, nipples and all the rest.

She forced me to take my first pill right away and sat staring at me as though waiting for an immediate response. I waited another month before the full effects of the drugs kicked in, and I rediscovered my love for sweet Sheila and Garret, Tara and Ian, and my Mary again.

I also returned to management of our finances. Mary and I went over the accounts.

"We need help, Bria."

"We'll be fine. Things will get better."

"Not all on their own they won't. Call Jack."

"No."

We went at each other for a long time. She would not back down. Finally, I threw her a challenge. "Here's the deal, Mary. I'll tell Jack about our twins when you call John and demand he pay support."

"Fine. I will."

Wasn't I surprised? Not to mention cleverly trapped. "What?"

"You heard me, I'll call him." She pointed at me like an accusing avenger. "And you do what you should have done from the very beginning."

I ducked. "You first."

"Give me the phone."

She dialed. "Hello, John, Mary here. I have something to say to you, and you're going to shut up and listen. For six years now, I've waited for you to act like a man and do right by our child. You are no kind of man at all to expect Bria to support your son and his mother with only my pension to help us."

During the pause, I heard a tinny version of John's voice but not his words.

"Yes, it was my choice to have the baby, which does not exclude you from responsibility. We made him together, didn't we?"

The tinny voice grew louder but no less indistinct.

"Anger won't save you. If you don't help us, I'll instruct Bria to file against you in court. You'll be ordered to pay, because that's the law, and everyone will learn the truth about the great Captain John Connelly."

Mary took the phone and shut herself in the bathroom. Blown away by her calm attack, I hoped he was sober. She finally came out, pale but still serene. "I gave him to the end of the week to decide what he wants to do." She thrust the phone at me. "Your turn."

"I can't call him now. It's too late in New York. Don't look at me like that. I'm not trying to weasel out of the agreement."

"You'd certainly better not be."

"Jack's never given me a home number—just as well—but I can reach him at his office. Mary, I'm not going to blurt this out over the phone. If you're comfortable without me for a couple of days, I'll ask if I can talk to him in person."

She regarded me suspiciously for a second. "Whatever gave you the idea I couldn't handle this lot?"

Oh, nothing but nine months of whining, I thought, wise enough to keep it to myself.

The next morning, right after the school bus whisked off Tara and

Ian, Mary pointedly asked, "What's the time in New York?"

"Ten-thirty with the two hours difference. I'm calling now, okay?" I dialed the number from my address book, heart pounding, pulse racing.

"Mr. Connelly is not available. May I help you?"

I entrusted a message to the woman who answered. Mary glared at me as though I had purposely made him leave his office. If I could have, I would.

I spent the morning playing with Sheila and Garret on a blanketed patch of floor, watching their fun as they rolled from front to back. On their fronts, they lifted their heads high, not wobbly now, but strong, full of purpose.

Sheila was more agile than Garret and angry at not being able to do as she wished. When she wanted a toy and couldn't reach and grasp it, she screamed in frustration. I swear she already tried to drag herself over.

Garret, on the other hand, was a placid baby. He lay quiet, staring at the toy, happy as July. I thought he was calculating: how can I take that apart?

They were remarkably attuned to each other. I lay on the floor beside them and wondered what was it like to share a womb with someone else, to come out together, to grow together. Had they listened to the other's heartbeats along with mine? I hoped they'd enjoyed a beautiful symphony.

Whenever I thought of my brush with the grey oblivion, I felt deeply ashamed. I don't know why. I should have been better, I suppose. I wasn't afraid any more. My children would be fine. They had the best mother in the world—Mary.

She seemed to grow younger each day. A minute ago, she'd peeked into the room, seen the babies and me, and smiled to herself as she hustled away, happy running her house and family. I used to see the same look on her face when I played beside Tara, a girl myself.

I had no regrets over pushing her to call John, not that I wanted him in Ian's life; I didn't, considering his track record as a father. He should pay because he was a son of a bitch: Jack's favorite term.

Of course, the moment Jack entered my mind, the phone rang and I started in apprehensive anticipation. *It must be him.* I trembled. "Hello?"

"Bria? Abe Metzger, the bearded guy with the shitty office. How're ya doing?"

"I remember you well and I'm fine."

"You must have had that baby by now. What was it, boy or girl?"

"Both—twins."

"Well, well, I like that, an overachiever. Congratulations. Thinking about going back to work?"

"Soon. But Abe, I must tell you, I didn't find a placement last year. I worked on a horse ranch in Wyoming, instead. Needed the money. The point being, I'm not yet accredited, nor even accepted as a student-at-law, although my foreign credentials are approved."

"I know, checked at the Law Society. I hoped you were still available. Are you looking for a placement?"

"Yes, I am."

"I want you for a spot coming up. I discussed your background with the board and they want to meet you. We think you'll fit like a glove."

"Um…tell me where and what." *Don't sound too eager*, I told myself and then figured, *what the hell, why not?*

I couldn't believe my ears when he answered. "The Elizabeth Fry Organization is looking for a student-at-law to represent and advocate for women convicted of crimes. Is this something you'd be interested in?"

Cool as a cucumber, I said, "Yes. Can you tell me more?" Inside I screamed, yes and yes and yes. *Thank you, you wonderful man. I would kill for that job.*

"Can you get away Thursday? I'll take you there and we can talk."

Thursday. What day was today? Oh, God, I can't believe this. "Yes. I can. One question: who would be my principle? I'd like to research the name and walk in prepared."

"Oh, you're prepared enough. It's me."

From despair to exultation, my whole attitude changed. The job would be perfect, exactly what I wanted.

"I'd be honored to work with you, Abe."

"I hope honor is enough. We pay peanuts, but we will get you started in your articles."

"Abe, I don't care about the money. Honest, if I had more, I'd pay for the privilege."

"Well, another thing: space and books. You're welcome to use what I have here, but you've seen the place, not much room."

"I can always use the court library, and I plan to build an office on my property. If you'll put me on your list for Westlaw, I'll find a way to get books and subscriptions."

"We'll work out the details on Thursday. Glad you're aboard. We think you're perfect for the place. See you then, say nine. Meet here at my dump."

I hung up the phone, Jack and my task at hand forgotten. "Mary, I've got a job—a wonderful job."

I took her hands and danced her around the room. She let me lead and followed limply.

I stopped and flopped back on the floor with the babies. She looked at me through dazed eyes, bemused. "Did I hear you promise to build an office and buy a legal library? The last time we talked about this, back when we thought we had money, you had a budget of over $25,000. Are you out of your mind?"

"I'll find a way. I will. I have to."

"You can find a way to do build an office but I'm forced to call John and demand money? Bria, really!"

Too thrilled to let her grumbling get to me, I said, "Oh come on. You should have done it on principle."

"Well, you're still talking to Jack—on principle."

No sooner had she spoken than the phone rang again.

My elation evaporated. Well, not completely, but my heart did start racing.

Mary grabbed it. "Hello, Jack, wonderful to hear your voice after all this time."

I died a quick death, hauled my dead self off the floor and took the phone. I motioned Mary to watch the babies and went into the kitchen.

"Hi Jack. How are you?"

"I'm well. And you?"

"Never better. Today, not five minutes ago, I received some terrific news. I'm going to be counsel for the Elizabeth Fry Organization."

"The who?" His voice sounded warm and interested and, I hoped, happy for news of me.

"It's a Canadian organization – well, started in Britain, actually—that provides help and support to women convicted of crimes. I'm so excited." I spent the next five minutes spouting everything I knew about the group and the history, even went so far as to speculate on what clients with which problems I was likely to encounter.

"Good for you – the kind of work where you excel and can enjoy. Thank you for letting me know."

I wanted to end, as if I'd called to boast of my latest achievements as had always been my habit, but Mary stood in the next room. She glared at me and crossed her arms over her chest.

I eased into the subject. "How's Helena?"

"She's an ongoing miracle. You can't imagine."

Oh yes I can. "So everything is good, right?"

"Yes, Bria, all is well. I'm working with some fine people, very talented. I enjoy it."

I had to ask; I would be impolite if I did not. "I got your letter a while back. How is Leslie? I mean did the reconciliation work out for you?"

"Will you hang on a minute? I want to close the door."

Me too, I thought, looking at Mary's set face and body posture. *If only I had a door to close.* I settled for turning my back.

"Bria, I don't know what to say to you. I felt wrong somehow, leaving you there in Chicago. On the flight here, all I thought about was you and how, out of all the people in life, my best and happiest times were those I spent in your company."

He sounded despondent and I wondered why. "You didn't answer my question."

"I wanted to say my piece first. Leslie, she's not an easy woman to live with but I have to try. For better or worse, that's what I promised and my reward is Helena. Is that an honest enough answer for you?"

I took the leap. "Jack, I wondered, can I come and see you? Talk to you?"

I waited through a long pause. He came back on the line husky voiced. "I don't think that would be a good idea. Leslie…I need to make a decent home for my daughter. I must work this out."

I didn't say anything.

His speech broken-sounding, he added, "I don't think I can do that if I see you right now."

"Okay, Jack. I understand. I still love you. Wait a minute will you?"

I walked to the kitchen door, caught Mary's eye, shook my head and mouthed, "Can't go."

"Guess what Jack? The real reason I called, my big announcement: I'm the mother of twins, a boy and a girl, Sheila and Garret."

"Oh?" His voice sounded stronger again. "Sheila and Garret what— Did you marry that cowboy of yours?"

"No. I told you years ago, I'm never going to marry. Don't you ever listen?" I waited for his chuckle and got it. "Their name is Connelly, same as mine."

"Congratulations." His voice changed. "Or is there a problem?"

That's my Jack, I thought to myself. "No, none at all, just wanted you to know."

"Once again, congratulations to you and Ted."

"I'll pass that along. Well, hope to see you sometime. I love you Jack. Goodbye."

For the second time, I set Jack free.

I walked out to Mary. She still had her arms across her chest and her face was a question mark. "Well?"

Blatant as any brat I said, "I told him: twins, Garret and Sheila. I did, and you can't say I don't keep my word."

"And what did he say?"

"Congratulations to Ted and me."

I held up my hand to her, aware of her anger, "Don't!" and went back to playing with my babies.

Wouldn't you know it? The phone rang again.

Mary flew like a wildcat to pick up. I prepared to charge across the room and show her my crosscheck if it was Jack, doing math and calling back. I was thinking I might even enjoy that, when I realized she was talking to somebody else.

She held out the phone. "Mrs. Friesen wants to talk to you."

Oh, crap! I bet Mary called her again. I mouthed, "You bitch," at her as I took it from her hand.

She stuck out her tongue and flipped me the finger.

"Hello, Mrs. Friesen. How are you?"

"I haven't heard from you for almost a year and I wondered why."

You don't lie to Mrs. Friesen. I learned years ago; the attempt was a waste of time. *Didn't mean one couldn't show a little attitude though.* "Well to tell the truth…"

"As soon as anyone says that I assume they won't. Spit it out. I have some business with you."

"Okay, I was scared to call you because I knew Mary had. Better?"

"Succinct, eloquent, and immaterial to anything I have to say. I understand congratulations are in order. It was that interesting fact brought you to mind for some help on a follow-up study I'm conducting."

"What can I do?" Today was getting to be a pretty big day.

"I'm following the adult course of several of my child clients from past years, and an interesting common point caught my interest. I applied for a grant to pursue this research and a number of my cases now live in

Alberta, probably lured by the oil money, and stuck now, I imagine. Are you willing to interview for me and report back?"

"Uh, yes I am. Of course I need more information."

Mrs. Friesen's dry voice lectured. "Here's the premise. I noticed a high percentage of women who suffered sexual abuse between the ages of ten to sixteen give birth to children at a younger age than the norm. One thing led to another; we widened our horizons and examined the histories of other girls who come into care for a variety of reasons: abandonment, frequent change of homes, battery or neglect. We found the same high statistics. Interesting, don't you think?"

Mesmerized, I needed a few seconds to realize she was waiting for a response. "Yes. I'm sorry if I seem stunned. You started a chain of thought in my mind."

"Good," she said, her way of giving you an 'atta girl.' "We believe we have stumbled upon an interesting hypothesis: is there a syndrome in emotionally deprived girls that compels them to give birth at an earlier age, or in conditions less than ideal?"

"And one of those case studies might be my own. Yes?"

"Oh, most definitely and I think you're precisely the person for the job. We already know we work together well, and I was impressed with Jane Does one through eleven, those early cases when you were trying out your wings. I'm sure your recent experiences will give you a sharper perspective."

"What does this entail?"

"We need to ascertain if our statistics are supported by anecdotal evidence. I'm offering you eight cases in Alberta. You'd go in blind, knowing nothing of their previous histories, document the case and complete our report, along with your personal notes and observations."

"I'd love to, Mrs. Friesen, and thank you for thinking of me."

"I can only afford to pay $500 per case study, not a lot for what is bound to be six weeks work."

"It's the second best offer of my entire professional career. I'm honored to join your team. Thank you."

"Good. Oh, and Bria, pharmaceuticals are not the answer to depression. Process is and as I know I explained before, our demons always come back to haunt us, usually when we're stressed and tired. We must fight them many times over. Good night."

I hung up.

Mary stood less than two feet away from me as she had throughout the conversation. "Well?"

"Oh, you didn't hear?" I looked over at the babies sound asleep on the floor. I had some thinking to do.

Revelation arrived in a flash. Why had I done it? I needed someone of my own blood to love—my children. I wondered if this were true of other girls, unloved, neglected, exploited and abused. Did Mrs. Friesen's proposed syndrome relate in any way to the new rush of teenage mothers and their decision to keep their babies? A good thought, one to file away for a future project and research. Round and around the stream of ideas carried me, until Mary grabbed hold.

"Bria, why didn't you tell Mrs. Friesen your other news of the day? I'm sure she'd like to hear."

"Professionals don't discuss one client with another. Which leads me to something: I'd like your input, Mary. I respect your commonsense, but you have to swear on the Bible anything you see or hear about my work stays between us."

"Thank you. I'd love to participate in any way. But you did inform Jack, not five minutes ago, and in great detail." She coughed. "I couldn't help but hear."

"Ah, well Jack is my lawyer and will never tell my secrets."

Thirty-seven:
"Families come in all shapes and sizes."

1986
Mary

I am fifty-three years old today. I look at my life and consider myself the luckiest of women.

I have a family: five wonderful children, ages four through twenty-nine—three girls and two boys. The two little ones call me Nana, but Bria and I both know the truth. The way things worked out, she is busy earning a living for us and doing her best to change the world and I am the one at home caring for the children. Families come in all shapes and sizes.

My eldest is a lawyer and a social research professional. She carries a stack of business cards and hands them out at every given opportunity.

B.J. (Bria) Connelly, B.Sc, B.Ll, M.Ll
Barrister and Solicitor (Cdn.)
Attorney at Law (U.S.)

She spends a lot of time in her office over the garage, the one Annie loaned her the money to build. Of course, we now have Annie's name with ours on the deed to this property, although she didn't ask. But Bria insisted. "It's a good investment. Real estate values are going up now. Alberta is building again and we're only a half-mile from the growing town of Chestermere."

I'm told the land will make us a bundle one day. It just might. I look at Chestermere expanding rapidly with a shopping mall and a supermarket and neighborhoods full of upscale homes. It was a struggling village when I first came here. The reservoir, the pride and joy of the place, I remember not too long ago as a stinking, alkaline slough, fit only for ducks and leeches. Today the shores are ringed in fancy houses, and sailboats slice up and down the man-made lake.

Bria does important work, advocates for desperate women and children, and comes home some evenings in dour temper, fueled by the misery she encounters every day. She is a lot like a policeman that way. When she can't stand the stress anymore and needs a break, she takes time out, flees to Wyoming and runs wild with Annie and Ted.

She is still young and passionate and I hope she never changes.

A few months ago, she became a partner in her law firm of two, the most prestigious law firm in the city, judging by the festivity of the party we had. Her mentor, Abe, a disturbing man, looks like a pit bull terrier and acts the same way. Abe is three times divorced. I don't wonder why.

If not for Ted and his friendship with her and the children, I would worry about Bria and Abe. In many ways, he is an uncouth Jack.

You can't help but like Ted. He's a puppy of a man, full of simple good nature, wanting to love and be loved. I sometimes wonder about the relationship. He is not her equal in so many ways, but he seems to give her something she needs and their ties to each other stretch back to childhood. I have never known Bria to date anyone else. Who am I to question?

She still rides professional rodeo, working on her fifth World Championship. Racing may take her away but the money she earns more than makes up for her absence, she insists. She and Annie are so close they sometimes leave the bitter taste of jealousy in my mouth, and I chide myself for my pettiness. Annie is a lady, a good woman and my dear friend.

Tara is seventeen and in love for the first time. I found Bride magazine on her bed one day. I almost choked. He's not a bad lad, only young and stupid.

I heard Bria give her condoms and a lecture, and Tara's reaction, "I know, I know, Bee. I'm not exactly an idiot. I'm seventeen, not some kid." I laugh at them and pretend not to know, easier for me, and for the girls, too, I imagine.

Tara dreams of a career in veterinary medicine, but her grades are not impressive. Bria and I convinced her to take the two-year vet-tech course at the Olds Agricultural College. The credits are transferable if she does well. She's happy with that. If we can keep her away from the altar long enough, she just might make graduation.

Ian, my own flesh and blood, is a boy of ten whose passion is entomology. He spends his time outside, digging through cow patties and pulling out maggots, which he hatches in a bath of banana and yoghurt. I don't want to think what he does with them once they hatch, so long as the creatures are not in the house—not since the ant farm fell off his desk and smashed all over the floor.

Bria bought him a microscope last Christmas, his prize possession. His little brother, Garret, treated to the sight of pond water under magnification so Ian could educate him, showed more interest in the equipment itself.

Garret is the second sweetest boy on the planet at age four. He can strip down a lamp into components faster than you can move to stop him and sits for hours puzzling how to put the thing together again. I wouldn't worry so much if we could only teach him to unplug them first. I'm amazed he hasn't electrocuted himself.

Sheila, a miniature of her mother in so many ways, as dark as Bria is fiery, is a broody child, given to agony over the simplest things: one of the puppies died or some gopher found in the field, killed by the dogs. She feels too much. Often she wakes full of nightmares and likes to crawl into bed with me at night. I know I should put a stop to it, but don't have the heart.

Bria still hasn't told Jack he has two more children. She promises by the time they are twelve she will do so. Jack, she says, is good with twelve-year-old kids and she can vouch for that. In the meantime, she tells them stories about their father: what a fine man he is and how he waits for their visit to New York to meet him as soon as they are old enough. It never enters her mind he may let her down.

There are packages under the Christmas tree every year with labels in Bria's handwriting that read "to my sweet daughter Sheila" and "my wonderful son Garret, with love, Daddy." Same at their birthday.

A portrait of Jack and Bria, taken at some rodeo or other, sits on the mantel of the fireplace. Jack lives in our house, not only in his portrait but also in the faces of his brother, son and daughter. God bless him.

The sole comfort missing in my life is a cuddle at night and the warm body of a man sleeping next me. I still yearn for that. My Ian came to me through this simple need.

John wasn't a bad man, just a closed-minded one who hurt himself far more than anyone else. He did send us ten thousand dollars when I told him of our situation, but nothing since.

Our neighbor, another John, a widower and a quiet, thoughtful man comes by and has coffee and a chat regularly. He invited me to travel to

Hawaii next winter and we went to Las Vegas last month for a four-day trip.

Bria teases me unmercifully in the crudest terms. "How handy, you don't even need to change the name you call out in passion."

And of course, out of habit as familiar as breathing I say, "Bria, don't be vulgar." If she is within reach, I rap my knuckles on the back of her head.

I sometimes think Bria will never understand, but she is still young and lust is the province of youth. Passion quickly fades and when it does, you are left with the real reward: friendship and sharing. That's how I see love.

A friendly ear to fill with your fears and your triumphs, the comfort of arms that go around you, the cozy companionship in sharing a bed, and when you're feeling beat up, a voice that whispers, "Everything will be all right." That's all. What else is there?

The End

A preview of the next Bria Connelly novel
Fly High, Fly Blind
By Lynda M. Martin

1989
Bria

I sat at my desk in my Calgary office, busy proofreading a motion for sentence relief due in court in the morning. An appointment sat waiting, reading a magazine just outside my door. A courier had delivered a fat envelope, hopefully the report I expected yesterday, one certain to require my full attention for at least two hours. On my desk sat a pile of correspondence yet unanswered.

My eyes needed a rest, and I treated them to two minutes of the view outside. Busy admiring the beautiful sandstone courts center visible in the lower corner of my seventh floor window, I jumped when the intercom rang.

"Bria, you need to take this call—Natasha Prutko, long distance. She says it's urgent."

"Thanks, Dot," I said to my assistant and picked up the blinking line.

"What can I do for you, Natasha? I thought you had an appointment with Ms. Watson from the Urban Justice League today. Is something wrong?"

"I need your help." Her voice sounded strange, so strange the hairs on my arms stood up.

"Okay." For a moment, my mind ceased working. "Why?"

Sobs and gasps for breath streamed into my ear. I quailed as I waited for her response. She was only supposed to meet a lawyer to clear up a long-standing custody dispute, one that had eluded two years of long distance efforts. I had set everything up. I wanted to scream at her, "What could possibly go wrong?" I bit my tongue instead and waited.

Someone else took over the line. "Hey, Bria."

I recognized the voice and native accent of Edna Running Bear. *Oh, crap!* Edna was a major irritant, constantly around, joined to Natasha at the hip, poking her nose into everything I tried to do, always ready with her stupid opinions, whether wanted or not. The odd couple, we called them.

I wondered what had possessed Natasha to take her along on the trip. I had so carefully arranged her airline ticket and talked to her friend Rosa Perez, myself to ensure she had a safe place to stay and wouldn't be alone. I hushed my internal grumping and listened.

"We got a problem, eh. We never made it to that lawyer. Tasha's old man showed up at Rosa's Sunday night."

In the interminable pregnant pause, I fought down a quick flash of annoyance and summoned as much patience as I could. "And?"

"She killed him."

After a few moments of stunned silence, I exploded. "What?"

"Yeah, shot him dead."

My professional demeanor deserted me; I couldn't put one thought together. A million questions flooded into my brain, and I struggled to pull out the important ones. "First, where are you?"

"By the I-80. Someplace called Cleveland. A motel, eh." Edna's voice, as flat and monotone as always, betrayed not a trace of fear or nervousness.

"Give me the phone number – now—in case we get cut off or something." I grabbed my notepad and pen, and wrote as she slowly recited, then I read it back for confirmation. Natasha's gut-wrenching sobs still echoed in the background, so it would be pointless to ask to speak to her. "Tell me what happened. Start with where you were, what you were doing and how he found you."

"We arrived on Friday. We cashed in the ticket and drove down, eh. My idea. Let's see a little on the way, I said. I made Natasha take the wheel once we got there. That's one hell of a big city, eh. She knows her way around, not me. I wouldn't drive in that place for nothing."

I swallowed my impatience, knowing from miserable past experience it was useless to try to hustle Edna to the salient points. While I listened to her detailed descriptions of the big city streets, the bustling traffic and her impressions thereof, I pulled out one of the several thick files holding the case of Natasha Prutko and her daughter, Lara.

I opened the summary file where I kept the basic information, and found the name Rosa Perez and an address: Apt. 19, 562 West 174th St., New York, N.Y. 10033. Suitably armed, I interrupted. "You stayed with

Rosa Perez, right?"

"Not exactly."

Oh, God save me from this woman. "Edna, let's try a new approach. I'll ask questions and you give me the shortest answers you can." I started tapping the pencil on the desk. "Where and with whom were you staying?"

"At Rosa's, but she flew to Panama City to a wedding, eh. She left us a key at her neighbor and said we could crash there."

"Is that where Charles Stoughton found Natasha?" I wrote the words as I asked, followed by a line of huge question marks. Her presence was prearranged, and Rosa had to go to Panama—unexpectedly – for a wedding. That smelled ripe.

"Yeah. Outside. Real late. He came at her in the street." Edna drew in a deep inhale, and I realized she'd lighted a cigarette. At least, I hoped it was a cigarette. She had served two years plus a day for possession with intent. I pictured her big boned hands in the act, and the prison tattoos on her forearms.

I took a deep breath and tried again. "In twenty-five words or less, what happened?"

"He showed up. She shot him. I put her in the truck, and we got out of Dodge."

All my fault, I decided. I told her to be thrifty with her words. I tried again. "You were present? You saw this?"

"Not exactly."

"A yes or no question is not answered 'not exactly,' Edna." I sighed in exasperation and doodled arrows and crosses on my notepad while I thought through the information I had received so far.

It dawned on me those frightful sobs had ceased.

"Let me talk to Natasha."

A few seconds later, her voice addressed me. "I'm okay now, Bria. Weird, the panic seems to come and go. I feel like I'm dreaming and want to wake up."

Classic shock, I thought, suffering a little of that myself. A mantra played in my head: *what to do, what to do, what to do.* I tried to hush the clatter in my mind and think like a lawyer.

One truth beamed through loud and clear: it was only a matter of time before they'd hunt Natasha down. Our twenty-four month campaign to bring her miserable, wife-beating, child-molesting, coke-snorting, low-down-dog of an ex-husband to justice would leave a glowing trail clear enough to follow in the dark. This was a fact.

Also, the matter of privilege in such a circumstance was maybe a darker shade of gray, skirting on the edge of perpetuating an ongoing crime (assistance to a lawbreaker attempting to flee). As an officer of the court, my first obligation had to be to the law.

What I could not do was provide Natasha with legal advice to help her evade the consequences of her actions. I tried to sort out my scrambled brains. I was a children's advocate, not a criminal lawyer, and where the hell was Abe when you needed him, anyway?

"What are you thinking to do, Natasha?" I flipped through the Canadian Criminal Code under the related sections as I spoke. By experience, I knew penal law really didn't vary much from one jurisdiction to another.

"Come home and talk to you," she said in a small childish voice.

"No! Do not cross the border. Bad enough you left the city and the state. Don't leave the country. You can't run from this. Yours will be the first name up."

"I don't intend to," she said calmly, sounding more like the Natasha I had come to respect, in spite of her choice of companions. "I only wanted to talk and get your advice. I did it. I killed him and I'm not sorry one little bit."

"Don't say that to anybody else. Understand?"

"Uh-huh."

I came to a decision of sorts. There was no point in trying to get all the facts by phone. I already knew more than I was comfortable with under the circumstances. I wanted to meet them, but first I had to ask, "Are you willing to turn yourself in?"

"Yes." Her voice hardened. "I have nothing left to lose. At least now Lara will be safe. You're right; I can't run and I don't want to. What would be the point? Fix it, Bria and tell me what to do."

"Here's my advice." I found some remnant of professional demeanor and jotted down my thoughts on the notepad as they came to me. "I'll help you turn yourself in, and I'll make sure you get the best possible legal representation we can find. I'm going to contact the proper authorities in New York and try buy us enough time to meet and pull some kind of plan together."

"I want you to represent me." Natasha's tone was firm .

"Not a good idea." A jolt of fear ran through my body, so strong and sudden I almost yelped. "I've never even visited New York, let alone practiced law in the state, and I haven't a whole lot of experience in this kind of criminal law." Such an understatement: I had none. "We need to get you an attorney, and I'll ensure whoever we choose has the benefit of all we've done over the past three years." My eyes wandered to the still open file drawer where a long row of thick files marked 'Prutko, N & L' occupied half the space.

"I need you, please."

"I'll be there the whole time, but not in the front row."

"You don't understand. Maybe you can't and never will. I *need* to tell my story. I don't give a damn what price I have to pay." Her voice vibrated with subdued rage. "And I want *you.*"

"It wouldn't be in your best interest to have me represent you." I wandered further out into the gray area lawyers aren't supposed to visit. "In the meantime Natasha, I want you and Edna to find a small motel away from the interstate, pay in cash, not by credit card and let Edna register. As soon as you're done, call back here, leave the phone number and address with Dot. Got it?"

"You'll help me? Oh, thank God. We'll do as you say."

"Good. Now, give me time to think and get some advice. I'll call you later today, maybe even tonight and by then, I should have a plan." I hoped I sounded more sure of myself than I felt.

"I knew I could count on you," Natasha said, obviously comforted by her completely unwarranted confidence in my abilities.

"I'll get back to you." I had an important thought. "Natasha, if the police get to you before I do, say nothing to them. Absolutely nothing. Say you're invoking your right to silence and to contact me, your attorney, and then shut up. Do you understand?"

"Yes." She started crying again. Her sobs cut off abruptly as she hung up.

I sat stunned, my head in my hands, when the door opened and Dot walked in. She glanced around disapprovingly at the stacks of files and books on the tables and the wall of papers on my desk. "I need you to spend some time at your home office, Bria, so I can get this cleaned up."

Her cultured British accent intimidated me somehow, and I rarely dared argue. Besides, I hated filing and always left the dreary but necessary task to her competent attentions. I looked up at her soft pink, finely lined face under a thatch of white curls. "Is Dawn around?"

"Yes, she's back from Child and Family Services. Why?"

"Would you ask her to take Shauna's case history? She's waiting outside. Something came up and I wouldn't do it justice."

She was back in two minutes and to my relief, flashed a thumbs-up as she walked in the door. "Dawn's got everything under control." She sat in one of the chairs in front of my desk. "What has you looking so worried and how can I help?"

"I can't discuss it yet, but I'll tell you something you can do. I need all the back files on the Prutko case, every scrap of paper amassed over the past two years pulled and taken to the small conference room." I ran my hand across my face, trying to pull myself out of the thick fog of mind-numbing shock, and into some semblance of an intelligent mental process.

"Dot, is Abe in?"

"No dear, he's going to be out all day and tomorrow, too. Don't you remember? He's in court on the foster home outrage – the poor mother of that little dead boy. Fancy that: she sitting in jail, and her child killed while in care. Monstrous."

"Oh, of course he is. I'm sorry, Dot. I'm a mess right now, and I was hoping to talk to him before I have to act. I guess I'm on my own."

Dot gave me a motherly pat on the hand. "Will a coffee help? I'll fetch you one and get Cindy to pull those files."

"Thanks and may I ask another favor? I have two appointments this afternoon. Can you reschedule them? And would you please call Mary and tell her I'll be working late tonight."

I glanced at the clock: noon here and two in New York. I had to pull a plan together in short order. The more time passed, the greater the damage to our contention that after a brief and understandable period of shock and panic, Natasha did the right thing. This may mitigate her treatment at the hands of the law, if justice did exist in this world. Should the police find her beforehand, that claim would be shot to hell. I had two or three hours at most.

By two thirty, I had the beginnings of an idea. Justification. A stretch, no doubt, but it offered a glimmer of hope. Would it hold credence? I imposed on the good will of two criminal lawyers I knew well and picked their brains. With reluctance, and a handful of qualifiers – "I can't speak to the laws of New York, but…" – they offered opinions and wished me luck, this last delivered in the thin, half-amused, disbelieving voice of the cynic.

In the end, both agreed all depended on the caliber of her defense attorney and that in turn required money. Natasha had none. Her parents had already given all they had in an effort to save Lara. Still, there was a chance; at least I thought so, but criminal law was not my forte.

I reminded myself I had not heard the details of the events of late Sunday night. I buzzed Dot and asked her to book me a flight to Cleveland and a rental car for tomorrow, then changed my mind and thought if I go, I'll go standby. If things worked out, I might add on a leg to New York, hopefully for Natasha and me.

I suggested she clear my calendar from the morning's motion to the end of the week, left the conference room littered with papers and returned to my office.

Dot popped her head in. "Edna phoned in an address and phone number in Cleveland. I called Mary and informed her you were working late tonight and leaving town for a few days tomorrow. She'll pack for you. I've rescheduled everyone, but I must say you're facing a busy two weeks on your return. Abe checked in, and now knows you want to speak with him. He should be in the office at five. Anything else, dear?"

For the millionth time, I blessed Dorothy and the powers that had brought her into my life. "One more favor please: all the papers in the conference room marked with a sticky note and a number, I need them placed in that order in one big file. Would you mind?"

I sat alone in my office, staring at the phone, undeniably nervous about what I had to do next. I pulled up my purse, opened my wallet and took out the business card I kept in the back pocket. Looking at it made my pulse race. Seven years had passed since I last saw him, six since we spoke. Still, he was the one person who could and would help me—a fact as rock solid and irrefutable as the law of gravity that kept me from flying off into space. Fortified by the thought, I reached for the phone and dialed the number

A woman picked up on the third ring.

I drew in a deep breath. "May I speak to Jack Connelly please?"

"Who shall I say is calling?"

"Bria Connelly." For the first time in years, I found myself chewing my fingernails.

I sat on hold for a few minutes. Just as I decided he was out and composed a message in my mind, his deep voice came across the thirty-three hundred kilometers of wire between us.

"Hello, Bria. A lovely surprise." He sounded warm and welcoming. Along with an unexpected rush of pleasure, cold and clammy fear (or was it guilt?) settled in my guts.

"Hello Jack." I paused, unsure of what to say next and forced out the usual banalities. "Yeah… it's been a long time. Um...how are you?"

… This Novel Coming Soon

© Black Rose Writing

LaVergne, TN USA
01 February 2011
214788LV00003B/4/P